THE

TWO BARONESSES

A Romance.

BY

HANS CHRISTIAN ANDERSEN,

AUTHOR OF THE "IMPROVISATORE," ETC.

Fredonia Books
Amsterdam, The Netherlands

The Two Baronesses
(A Romance)

by
Hans Christian Andersen

ISBN: 1-58963-809-3

Reprinted from the 1879 edition

Fredonia Books
Amsterdam, The Netherlands
http://www.fredoniabooks.com

In order to make original editions of historical works available to scholars at an economical price, this facsimile of the original edition of 1879 is reproduced from the best available copy and has been digitally enhanced to improve legibility, but the text remains unaltered to retain historical authenticity.

CONTENTS.

———◆———

CHAPTER XI.

CHAPTER XII.

CHAPTER XIII.

CHAPTER XIV.

CHAPTER XV.

CHAPTER XVI.

CHAPTER XVII.

CHAPTER XVIII.

CHAPTER XIX.

CHAPTER XX.

CHAPTER XXI.

CHAPTER XXII.

CHAPTER XXIII.

CHAPTER XXIV.

CHAPTER XXV.

CHAPTER XXVI.

CHAPTER XXVII.

THE TWO BARONESSES.

CHAPTER I.

IN AN OPEN BOAT. — THE OLD MANOR-HOUSE.

IT was a fresh breeze from the northeast. A heavy sea rolled through the Great Belt, and dashed its waves against the narrow wood-grown island, Langeland, which Oehlenschläger calls " a rose-branch cast into the water," and which he has so prettily celebrated in song in his " Travels in Langeland." *We* have only to say of it, that a party had assembled there at the north point, and had sat down quietly around the provision basket: the carriage that was to convey them back to the manor-house, stood close by; the surges rose higher and higher, the champagne exploded, and the wind took hold of the napkins and the ladies' cloaks, which they had only half on, for it was late in autumn.

" It is almost a storm ! " said the elder lady.

"O, it is so delightful, mamma ! " cried the younger one ; " if we could but see a shipwreck ! "

" God forgive you your sins ! " said the mother.

" But the stranded men should be well treated ! we would give them ham and champagne, and make up beds for them at home " —

" Pray be quiet—it is terrible ! And only see, there is a small vessel out there ! Good gracious ! it will be upset — it cannot go on ! Thank God we are on dry land ! "

Far in the distance was a large open boat ; it came from the Sealand side of the Belt ; there was only one sail up, which swelled in the strong gale, and drove the boat like lightning through the high waves, now lifting it so that one could almost see the keel, now almost burying half the sail in the hollows.

"She goes well there!" said an elderly man who was of the party; "but when they tack outside the sand-reef, it will be a hard trial for them. It will be difficult to run into Lohals, and they cannot get to Funen unless they have smooth water."

"See — how delightful, mamma!" cried the young lady, as the boat heeled on the top of a wave, and the water rushed over it.

"It is dreadful!" said the mother, "but interesting."

We shall now see how interesting it was to those in the boat.

The boat was from the fishing-village, Knudshoved, north of Copenhagen, and consequently had made a pretty long voyage; a man in a yellow oilskin jacket and trousers, and a broad-brimmed hat of the same stuff, which hung down over his shoulders, sat at the rudder. This man was dressed as if he could have gone through the sea with a dry skin; he was the owner of the boat, Ole Hansen, from Knudshoved. By his side sat a handsome young man, also in a seaman's dress, but the cloth of his coat was fine, and the cut fashionable; he was Count Frederick, a young student, whose father's estate lay in Funen. Two other persons, well wrapped up, sat before a large basket of provisions, from which one of them continually helped himself; a fourth lay stretched out at the bottom of the boat, but covered up well with cloaks, though they were now soaked with the sea water. He was suffering much from sickness, and his fine face, to which his wet black hair adhered, was deadly pale. He looked like the corpse of a handsome young gladiator.

"Let me steer her, Count," said Ole Hansen, as they shipped the heavy sea we have just mentioned, and which drenched from top to toe the sick young man, who now opened his eyes, — two dark and shining eyes, as though they had first received light from an Italian sky.

Ole looked steadfastly on the waves as they rolled forward, and which, as the boat now changed its course to make the point, would wreak their utmost fury upon it; but he knew with his own peculiar sagacity how to baffle them. The gunwale was split by the heavy wave, which seemed for the mo ment as if it would upset the little bark, but it appeared to dive down and let the fresh wave lift it up again high into the air.

"Gloriously steered, old Ole !" shouted Frederick. "This is delightful ! we fly like the sea-birds ; and see how the wind takes hold of the mast-top, so that it smokes again ! There is a rainbow in the drops."

"We shall soon have some other drops !" said Ole, as he pointed towards a cloud. "That gray fellow up there will soon give us water enough ! We must manage to take the wind off a little — lee-sail !"

Quick as a practiced seaman, Count Frederick executed the desired maneuver ; a heavy sea nearly heeled the boat ; the two who sat by the provision basket sprang up ; even the sick young man was on his legs.

"Sit still !" shouted the old man, with a powerful and imperative voice ; "bale the water out !"

They obeyed ; and the boat now went, with half-reefed-sail, further out from land.

"And you, who should be the gayest of us !" said Count Frederick, as he looked at the sick man, who had again laid down, "you are truly very amusing after a new fashion. We might as well land you as contraband goods on the island of Funen ; no one would know you !"

It began to rain, and the sun was about to set. Their continual tacking had as yet only brought them a few miles to the western side of Langeland. The estate, which belonged to Count Frederick's father, and whither they were bound, lay on the coast of Funen Svendborg and Faaborg, so that they had still a considerable distance to make ; and wind and tide were against them. There they sat dripping wet, having already passed one night from Copenhagen on the open sea.

"We shall not reach Svendborg by this day's light !" said Ole ; "we must try and get in under Funen."

"Now," said Frederick, "it is not much more than a good three miles' walk up the country to the old manor which my father has bought and intends to rebuild for me. Shall we not go there ? It is a veritable robbers' den to look at, but quite romantic, and, what is still better, we shall have a roof there over our heads, and people to wait on us ; there is a manager, with a dairy-maid, and a whole pack of servants. We shall neither suffer hunger nor thirst. Just steer for Svendinge church tower ; there it is ! sticking up in the air there like a bottle ! There is a little rivulet on the coast here which runs out between the bushes at high water, which it is now. We can run right up it, and the boat will lie as snug as behind a baker's oven."

"Yes, you have got us on a sailing tour with a vengeance," said he who sat by the basket ; "had I not had this blessed appetite, I should long since have lain like Herman there ! " and he pointed to the sea-sick man.

It became darker and darker ; the boat rocked like a swing, and although old Ole looked sharp out, and steered well, they shipped a few heavy seas : the rain that fell had, on the contrary, but little effect upon the soaked voyagers.

"Are you steering for it, Ole ? " asked Frederick, as they made at a rapid rate for the coast.

"Here's the creek ! " said Ole ; and there it was sure enough ; his knowledge of the current, and his practiced eye, had led him to it ; the sail fell, and with one bound he was on land. "Holloa ! " He dragged the boat to the side, and threw the rope round one of the large stones. The yard-dog at the fishing-house close by barked his welcome.

A walk of about three miles would be of great benefit to the dripping wet and benumbed young men ; accordingly, they resolved to set out directly for the old ruined manor-house Ole was to remain with the boat ; he could lodge at the fisherman's house, so the little bottle of rum and the whole of the provisions were delivered up to him.

"My knapsack is the lightest," said he who sat nearest the provision basket. "I have at least one shirt for each of us, and that is something."

They began their walk ; it was dark, the road was heavy and sandy, and the rain fell fast.

"We cannot say that we have as yet got on dry land," said he who had been so sea-sick. "I have a feeling as if I walked at the bottom of the sea, and that every now and then it capsized me."

" Hear how the wind whistles through the trees, ' said the other ; " it gets worse and worse. Are you sure that you know the right road, so that we may not be footing it the whole night, or be obliged to knock at a peasant's door, who will not even open it for us ? I must take hold of your coat, for I cannot see a step before me." At the same moment he fell down at full length, but got on his legs again, whilst the others shouted with laughter.

They had now wandered for above an hour, when Count Frederick assured them that they must have gone in the dark past the place where the road turned off to the old manor-house. They listened, and thought they heard the barking of a dog borne on the wind. No! they were mistaken. This is indeed a pleasure excursion ! They listened again ; a moaning sound reached their ears.

"What is that ? " they asked each other.

" It is the wind," was the answer each gave ; but the moaning tones were heard again.

" Nay, but what is it ? " said one to the other ; but not one was able to explain it. They stood still a moment, and then went on. We shall afterwards know from whom these deep sighs proceeded.

Suddenly a light appeared before them.

" Now I know the way," said Count Frederick ; " there is the manor ! "

At the same moment the light disappeared, but they bent their steps in the direction whence it came.

" My boots are already so full of water," said he who was nearest to their leader, " that I really don't know how deep I am wading. It seems to me, however, that it is rather a fresh cold about the feet, — have we not got into a morass ? "

" Yes, that we have ! " said Frederick, " but it is the shortest way, and we can touch the bottom very well. It is what they call the dry side of the old moat which we are now passing through. Now we are close to the house."

They were close to it, and would without doubt have run their heads right against the wall, if the light had not appeared again at a window above them, at scarcely an ell's distance. They shouted aloud : "Halloo ! " as if with one accord.

and were answered by the barking of three or four dogs. No one appeared : the wind howled and blew large drops of rain in their faces. They tapped at the window panes, and then came one face and then another behind it, though without speaking a word, or opening the window. The young men made a greater noise. Count Frederick broke one of the panes and called upon them to open the door.

"Come with a light, you blockheads : it is I, Count Frederick ! open the door directly, and don't make us stand here in this villainous weather."

"Lord save us !" was the answer, and then there was a bustle in the house ; the light was withdrawn, and the travellers stood in pitchy darkness : the barking of the dogs increased, —at length the wicket creaked in the closed wooden gate, a lantern shone, and a man and girl received the travellers with the exclamation : "Lord save us, in this weather !"

"We are from Copenhagen," said Count Frederick ; "we came by sea in an open boat, and got on shore on account of the bad weather. Now get the saloon in order, over there by the tower ; that is certainly the best place in the house !"

"It looks terrible !" said the man : "but that room is the best, and we can put something into the windows to keep out the weather."

"Gentlemen !" said Count Frederick, "we will now make our entrance into my little property ! I hope it will this day twelvemonth show itself in a better form, and then we will have our house-warming with sparkling champagne. Only tread carefully, for here we seem to be all at sixes and sevens. In the mean time get us something hot, — what have you got here ? You have at least ale and eggs ; but I suppose rum and lemons are quite out of the question ?"

Yes ! nodded the girl, and showed her red, cheerful face out of her apron, which she had hastily thrown over her head to keep the rain off.

They went on, but stumbled every moment over stones and clumps of wood. The man led the way with the lantern down a slope overgrown with nettles, and now and then he righted a few planks, which, however, did not lie any the better for his pains.

"This is the second moat we are now passing over," said Frederick; "in former times there stood an old manor-house here, with walls and ditches; half a century ago it was all pulled down, except one tower, and they plastered up a great wooden frame-work building instead of it, which soon went to ruins, while the late General Maag owned it. My father has bought the whole lumber, the land belonging to it being capital. We have a fine wood, and the site of the building is admirable; the whole affair is to be pulled down next spring, and a new building erected in its place."

They now stood in the inner court-yard, which was inclosed on three sides by a building of two stories; a large and splendid linden-tree extended its branches on all sides: the building itself, by the dim light which the lantern afforded, looked imposing.

"Come, this is something like," cried one of them, — "a fine large door, too, in the centre of the house!"

"But no steps," said Frederick, as he turned the arm of the man with the lantern. They now saw that the broad stone steps had been taken away; a rusty iron railing which had belonged to them stood against the door, which, on a closer examination, they perceived hung only on one hinge, and the panels bulged out.

"Hold the lantern up that we may see the place," said Frederick. The lantern being raised, showed that there was scarcely a whole pane in the windows, and that a couple of the frames had started from their fittings, and in the walls themselves there were large crevices, as if the whole building had lately undergone the shock of an earthquake.

They now passed through a small door and entered a narrow passage; where they had to stumble over rubbish, stones, and a broken-down wall, and then they came into a chamber where the torn paper-hangings literally moved in the wind. They passed a large chimney, which, the lower part being cracked, was held together by beams and stays: the wind whistled through the crannies there. They next passed through a row of dilapidated rooms in which the floors, or at least parts of them, were broken up; a single piece of old furniture, with garden implements, and whitewashed, clumsy stone figures lay in a corner.

At length they reached a large corner room, which bore milder traces of devastation. The walls here — even the wainscots — were almost hid by worm-eaten family portraits, as old as the days of chivalry. Here stood venerable ladies with their dogs on their arms, or with a large tulip in the hand ; knights, with falchion and dogs of the chase ; and priests, with psalm-book, Latin devices, and the date of the year. An old open harpsichord stood in the middle of the floor.

" An instrument into the bargain," cried one, and struck a note upon it ; they heard the clapping keys and three grating strings. The player executed one of these comical leaps that a person makes when about to fall, and he nearly did so, for at his feet lay the old door to the clock-tower. The candle was taken out of the lantern and stuck in a bottle which accidentally lay on the old harpsichord.

" More lights," said Count Frederick, " and bring us some of your clothes, Christen ; but they must be clean. Don't you see we are soaked through, and that the water is dripping off us ! As many horse-cloths as possible, and some bundles of straw, into the tower there ! but it must all be done in a twinkling ! The girl must kill some chickens, and prepare the best meal she can ; but first of all the straw, that we may warm ourselves ! in a twinkling, Christen, in a twinkling ! "

And it was done in a twinkling ; Christen brought all his best clothes, and a large fur-lined travelling-cloak, which belonged to Count Frederick's father. One wet garment was thrown off after the other ; the knapsacks were in the mean while opened, and everything taken out ; a pair of swimming-drawers was found packed in by mistake among the handkerchiefs.

" It is a decree of Providence ! " said our sea-sick student, who was now mirth itself. " Here is a great want of inexpressibles ! — small contributions gratefully received ! — I am, however, the most accustomed to these things, so I shall take them and the cloak. With swimming-drawers and a fur cloak a man may look tolerably smart ! My dear ladies," — here he bowed to the grim portraits round about, — " I trust you will excuse my dressing myself in your presence ! " — and the transformation took place directly.

"The clergy must have Sunday clothes," said he, as he drew out the only and best dress he had brought with him.

"Assuredly. Our good and reverend tutor must cut the best figure amongst us."

They spoke of the eldest in this little party. He was a Holsteiner, by name Moritz Nommasen, and he had prepared the three others for their degrees in philology and philosophy, an examination which they had just passed. The leader of this adventurous tour, Count Frederick, whose father's property, as we have stated, lay in the eastern part of Funen, had been accustomed from his childhood to sail about in his own boat; when a boy he had made a tour to Als and Angeln; nay, after his first collegiate examination he had twice tried a sea-voyage in an open boat with Ole Hansen, from Copenhagen and home. A similar one had been now arranged and completed: his tutor was with them, and two young men of his own age, Baron Holger and Baron Herman; but the result of this expedition, as we have seen, was not the most fortunate.

They were now sitting under a roof and in dry clothes; five large candles, not wax, but tallow-dips, were lighted, and stuck in haste in different-sized candlesticks. A capital family bed was made in the tower with straw and horse-cloths; the punch-bowl steamed, and after the first glass (not the room but) the friends danced a round, the rain poured down out-of-doors, and the storm shook the frail building.

"Herman!" said Count Frederick, "now if the door were only to open, and your grandmother enter, with you amongst us! you who durst not come to Funen."

"I cannot understand that woman," said the tutor.

"Nor is she to be understood," interrupted Herman. "There is sometimes what I should call a little too much originality about her; but at other times again so much of what is good and noble. In almost everything she does her temper peeps forth; but the poor bless her, and it is only with us, her nearest relatives, that she is somewhat severe. Myself, for instance, she could never quite bear to see since I was born!"

"Yes," said Frederick, "when *he* speaks of her, then she

appears to be a reasonable person ; but she is mad, nevertheless ! I beg pardon : I know well that she is your grandmother. When in Italy, she fell in love with Guido Reni's
picture of Beatrice Cenci, painted shortly before she was taken
to the place of execution, and therefore the Baroness had
always one particular execution-dress, prepared *à la phan-
tasia.* She has varieties of them, — an execution travelling-
cloak, execution morning-gowns, and execution ball-dresses of
satin ; she had such a dress on at one of the greatest balls
last year ! "

" Yet, while we laugh at her dress," said Herman, " she sits
with all her girls and makes clothes for the poor ! "

" I don't find her so mad, after all," said Baron Holger ;
" now and then she says things that are highly striking. People arrive at the truth when they go to her. The other day
she invited a party of professed *gourmands ;* the dean was also
there ; she invited them to a ' feast of reason,' and they got
only boiled groats and cod-fish, together with a lecture, teach
ing how dangerous it is to spoil one's stomach ! "

" But she is an excellent woman," observed the tutor

" I have not seen my grandmother for ten years," said Herman, " and should she live, ten years more might pass away
before she would send for me here."

" Long may she live ! " shouted Holger : " the originals
must not die out, for they create as good an effect in the world
as uniforms in the theatre."

He raised his glass, and the toast was drunk, but as the
hurrah ended, a strange sigh was heard, and it died away ; all
four turned their heads towards the spot whence it came, but
no one said a word, convinced that it was only the wind they
heard.

Whilst they are merry we will pay a visit to the above-men-
tioned grandmother.

CHAPTER II.

ABOUT sixty years ago the lot of the peasant in Denmark was deplorable enough ; he was not much better than a drudge. After villeinage, which King Frederick the Fourth abolished, came bondage ; almost all the peasants were serfs, and obliged to do military service until their fifty-second year. Many young men endeavored to escape this service by hiding themselves, and others disabled themselves in order to be free.

The proprietor of the estate where this original Grandmother lived — her father-in-law — had been a reprobate fellow, one of the most barbarous men of his time, and about whom tradition has preserved the most cruel remembrances.

An opening was still shown in the gateway where the peasant was let down into what they called " *the dog's-hole.*" The damps from the moat penetrated through the walls below, and in wet seasons the floor was covered with mud and water, in which the frogs and water-rats gamboled at will ; here they let the peasant down, and why ? Often because he could not pay what was imposed on him for the miserable farm, which the proprietor had ordered him to take, and on which the peasant's little inheritance was expended. *The Spanish cloak,*[1] which many an honest man had been compelled to bear, still lay in the tower ; and in the centre of the court-yard, where there was now a fine grass-plot and Provence roses, once stood " the wooden horse," on whose back the peasant had often sat, with leaden weights fastened to his legs, until he became a cripple, whilst the baron sat in his hall and drank with his good

---

[1] A wooden dress in the form of a tun, with a hole at the top for the head to pass through, and resting on the shoulders.

friends, or flogged his hounds so that they howled in rivalry with the rider in the yard.

It is of that time, of that manor, and of that lord of the manor, we now propose to speak.

Some ragged peasant boys stood and peeped into the court-yard; there sat a man riding the "wooden horse;" it was long Rasmus, as they called him. He had once saved a little money, and therefore the lord of the manor forced him to take a miserable, half-ruined farm. Rasmus laid out his little all in the endeavor to improve it, but he could not make it much better, and they could not pay the rent and taxes. The proprietor had every stick and stone valued, and then turned Rasmus, with his wife and child, out of the farm. Rasmus wrote a melancholy song about it, and was put in the "dog's-hole" for his pains. When he came out, they let him have a house in the fields, with scarcely any land to it, unless a little cabbage-garden and a piece of land in the pastures, about two acres, can be so called; and for this wretched shed and strip of ground he and his wife were obliged to work and drudge most of their time on the estate: he had that morning complained that it was too hard a life, and for this he now rode on the "wooden horse." This horse was a narrow plank raised on two poles, and the poor sinner was placed across it; two heavy bricks were fastened to his legs that they might stretch them down, and that his seat on the sharp board might be more painful.

A pale, emaciated woman, her eyes filled with tears, stood and talked with the man who had a sort of temporary super-intendence over the sinner — she was long Rasmus's wife. The culprit had neither hat nor cap on, his thick hair hung down over his face, and he shook it now and then when the flies plagued him too much. The heavy bricks weighed his feet towards the ground, but however much he stretched out his toes, he could not reach it to get support.

A little girl, three years of age, his and Hannah's child, and beautiful as an angel, toddled about in the grass, and whilst the mother spoke with the man who kept guard, the child approached her father, and, either from the mother's in-structions or from childish instinct, she pushed a stone noiselessly under one foot, so that he could rest on it. The child had already taken a stone up in the same way, to slip it under the other foot, and looked, with her beautiful, intelligent face, up to her father, when the baron stood in the gateway opposite to them with his great riding whip. He had observed what passed, and the whip cracked around the poor child, and it uttered a painful scream from the blow : the mother threw herself between them, but the baron kicked the poor pregnant woman, who fell down on the pavement.

We will turn from this horrid scene, of which, in the so-called *good old times*, there are too many to tell, and only state that this child, whose neck and arm were swollen with the blow of the whip when she pushed the stone under her father's, long Rasmus's, foot, as he rode on the "wooden horse," was no other than the old Baroness, the Grandmother ; for this child, whom he struck, became in time his son's wife.

So dark a scene of her childhood as that we have communicated, lived in the memory of the old woman whose originality has been mentioned and laughed at. She herself had been mistress for many years of that manor where her mother had been kicked until it brought on a severe illness, where her father had sat in the "dog's-hole," and ridden the "wooden horse ; " and now she had planted the finest roses on that place of punishment.

Many a tradition is told of that wicked lord. His magnificent marble monument stood over the family vault of the church, surrounded by angels, and with gilt inscriptions : he himself had during his life sent for all this splendor from Italy, and placed it in the chapel. In a wild and merry humor, he and his companions went into the church, where he sat down in his coffin, and there drank his own health, his comrades' health, and, last of all, the devil's — and he sat there dead in the coffin. Some said that he had had an apoplectic stroke, but most people knew better, — it was the devil who had twisted his neck.

The Baron's son, the only one he had, was just as rude and wild as his father, but not so cruel or wicked. He led a reckless life, but at last he fell really in love, and that was with the schoolmaster's foster-daughter — a beauty, such as the country has but few of. She was the daughter of long Rasmus ; a courageous girl and merry to an excess, yet, strange to say, virtuous ; and spite of himself, the Baron was obliged to take her to wife if he would have her.

Now it is certainly told by some that he had allowed himself to be ensnared ; that he was just about to drive off to Laaland, in order to marry a young lady of noble family, but that he saw the beautiful Dorothea near the schoolmaster's house ; that the latter had got him to drink, and that an old hussar, dressed as a priest, had married them ; but this is only a lie and invention ; the church register tells a different story, and it is quite sure that he never parted from Dorothea, who now became a fine lady, though it is true that she was often harshly and badly treated by him.

They had several sons, who all died before they arrived at man's estate ; at length, many years after their marriage, they had a daughter. She grew up, and was a quiet child ; but whilst she was young the father died, and then Dorothea's government began. They said, that if her life before had been one of seclusion, it now went on as merrily as with pipe and tabor. It is true there were none of the first nobility in the neighborhood that visited her, yet she had the house always full of guests.

In the winter she visited Copenhagen, and there lived merrily, and made acquaintances enough with counselors' wives, advocates' wives, artists, and widow ladies ; and thus she had her house in the country always filled with guests during the summer, and was quite the fine lady. She was not in want of sense, and had even genius, but it always ran wild : she had also a heart, but caprice directed it in an unaccountable manner.

She travelled to Italy, became a connoisseur in art, and dressed herself *à la Beatrice Cenci*, in the dress in which the latter was executed : all the letters from her countrymen in Rome, at that time, contained amusing anecdotes about the Funen lady. A Baron Buncke Rennow, from Holstein, who was not a very young man, resided at that time in the city of the Pope : he visited the Baroness and her pretty daughter, the latter of whom, it was already said in Copenhagen, had made an impression on him. All at once, it was reported that they were betrothed, and soon after, that they were married. The following year, they all returned to Denmark.

Buncke Rennow was not the eldest son, but he had a considerable annual income from the family estate, and, besides, had a good place in the German board of justice and home department, in Denmark, and accordingly, as the saying is, he could afford to keep a wife. With the son-in-law, there now came several grown-up sons of the first families to the mother-in-law's house; they wished to see her peculiarities, and felt a desire to speak about them. She was soon known and sought as an original, who furnished materials for conversation in their meagre saloon life.

Soon after their return from Italy, the young wife gave birth to a son; his skin was dark and his eyes jet black, like Italy's children, in whose sunny clime she had borne him under her heart. This child was Herman, our young student, whom we first found sea-sick in the boat, and whom we left last in swimming-drawers and fur-lined travelling-cloak, before the punch-bowl.

However fond the parents might be of each other, it seemed, nevertheless, as if their love did not meet in this child; it was said, that from the first moment it was shown to the father, he regarded it coldly, and without saying a word. The mother's feelings for it were sadness or silent sorrow: there was a peculiar melancholy about her mouth, when she looked at the little one, and she shook her head, as if she did not approve of the thoughts that passed in her mind, then burst into tears and kissed the child. It was but a little more than a year old when it lost its parents; a virulent typhus fever carried off the father, and the mother, who attended on him night and day, drank in the contagious venom, and followed him, a week after his funeral.

The Grandmother sent the child away immediately to a respectable gardener near Odense, in whose family the boy remained until his ninth year. He had become a fine boy, full of life and vigor, wild and merry, for he had always plenty of exercise; but all were fond of him, for he had a good heart ; and he possessed considerable talent, particularly in drawing, in which he excelled ; but they were always comic subjects that he designed.

He was, as we have said, nine years of age, when his grandmother determined on taking him home to live with her, in order, as she said, to educate him herself, to be " a Christian robber." He came, was in the house with her for three days, but she found that he made a fool of every one and everything ; he was " a little blackguard," — but this we must positively deny, — he should, therefore, be sent away again, but not to the gardener's family, for they did not understand how to root out weeds, she said. " The man may understand, well enough, how to look after cucumbers, and his wife to gather currants, but they do not understand how to ennoble slave-seed."

The boy's family, on the father's side, cared nothing about him ; and his guardian, who was the clergyman of the place, obeyed the gracious old lady in everything. Herman was therefore sent to the Latin school at Herlufholm, whence he was removed to the university, where in one year he grew up a handsome man. There was something in his whole person that bespoke innate chivalry. He was of a lively and merry nature, and had no small share of eloquence. His excellent talent in drawing comic figures, and the fact of his being by birth a baron, had in particular bound Count Frederick to him. They had formed an acquaintance whilst frequenting the lectures at the university, and continued it with their common tutor : the third young friend, Baron Holger, joined them in their preparatory studies and friendship.

Herman knew that his Grandmother had set out a week before for Holstein, where she was to stay for at least six weeks. He had therefore allowed himself to be persuaded by Count Frederick to make the sea-trip to Funen, whither she would not allow him to go. He was obliged to write to her every month, and the following post-day he regularly received a few lines. She had lately written to him and said, " I mean once more to see you, but we can very well wait for some time yet ; yes, both of us. Do not come before I invite you, for it will be a dear-bought pleasure to you ! "

Thus, after an absence of ten years, Baron Herman came to his native island, where the party intended to pass a few days in shooting, and other sports. A ride out past Grandmother's manor, a peep into the garden there, now that she was away, might very well be undertaken without its coming to her knowledge, for no one knew who he was.

They had sailed out from Copenhagen with a good wind ; but, as it afterwards changed, they had only been able to reach Jungehoved on Sealand, where they lay in the open boat the first night, and had now, as we know, come the next evening to Funen : not to their place of destination, but to the old ruined manor-house, where we will again visit them whilst they are drinking toasts to the deceased ladies and misses, whose worm-eaten figures formed the ladies' part of the company in the saloon there, where a strange adventure took place that same evening.

CHAPTER III.

THE STUDENTS' DAUGHTER.

HERMAN had drawn an amusing little picture in his sketch-book of the whole party as they were then dressed, and on another leaf a sketch of himself, as the sea-sick student — a picture that was very successful, on account of the resemblance. The conversation had taken another turn; the wind had fallen somewhat, but the rain, on the contrary, poured down faster: the water ran in streams from the windows, down the walls, and along the floor in a sort of channel, which it had formed for itself.

They were in the middle of their sporting stories, and Count Frederick related his last badger-hunt so vividly, that Herman, as he said, really thought he felt the charcoal creak in his boots.

"Such animals I can shoot!" continued Frederick; "foxes, martens, and large birds of prey; but a stag, a roe — no! I am not a true sportsman! Only think of standing on the watch, waiting, lurking, and looking at the royal animal, springing by so light and hovering; and then to send the ball hissing after it, to set the dogs on it, to see them catch and tear that shining, brown skin; and then to see the expanding eyes of the animal! it is like a human being in the deepest affliction! I have seen it, and I threw away the gun; there was something in the animal's eyes that made me abashed and sad! No, I would not be a sportsman, but a seaman! it is a free and proud life! it is something to wrestle with the wind and the storm, and to become master over them!"

"For my part," said Herman, "I am not fond of wrestling with the sea, neither in one way nor the other. I have had enough of it these two nights past; but with respect to seal-hunting, I have been once on such a tour; it was during a vacation! How strange we looked in our clothes; much the same as this evening, yet in another fashion. I had sledge-boots on: it was quite early in the morning, cold and foggy, when six of us sailed out in a large open boat; each of us was set on one of the many stones in the shallow water, about half a mile off. It was strange enough to sit there alone on the stone, slimy as it was from the bodies of the seals: the sea-weed lay round about; I imagined myself alone on a desert island in the wide ocean. The water beat against the stone, and now and then I heard the hollow, ugly bark of a seal; all at once there was a splashing close by me: I lay on my stomach, the wind blew right in my face; I, however, lay quite still, when a seal rose suddenly up from the side whence the wind blew; he rose straight up against the barrel of my gun, and I pulled the trigger; the whole was but the work of a moment, but I had looked into his large brown eyes, which he darted on me, and it was just as if I had shot a man."

"I am sure," said Count Frederick, "that it is the seal with its intelligent human eyes, that first gave the idea of mermen and mermaids; often, when I was a boy, and when I lay under the trees by the sea-shore, have I seen them rise up, and when the fresh sea-grass hung down over the animal's head, it really looked like a human being!"

He stopped suddenly, and looked towards the side room: the others did the same; they had all the same thoughts, and the same words escaped their lips,— "We are not alone here!"

Count Frederick seized a candle.

"It is not yet the hour for ghosts to walk abroad," said he, and looked at his watch. "It is only eleven. Every one take his candle; half of them will go out from the draught."

They now heard a sound as of crying, quite distinctly; it might be the voice of an infant, or it might be a cat. The door was not easy to open, but a kick with the foot was of some avail, and they now stood in a quite empty room, and the wind blew the flames of the candles nearly out. The door of the next room was taken off its hinges, and placed length-wise across the doorway, whence the sound proceeded, and they held their lights into the room. The wall towards the garden was half dilapidated, and there, in a corner, upon some pea-straw and torn-down hangings from the walls, lay a human being, a woman, who, when they entered, raised herself up, and lifted a little naked child towards them.

Count Frederick was the foremost: he stopped, and the woman sank back with a sigh. Her hands fell, with the child, against her breast, but in that short moment she had fixed her eyes on Frederick, with an expression of pain, deeper and greater than the wounded hind, whose look he had so lately described.

"My God!" he exclaimed. The child cried; the mother, they found, was either dead or had swooned; they lifted her arms, but they fell back powerless.

"It is a new-born child," cried the tutor. "Poor little thing! And the mother will die here in this wind and rain," — and away he sprang to fetch a pair of the blankets that were intended for their beds, and threw them over her.

"Who can she be?" said Frederick. "We must see after some of the servants, and get her to bed. But stay; none of you can find the way here in the dark except myself," — and away he ran.

"Poor little thing!" said Herman, as he took the child from its mother, and wrapped it up in his thick travelling-cloak. "Little did I dream that I should play the part of a nurse to-night. You may be sure that it was the mother we heard in the fields there, moaning so, this evening."

And this was indeed the case. The suffering mother, from being out in such dreadful weather, had become ill; in her misery, she had made her way to the old manor-house, where she knew the yard was open and deserted; and here, in that dark corner, on the torn-down hangings, she had given birth to a child. The young men took the corpse — for she was dead — and bore it into the large and better sheltered room, where they had sat around the punch-bowl. They still hoped that it was but a swoon.

Count Frederick now returned, with Christen and a couple more of the servants.

"It is the musician's wife!" said Christen; "that strolling musician's — he who turns the barrel-organ, and plays on the reeds which he sticks into his neckcloth. The wife is a young girl; she beat the triangle and sang songs; I saw, well enough, the last time she sang here, how it was with her, and now she is dead and gone!"

"No, no!" said Frederick; "let us only get her into the tower, on the straw, where we should have lain, and do you mount on horseback, ride as fast as the horse can carry you, and fetch us Madam Sorensen, the midwife, from Qverndrup."

"But the woman is dead, Sir Count!" said Christen; "her hands are already cold."

"Do as I say!"

And Christen was obliged to mount the horse, however much it was against his inclination, and set off to fetch the midwife, who could render no assistance.

The dead woman was laid in the tower, on a bundle of straw, and covered up warm. One of the milkmaids got the child, which was wrapped well up, and had orders to take it to bed with her.

"Yes, only let me be rid of it," said Baron Herman, as he gave it to the girl; "I am afraid of its falling to pieces with me. It looks like one of these young copper-colored Indians!"

The child was a girl.

"We must all stand godfather to her," said Herman; "and I hope in time we may not be ashamed of her! though one dare not hope the best of a young lady, who, the first time she is introduced into the world, lays her head on the breast of a gentleman in swimming-drawers!"

"O, on her father's heart she can surely rest!" said Holger.

"But I will not be her father!" answered Herman. "You have all as great a part in her as I; but I will willingly contribute my share towards a Christian education."

"Did you see the eyes the mother looked on me with?" said Frederick.

"Yes, she intrusted the child to you, that's clear; but as we have all taken a part in it, we must also share the burden! Herman will contribute his share; I also. What says our tutor?"

"We have come to a christening this evening ; but who will take care that she gets into good hands, and who is to be father to her ? one of us must be ! so let us draw lots." And they did so.

"The lot has fallen to the tutor ; therefore as she is his daughter, she must be christened as such !"

"No ! the Students' Daughter !" said Moritz.

"Well, let it be so, then, —'the Students' Daughter' — it has a good sound with it ; but you are her guardian !"

"But, if the real father announces himself !"

"Why, let him ; but I do not think he will do so ! Let us now, in the mean time, think of getting a little rest, that we may proceed further to-morrow with better wind and weather. Good night, and a health to the Students' Daughter !"

"A health to her guardian, and long may he live !" and they raised their glasses and struck them each against that of Moritz.

"Nay," said he, "if you will drink my health, then, rather, — yes, why make a secret of it ? drink to my betrothal !"

"Betrothal !" they all cried.

"Yes, the evening before yesterday, just an hour before we started, I was betrothed ; and it was on that account that I bore the voyage so well. I thought of her, and therefore I smiled, and not at the high waves, as you thought. It was at her express wish that I accompanied you, or I would, sincerely speaking, rather have been at home."

"That is not so unreasonable !" said Frederick ; "but who is the intended bride ?"

"Miss Heimerant, the Councilor's daughter."

"What ! is it she ? now I understand. She had a seat at the theatre every Tuesday last year, and therefore you went to see all the pieces they performed on the Tuesdays."

"Now you will of course write home directly, and let her know that you have got a daughter," said Herman, laughing. The glasses were struck, and the harmonious ! "Hurrah !" sounded merrily, close by the dead woman.

An hour afterwards they all lay stretched out on blankets and bundles of straw : they slept soundly and well after their two days' sea-trip, and the events of that evening, — they slept without dreaming, all except Moritz, before whom hovered the image of a young lively girl, delicately formed, graceful, and laughing, the picture of mirth itself: with her two brown eyes she looked into his very soul; this was his betrothed, Caroline Heimerant.

CHAPTER IV.

THE GENTLEMAN OF THE BED-CHAMBER.[1]

NEXT morning the weather was delightful; the sky looked as if it were a holiday; not a cloud was to be seen. The friends wandered down to the strand, where Ole got the boat in order, and with a good side-wind they went briskly along the coast toward Svendborg-fiord.

"Our northern mythology's Archipelago begins here!" said Frederick.

"How do you make that out?" asked the tutor.

"Here lies, as you see, Funen, where Odin dwelt; one of these days we should drive up to Odense, Odin's old city; there before us is the island of Thorsing, which speaks of Thor; and there lies Thur Island, where Baldur slew Thore."

They soon entered the sound, which here resembles the Rhine in its broadest part, but with more of verdure; the fresh stream runs in bold picturesque curves between tall oak and beech woods.

"Here Svend Tveskjæg and Palnatoke rioted, and caused many a broken head; here the northern Vikings, our Argonauts sailed. There, in the wood, you see St. George's hall and church, and there he combated with the dragon. Its abode was in Nyborg, whence it crept about the country, and craved its victim every day: the lot fell on the king's daughter, and the knight George rescued her. The north also has its Perseus and Andromache!"

"Translated from the Greek," said the tutor, with a smile.

"No, it lies in the soil," said Holger, and laughed. "Let the peasants here tell you how great gates of copper under-

---

[1] In Denmark this title is not only given to those in actual service at court, but is granted as a sort of rank, and not confined to numbers, or personal qualifications, in order to gain admission to the court.

ground are opened and shut every midnight. There magic lights burn over sunken treasures; and in the fields in Funen you can see large stones, like houses, that have been thrown by the witches across the sound from the high hills of Thorsing!"

"Yes, we sail here right into the kingdom of Sagas. Ly Island, which you will soon see, was once overgrown with trees; but there was a skipper, who, when he went from home, received three knots from his mother. If he undid the first, he would have a fair wind; if he undid the second, there would be a fresh breeze; if he undid the third, then — yes, he undid it at Svendborg, and then it blew such a storm that the wood on Ly Island was swept away; and one can still see that that is true, for there is not a tree to be seen on Ly Island!"

"Now I see my Funen tree!" cried Frederick, and the boat was steered towards a tongue of land thickly covered with underwood, where there stood a tall old tree, not withered, but almost leafless from the wind. A thousand birds flew screaming away from it, as our party sprang on shore; close by a noble stag darted off, lightly and flutteringly; and a hare started away in an opposite direction, — everything bespoke that it was a paradise for the sportsman.

Wet through from the previous night's rain, they directed their steps through the long grass towards the forester's house, where Eiler and his wife, an old couple, lived in the silent solitude of the woods, and looked after the deer in the inclosed grounds. Their whole world was this tongue of land, their metropolis the manor-house, which they perhaps visited scarcely twice a year; as to what passed in the real world itself they knew nothing at all, except when their son Hans, who had the good fortune to be a footman at the manor-house, let a few words fall that he had read in the newspapers, but that news was forgotten directly. Hans was just then with the old folks, and he ran immediately to meet the young party. The old woman took her wooden shoes off, and stood in her stocking-feet on the paved floor.

"Why do you do that, dame?" asked Frederick.

"Because I know well," said she, "how to honor those to

whom honor is due ; " and she smiled cunningly at the gentility she had shown. She then spread her petticoat out on one chair, and her husband's jacket on another, and begged the company to be seated.

"It was fortunate," she said, "for the Count, that he should meet with her son here, so that he could now learn how matters stood up at the hall ; it was in order to console his sister, Anna Livbets, that he had come. She had been married a little more than a year to a clever seaman, master of a vessel belonging to a merchant in Faaborg ; he had been washed overboard by a heavy sea, and she had also lost her little child, a few days ago."

"There, we have a nurse for the Students' Daughter !" exclaimed Holger. "It happens as excellently as if it had been arranged, — and so it is in reality ; but if one reads of such things in books, criticisms are made on them ! "

"What strangers are there at home, Hans ? " asked Count Frederick.

"O the Gentleman of the Bed-chamber has come — he who has something to wash every evening, and yet goes about with a leather shirt ! " And Hans smiled sagaciously at the idea.

"What ! has he come ? He will stick as fast as a leech for several months, for he lives here as if he were a regular boarder ; he is one of these who wish to be regarded as persons of quality, and yet are almost dying with hunger. His whole aim and endeavor through life has been to become a Gentleman of the Bed-chamber."

"Does he wear a leather shirt, and yet has something washed every evening ? " asked Herman.

"Yes," replied Hans, who saw by the faces of the gentlemen that he could join in the conversation which he had begun. "He has so few things with him that they must wash for him every day ; though the trunk gets the blame for holding so little. He is very polite and free towards us servants, except with drink-money. There's the pinch ; but then we get civility ! "

And Hans grinned.

"And who is there besides ? "

"There is the Councilor of War, from Odense, husband and wife."

"They are also a pair!" said Frederick. "He once travelled abroad for six weeks; he was half a day in Hanover, and three hours in Brunswick, but then he was a day and a half in Cassel, and he now speaks of that journey so that you would think he had been twenty years away from home. He has either met with persons who were nearly related to the most celebrated men, or he has travelled with a person who was so like this or that person's portrait, that he is almost sure it was that personage himself. Nay, he durst almost swear that he had sailed down the Rhine with Napoleon, on a timber-raft. But the most amusing thing to observe is, that his wife has heard him relate his travels so often, that she can supply any deficiency in the story when he stops. Most of the time of the six weeks' travelling, he passed in diligences and on the high roads; but, as I have said, he always met with the most remarkable persons — Napoleon, Lavater, and Fru Krudner. "And is that the whole company?"

"Fru Bager from Middlefart — "

"Well, that is one reasonable person, at least. Now let us be off! Zamora! — my own boy!" he exclaimed and whistled, as a splendid pointer sprang to meet him, jumped up on him, rolled on the ground, wagged its tail, and again sprang up, barking all the while: he clapped it, and away it darted towards the hall, returning again and again to repeat the same maneuver.

"Zamora is not at all related to the Spaniards," said Frederick, "but it resembles a pointer that my father got of Zamora himself; and which, when the Spaniards broke up their quarters, sneaked on board with him at Nyborg."

The out-buildings of the manor-house, with their fine red walls, now shone, between a row of splendid linden-trees, as if they had been lately erected; the date of the year in iron, and the old inscriptions, told, however, that they were three hundred years old: the roofs had been lately thatched, and a gilt weather-cock turned with the wind on the gable-end.

As the friends approached, a travelling-carriage drove from

the lane in at the gate, but Hans neither knew it nor **the**
livery.

The court-yard was well-paved ; a low wooden trellis-work
was fixed to the white walls of the stables, up which grew
apricots and figs in the sunshine.

Several of the servants stood before the carriage, out of
which Count Frederick's father assisted two ladies — mother
and daughter. The former one might still call a beauty, for
she had a high-bred bearing, noble features, and expressive
brown eyes. The daughter was the express image of her
mother, only that she was more finely formed : here, indeed,
was youth in all its blooming freshness.

" It is Clara ! " exclaimed the elder Count, and his eyes
beamed on seeing such a paragon of nature's making.

Frederick pressed forward and seized his father's hand.

" My boy — you here ! " cried his father, pressing a kiss on
his forehead, and shaking hands with each of the young men,
whom he bade welcome. He then conducted both the ladies
to the rooms set apart for them. They were the widow of
Admiral Schleysner, and her daughter, both from Jutland, and
now on their way to Copenhagen, who had taken up their
quarters for the night at the Count's house. Next morning
they intended to continue their journey, but half a day and a
whole evening will bring many events to pass, or at least lay
the foundation for them.

" I must look to it myself to get us lodged," said Frederick. " Are you in order in the green passage ? " he added to
a servant.

" Sir Count ! " said a little and particularly thin man in a
friendly tone, as he shook hands heartily with Frederick.

" Ah ! Sir Gentleman of the Bed-chamber ! " said Frederick, laughing ; " I heard as soon as we came on shore that we
had the honor of your visit ! Now you must really be amusing, and play something for us — some dances. You saw what
a dancing partner we got ! "

This was said kindly, — kindly as when one whistles to
one's dog, — in this way at least the party concerned felt it ; a
slight blush passed over his face, on which however, the most
prominent expression was a good-natured smile. This then

was *the* Gentleman, who, according to the servant's account, wore a leather shirt and false collars. He was about twenty-five years of age, and if the expression may be allowed, for it is at least significant, he looked famished.

The whole company assembled at the dinner-table ; Count Frederick conducted Clara, who made a remarkable impression on all, which she could hardly fail of doing. A poet now would recite in verse, to the effect that here was the regal deportment, and that lightness which one sees in the fleeing hind ; that here was that freshness which enchants us in the first budding rose, or the young vernal green when the snow melts. There was something so singularly transparent in the whole appearance of this young creature ; it was the freshness of youth with all its innocence and happiness, — all its confidence in man and the world.

"She is quite Raphael's Madonna in Dresden," observed the Councilor of War from Odense, and whispered his remark to the tutor, his neighbor, though he at the same time added, that he had not been in Dresden, but that he had seen an excellent copy in Frankfort before he had travelled.

The Gentleman was not at table, nor was he missed : no one mentioned him ; the conversation was carried on briskly ; the young gentlemen's sea-trip, the visit to the ruined manor on the previous evening, the little child there, and the dead mother, afforded them abundant subjects. Herman was obliged to produce his drawings, which particularly awakened Clara's highest admiration. "He was a man of talent, a genius," she said, "and the representation of himself, as seasick, was masterly." The admiral's lady spoke about her acquaintances in Jutland ; the War Councilor was led on to recount similar tales to every one that was related, of things and persons he had witnessed in Germany, when he travelled there ; his wife assisted his memory ; Fru Bager made short but pertinent remarks, each characteristic of her cast of mind. But Clara was the sun that illumined and gave warmth ; her eloquence lay in her smile — and she smiled often.

It was dark evening long before they rose from table. Clara sat down to the piano ; she knew only one dance by heart, and, as she said, all her music was packed up. The dance was played, and the gayety of the ball-room beamed from every eye.

"O how I love music!" she exclaimed, "but I cannot play myself, at least not without notes. Who plays?"

"The Gentleman of the Bed-chamber," said Frederick, and gave one of the servants orders to tell him that they waited for him; that it was not a time now to have the tooth-ache.

The Gentleman came, yet with a swelled cheek, but the pain had ceased. Fru Bager clapped him on the shoulder, begging him to give them, as she called it, a musical lecture; the poor man excused himself by saying how little he felt dis-posed to play that evening, after such a violent tooth-ache, but yet he sat down directly to the piano, where Clara, with her speaking smile, looked in his face, so that the blood rose to his cheeks, and he executed a prelude.

"Nothing of your own, if we may beg," said Frederick; "you play whole pieces from 'The Barber of Seville' so ex-cellently."

The old count persisted in having "the musical lecture," and Fru Bager laid a few pieces of national melodies on the piano. *The* Gentleman had during the previous autumn read to them scenes from Goethe's "Faust," and before and after each scene had depicted the situation in music; he had performed this "work of art," as Count Frederick's father called it, with several Danish poems, and really succeeded well.

"But don't turn the leaves over," said the Count; "take the first that comes to hand; it is sure to be the most inter-esting. Here is the ballad about 'Elina of Veller-wood,'" — and it lay open.

The Gentleman of the Bed-chamber seemed perplexed; the admiral's lady looked kindly on him; Clara smiled, and a conversation began in an under-tone amongst the young gen-tlemen, as the prelude sounded, and tones came forth that in-timated the rushing of the wind through the forest, and the lightning dismissed from the cloud, described in a short but glorious harmony. The player then began to read quietly:

without possessing any particular compass in his organ, his voice was pliant : —

> " In the North Sea there lies an isle,
> There a peasant intends to dwell."

At the end of the third verse he ceased, and then followed a sort of ghost-like music, something demoniacally whirling, so that one might really have imagined one heard the seven hundred demons who came and would do the peasant mischief, and carry off his wife, as a punishment because he built his dwelling there. And he read on, the music all the while preceding or joining in what he read. One heard the combat of the demons, and the pious folks' prayers. The whole was like a varying song, with alternate demoniacal howlings and psalm-singing.

Where the woman calls to Jesus Christ for the third time, and the spell is broken, and the least demon below stands a handsome knight, the verse was followed by a beautiful exulting melody, which, if it was then actually improvised, might be called masterly, or if it was another's composition, it was well chosen.

Clara's feet kept time, and the Councilor cried " bravo ! " It reminded him of a distinguished pianist he had heard in Frankfort. After having ended the explanation of the poem, where the saved knight marries the peasant's daughter, he played, " God save the king," which was well calculated to entertain his auditors. It was a splendid thought, said the admiral's lady, for the knight was king of England, and the peasant's daughter became an English queen !

Great applause followed the conclusion of the piece, and the Councilor's lady assured them that, hearing this music, she now for the first time understood the ancient Scandinavian ballads.

Clara stepped up to the piano and laid her hands on it : two beautiful eyes looked into his, and there was music in her words: *the* Gentleman blushed still deeper, but did not cast down his eyes. Music was his world, it still whirled around him, and, at a word from Clara, the light, dancing melodies sounded again.

" Bravo ! " cried Count Frederick.

" Bravo ! " repeated Herman and Holger.

But it was Frederick who danced round the saloon with **the** hovering, lively young girl. " Here are more ladies ! " he exclaimed while dancing ; but the Councilor's lady was the only one who allowed herself to be moved by the invitation, and she was led out by Count Holger.

Moritz had taken his place by the piano, and regarded the meagre and sorrowful face of the musician, which, while he played, put on a peculiarly animated expression ; the piano and the man seemed thoroughly to understand each other ; the tones had their source from his feelings, as surely as the blood circulates through the heart. There seemed to be something more in " the Gentleman " than those by whom he was surrounded understood. That at least was Moritz's opinion. He now regarded the dancers, and even *he* found Clara beautiful ; he compared her with his bride, Caroline Heimerant, and if he had spoken his thoughts aloud, and honestly, they were, — " It is a delight to look at her ; but there is another beauty, the mind's ; there is another still more lasting, and my bride has both these ; Caroline is prettier ! " He was a lover who judged thus.

Baron Herman now took Count Frederick's place in the dance, for Clara assured them that she could dance her whole life through.

" And I in eternity also ! " said Herman, who certainly entertained his partner excellently, for she laughed aloud ; laughed so that she could dance no longer. There was then a chattering and a noise, and while this was going on, the admiral's lady begged " the Gentleman " to favor her with the overture to " The Caliph of Bagdad." It lay on the piano, and in another moment it sounded from the wires, whilst the conversation began, first in a whisper, afterwards louder ; some went out and came in, and when the piece was ended, they withdrew to a tea-table in a side room ; the Gentleman remained behind, buried in fantasies, until Count Frederick clapped him on the shoulder, and said, " Now you shall rest, and we too."

The Gentleman sprang up, bowed in a perplexed **manner,**

and accompanied him to the tea-table, where Fru Bager said he had certainly deserved his cup.

The admiral's lady and her daughter said they must go early to rest, as they were to depart at break of day, and must therefore get up by candle light, — " Long before the gentle-men rise ! " said Clara.

She smiled to the Gentleman ; his best music could not ex-press that smile. She bowed to each of the gentlemen, except *the* Gentleman, to whom she gave her hand. " You have had work enough," said she ; " a thousand thanks ! " and she was gone with her mother.

" There was nothing more to be said or done for the rest of the evening," said the young gentlemen, as Count Frederick accompanied them to the green passage.

" She is charming," said Frederick.

" You are in love," was Herman's reply, who wished to conceal his own stronger love by attributing love to another.

" Yes, Frederick, you are in love ! " said Holger, who was more so than any of them.

Frederick laughed outright. " Yes," said he, " violently in love ; " but he was not at all so.

" Do you want any initiation or preparation ? " asked Mo-ritz.

" *Ars amandi* is certainly easy ! " said Herman. " Ovid does not belong to the human *auctores !* "

One light disappeared after the other in the chambers of the guests ; the last that burnt was that of the Gentleman. His door was well fastened ; one part of his dress was care-fully hung on the door-handle within, so that none of the ser-vants might peep in at the key-hole and watch him. He studied thorough-bass, and mended his own clothes — a tal-ent which the world did not know that he possessed, and must not know it. The cock began to crow before his light was put out, — before the bed-clothes were drawn up under his chin, — but when that was done, he slept immediately after ; he, however, dreamt not of Clara, and yet she was in his thoughts, between the thorough-bass and the art of tailoring.

When he made his appearance next morning both she and her mother were gone. The other young gentlemen had risen to take leave, but not *the* Gentleman, and yet it was remarked, he was the only one to whom Clara had given her hand the previous evening, on bidding good-night.

"The sun is gone down before you get up!" said Frederick.

"Down in Nyborg, to pass over the belt!" were Herman's words.

A carriage stood before the door; the young friends had determined to have a drive to the forest, and the Gentleman was to go with them, for there was room enough. Zamora sprang about before the horses, and the yard-dog gave a single bark. The servant-girls took a sly peep from the kitchen door, where they stood, and pushed each other, so that their wooden shoes clattered again.

The party rolled away from the field road over the highway into the forest and out of the forest, and it was splendid there; — the foliage was a copper-red; the brackens were still of a fresh light green by the blue-green bramble-berry bushes and lilacs. Stag and roe stood in large herds, and listened with their heads erect; one darted off, and the whole herd trooped away after it; no practiced maneuver could go off better. There were magnificent beeches, high, straight, and broad-crowned, as any land might be proud to own, and the sun shone on the wet trunks: one might have seen the shadows of the horses, the carriage, and the whole party pass rapidly by them. The green woodruff flowered again; and in the wet, fallen leaves, a brown-yellow frog sprang about, as if it were a leaf that had received life.

"Don't upset us!" said the Gentleman, half jestingly to Herman, who sat with the coachman, and held the reins, which was something he did not understand; besides, the conversation in the carriage was so lively that he could not avoid listening to it, and they would soon have been half over into the ditch if the coachman had not helped him to guide the horses, but *he* also now seemed to have more ears than eyes.

"Are you afraid?" shouted Frederick. "O, I know you; you were excellent last year when we drove with Count Borihs:" and he turned to the others as he continued: "the youngest daughter, Hermanine, is a little wildcat, and indulged in everything; but it becomes her. She sat with the coachman — they allow her, because she is so daring — now he had given her the reins, and she was to drive a carriage with four horses."

"And she is only seven years of age," said the Gentleman.

"But that is just the most amusing part of it," said Frederick; "she drove us down the high-road close by the deep ditch, but *he* sat with his heart in his mouth, and when the coachman cracked his whip a little to make the horses go quicker, and they sprang to the side, he would sit no longer in the carriage."

"But you have certainly not learned to drive," cried the Gentleman, seizing fast hold of Baron Herman, who swung to and fro, and actually rolled them all into the ditch at the same moment.

There was a momentary silence. The horses stood quite still; each of the young men crept out, the Gentleman was the last.

"O my God, my hand!" he sighed; "it is broken! It pains insufferably! We have not come so far away from the house but that I can go home again — you drive on."

"We must be at least more than four miles from home," said Moritz. "We will return, or I will go with you."

"You have sprained your hand a little," said Frederick; "only don't fancy that it is broken."

"Perhaps you are right, Sir Count," he replied; "you have more understanding than I;" and he sprang over the stile, and with his lame hand held by the other, they saw him hastening homewards through the forest.

"He was saucy," said Count Frederick; "that parish beadle! Now he has not broken it, but it was only to get out of the carriage — the coward!"

"My dear Count Frederick," said Moritz, "I know you by this time so well; know that you are really an excellent young man, but you have, from the first moment we came here, shown yourself strangely severe against that man. He is your father's guest, and he is really a man of talent, not a mere Gentleman of the Bed-chamber, if I may use the expression. You are too good to behave in this manner; and he is, I also believe, too good to bear it."

"You lecture me!" said Frederick, half surprised and half good-naturedly. "Now it is you who disturb the trip; we can return, but it would be very stupid."

"Yes, I will go to accompany him," said Moritz.

"Turn round," said Frederick, surprised, and the coachman was obliged to return — he was also surprised, for he drove almost at a walking pace. They were almost close to the manor-house when Herman pointed towards the ditch, where the Gentleman sat, pale as death, with his shirt unbuttoned. Overpowered by the pain and quick walking, he had felt himself about to swoon, and now sat here with his hair quite wet, as if he would cool his forehead.

When they arrived at the house the doctor was by chance there. He declared that the wrist was sprained and broken, and desired the greatest care to be taken, otherwise the hand might become stiff forever. A fever had commenced, and that delicate, slender body seemed as if it could bear nothing : it afflicted Herman deeply that he was the cause of it.

"O this is the whole of it," said Count Frederick; "he will soon recover the use of his hand, and in the mean time he will be well nursed here; they have taken care of him for a couple of weeks already. Yes, I have a personal feeling against him : it is so pitiable to wish to be what one calls a *noblesse*, to wear out the carpets for an invitation, where one has not even clothes to appear in. Rather a good tailor than a poor *gentleman*."

The sick man lay in a fever; Fru Bager had left; she had lately visited him. Many thoughts passed through his feverish brain.

"My hand useless! Music is over! O my God, how unfortunate I am! What will my future life now be!"

CHAPTER V.

"THIS is a punishment because I have come here to Funen against my grandmother's commands," said Herman, whom the upsetting of the carriage troubled in a high degree ; "this is a punishment because I would drive, and have never learned to do so."

"My dear friend," said the old Count, "such a thing might have happened to the best coachman. Come with me, you shall see my orchard ; I will show it you myself, and I must tell you that it is my pride ; persons often come here from a great distance to see it."

They then went into the garden ; it was the day after the driving party. As they came into one of the side walks they saw two ladies, accompanied by the gardener.

"They are certainly strangers, as the gardener is with them," said the Count ; "many come here to see my fruit-trees, and how the whole garden is laid out."

When they came nearer, they saw that both the ladies were old. The elder of the two, a little broad-shouldered woman, with a bold face, which had certainly once been handsome, stepped briskly up towards the Count. She was dressed in a white travelling-cloak, and had a sort of turban on her head, of the same stuff as Beatrice Cenci's costume : — it was Baron Herman's grandmother. She had, contrary to her intentions, left Holstein, and as she passed the Count's house on her way home, had ordered the carriage to stop, and descended, in order to view the grounds and garden.

"You, Sir Count, I did not intend to see," said she ; "but your fruit-trees, and your hot-beds. You too would certainly rather be free from visitors ; one only troubles the

other ; but now we are here, and the fault lies with neither
of us."

The Count, surprised and perplexed, on account of her sudden appearance directly before her grandson, who had been
prohibited from coming to Funen, and was his guest, stammered forth a few words in a perplexed manner, and naturally
avoided presenting them to each other.

Herman knew his grandmother directly, on their first salu-
tation ; she, on the contrary, did not recognize him. It was
in his sixth year when he was with her, and since that time she
had seen him but for a few days, in his ninth year ; now, as
we know, he had grown to man's estate, and had a fine black
beard and manly features.

The Count insisted on accompanying them instead of the
gardener, and added, that the ladies would, he was sure, do
them the honor to stay to dinner, which the Baroness refused
in the most positive manner. She, however, took his arm, and
they went into the nursery-ground. Herman recovered himself, nay, even became eloquent, and the old lady seemed to
be pleased with him.

"You do not want oratorical powers," said she ; "but do
not imagine that I believe all you say ; I do not believe people who have eyes like yours ! The Black Sea is deceitful,
they say."

An involuntary feeling that he had been recognized drove
the blood immediately into Herman's cheeks ; at the same
moment a servant came and informed the Count that the Organ Man, the father of the new-born child, had been sent up
to the manor by the magistrate, and that they were all in the
billiard-room. The Count gave the old lady a short account
of what had occurred.

"Poor child !" was all that she said, but her laughing face
became sad, and tears came into her eyes. "I shall not dine
with you," said she ; "but I will certainly attend the examination of the man. I may perhaps be able to ward off a blow,
if he should run the gauntlet."

She accompanied the Count, and Herman offered his arm
to her companion, a genteel, but not very young person. She
was a Madame Krone, a widow ; she was mild, phlegmatic,

and discreet; formed, as it were, to live with the old lady,
who found pleasure in treating her superciliously, in teaching
her, and yet now and then be obliged to give way to her.

The only — if one may call it so — characteristic room in
the whole manor-house, was the billiard-room, for here the
gentlemen assembled after dinner, and smoked, chatted, and
played. Here, in the gray, painted walls were twelve parti-
colored gilt fields, walled in, wherein were projecting stags'
heads carved in wood, of a natural size, with the real horns of
that splendid animal, which had been shed centuries before.
Some had thirteen, others fifteen points on the antlers, all
richly gilt; they had once adorned the armory in the original
ancient manor-house. Old arms were hung up between the
windows, and on the opposite wall, along which was a sofa the
whole breadth of the room, there hung two old portraits of
ladies belonging to the family, both painted as shepherdesses,
and each with a little lamb, which she held by a garland of
flowers. The billiard-table stood in the middle of the room.

The chief person now here was the Organ Man; he had
been to the magistrate of the district, and there made a dec-
laration; his wife had left Nyborg during that dreadful
weather, whilst he was playing in the inn, and had been seized
with the pains incidental to her case. She knew the deserted
part of the building well, and as she was nearest to it, she had
made her way thither, given birth to her child, and drawn her
last breath there. The body was to be buried at the expense
of the parish; the father knew that the young Count and his
friends had taken care of the child, and now we shall hear a
little about its parents.

The Organ Man stood in the middle of the floor when the
party entered the room from the garden. The poor man had
on a threadbare coat of a fashionable cut, but one could see
immediately that it had been made for a stouter person than
himself, as it hung much too loose on him. A red velvet
waistcoat, with a broad binding, evidently put on at a later
period to cover the ragged edges, and a pair of well-worn,
shining trousers, were the most striking parts of his dress;
his cap, which he held in his hand, was embroidered with
woolen braid, and had a long woolen tassel. His face was

pale, and the unsteady look of his eye, as he endeavored to fix it on the ceiling with a visionary stare, seemed to indicate a striving after repose; a cunning smile played around his mouth; one saw through his glassy eyes, as it were, right into the man, and yet one saw nothing. He was told to give an account of himself, and with many gestures, and in a highly affected manner, he began to relate his life and adventures.

"I was born in the Imperial City, by the Danube. My father was an actor at the theatre in Vienna, but he did not play any great parts; he brought in a letter or a message, or stood as a herald. I never got permission to go on the stage. He had observed an immense talent in me, and that he would not have awakened, so that I almost believe there was a little jealousy in the business. The son must not be the first where the father was but an attendant — so I was put out apprentice to a painter. I had certainly an unusual talent, and much sensibility, and, therefore, felt myself mortified by degrading treatment, which was carried to that degree that they made me take care of a child, sit with it and stick a rattle in its mouth; so I ran away, — that was just a year before the expiration of my term, and I became a strolling player. I had many happy moments, but, also, many vexations. My talents were too great for a little boarded floor; my movements and action, which were suitable for the theatre in Vienna, la Scala, or St. Carlo, were ridiculous on a small stage. High tragedy approximates nearest to the comical; I was laughed off, because I was born for something greater. Yes, one can, like you, gentlemen, laugh; I myself have laughed at it."

"And so you became an organ player?" asked Frederick.

"No, I had so many talents, which, each by itself, if developed and encouraged, might have placed me on no mean footing in society; I was in an uncertainty as to what talent I should avail myself of. I could paint, write verses, and sew stage costumes; I am convinced that if I had been born and educated in Paris, I should have been one of the first man-milliners! I could cut out the prettiest things in paper with a pair of scissors; that I could do even when a child, and in many families they still preserve my clipped papers. I now became manager of a *theatrum mundi.* There were really highly interesting things to be seen ; the majority were taken from Napoleon's life ; but they did not fill the house, so I was obliged to leave the theatre in the lurch — and stood — yes, I assure you, stood with bare legs in my boots, and the wide world before me ! "

" And your wife accompanied you ? " asked the old Count.

" I was unmarried then. It was wondrously long before the feeling of love became awakened in me. From this, one may well imagine that no great qualities were implanted in me, as it is well known that all real geniuses have very in-flammable hearts. I cannot say anything about this, but in nature there are always found exceptions enough ? I travelled to Norway, and became private tutor to four pupils."

" Private tutor ! but what did you teach them ? "

" Teach ! I taught them in point of fact everything, for they knew nothing, and I myself was extremely diligent. I read over every morning what I had to examine them in ; and I often said to them, ' To-day we shall have a very difficult les-son ; how long have you studied it ? I, myself, read for a whole hour.' They learned geography very well, particularly about Vienna. I fell in love with the eldest of my pupils, and her father drove me away ; so I went to Russia, and read lectures. I read from Schiller and Goethe, but they were nothing to the Russians. They cannot have understood it, for they hissed both authors ; that is to say, I had to stand the brunt of the hisses. Two years afterwards I returned to that ' proud Nor-way,' where I again met with Stella. Yes, my pupil's name was Stella. Is it not a pretty name ? The father was dead, the children separated ; she attached herself to me, became my wife, and so we travelled to Copenhagen, where we have experienced two severe winters ; but we could not succeed, and so I took to the organ, for we intended to go to the Impe-rial City. Death took her to a better city."

The Organ Man ceased his affected narration, and pressed the woolen tassel of his cap firmly to his eyes, for he actually shed tears.

" Much of what you have just told us is certainly not true ; eh ? " said the elder Count.

' Most of it, your Excellence. It is truth and fiction, as the

great Goethe says of his own life and adventures; and yet **no**
one calls *him* a liar. I have the talent of being able to *group*,
and I have done so here."

"Only hear!" said the old lady, who had listened silently
to his long narrative, and now went straight up to the man.
"Your story is a made-up one throughout," she added;
"there is something silly in your whole person, and I am not
to be made a fool of by you. I shall take care of the child,
however; but I will not have your visits. I will not have any
letter-writing, nor any claims upon it, should the child turn
out an honest man."

"But it is a girl," said Herman.

"Well, Mr. Jackanapes! then I shall make a wife for **you**
of her," was her answer.

"It is really kind," said Frederick, "that your ladyship
will take care of the child. I only hope you may not regret it."

"That you will leave to me," answered the old lady, with a
slight toss of her head, and she laughed.

"I must, however, tell you, that we young men have sub-
scribed together for the support of the child during its early
years. He yonder, the tutor, and *candidatus theologiæ*, is
book-keeper; he is the child's guardian, and the child itself
is sent to Canute Caspersen's widow."

"That is more reasonable than I should have thought you
could have been," she answered. "The theologian I don't
know. But Caspersen's widow can remove to my house, for I
will have the superintendence of the child. And don't believe, gentlemen, that you shall go free from paying your con-
tribution. I will have board wages for it. Each of you shall
pay a penny yearly for the nurse, and a half-penny for the
child; and that I shall lay aside against my Christmas-eve.
It is my serious intention; and so it must be. Is it not so,
Sir Count? We two old folks must hold together; and
now I must be off. I shall send the carriage this evening for
the nurse and child; but the penny directly, and the half-
penny too."

"We are four," said Frederick, "therefore it will be just a
groat and a half-penny. Here is a groat and a penny; I have
not a half-penny, but you ought to have interest."

"No foolery!" said the old lady; "I shall send you your half-penny; it may perhaps be a lucky one to you, so take care of it;" and then she nodded kindly to them all, looked for a moment at the Organ Man, and said to him, "I advise you to sell that story you told us; you will find some one fool enough to buy it!" She clapped Herman on the shoulder, and went away with her companion, Madame Krone, at the same time waving her hand to the old Count and Frederick, who would accompany her.

This was the Grandmother, the Funen original, as they called her. She had made a peculiar, but favorable, impression on Herman, who if she had remained much longer would certainly have said, "I am your grandson."

Long after she was gone this thought passed through his mind: "It is not right of me to be here against her command, and without her knowledge." It was continually haunting him, and pained him; "I will ride over and visit her. There must, however, be an end to this state of things between us. What a strange caprice of hers, that she will not see me; I who never injured or insulted her. There is certainly some heart under that strange shell."

His determination was taken, yet he, nevertheless, told it to Count Frederick, who immediately advised him not to take such a step; but he afterwards inclined to his opinion, though he at the same time requested to accompany him on this visit, as the storm might, perhaps, be averted by his presence.

"This evening our little foster-daughter is to be delivered up to her new guardian; to-morrow morning we must be out shooting, and after lunch we will ride over to see if the little thing has arrived safe, for we will not say a word here at home about our intended trip."

CHAPTER VI.

THE VISIT TO THE GRANDMOTHER.

A LITTLE vessel with several passengers, on their way to Kiel, was seen driving along before a good wind, in the fresh undulating sea, under Ly Island. The passengers were sitting around the provision basket; nor was table music wanting, for an Organ Man sat there and played "Noch einmal die schöne Gegend." It was the father of the new-born child, whose history we have heard, and who now left the island that contained his dead wife and living daughter. Not only his whole person, every word — even his thoughts — were affected and extravagant; yet there was a sorrowful string that vibrated in his breast at that moment, but no one could read it in his face, upon which was a foolish sentimentality that appeared to be assumed, by way of mockery of the melancholy tune. None of the passengers knew what his thoughts were; he had not yet told them his history, nor *grouped* it for them. One of the chapters was concluded in Funen.

One could see the vessel as it sailed alone from the high-road, and here Count Frederick and Baron Herman were just riding at the time, to tempt their fate at the old lady's. There were hedgerows on both sides of the way, and it was only when they passed a gate that they could get a peep into the fields. A messenger on horseback, from the old lady, met them on the way, and delivered a small but bulky letter to Count Frederick.

"Perhaps an invitation! no; what is it? a half-penny, a common copper half-penny. It is a dear ride, so many miles alone to deliver a single half-penny." The letter was as follows: —

"Sir Count, one must pay one's debts; herewith I send you the half-penny, and request a receipt.

"P. S. The child has arrived; a very nice child it is; the nurse is a little too sensitive, but a very respectable woman. Dorothea."

Frederick turned to the messenger: —

"I shall deliver the receipt myself, as I am riding thither;" and he now put his horse into a gallop: Herman spurred his, and they hurried off.

The exterior of the mansion afforded a rich subject for a painter. The old stones which served as gate-posts were overgrown with wild hops, the tendrils of which ran up over the thatched roof, which on the side next the road reached to the ground, and was covered with moss and house-leek; forming such a richness and variety of color as may be seen on a painter's palette. Opposite the straw roof was a yellow clay slope, from which hung wild rose-bushes, with their red hips. In the centre stood the main building, the walls of which were supported by thick brick pillars; but one did not see much of the red bricks in that half church-like building. They were hidden as with a curtain of close ivy, which grew fresh and luxuriantly up the roof, nay, even twined itself around the chimney. The side buildings were of frame-work, that is, they were of wood and brick-work; the projecting wings were covered with wild vines, which now, in the autumn, showed their vermilion-colored leaves to the greatest advantage. Here was window close by window, from the top to the bottom through two stories; the place looked quite like a large conservatory, and for that reason the whole mansion was generally called in the neighborhood, "*the greenhouse.*"

In the summer time palms, cypresses, and cactus stood outside in large tubs, and it was worth while to see the beautiful water-lilies that flowered here: they almost covered two long ponds, the remains of the old moat. The mansion lay in a wilderness of verdure; it was as if grown over and around with white and red thorn, linden-trees, chestnuts, and buck-thorn.

It must be allowed that the stranger was right who once said, it looked like "the palace in the sleeping forest," only a beauty was wanting therein.

Perhaps the little girl now there might grow up such a one.

Frederick and Herman were announced and admitted. Having first passed through a passage where two vines were trained through an open pane, and formed a whole leafy saloon covered with large bunches of grapes, they entered a a small cabinet, where two trees in tubs, grown round with moss, stood like sentinels at the door. Every conceivable color glowed upon their branches, and yet there was neither flower nor leaf. they were two artificial trees, covered all over with stuffed humming-birds, so shiningly beautiful, in red and green, in gold and colors, that regarded for the moment, the whole looked like richly beaming flowers. A double curtain hung down before the door; it drew aside, and one was in the Grandmother's sitting-room. Here, also, it looked like a conservatory; along the walls stood long, small tin boxes, in which evergreens were planted, and trained over a trellis work of fine canes. They formed an espalier, a living screen for the portraits, with which the walls behind were hung; the fresh green leaves hid the frames, and for the most part the figures also; it was only before the faces that there was a larger opening through the foliage.

"I have put my husband's forefathers in flower-pots," said the old lady. "Look at the commodore there, — one cannot find the star now, it has got a covering; what strange eyes he makes behind the green leaves! I erect an order of merit for the dead, but with living foliage. The fair lady there with the parrot looks pleased enough at it, but especially the parrot. But it is well you have come; you are both of you students, and well read. Here I sit and dispute with Madame Krone, who is a very excellent woman, but she does not know geography, and that is certainly the science one can least of all do without. Our geography always lies here on the table, that we may refer to it when we read the newspapers, and know where we are: I always use it in Copenhagen, when I read the play-bills. If the scene, for instance, be laid in Milan, I refer to the book, — 'Milan, a large Cathedral;' — so I know that. If one goes to the theatre, there the geography is just as useful as the play-bill, for one must know where one is."

"Yes," said Madame Krone ; "but just now my gracious lady will have it that Jutland is united with Norway, and that can never be ; Jutland is on the other side of Funen, and Norway is a long voyage above Elsinore. Have I not sailed up there myself from Copenhagen ? "

"But I will have a suspension bridge," said the old lady. "Madame Krone does not know that Jutland ends in a point, and from that point, which is called Skagen, they should make the junction."

"But the distance is pretty great," said Frederick, "and the open sea runs between, full eighteen Danish [1] miles across ! "

"I know it ; but it is for that reason I will have it that they shall make a suspension bridge ; then the post might go in the winter, and they could send corn in, and many other useful things besides. It is always good for lands to be joined together."

"But on what should that bridge hang ? " asked Frederick.

"On chains," said the lady. "They must make them fast to the Norwegian rocks, build a tower on Skagen, and then hang the bridge between."

"But, according to the laws of gravitation, the chains would, by dint of their own weight, sink deep into the sea ! "

"Then they must be braced tighter ! " said the old lady. "The engineer must understand that ! Have we not such a one in Copenhagen ? let him stretch them well out, and then it will hang. But Madame Krone cannot understand that ; she will have it that the way to Norway is from Elsinore. But why is the other one there laughing ? *Him* I mean with the beautiful eyes ! Well, laugh on, your teeth are very good, and laughing suits you ; an honest mind at least lies in the teeth — further in I shall not go — so give me your hand ! " She gave him hers, shook his, and said : " Thanks, comrade ! and the water-splasher there also," she added, and gave her hand to Count Frederick, saying, "I beg pardon, Sir Count, but you're a little foolish and sea-mad ! You shall both have a little present before you go ; but you have leave to stay awhile yet."

---

[1] Nearly eighty miles English.

"You say I have an honest mind, as far as my teeth," said Herman. "I have also one within, and that I will prove to you. You know not what an unutterable desire I have had for many years to see Funen. My friend there persuaded me to make one of the sailing party hither ; we have both passed our college examinations with success, and in such cases one does not begin to read again directly. We knew that you were in Holstein, but it never came into my mind that you would return so suddenly. I was certain that I should not meet with you, and in a few days would have been again in Copenhagen. Everything has happened contrary to expectation. You have made so good an impression on me that it would be dishonorable not to tell you whom you have seen, whom you have so kindly taken by the hand. I am Herman, dear Grandmother ! "

The old lady had looked at him intently from the beginning of his speech, and her face had become more and more serious ; she now gave her head a toss, and exclaimed, —

"I know it ! I knew it, but yet I would not know it ! They say I am a strange creature, so what should I know it for ? "

"Did you know him ? " asked Frederick. "But how was that possible ? "

"Sailor ! " said she ; and there was something peculiar in the tone which might either be of jest or anger. "Come, now you shall have the presents ; " and she beckoned to her grandson, but stopped. "No, a Count is more than a Baron ; besides, you belong, as one may say, to the house. Sir Count," and she drew Frederick with her into the first room. Here she looked on all sides, and suddenly cast her eyes on the tree with the variegated humming-birds. "Would you like that ? You are yourself a bird, a water-bird, and such a one is wanting at the manor. Do you like it ? But you must take it with you directly ; for I tell you, that from the moment you accept it, it must not remain any longer in my house ! "

"Then you would have me ride with it before me on my horse," said Frederick ; "but that is not possible, so I must lose your handsome present."

"Claus can ride with it." said she. "It is a fine Shrovetide rod,[1] is it not? And a Shrovetide rod might do you good."

She turned her back on him, and went into the next room.

"Now he has got his rod," said she, turning to Herman, "you shall have your present!"

She opened the door of the next room, Herman followed her, and the door was closed.

"Why have you brought him over here, Sir Count?" said Madame Krone; "the old lady is angry, extremely angry. I know her face!"

"No, she is not angry," said Frederick; "she received him in the most amiable manner, and we are both to have presents. Besides, what foolish idea is that of hers, that she will not see her grandson, a young man whom every one is fond of, and must respect."

"You don't know that — you don't know her. Pardon me, Sir Count, that I speak thus. She is good and benevolent, better than the world is in general, but she has her strange whims, and one must put up with them."

"Is it true, as folks say," asked Frederick, " that she lately made a velvet collar for you, Madame Krone, and embroidered her own name on it, — and that you are to wear it, but which you of course will not?"

"Yes, they tell such stories; but others which have more of truth in them, and are just as amusing, if you will, but which bear witness to her goodness of heart, they do not tell."

"Yes, they do," said Frederick; "the Councilor's lady told me one no later than yesterday, which is both comical and touching. You also play a part in it, although a secondary one. But you shall hear. The old lady was passing a wretched house down in the village, where an old woman, who lives with the owner of the house, and looks after it, stood and washed her linen; it was a single piece.

---

[1] In Denmark it is the custom on Shrove Tuesday to beat one's friends out of their beds with a rod; this practice, however, is not carried out, as, instead of a birch rod, a bouquet of artificial flowers is generally laid within the bed-chamber door.

"'How many have you of that sort?' asked the old lady.

"'God help me!' said the old woman, 'I have only this one.'

"'Every decent woman ought to have six!' said the old lady.

"'Yes; God help me!' repeated the old woman.

"So the old lady set off directly to Svendborg, bought some linen, and made five more. You know the story very well! and the old woman was happy, and the Baroness also, and she then said : —

"'If I can do so much good for that bit of money, and get a little needlework, then I have more pleasure of the same kind. Tell me, dame,' said she, 'are there more in the village who have not six pieces of linen?'

"'Yes, God knows there are!' said the old woman.

"'Well, then, send them all to me.'

"The Baroness herself told the story from the beginning, and she said, 'there came so many persons to me, — girls and women, that I went to Svendborg, and bought linen, and Madame Krone and I sewed the whole day and half the night, during a fortnight, and now all the girls and women in the village have six.'"

"But is that anything to make a jest of?" said Madame Krone ; "is it not kind — is it not good? even if it be something out of the way?"

The grandmother and grandson came just then into the room ; both were laughing, and he had a splendid gold watch attached to a long chain.

"It is that he may know how time goes, and that one must do something, and not trifle it away. You, too, may learn a little from it," said the Grandmother to Frederick.

She and Herman, as we have said, both came in laughing, but it was too clearly depicted on their faces that something had happened ; that feelings quite different from such as call forth a smile were fermenting within.

"Now we should see our little foster-daughter," said Frederick.

"She is asleep," said the old lady, "and no one must dis-

turb her ; and now I thank you for the honor of the visit," —
here she courtesied low. "Each has got what he ought to
have, and I have had a great pleasure."

Both the gentlemen were now obliged to take leave. The
groom stood before the door with their horses : they mounted
and galloped off.

"Well," said Frederick, "she is a remarkable woman, —
we were in reality shown the door ! But you are not in your
old humor. Has she said anything mortifying ? How can
her words have such an effect on you, a reasonable being ! "

"O no ! " answered Herman, who became still paler. "I
know that every man has his Achilles' heel, where he can be
wounded, and she has found mine, and wounded me. Yet it
is not her words ; she has touched what I thought the invul-
nerable part of my heart ! Tell you it, I cannot, — I cannot
impart it to any one, at least not to-day — not this year. You
shall, however, be the first to whom I will tell it. But now all
this must be a secret ; you will give me your hand as an assurance. She has cast a brand into my soul which at this
moment destroys all pleasure — all happiness ! No, no ! " he
shouted violently, "it is not so — I will preserve my good
humor ! " and he spurred his horse.

Count Frederick, in the greatest astonishment, and uneasy
at the change that showed itself in his friend's face, rode side
by side with him. The old lady's servant could not keep pace
with them, but went at what the peasants call "a jog-trot," behind them, as well as he could, as he bore before him on the
horse the whole of that artificial tree, with the variegated humming-birds, which trembled with the motion, and shone in the
sun with a thousand colors.

CHAPTER VII.

IN THE STREET, AND IN THE BALL-ROOM.

WE will now accompany the friends to Copenhagen; the
return voyage was much better for them than the voyage out; it was in November, in what we call our bad season,
with rain and drizzle; and with its eternal blasts, one imag-
ines one's self in the cavern of the winds. It was in the real,
Copenhagen November days; with gray skies, twilight instead
of daylight, and muddy streets, so that umbrellas and galoches became a necessary part of the human machine —
its limit above and below; added to this, as the only change,
a raw, thick fog, such as one can positively taste. The whole
air is a cold damp, which penetrates through the clothes, and
into the pores of the body: it sheds its clamminess over gateway and door, over the wooden balustrades, and through the
entrance halls; one feels one's self in an element suited for
frogs, and not for warm-blooded animals. The dustman and
scavenger's wagon, with its drenched and ragged driver, who
helps the dirty servant girl to empty her tub of dirt and
sweepings into his filthy receptacle, is the bouquet of such a
Copenhagen November day.

Leaving this weather and these streets, we will enter the
minister's saloon, and see lights and colors that remind us of
the summer sun, and we shall breathe there. Orange-trees
are placed on each side of the broad staircase, which is covered with variegated carpeting, fastened with bright brass rods.
Servants in splendid liveries, with shoes and silk stockings,
fill the lobby and throw open the large folding-doors; a mild
scented air streams towards us, from the lustre, from the chan-
delier under the ceiling, and from the astral lamps on the
tables. A suite of rooms thus lighted up lies before us, all
covered with rich carpets, long, splendid curtains, silk-cush-

ioned chairs, and velvet-covered sofas, which, impelléd by the slightest touch, roll to whatever place one would have them. Here stand tables with richly bound English and French books, engravings, and journals. Paintings hang on the walls, and in one room, between the prettily arranged flowers, stands a beautiful statue.

Some of the elder part of the company now go to the card-tables, others sit in conversation, or silently watch the groups of young ladies whom the gentlemen join, and converse with, in a lively and laughing tone, and amongst these Clara is the prettiest: one can see that in the mother's face, which says: "She is my daughter; eighteen years ago I myself looked like her." Baron Herman is the leader of the conversation, which is, if one may call it so, that of repartee, such as we read in "The School for Scandal," though there is no intended malice in it; being a few stories about some well-known man, to whom at least one may always attribute stories of that kind. Count Frederick and Holger make lively remarks, but Herman is the liveliest; no one observes the gloom that has sunk deep into his soul since his conversation with his grandmother; no one suspects that that laughing face can, at home, in solitary moments, wear the expression of pain itself! He stands before Clara; her eyes shine into his soul, and fill it, and he is fascinated.

"You have really drawn his picture of whom you spoke?" asked Clara. "You do it excellently! you are truly an excellent man."

"He knows how to take us all off from the wrong side," said Frederick.

"And I also?" asked Clara. "You must draw me in caricature; I shall certainly look frightful; but it is of no consequence."

"I know no wrong side to take you from," said Herman, "I must at least see you oftener, and watch you."

"I laugh so much," said Clara; "there you have a subject," and she laughed with her rosy lips, beautiful teeth, and sparkling eyes, so that it was still more difficult to catch an ugly or comic idea.

The servants came in with ices, the conversation changed,

and the piano sounded. The music-master had obtained permission for one of his poor pupils, a young girl, to play in that high circle. She was very pretty, and had much talent; a few eye-glasses were directed towards her from the card-tables, and one old lady rose from her chair, stood a moment by the door, and cried, "*Charmant.*"

"Prettily played," said Clara; "but she has not a good carriage."

However, Clara was the only one amongst all the young ladies that spoke to the quiet stranger, who, after having finished playing, stood in a corner, between the piano and a group of other young girls, who showed that they had nothing to do with her.

Clara's words and kindness enlivened her features, and her eyes glistened. Herman approached. Was it for the girl's sake or for Clara's?

It was late in the night, and he was still by Clara's side, when she and her mother got into their carriage. It rolled away in the raw damp air; the fog hung like a close white veil over the carriage-windows, and the ladies drew their cloaks closer around them.

"You had all the young gentlemen about you, Clara," said her mother. "That is always the case at your age, and with your exterior. Be a prudent and sensible child; and do not be hasty. You did not, however, keep yourself quite erect. Else it is remarkable how you resemble me, when I was your age."

"Count Frederick was very amiable," said Clara, though she at the same time really thought of Herman, whose liveliness and whose attention to her were not without their effect.

"Count Frederick is an excellent young man," said the mother; "and the family is one of the first."

There was a pause; she then kissed Clara, and they stopped before their own house.

Herman ran through the slushy streets in galoches and with an umbrella; the fine cold rain that fell with the fog forced its way into his face, but he did not feel it; all was flame within him, all sunlight; his whole thoughts were bound up in Clara, and yet he did not then know that it was love, — his dawning first love.

We are again at a ball, a great court ball. It is like a bright sunshiny day, so splendid is the light; no flower-bed can be more variegated or rich than this vast assembly of red uniforms, with stars and orders: the ladies' dresses are so tasteful, so various; and it is precisely the dresses that the admiral's lady is reviewing and talking about with an elder lady, whose golden turban, which looks like a saucepan, and her bright yellow satin gown, trimmed with blonde, do not betray the very best taste.

The music is excellent; it even sets the old Excellences' legs in motion, and they think of dances in days of yore. The lackeys move like Caryatides, with refreshments, through the closest circles; in a recess of the window stands Clara, prettier, perhaps, than she ever was before. She is in a white transparent dress, which falls in full, vapor-like folds, as if it were woven of air and snow. Small bouquets of moss and violets seem as if they were thrown on it. There is, as it were, a transparency in the face, in the arm, in the whole figure. There is an expression of bliss in that youthfully fresh, charming face — a smile that owns more magic than music and poetry; never before has she been so beautiful, never before has she smiled more happily, — she is in conversation with one of the princes, who leads her to the dance. Frederick stands not far from her, in a blue velvet court-dress with large diamond buttons; he sees her happy smile, he is angry with her without even being able to account to himself for it.

They meet in the dance and part again. Holger enters just at this moment. Clara has promised him her hand for the third dance, and yet he is the last that arrives; but we must know the reason.

Holger was yesterday made a gentleman of the bed-chamber. His tailor has been sewing the whole night and day at his uniform, made impossibilities possible, got it ready for this ball, and only half an hour ago was it delivered.

The red gold-embroidered coat sits well; the tight kerseymere trousers are made to admiration. Holger is strikingly handsome ; and he knows,it. This is the first uniform he has ever worn ; it is the first title he has received, except that of baron by right of birth, and Clara has already discovered him, and smiled to him. How much youthful spirit and happiness can one heart not find place for!

Count Frederick, on the contrary, appears all at once to be quite dissatisfied. The ball tires him; Clara's smile is not pleasing to him, and not one dance has she for him. "Fourteen days ago, I was engaged for them all," — has she said with a smile, which he, in his present state of feeling, thought was coquettish, — "and now she dances with Holger!"

They are a handsome couple, and they are noticed. There is to them both a present feeling of, "the whole world is ours! — all the rest only figure around us!" — is it Clara's smile; is it the music, or the new uniform, that fits so well, or perhaps all three, that have their influence? At this moment it is clear to Holger, as it never was before, that he loves Clara, that he must tell her so, that he would dance with her thus life through; there is no sorrow, no sickness, nor death!

They now retire to a saloon; the champagne explodes. Holger is happy as a god, eloquent and gay, and as he again enters the ball-room with Clara, his resolution is formed, — before the ball is ended she must know his feelings, know that he loves her — that this is his first, all-powerful love!

He has spirit, and he has a will, that must be acknowledged ; and at this moment Herman sleeps quietly at home ; at this moment Frederick is meditating if he shall, or if he shall not, drive Clara to-morrow at noon, with the great sledge party to Bellevue. The music of the dance is to the low-spirited wretch like surging waves, that make his spirit still more a wreck, but the glad and happy they only lift still higher. Clara has quite forgotten Herman's amusing, genial pictures, forgotten Frederick's lively sketches of his sea-trip — which she before had listened to with so much delight. Holger is the best dancer, the most attentive of all, the most amiable. In the dance which is now to begin he will lead her out.

With the whole expression of a happy being in his eyes and mien, he stands before Clara, his blood and thoughts like champagne : he bows low ; with a jesting smile he then raises himself a full inch higher than his wont, and then — is there magic at work ? One would think so ! Are men accompanied by an invisible spirit, good or bad ? At the moment that Holger rises, there occurs suddenly, as it were, a transformation in him ; his face becomes deeply crimsoned, his movements are forced ; his words are no longer buoyant ; something of importance has happened ; his whole thoughts are divided between Clara and — nay, it would sound too terrible to pronounce the word suddenly.

The least causes have often the greatest effects. Holger no longer moves as before — he even returns quite preposterous answers.

This night he will not propose. Clara still exists for Frederick, for Herman, for him whom no one knows — for anybody. In the midst of fascination's brightest moment, on the eve of love's bold revelation — yes, perhaps, more than one who has been in the same situation, knows the agony with which a man loses all his moral courage at such a moment — and this Holger has lost : the joys of youth, the pride of his new title, of his well-made uniform — all are vanished. Clara regards him with an anxious look ; the thought strikes her, — the unjust thought — it is the wine ! he has drunk too much champagne ! — and the halo around him is extinguished. She knows not what injustice she does him ; her eloquence becomes mute ; she involuntarily seeks Count Frederick ; her eye meets his, — it is as if he smiled, as if he understood her position, — inclination is renewed, and she inclines for Frederick. Holger creeps behind the window-curtain for a moment, and makes his appearance again, but he is no longer the same man. The whole affair has been the most unfortunate, but most innocent situation at a ball that ever happened. It is reality's most fearful prose that has overwhelmed him. When a man is to be executed, it is the custom to say, " he is to lose his button," that is, to lose his head, and Holger has lost a button, and with that his head. The brace-button behind has come off his tight kerseymere inexpressibles — now the word is out, and now we can conceive his sudden blushing, the forced deportment, the distracted thoughts, and the preposterous answers. With that button went courage and happiness, and Clara's rapture; she accepted Frederick's invitation, and they both drove next day in the sledge together to Bellevue. The train, consisting of forty-seven sledges, went from Amalienborg, the royal residence; princes, diplomatists, and young noblemen formed the *cortége.* The bells tinkled, the variegated nets fluttered over the horses' backs, and the whips cracked. Frederick, in a bear-skin cloak, with seal-skin boots, and fur cap, had Clara in his sledge, and they were soon out of the city; the crows flew over the white snow, — "caw, caw," — every one greets in his own way; where the snow was deepest, there these two were upset; it was like a play. It was a little adventure, it was a splendid trip. "It was an important trip," said the admiral's lady — and why?

The same evening Frederick wrote to his father that he loved Clara, that she had accepted him, and that her excellent mother had no objection to the match, provided his father sanctioned it.

"That button," said Holger, when he heard it, "that d—d button is the cause of the whole!" and he fell into deep musing.

Herman tore all his drawings to pieces; they were too ideal, he thought; everything was far more discordant, far uglier. Copenhagen was the most insupportable place, the men and women, with very few exceptions, — in fact without any, — a collection of caricatures and tediousness. Nay, not only Copenhagen, but Sealand, Funen, the whole country was insupportable to him.

Was it Clara's betrothal that cast this shadow over the country and inhabitants, or had that poisonous seed his grandmother's words had sown in his heart, now shot up and become an upas-tree, that poisoned all around him? Such moments in a mind like Herman's, nourish thoughts and determinations that often decide one's whole future life.

The ball-room on a winter forenoon, after a ball, is an uncomfortable place; its lustre is extinguished, the music is mute, all the fresh joys of youth are gone, the curtains hang heavily with dust, the candles are burnt down in the sconces, the bass-viol, and such like mammoth instruments, lie like mummies, and point to a life that was.

Thus it looked next morning in the royal ball-room : in the middle of the floor there lay a shining button, which the woman swept away. That button it was that had caused Holger's heart to look like the ball-room now, — void, uncomfortable. a mausoleum for a button.

CHAPTER VIII.

CAROLINE HEIMERANT.

AS we have now followed the three young friends and fellow-travellers, we may as well look after their tutor, or, what sounds shorter, Moritz. We shall not meet with him at court, nor in the great saloons ; his world is Councilor Heimerant's comfortable parlor.

Here perhaps we may rest awhile after the many balls. Here Caroline was the soul. She lost her mother early, and grew up like a boy, with her wild brothers, who were now dispersed about the country ; she had caught from them all their bold Copenhagen phrases, which, to the initiated, often sounded highly strange, from that pretty, lively girl's mouth.

The father was one of those good-natured, laughing persons, who, in the theatre, are a blessing to the farce-writer whose piece may happen to be played ; for he laughed on the least occasion. In business he was as accurate as a correct sum in arithmetic without fractions, and a father with his whole soul. The family lived entirely to themselves, formed their own fixed family circle, and in this Caroline shone ; they knew her excellent qualities, and amused themselves with what strangers would, in her, call bad habits.

As we know, Moritz, the evening before his departure for Funen, had proposed, and been accepted, but at the same time she declared that he must not let the voyage pass over, but that he should have his sail for a few days, as if nothing had happened.

"We will not begin by hanging over and about each other," said she. " I have seen enough of that with my eldest brother and Louisa. Good dear wife she is, but a hanging tree she was. Sail, but don't upset, for I have no desire to be melancholy ; there is no pleasure in it."

She smiled, but yet there were tears in her eyes ; Moritz thought she was charming.

And Moritz sailed to Funen, as we know, and everything that happened to him and the friends there we also know, and that he was now again in Copenhagen ; but that he, on his arrival, got the first kiss — that we do not know ; but he got it, and there was much to tell about, much to say.

"Do you think I can keep all the nonsense I have heard ?" said she. "No, we are now two to bear the burden ; so you must take your share."

They must also drink *thou* together, or else she could not address him properly when he was to be chid.

"You are a strange, blessed being !" said he ; "I have often thought you resemble Undine."

"That was a very romantic woman you sought out to compare me to," said she. "Yes, I am somewhat eccentric, as you say, but yet it is that which had made me interesting to you ; we two certainly do not resemble each other in the least."

A friend of hers now came to visit her.

"Will you see the fellow ?" said she. "He is a little quiet yet ; but I shall put him in trim. Next winter he shall run on the ice with me. It is so tiresome with many gentlemen. When they *will* accompany me home in the evening, they are so afraid because I speak so loud ; and then I must not slide on the ice when there are boys. It is pleasant to be a street-boy now and then. 'Off the slide !' I shout, and slide away."

"If one did not know you, Caroline," said Moritz, "one might" —

"She knows me better than you do. We have gone to school together ; we went in the month of March with cloaks, muffs, and a large parasol, which we held before us against the wind, and the sun shone on our necks, so that our shadows were in the parasol ; at every street corner, on the right side, we changed to carry it, and we held it straight before us, and not before our faces, for the wind obliged us to do so. And so you think that she does not know me ! It is more for two persons to go under one parasol than to exchange gold

rings. Can you understand that?" And she laughed with
her eyes as well as her mouth.

All the servants were fondly attached to her, for she was
kind-hearted, and always spoke so confidentially with them ;
the old serving-man would go through fire and water for her ;
but then she always nodded so kindly to him, even at the great
party that was given once a year, and where there were privy
councilors, and even the head of the police. "Not that look,
George," she would then say ; "besides, I am betrothed."
For the servant-girls she wrote letters and verses to their
sweethearts. She had also her own language for the servants.
"You are a slave this evening at nine o'clock," sufficed for
George. "You will come at that time and fetch me." No
one in the theatre was more easily affected by a tragedy than
she ; no one shed more tears at the conclusion of an affecting
book, and at the same moment she could jest at it. "I have
a wonderfully great talent for the sentimental," she would say ;
"if I would only perfect myself in it, I might become a salt-
spring for the country." Her prettiest talent was, however,
the performance of small pieces of music and accompaniments
to songs on the piano. It is true she had no great power of
voice, but all that deep feeling which a poem inspired her with,
she seized directly, and it ran through the song ; it was a
pleasure to hear her perform Reichardt's melodies to Goethe's
poems. Humor was, however, as we have said, the most pre-
dominant in her. Moritz's adventures in Funen, and the
drawing of lots as to who should be the little child's father,
she thought at once merry and touching ; it amused her to tell
acquaintances when Moritz could overhear her : "My betrothed has a little daughter in Funen."

"My dear girl," said he, "you must really tell the whole
story, or don't tell such things about me."

"He is afraid of his reputation," cried she, laughing.

On her chefonier she had a collection of small figures : two
game-cocks made of feathers, and a sailing-vessel of blown-
glass, but the prettiest were five small porcelain figures, representing Cupid in different characters. First the naked little
fellow with bow and quiver of arrows ; then Cupid as a chim-
ney-sweep with a ladder ; then as an officer with a general's

hat on his head, a sword and belt round his waist, and large riding-boots on — otherwise he was naked; number four, as a watchman with his morning star and helmet-hat; number five, as a sailor with a glazed hat, short jacket, and an oar in his hand.

"You only want him a priest," said her friend.

"There I have Moritz. He is a large edition to be sure, but then he is also more dressed."

"You will really resemble the old Baroness in Funen," said he; "you speak almost like her, and have so many of her ways; it may do well enough now that you are young, and it may suit well enough yet, because I myself am blind in these days of betrothal; but when you become old and " —

"I shall be quiet and tiresome enough," said she; "when you get me up to the Faroe Islands or over to Bornholm, then you will see how considerate and tiresome I shall be. Then you will wish me my humor back again."

The winter was past: it was one evening in the early spring, and Caroline, like all other persons, had caught a cold.

"Yes, and in such a degree," said she, "that I must use sheets, and not pocket-handkerchiefs."

Moritz was in a bad humor, and vexed himself because Herman, whom he was fond of, and who was so good and clever, had got, as Moritz expressed himself, one of his Funen grandmother's mad fits. Herman had suddenly ceased to study, and would be a painter, or — what he had most at heart — he would go to Italy. It is true he had six hundred dollars a year secured to him, but how far would that sum go abroad, and what was his future life likely to be if his grandmother disinherited him?

"I have preached to him," said Moritz, "but it is of no avail. Everything is in readiness for his departure. And it is certainly the General who is so fond of him, who has spoken so well of him to the King, and got permission for him to go with the frigate which sails to-morrow for the Mediterranean. He will quite spoil his future prospects! spoil everything with his grandmother. But it is some of her nature that is coming out, and I have told him so."

"I am not the cause of it," said Caroline; "you must not

look so angrily at me. If it be from an unfortunate love to me, then it is you yourself who are the cause; why has he been allowed to see me, and learned to know my matchless amiability?"

Moritz looked gravely at her, on account of this jest, now that he was in such low spirits; she smiled, and imprinted a kiss on his brow. "Do not take it so seriously to heart," said she; "of what use can it be if I were also to sit and hang my head down? One must suffer and one must die, is what I always say."

Herman was to go on board this very evening; he had prepared himself very quietly for his voyage during the few last weeks. We will not describe his leave-taking of his friends; the few he has he hastens away from as if he were going on a journey for two or three days. We will not look into the pain which dwells within him. Who misses him here? who thinks of him when, in the early morning hour, they weigh anchor in the roads? — not Clara, — no, Caroline Heimerant. She thinks of his sorrows, thinks of the beautiful Clara, and excuses her; one can love but *one*, and she loves Count Frederick.

No one speaks more about Herman; but of the first violets and of the storks that had come; of the new operas that would still be performed before the close of the season. The summer comes, the harvest succeeds, and the year's wheel has revolved once more since the four friends sat together in rain and storm, with full glasses, and adopted their little daughter. We will turn the year's wheel four times more, and Clara is a countess; Holger is attached to the embassy in Stockholm; and Moritz, — yes, Moritz, he is also gone; he has got a living at Halligers, on the coast of Slesvig; he has now been there full six months, and in the approaching harvest will come to fetch his bride. She is the only one of our acquaintances who still remains in Copenhagen, pretty, lively, and jesting as ever. She has borrowed a lover in Moritz's absence, she says; "quite a little one!" it is a child, a boy four years of age, Moritz's sister's son. The mother is a widow, and has gone to Jutland this summer; the little fellow does not miss her, for he clings with his whole heart to Caroline. "She does not know how to talk to children!" said Moritz frequently, thereby showing how little he knew about them. Children are most amused with new expressions, and being spoken to in an unusual manner. She was just as zealous in painting the boy's top and fastening the lash to his whip as she was in sewing for her approaching marriage. If she fell short of stories, she took "The Advertiser" and read for him, with a strong emphasis and pleasure, all the dishes that it was stated one could get at the dining-rooms, and every dish was for the little boy, as the most beautiful strophe in a poem is for us. The same paper in which she read to him ended its service as a three-cornered hat, or a boat, in which he could sail over and fetch Moritz.

She dressed herself and the boy out, and then they formed a *tableau*, and no one saw it except Ragatzo, the old dog, and he was so fat and lazy, so unsuited to play with, that he lay down to rest, even when the sword was bound round his body, and he, Caroline, and the little boy, were to play a band of robbers. These plays often caused her to sit up long after midnight, but then her fingers plied the needle quicker, and the scissors too; there was both woolen and linen in preparation for the parsonage at the Halligers. At the same time she managed the house for her father, with one girl. Everything went on well; there was time both to play and jest, at least so it appeared. The autumn came, and the little boy's mother, Hedevig, was to come in the course of a fortnight, but Moritz was expected still earlier. Two evenings before his arrival, the little boy was taken ill, very ill, and Caroline sat up with him, and nursed him; she was unceasing in her attentions to him. The doctor could not as yet say what ailed the child. He would always have Caroline with him; she sat up with him again the next night: it was typhus. The doctor had just pronounced this to be the child's illness when Moritz arrived. He was to remain some weeks, then the marriage was to take place, and directly afterwards he was to depart with his fair bride to the Halligers, by the foaming Baltic. The joy of meeting was mutual; they were both afflicted on account of the little boy, whose mother was absent, and whose only joy he was.

5

The child's bed stood in Caroline's chamber, for she could not leave the sick boy; she also was attacked, and lay suffering when they bore the little child, as a corpse, out of her chamber.

Moritz had come with his heart full of summer's pleasures; for months and weeks these days had shone before him as the days of happiness, and now he sat beside — perhaps a death-bed. It was a wet, raw night, one of the coldest that the autumn had yet brought with it; the windows stood open, and the little dead boy lay in an adjoining room. Caroline had fallen asleep with her head on Moritz's arm; he could not find in his heart to withdraw it, although it pained him. Her long hair had fallen down over her forehead, and a hectic flush stained her cheeks. It was quite still, and in the middle of the night, when the door of the room in which the little dead boy lay sprang suddenly open. At any other time there would have been nothing striking in it; the door had often sprung open in this way, but that it should occur this night was somewhat strange. The lamp was placed so that the light should not fall on the face of the sufferer, and it now cast its whole light on the face of the dead child, which lay there clothed in white, and with a wreath of flowers around its head. Caroline opened her eyes at that moment, and gazed on it. "Yes, I knew well that he was dead," she said, in a low voice. "I shall also die, but do not grieve for me. I once thought it would be so terrible, but now I do not think it at all so. I can even bear the thought that you remain behind; it seems to me as if I shall only say good-night to you; we shall see each other to-morrow, — then I shall not fail to joke with you, but now I cannot: good night!" and she laid her head down again.

It was so still in the chamber — so raw and cold. A bird screamed in the garden. Was it death's bird? In the adjoining chambers there lay two dead bodies — the little boy's and Caroline Heimerant's.

CHAPTER IX.

THE MYSTERIOUS CHAMBER.

COUNT FREDERICK and Clara, who had now been married a year, returned just at this time from Paris and Switzerland Frederick heard of Moritz's misfortune with much sorrow and sympathy, and begged him in the most pressing terms to come over to him in Funen, and pass some days there ; it lay on his way home, and the neighborhood and society there would not, as in Copenhagen, continually remind him of his loss ; his sister, Hedevig, who, after the death of her lively little boy attached herself more closely to her brother, and had determined to accompany him to the Halligers, and keep house for him, was of course also invited. Moritz accepted the invitation, as he felt a suffering in remaining in the Councilor's house, where the soul, the sunshine, Caroline, was present no longer. Besides, he had a great desire to speak with the old Baroness about the little girl. Elizabeth was her name ; the poor child had no one in the world but him to look after her now ; and this he felt deeply in his sorrow, for the child, now five years of age, had suddenly fallen under the Baroness's highest displeasure, and been sent out of the house for her " cunning," as it was stated in the last letter.

In order to learn this " cunning," we will also join the travellers to Funen, and even go a few weeks back in time, to the 14th of August, the Baroness's birthday, as it was called, but which in fact it never had been.

" My birthday was a stupid day," said she ; " I celebrate it very quietly, and no one shall know it ; but I have looked out the 14th of August as my birthday, for I like the look of it in the almanac, and I will make merry on that day."

It was whispered about that it was on that day her father,

long Rasmus, had ridden on the wooden horse; there were also several stories about a little chamber that was always kept locked, and only opened once a year, just on that very morning, when the old lady went into it; and when she came back she was as merry and lively as if she had been drinking a little.

On the 14th of August all the poor in the neighborhood were assembled at a sort of audience; the old lady knew them all by name, and even their whole life and history, and after this knowledge they were all rewarded. The great saloon was then a perfect bazaar, where she and Madame Krone sat and distributed the presents. Every one got something. The married folks, grits, butter, and meal; the young girls ribbons, and colored neckerchiefs; the peasant boys, a horse with a whistle attached to the tail, and that the old lady herself blew first of all, before she delivered it. Several hundred dollars' worth of things were thus given away.

Against this time — as early as the month of July — the old lady and Madame Krone were always found busily occupied, sewing clothes for the men and women, all made after the Baroness's own orders.

When they had all got what they were to have, the old lady clapped herself and Madame Krone on the shoulder, saying, —

"See, now, we two have been decent folks. Now I mean to be ' *her ladyship* !' "

And then she dressed herself in her best apparel, and carriages began to roll into the court-yard; great and rich guests came to a grand dinner-party, and after that was ended, all were obliged to go down into the garden and the adjacent wood.

Every year there was one or the other arrangement made calculated to surprise the guests. It was generally a living picture, or tableau, and often arranged with picturesque taste and effect. Thus: as a visitor walked in the wood, and came where it inclosed a little lake, flames suddenly rose from the surface; a few fishermen lay in their boats with outspread nets, others stood in the water up to their knees; the women worked, and the children danced about. The whole was always performed by the peasantry, who were themselves well-pleased with this comedy, as they called it, and besides, they got money for it. Another year, when the guests came into a ravine in the wood, they stood in the midst of a gypsy camp, where the fire blazed under the large soup-kettle, and the old gypsy hag beat the youngest boy with the ladle. After such a tour, they returned to the great saloon, where they found everything served up in a festal manner.

On the table stood an immensely large cake, and in an undefined place in the cake there was placed a nut, baked with it; the cake was then divided equally amongst the guests, and the one who got the piece wherein the nut lay, was called "the second birthday child," was congratulated, and got a present from the lady of the house, which was always bound round with roses gathered from the grass-plot in the court-yard, where, as we know, the wooden horse had stood.

It was just towards evening of the day previous to this festival that the old lady was busily engaged in arranging everything in the wood. This time it was to be "the Elves'-dance;" it had first been her intention to give "the Greek gods," but Madame Krone had most seriously opposed it, and at last had gained her point; for it would have been scandalous, she said, if the old lady had arranged the affair with sea-nymphs, as they should have been naked peasant women, who waded about in the lake. That they might become ill by performing such a *comedy* moved the Baroness to give up the idea, but not that it could be called immoral, "for all virtue was immorality when immoral persons judged it," said the old lady.

Little Elizabeth, now a girl of five years, a singularly still child, and rather naughty, as spoiled children generally become, sat on a stool at some distance from Madame Krone and the Baroness, both of whom were busy sewing, as they were not quite ready with the presents for the next day. There was a woolen under-jacket unfinished for an old and infirm cottager. Elizabeth had her little table before her, covered with playthings, but they lay untouched; her doll was thrown on the floor, and the child held her hands in her lap, and looked thoughtfully before her with her blue eyes.

"You must not sit and think, Elizabeth," said the old lady; "let that alone till you grow bigger, and if it be sleepiness, why then, to bed. That is the best, too, for to-morrow you are to stay up, like a grown-up woman."

"O, to-morrow!" exclaimed Elizabeth, lifting her little hands, and then sitting again thoughtfully.

"It is all that she sits and thinks about!" said Madame Krone, half aloud. "She hears nothing else talked about amongst the servants at this time, and she sees how busy we are! Little pitchers have ears as well as large ones · how happy she was last year, and the year before; but now she has more understanding."

It *was* the following day that was running in the child's head, but in another way than that which Madame Krone and the old lady supposed; the little ears had heard and retained much of what the servants had related. There was more wisdom in the old lady's "you must not sit and think," than any one imagined.

Elizabeth must now go to bed. She slept in a little chamber close to Madame Krone's, who led her thither, got her undressed, and to sleep, when the sewing began again. At one o'clock, however, all were to go to bed that night. Madame Krone looked in to little Elizabeth — there was no one in the bed. She sought for her everywhere, sent a message to the kitchen, ordered the servants to search the yard and the garden, but Elizabeth was nowhere to be found. Madame Krone would, in her anxiety, have gone to the Baroness and told her of it, but stopped, turned round, and went down into the servants' hall, where she gave orders that they should all go with lanterns and poles, and search the garden once more — but the child was not found.

It was early morning; the candle was lighted in the old lady's chamber, who, as yet, knew nothing of what had occurred; Madame Krone was on her way to her, but stopped, as the old lady had gone to the private room, the secret of which Madame Krone did not know, or would not acknowledge that she knew; she therefore waited until the old lady's return.

There, between four walls, was inclosed the mystery of the

house, and the whole neighborhood; and this was often and often spoken of amongst the servants; little Elizabeth had frequently listened to all this, and when they least imagined it, had sat and thought about it.

Some said that there was nothing in the chamber but a pair of wooden shoes and a milking-pail, which her ladyship herself had worn and carried when she was a poor peasant-girl, and which, on the occasion of her visits, she put on, saying, —

"So I was, and so I am now!"

Others said, that she had concealed a little man there in a bottle, who told her everything that was to happen during the year.

Elizabeth thought of nothing else but to get into the chamber and see what was there. The key, which she knew lay in the little casket on the drawers, she had taken and very cunningly put down into her stocking. As soon as she was in bed and Madame Krone gone, she got up again, put on her shoes, lighted the candle at the night-lamp, and crept along the passage where the door was. She succeeded in opening it directly, and, with the candle in her hand, she now stood in the little semicircular tower-chamber. There was nothing to be seen but a large old portrait of a man, placed in the middle of the chamber, on a board which lay over some rotten wooden piles that appeared to have been pulled up out of the earth. He had on a very large peruke, a red vest and coat, and exhibited a very angry face. Elizabeth looked into every corner to see if she could not find the bottle with the little man in, or at least the wooden shoes and the milk-pail; but there was nothing at all to be found, and therefore she was going to creep away just as stealthily as she had come, but the door had fallen to, the key was outside, and she could not, or did not understand how to open it. She put the candle down on the floor, and pushed against the door with hands and feet, but it was of no use: she was about to cry, but restrained her tears by force. She looked at the old portrait; the full light of the candle fell on it, and she felt the most terrible dread; she fancied that the picture became living; the tears streamed out of her eyes; she shouted aloud, but at the same moment she remembered the old lady, and, through fear of her, became suddenly still, and seized the candle again, but it fell out of her hands, and was extinguished, the long red wick alone showing where it lay. She tried to blow it into a flame again, as she had seen the servants do, but in vain. Her improper conduct, which she well understood, and now the darkness, and the mysterious chamber — everything shook her with terror. The chambermaid Trina, who was to go shortly to Copenhagen to be married to her sweetheart the shoemaker, had told many stories, which she called comedies and ballets, one of them in particular, about Ralph Bluebeard, was very shocking. He had murdered his wives and hidden their bodies in a chamber where no one durst come. This story little Elizabeth could not forget, and thought that the chamber here was just such a one. She thought of the dead wives, who, as Trina had said, danced in their white gowns, and the little child sobbed aloud, crept further and further up into a corner, and as she began to be cold, she drew her little bed-gown up over her head, sat thus, and fell asleep.

It was not daybreak, when the old Baroness was up; she missed the key directly, and to her amazement she found that it was in the door. Scarcely knowing what she did, she pushed the door open with such violence that Elizabeth woke up and stared around her.

The old lady looked about her, and when she discovered the child, she started back, uttering a strange short scream. Her face was distorted, and she seized the child by the arm with the violence of one insane.

"Vagrant!" she muttered, "a key robber!" and she dragged Elizabeth before the picture; here she raised her arm to strike her, but suddenly stopped, and looked at that portrait with a disturbed countenance; the light at this moment fell full on the face of the portrait.

"No, *thou*," said she to the picture, "*thou* shalt not see even a guilty child punished! — ride on thy horse!" and then, like one deranged, she spat on the portrait of him who had kicked her mother, struck herself with the whip, and made her father ride, for derision and contempt, on the wooden horse, which now stood here, a worm-eaten, rotten piece of frame-work, the pedestal for the portrait. It was the wicked lord of the manor, her husband's father's portrait, with the remains of the wooden horse that was kept here.

Elizabeth cried and sobbed.

"Silence!" shouted the old Baroness; "you are bad, wicked; you would lurk and watch, would you! you are, or may be, everything that is bad, — and out of my house you shall go!"

She dragged her along with her and locked the door. Elizabeth, pale as death, stared at her with tearful eyes, whilst all her limbs shook with terror and cold fits.

"I am firm even when I would be bad!" muttered the old woman, and burst into a violent fit of weeping.

Madame Krone came up just then.

The Baroness pointed to the child.

"Away with that creature — away! to bed — to bed! — don't look at me — away!" and she pushed the little girl away from her, then hastened into her room, threw herself into a chair, and wept bitterly, whilst all her limbs trembled.

At once she sprang up again, clutched the key to the secret chamber fast in her hand, made a step towards the door, but stopped again.

"No," said she, "I have seen him — I have insulted him!" and she rested her hand on the table, and was standing thus when Madame Krone came.

Elizabeth should be sent out of the house that very day, said the old Baroness; Madame Krone might give her to some peasants, put her in the pig-sty, or do what she liked with her; and that day they should write to the clergyman to whom the yearly account had been sent. "It has been all jest and nonsense that he has had before, now he shall have earnest," said she; and her will was a fixed and determined one.

Madame Krone was obliged to send Elizabeth away to the old clerk of the parish. Trina, who knew so many comedies and ballets, had, in the name of Madame Krone, to put all in order, and it was a very affecting business for her, as she was fond of little Elizabeth; and "however much good there might be in her ladyship, she was, to say the least, unreasonable," said Trina ; "nay, at times, the Baroness is just as if she were mad. God forgive me my sins for saying so ! "

Whilst Trina went with Elizabeth to the old clerk's, the feast for the peasants began. The old lady gave out the presents to them ; but the peasant children, who were always accustomed to hear her jest with them when she handed the presents over to them, got to-day serious admonitions and reprimands.

"Her ladyship is not in right sorts to-day," said they. But the great guests who came afterwards observed nothing of this — she was then mirth itself. No one asked after little Elizabeth, who sat still and dreaming in the clerk's house, with the honest, but highly superstitious old folks. Trina wept ; Madame Krone was silent, but she thought so much the more.

CHAPTER X.

TWO months had nearly passed away since the above event, and during all that time Elizabeth had remained with the clerk and his wife. It was at this time that Moritz, with his sister Hedevig, came to Funen; he would himself speak with the old lady, and know how matters actually stood with the child, for it was not possible to calculate what that strange old woman might get into her head. Hedevig, who was quite absorbed by the loss of her little son, saw, as a mother, her own child in every little one, and therefore heard, with the greatest sympathy, what was related about Elizabeth, who was now at the clerk's, a very honest old couple, and the willing receptacles of every superstition.

Hedevig determined to accompany her brother to the old Baroness's, not to visit her, but in order to learn what sort of folks the clerk and his wife were, and to see how the child was taken care of.

The honest old clerk was called Mr. Katrineson; and by that name we may understand that he was from the little island of Oro, where the unusual custom exists, that the sons generally take their mother's name, when she has been well known as a clever woman. Thus the clerk was called Katrineson after his mother, whose name was Katrine. His wife was also from Oro, somewhat younger than her husband, of a very lively disposition, and highly industrious: it was particularly on account of this last quality, that Madame Krone was fond of her. Madame Katrineson made excellent soup of hips and elder-berries; her tea was native manufacture, a composition of marsh-marigolds and millefoil. Her coffee was mixed with chickory-root from the fields, and cleared with dried flounder-skin. No one had better starch than she had:

the potatoes were riven on the grater, and the refuse was washed again and again, until the white starch lay on the linen to be bleached in the sun.

But all the superstition from Oro, as it is there reflected from the whole country, was, as we have said, removed with the good couple into the clerk's little dwelling, which was very comfortable and cleanly, but presented an appearance of all those amulets that the peasant has against superstition. On the threshold of the door there was a horseshoe nailed fast, with the open part outwards, so that no wher-wolf or sprite could slip in. The parlor, which was in all other respects extremely neat and clean, had a ceiling that quite shone with what the peasant's call " the herring's soul," a long shining part of the herring, which is always taken out and thrown up against the ceiling where it remains hanging, and insures the party who eats against fever during the whole of that year, "the cold one," as it is called. St. John's wort grew in the crevices of the beams, and prophesied a long life to the old couple.

Mr. Katrineson was a round, little person, — the Baroness called him an apple-dumpling with legs ; his wife, on the contrary, was the type of scragginess, fine and slender : in her youth she had lost one of her eyes, and, in order to hide this want, she always wore a false lock of hair over it, but this on account of its immense size, and the awkwardness of its arrangement always drew attention to it. Besides the married couple, there were in the room, when Moritz and Hedevig entered, little Elizabeth and the chambermaid Trina, who, in a couple of days, was to go to Copenhagen to become the shoemaker's wife. She was immoderately fond of the little girl, to whom she had told ballets and operas, both Ralph Bluebeard and Cinderella, and had sung so many songs for. Trina knew a great number, and had a clear, strong voice. She would now, however, see her sweet little Elizabeth once more, to whom she had brought with her, as a remembrance of herself, a printed song-book, — that out of which Trina had so often sung, — and in which she had written on the binding, " To little Elizabeth, from her affectionate servant, Trina, betrothed to the master-shoemaker, Hansen."

As soon as she saw Mr. Moritz's sister, she exclaimed : —

"Good God, madame, is it you !" This exclamation showed a sort of earlier acquaintance in Copenhagen.

"It is many years since we met," said Hedevig ; I really thought you had gone on the stage."

"Much water has run into the sea since that time," said Trina ; "it was no place for me, as Hansen also said, — there may be very decent, honest persons there ; but appearances, madame ! it is that one looks at !"

Moritz explained to the old folks who he was, on what occasion he had come, and that he would go up to the manor to speak with the Baroness.

"It is kind of you," said Madame Katrineson : "for what is to become of the child ? With our best will we could not keep her, — we are old folks, and good as 'Lizabeth is, she is hard to master : a compliant child she is not, and at times, when she sits alone, and stares with those strange eyes (here the old woman spoke in a lower tone), one would think the child did not belong to Christian persons, though her body is very regularly shaped."

Moritz answered what he could answer, and then set off to the old lady's. Hedevig stayed at the clerk's ; her old acquaintance with Trina was a point of attraction. Madame Katrineson went to fetch the coffee-can which, on account of Trina's visit, had been set on the fire.

"Have you been on the stage ?" asked Madame Katrineson, as she stood a long time and thought of what she had just before heard. Trina blushed, laughed, and nodded.

"That certainly you never have," thought Mr. Katrineson.

"I never liked to speak about it, and Hansen desired me not to do so. I have — that is to say when I was a little child — been 'the god of love,' with wings, and spangles on my shoes. Yes, they even applauded me. I was with the dancers, ran about the whole day up in the dancing-school, and had to go to the baker's, and buy buns for the ballet-dancers. Alas ! it was a miserable life ; there is much chicanery in it, and appearances were always, at least at that time, against dancing ; and appearances it is that one looks at. When I became older, and Hansen was a journeyman, and courted me, he told me that it was so much against his wish that I should go and spring about there ; and the dancing-master always scolded so much, and set me amongst the last, so I went into service — it is now eight years since. The Baroness here has been a good mistress to me, for she is good, however strange she can be. Now Hansen has become a master, and if I do not live as I have been used to live here at the manor, I shall at least have my own house, for he is a good man I shall have for a husband, and one I am really fond of! and I shall be free from the world's talk — for appearances, Mr. Katrineson! it is every one's, and particularly every woman's character!"

That Trina should have danced with spangles on her shoes and wings on her shoulders, made a strange effect on Mr. Katrineson. He had stepped some paces backward, his hands folded involuntarily, and he looked at her with a sad and sorrowful expression. Little Elizabeth, on the contrary, went straight up to Trina, laid her elbows in her lap, and looked up in her face without removing her eyes.

"May God grant you happiness in the married state," said Hedevig; "you are a good girl, and that theatre-life is a heavy road : the world likes best to speak ill ! "

"No one escapes," said Trina, "not even Hansen ; but that makes no difference to me, *I* know him, and people look differently inwards to what they do outwards. Now, there is my lady, the Baroness : — they laugh at her many call her mad, and yet she is wiser and better than most ! There is a good principle in her, hard as she is towards little Elizabeth — who has been a very naughty child," she added, and looked as severe she could at the little girl, but only for a moment ; then kissed her brow and stroked her curls.

"Had you nothing else on but shoes and wings, when you danced ? " asked Elizabeth, who seemed to have remained with all her thoughts fixed on that point, as the most interesting in the whole of Trina's conversation.

Madame Katrineson now came, with her bright, polished coffee-can ; cups, saucers, and slop-basin were set out ; Katrineson drew his chair nearer, and gave Trina a piece of paper.

"I did not know," said he, "that you had been a dancer, or else I would have added one pious verse more, because it has fared as well as it has with you. It is a song for you; you can sing it at the wedding; you can read it, just as you like, for I have composed it."

The verses were set to a psalm tune, and the words were as melancholy, as if they were intended for an execution. Katrineson read what he had written, and wept at the second verse; then Trina wiped her eyes also, and afterwards the others did the same.

"I don't think that the parson could write them better," said Madame Katrineson, and she looked proudly at her husband.

"Had you nothing else on but shoes and wings when you danced?" asked Elizabeth again.

"Don't look with such eyes, little 'Lizabeth!" exclaimed Madame Katrineson; "you sit down to your doll;" and she drew the child away from Trina, for, as she said to her husband, "She set up grandmother eyes."

"Grandmother's!" repeated Trina, and shook hands with Katrineson once more for the pretty melancholy song.

"That is our way of speaking: we have it from Oro. Katrineson's grandmother was made blind by the elves: did you never know that?"

"She could not see," said her husband, "and yet it looked as if she could, and little 'Lizabeth has often such eyes.

"Grandmother was a midwife in Dunkjer on Oro; she was fetched to the elf-queen, who was in labor, and she got some salve to rub the elf-child's eyes with; some of it stuck to her fingers when she came out of the hill, and she happened to ub her own eyes with it: then she was clear-sighted; she saw the little elves swarm forth in the rye-field, and cut the ears off the stalk.

"'What are you doing there?' said she.

"Then they all screamed out, —

"'If you can see, you shall see!' and then they blew her eyes out. Certain it is," he added, "that as long as I can remember, she was blind; but now and then there came a lustre on the gray-blue dead eyes, and then it seemed as if she could see ; and it was for all the world just as 'Lizabeth looks at times, when she does not say a word."

"Yes, if it were not Madame Krone who had spoken for her, we should not have had that child," said the clerk's wife. "I wish all was well again, and that she was up again at the manor and not here in the house ; does she look like a Christian child ?"

"She thrives, but she is skin and bone ; eats as much as three, and has such a memory that it is enough to terrify one ; and that is not the worst of all !"

"She is clear, clear-sighted," repeated Katrineson, and continued, as Hedevig shook her head : "I shall give you ocular demonstration, madame. She was with me in the church-yard last night : it was clear moonlight, — 'What is that there ?' said she to me, and pointed to the church-wall. I looked, and it appeared to me to be her shadow and mine. 'It is surely my horse,' said she ; then I thought of the hell-horse,[1] thought of what eyes she had, and that she could see better than I, and I sang a psalm aloud, when I felt that she trembled like an aspen leaf."

"You have frightened the child," said Hedevig ; "there is no hell-horse ; who believes such things ?"

"That do I !" said Madame Katrineson, "and so did my father too, for he knew the hell-horse, knew him better than you or I. My father was a watchman in Areskjöbing, and he saw the hell-horse hobble away every night on his three legs from the church-yard to the place where one was to die. Once he went straight towards our house, where my mother and I lay — it is true, every word I tell you. 'Ho, ho !' said my father, 'don't go there,' and then he named our Lord's name ; but the hell-horse is surely a spirit, though it goes our Lord's errands, and therefore it continued to go straight towards the house ; then my father set off after it, and sprang at once on its back. My father was a courageous man, and as he sat on the hell-horse he had it in his power : he held his mace before him, and rode so that the horse clattered on. He ran straight up to the town-hall, where there was a large tree, and he bound

[1] A fabled three-legged horse (from Hell, the northern goddess of death).

the hell-horse fast to it, for it wanted to get away but it could not, and my father stood and looked at it, and saw that, as the day broke, the horse became more and more like a mist, and when the sun rose there was no horse to be seen, but a long shaving hung to the tree, as if it had just been taken off a coffin."

"O Jesu, mother!" screamed Madame Katrineson, and let the basin of coffee fall, for little Elizabeth stood close up to her, with fixed eyes: it was as if she heard with them.

"Was it that hell-horse we saw last night?" asked the child.

"'Lizabeth will be my death!" said Madame Katrineson; "she is frightful to look at."

"Poor little thing!" sighed Hedevig, and drew the child towards her; "she has an intelligent face; there is something in it, though I know not myself what it is, that reminds me of my sweet boy! and he was just her size!" She wiped her eyes and looked at Elizabeth.

Madame Katrineson then confided to Hedevig and Trina, what, as she said, was not confided to any one. "This child is not like others. The little innocents sleep their sweet sleep at nights, but *she* there — I have seen it to my horror — gets up! she has done it twice, and the last time it was just on the stroke of twelve. She went along the floor, right up to the door, and there sat down, and drew her night-gown up about her head; ''Lizabeth! in Jesu's name!' I shouted, and then it fell down as if dead on the floor. Now, I have laid a wet cloth with hemp-seed on it, before the bed: if she treads on that then she will turn back again; I learned that of grand-mother! No, that child is not one of our kind!"

"She never walked in her sleep at the manor," said Trina, in the most positive manner, and she was right; but Madame Katrineson was also right. She had seen Elizabeth rise from her bed and go straight up to the door, but the whole was a comedy, which Madame Katrineson herself was the cause of; for one night, when Elizabeth was awake, she had got up in bed to look at the pendulum of the clock, as the moon shone on it, and Madame Katrineson had said quite

6

aloud : "Jesu's mother! now she is getting up like a ghost!"
and this remark had given Elizabeth the greatest desire to do
so, but as Katrineson himself now awoke also, and spoke to
her, nothing came of it on that night, but on another. Both
husband and wife had chatted so much of their foolish nonsense to the poor child, that it almost believed itself to be a
witch. Elizabeth had never before stared as she did now,
with her eyes; she heard that they took notice of it, spoke
about it, were terrified, and all this she found to be very amusing. This was the real state of affairs.

Moritz now returned from his visit to the old Baroness,
where, however, something had been done.

"The kernel is good!" said he ; "it is as it has come from
our Lord, and the world has given the shell its color. She is
certainly a strange woman! 'I will give two hundred dollars
a year to the child,' said she ; 'but it is not for the child's
sake, for it is a good-for-nothing! but for my conscience, and
for that I will pay two hundred dollars! When Elizabeth is
fourteen years old, then that is over, and she must provide for
herself, and I know I have paid my entrance money for the
"Lying Comedy" her father told us!' The woman is singular," he continued, "but she is better than she wishes to appear, and better than the world sees."

"Yes, if people only knew each other," said Trina, "they
would not judge as they do."

The clerk and his wife would not keep Elizabeth, not for
twice two hundred dollars! Where should the child be sent
to? Madame Katrineson thought it might be a good help to
Trina, now that she was to marry, to have the money.

"Nay, God preserve me!" said Trina ; "it would fall heavy
on my shoulders if I came to be married, and had such a little girl with me — nay, not for all the money in the world.
Then I might just as well have continued to be a dancer.
Appearances, Madame Katrineson — it is that one looks
at."

Hedevig took hold of her brother's hand.

"Elizabeth is the same age as my little boy was : she can
sit with me as if I had him, and I will take her, brother, if
you have nothing to object."

Moritz looked kindly at his sister, and Elizabeth's fate was lecided — she should accompany them to the Halligers.

"Farewell," said Trina, and kissed the child once more, and begged her to take good care of the song-book she had given her. Elizabeth hung round her neck, cried, and then asked her, for the third time, "Had you only shoes and wings on?"

"Are you still thinking of that?" said Trina. "Alas! I was dressed like the angels on the stage, and they have clothes that look as if they had no clothes on."

"It is appearance," she was going to say, but did not; she kissed Elizabeth, kissed Madame Katrineson, and shook hands with all the others.

"Now be a good child," said she; "and if you ever come to Copenhagen, Hansen shall make you a pair of red boots, and you shall go with me to the theatre to see 'Cinderella' or 'Bluebeard;' you sweet child — perhaps we may never see each other again! I thought that you would grow up in the good old manor-house, and live to close the old lady's eyes! You are now more deserted than even I was; and you are to go a long way off! — so far — so far!"

Moritz clapped her on the shoulder.

"I am glad to see that there is one who is fond of the little thing. May God let me cause the good that is in her to thrive well!"

"Yes, she also, little soul!" said Trina, "she, also, your Reverence, has appearances already against her."

She nodded, kissed Elizabeth and Madame Katrineson once more, then shook hands again with the others, and went — to be married to her Hansen.

Hedevig took little Elizabeth by the hand, imprinted a kiss on her brow, and promised in her heart, "I will be to her a good mother, for his sake whom our Lord took unto Himself;" and the child looked with its intelligent eyes on the new mother — the real one had lain many years already in her grave; no one knew the place, and the grass grew high above it. Her eyes were filled with tears, but they were for Trina, who was to be, though no one thought of that, a mother to Elizabeth — a refuge, the only one in her abandonment.

"Thus we do not see it now, for appearances — yes, it is appearances one looks at !" said Trina.

But we will now travel with Moritz, Hedevig, and little Elizabeth over to the Halligers — the peaceful islands in the stormy North Sea.

CHAPTER XI.

WHAT HAPPENED AT DAGEBÖL.

A T two o'clock in the morning a large Holstein wicker-
wagon well packed with baggage drove out of the
town of Flensborg; in it sat Moritz, Hedevig, and little Elizabeth. They were obliged to start at this time in order to be
sure of arriving at Dageböl in time for the tide. It was
clear moonlight, but cold. They drove at a walking pace up
the bank, nor did they go much faster when they arrived at the
top, where the country extended itself in sandy fields and
moorlands. A long part of the road, which had collected a
mass of rain-water, was not at all a road, but a canal, through
which the horses waded. They afterwards went on through
heavy sands, seldom passed a house, and still more seldom did
they see a church tower; the noise of a croaking bird was
heard at a distance, otherwise all was monotonously silent;
not one of the travellers spoke; they each sat buried in their
own thoughts, and little Elizabeth fixed her eyes on the moon.

They had sailed in an open boat from Funen to Als, and
from the latter place had been driven by way of Gravenstein
to Flensborg. The beautiful woodlands, the alternations of
fiords and lakes, high banks, green meadows, and moorlands,
the different dresses of the people, the strange language, — all
these new impressions filled little Elizabeth's mind, whilst they
glided unnoticed past Moritz and Hedevig, each of whom
thought of what they had lost in the world.

Shortly before daybreak they reached the first baiting-place,
which lay in the outskirts of a little village.

Towards morning the air became colder than before. The
road-side inn which they entered was highly uncomfortable:
half emptied tankards and glasses stood on the table in the
guests' room; a tallow candle with a long snuff burnt in an

iron candlestick ; the floor was thickly strewn with wet **sand**. The girl, who should have put life into the whole, stood half-asleep, with her clothes thrown loosely about her, and took several letters up from the floor, where they had fallen down ; every one of them as clumsily sealed as they were folded. They were all sent as occasion offered, that is to say, with the butcher or peasants who came into the place ; piled up in the window, where every one could read the address as he passed by. Every letter now remained here, and waited for him to whom it was addressed, or till an acquaintance of his should come that way, and thus, frequently after several weeks and days, it might arrive at its destination. The snail-like mode of this reciprocal transmission of letters seemed to be imparted to all the inmates of the house that morning. To get a fire made, and a basin of warm ale and eggs prepared, seemed as if it would make such an inroad on time that they determined to put it off until they arrived at the next baiting-place. The horses had been foddered, and the driver promised that they should *now* go briskly forward, though they could not do so when they got into the Marskland, as the roads there were almost impassable, he said, and the horses would sink down to the girths. Nevertheless he thought he could bring them to do two miles an hour !

The clouds became redder, the moon paler, and the daylight came : they saw the birds above them and on the wayside, the sheep on the moors, and at length a few men here and there on the road, the majority on horseback, and also women.

" Moritz, the day will be fine," began Hedevig, as if driven to speak by seeing the awakening life around her. " Every morning is in fact a repetition of the creation, just as the Bible tells us it was. First we see the air, then the water ; the plants next appear, then the birds of the air and the beasts of the field ; and lastly, man ! "

" Certainly," said Moritz ; " Moses's Bible was God's great nature. He read it in the desert ; from that he got as much wisdom as from the wise men of Egypt, and the sagas his own people gave him."

Moritz again sat silent, and looked contemplative. **Hedevig** would have spoken but stopped; the driver took his post-horn, and blew it as miserably as he could, though it was not his intention.

"I understand German," cried little Elizabeth, when she heard the children speak at the next baiting-place. "I understand almost every word."

And she did so, for it was Danish she heard. Here in the whole district, from Flensborg towards the Marskland, the language is Danish, German, and Frisian; the three languages are mixed with each other. The Frisian prevails in the Marskland, where the Frisians dwell, that ancient people whom Herodotus and Xenophon mention as having emigrated from Persia.

The flat, green Marskland lay extended before them; the long, still canals, had, from the continued rain, overflowed, and the whole district lay under water.

Groups of sheep appeared on the higher situated green spots, to which the shepherd was obliged to wade; the peas-- ants walked knee-deep in the water, and cut the unripe corn. The roads here extend in all directions on raised dikes of equal height, over marsh and meadow, like an intersecting railway; the traveller on seeing them is led to think of a railway, but with the same disappointed feeling as the caravans in the desert see in the *fata morgana* lakes and woods, where they know that it is but the desert sand. The whole dikes were so neck-breaking, full of ruts, and muddy, that they could not properly be called roads; the horses were every moment in danger of breaking their legs; and where the travellers met others in wagons, it was really a work of skill to pass one another without being upset into the water or a bean-field. The few villages generally lie with all the houses in a row along the dikes, from which cause they assume an extensive and considerable appearance; all the houses are built of stone from the foundation, with large thoroughfares, whence the smoke escapes through the large open gateway.

Houseleek and creeping plants flourished on the moss-grown roof. The whole made that lively, touching impression which the home of our childhood always makes on elderly persons. Moritz and Hedevig were, as we know, from Marskland, from the Holstein part, near Itzeho, where the land and buildings gave tokens of greater wealth than that district of country in the Slesvig part, which the brother and sister now passed through, — a remark which they also made in silence. But yet it was the character of their native home they saw ; it was that of the well-known houses without chimneys, with their gables towards the wayside, and with the broad, open gateway, through which one could see into the room, kitchen, and stable. How often had not Moritz and Hedevig, when they were children, sat and played in the open gateway, and watched the swallow as it flew in and out of the room, where it also had its nest and its little ones. The brother and sister had both the same thoughts at this moment, but they did not express them.

They now went forward at the rate of four miles an hour ; the poor horses reeked and strained themselves ; a thick, damp fog rolled on towards them ; it was " the shrew," as it is called ; its bitter cold taste forced its way into their mouths and eyes, and they soon came into a cloud, which was so thick and opaque, that almost every one, whether riding or driving, who came past them, had nearly run against the horses.

It will scarcely be possible to get from the continent to the islands to-day, and, in all probability, they will have to pass the night in Dageböl, the little ferry place whence one crosses over to Föhr.

It is not twenty years since that there was not, in many of the Danish towns, a single house that could properly be called an inn, or public-house. The traveller was obliged to apply to one or another tradesman, who had a spare room and would not refuse to be paid for its use ; it was usually the apothecary or shop-keeper. The unknown guest had a place at the family table, where the mistress of the house counted, and accurately remembered, how many pieces of bread and butter, bread and cheese, or bread and meat, or whatever it might be, that he ate, that she might put it down to the account afterwards. That custom belonged to what people in our convenient, well-managed times, call " that period's prose in a traveller's life," but which one ought to be glad is now past.

Now, in Dageböl there was neither apothecary nor shop-keeper to resort to, but, on the contrary, a wealthy Marsk-land farmer, a genuine Frisian, proud and selfish, a monarch in his own house, and fully persuaded in his own mind that Dageböl was the first town within a circle of several miles.

Dagebòl lies close up to the dikes, which protect it and the neighborhood against the inroads of the German ocean off the coast of Jutland.

The wagon jolted along over the terrible stone bridge, and at last stopped before the inn, if one may venture to give the farm-house that name.

A tall, broad-shouldered man appeared in the door-way, and looked at them, but without saying "good-day;" he seemed vexed at seeing strangers whom he did not expect. This was the landlord himself.

Moritz and Hedevig bade him "good-day," but got no answer. "We should like to have all these things under cover!" said they.

"Why, then, see to get them under," answered the landlord, and he turned round and walked in again.

Whilst the driver took the horses from the wagon, which had to stand before the house with all its baggage, — and where it in fact stood safe enough, — Moritz, with his sister and little Elizabeth, entered the room. It was pretty well filled with strangers, hot, and uncomfortable: near the stove, which was remarkable for its size, and its bright brass ball, and was besides hung round with half-wet linen that hung like banners in a sepulchral chapel, sat some women with large men's hats on, of fine felt, and two girls from Föhr, with silver plates, and large silver buttons in their bodice: colored handkerchiefs hung, turban-like, about their plaited hair.

The landlord had again taken his place at the end of the table, where all his attention appeared to be turned to the man by his side, a heavy person in a thick red flannel under-jacket, and whose waistcoat was so covered with small buttons in several rows, that it looked like the breast of a hussar's uniform. A blue woolen neckerchief hung loosely around his throat, and large gold rings, such as the women wear, were in his ears: his hands were remarkably large and red, everything about him was colossal, but his voice, on the contrary, was fine as a woman's; and he stirred the contents of his tankard with a bone spoon: this was the rich horse-dealer, Petters, who was on his way to Tönningen.

No one made a place for Moritz and his sister; it seemed as if they took no notice whatever of them; Moritz turned to the right and to the left, and as the door to the next room stood open, and which led to the kitchen, where any one could hear that something was frying in the pan, he walked in, followed by Hedevig and Elizabeth: he addressed himself directly to the mistress of the house, who seemed to be very busy, and looked angry and proud.

"I am the clergyman from the Halligers," said he.

"Yes, I know you well enough," she replied sulkily. "You have been here twice before; one cannot move about in one's own house."

Moritz patiently held his tongue. Hedevig, however, entered cunningly into conversation about all the trouble that the woman must have, all the great toil and drudgery that there must be in such a house, whereby she at length brought her into a milder humor, so that she allowed them to have a small chamber, and that too with a bed in it. This latter was quite characteristic: the head-piece was the half of the rudder of a stranded ship, and the foot-piece was real mahogany, with carved figures on it; it was a door which the sea had cast up, and which now served to shut in the legs of the sleeper: the walls were white and bare, and there was wet sand on the floor; this was the whole furniture.

After having taken off a great part of their travelling clothes, and, as they called it, put themselves a little in order, which, with Moritz, consisted in brushing his coat, and with Hedevig in tying her cap-strings afresh, and arranging her hair, they determined to return to the large room, where one end of the table was laid out for them.

The horse-dealer, Petters, with his fine, screaming, female voice, was the first and loudest speaker, and the subject they were discussing was one that, according to his calling, one would least have imagined — namely, baptism; that is to say, concerning christening the old church bells, when there were present both godfathers and a godmother, who, it was said, bore the bell, just as they bear a child ; and about this same godmother Mr. Petters related a very curious story, which was more broad than witty, and which he, like all garrulous persons, when they find their tales are well received, related again to the same listeners, and now repeated for the third time, as Moritz, Hedevig, and Elizabeth entered.

The rumbling of a wagon outside gave tokens of new guests, but the landlord sat still, and Mr. Petters raised his voice, for the story was to be finished.

Two persons wrapped up in seal-skin travelling-cloaks now entered the room. They were Vomme Leyson, the old commander, as he was called, and his wife. These were the two personages of most importance that Moritz had in his whole parish, and his most intimate acquaintances. As soon as the landlord saw who they were, he rose up from his chair, as they were persons of consequence, and then sat down again. Mr. Petters made his compliments in an equally polite way, and was quite pleased, as he laughed at the Greenland dress. The married couple were on their way home from Husum, where their only living son, "who had been so stupid as to study," so the commander said, was now a town judge, and had just married, and at the wedding the parents were obliged to be present, or else they would not have left their island.

"We were made much of," said the old woman ; "honored : I was like a queen ! and such a table as there was ! but they didn't understand how to stuff the capons, and that my son said."

"And there is our parson," cried the commander, as he saw Moritz ; "welcome ! welcome ! — well, where is the wife ? — where is the lady of Halliger-parsonage ? I shall make a little party for her to-morrow ! But can I appear before her for the first time in this costume ? and you, mother ! " —

Moritz pressed his hand, and in a few words told him his great loss, and presented him to his sister and little Elizabeth. The commander's smiling face became serious and perplexed. Without saying a word, he threw his arms round Moritz's neck and kissed him, then withdrew from the room with his wife, who uttered a sorrowful cry. They went into the next room, where they threw off their seal-skin cloaks, which the commander himself had brought from Greenland, and which on their journey to Hobro had proved of much use.

When they returned to the great room, Madame Leyson shook hands with Hedevig, kissed little Elizabeth, and related what *she* had lost in this world. The sea had taken all her sons but one — "my judge," as she called him ; and then she had a grandson, Elimar, her heart's pride, the finest boy, the wisest child : this was the grandmother that spoke ; he also was now out "on the wide sea, or down in it" — it was his first great voyage to Greenland. "Nay, the land is, however, firm ground," continued the old woman, "and it also gives us good bread, and many joys and pleasures. What a house my son has ; that was a wedding ;" and then she was obliged to tell them all about the festivity and about the dancing. "Yes," said she, "my old commander danced too, but I only went once round ; these new-fashioned dances are so difficult, and what are they compared to those in my grandfather's time ? I remember them still, though I was so little that I had to be lifted up in the servant's arms to see them. My grandfather was always the first in the dance at all festivals ; he was the king, as it is called. They were all in white shirtsleeves ; they all had small bells on each leg ; and when he had made a speech — it was in verse — their legs went and the swords went, for they always bore a sword in the dance, and they sprang over it, and they placed them in such a position as to form a rose, and then they held it above their shoulders as a shield, and the king stood on it, and was lifted above their heads."

"What ! the town judge !" asked Petters, who had not attended to the conversation, and thought that the whole was a description of the wedding-dance at Husum. "That was a devil of a dance !"

"Who talks about the 'town judge !'" answered Madame Leyson ; "I speak of old days, of my grandfather, of the old Frisian dancers. Do you think they dance nowadays with bells on their legs, or form roses in the dance ?"

"There was meaning in all our old customs," said the landlord; "there is not near so much of what is solemn now as
in ancient times. I always liked the old dances. Nowadays
it is, 'swing me here, swing me there' — it is meaning that's
wanting. And then that fine custom at the wedding, that
when the young wife was led home for the first time to her
husband's house, he drew his sword and stuck it into the
thatched roof over the door, and let her go in under it: the
marriage-sword was drawn over her."

"Have you now got into that nonsense?" cried a voice
from the kitchen; but the landlord was not to be put out of
his talk, and continued: "and then the old *Fenstern*, which
has quite died away, nay, is even forbidden by law."

"And I think it ought to be forbidden," said Moritz; "it
appears to me to be derogatory to all modesty, to continue
such a custom as that."

"It was highly moral," said Madame Leyson; "my grandmother was a highly moral woman, and she got her husband
by the 'Fenstern.' When they knew that all were in bed, the
young men went each to the house where *she* lived that *he*
would go a-courting to. The chamber windows were, as we
know, never fastened; the lover went very orderly into the
chamber, and sat down by the bed; there he could speak the
feelings of his heart freely, and if she did not like him, she
could creep under the bed-clothes as far as she liked, and then
he was obliged to go his way. I don't think that this was more
shocking than the long betrothals, and that eternal kissing
which accompanies it in these times; *that* I think immoral.
Not one kiss did they get in their night courtships. I know
it, for my grandmother was a woman of veracity."

The conversation thus fell more and more into the old customs and usages of the country. Out-of-doors there was
still a thick raw sea-mist, and as long as that prevailed there
could be no thought of crossing the water. At night the
moon would be up, and it might perhaps get the better of *the
shrew;* the travellers were, therefore, obliged to pass the
night in Dageböl; and as they knew it they drew nearer together: the conversation was about old and modern times.
Little Elizabeth listened with all the curiosity of a child, but

she did not understand the language ; tired and sleepy, she opened her eyes wider and wider, until they at length closed altogether ; she slept as soundly as all of us sleep at that age.

We will also sleep here, and awake again when she first awakes, and that was about midnight. She lay on a sack and some clothes, a horse-cloth was thrown over her, and she was placed close before the bed, with the rudder and door-head as a foot-piece, on which Hedevig and Madame Leyson had laid down, half undressed, and now they both slept.

The night had begun to be windy : the fog dispersed and drove in small patches past the moon, which shone into the chamber. The child awoke, and at the first moment she was terrified on finding herself in a strange place ; she rose up, and then remembered where she was ; looked to the bed to see if Hedevig was there, and as she found her and the old lady, who slept very soundly, she was quiet. The door out to the side-building kept clattering continually, as every gust of wind set it in motion — it was only fastened with a noose of cord. Elizabeth now got up ; she must know what was the matter with the door ; and when she got there and touched the cord, the door flew open outwards, as it was one of those doors that are more inclined to spring open than remain shut, and she fell on her head, but without hurting herself, as there was a good deal of straw there. She got up again and looked about her ; it was a great barn that she had tumbled into. Here stood several wagons, and between these lay something that shone in the dark like a star, and on which a ray from the moon fell. What could it be ? she must know it ; she must go up to it ; she stood for a moment as if debating with herself, then made a brisk step.

And we will also make one, though only a few hours forward in time.

It was morning ; Hedevig and Madame Leyson were both up, and astonished in a high degree, for the child was not to be found, neither in doors nor out. No one could give any account of her, and yet many of the folks about the house had been up before daylight. The horse-dealer, Petters, had driven southwards before daybreak, and the travellers from Föhr had gone off about the same time to Tondern.

Madame Leyson had been awakened shortly before daylight by a loud barking that came from the barn close by. The door to their chamber was open, she said, and as there was a strong draught, she had got up to lock it, and on that occasion she thought that she saw little Elizabeth lying where they had made a bed for her ; this, however, was not the case, as Elizabeth was then in the barn already. They saw that the child must have gone straight from the bed without either shoe or frock on, but whither ? — she had disappeared !

"Alas, my own dear Elimar ! " sighed Madame Leyson, "God knows where he is at this moment, — we can all be lost ! " And although there was no reason to suppose that Elimar also should have disappeared from the vessel he was with, or the vessel with him have foundered, she could not help thinking so, and expressing her anxiety, — yet she as quickly spoke consoling and pitying words to poor, despairing Hedevig.

The whole forenoon was passed in searching and inquiries : the brother and sister were now deeply affected, — there was nothing more to be done. Another day was added to their time of trial. Sorrowfully they entered the boat that was to bear them over to Oland. They commissioned the landlord in Dageböl, and the revenue officer there, to question every stranger, and then to send them every information directly that might lead to a trace of her. A great misfortune must certainly have happened to her.

The brother and sister stood at the fore part of the boat : they spoke not a word, their eyes were fixed on the dark swimming islands — the Halligers — the largest of which was the end of their voyage.

The white mountainous sand banks on Amrom rose high in the dark atmosphere ; the flat Halligers lay like a drift of sea-weed, whose motion has ceased.

The sea rolled its yellow-green, turbid waves, as the tide brings them in. They were obliged to tack ; a few strokes of the oars brought them nearer Oland, with its town and church. They saw two female figures approaching the shore ; others soon joined them ; every figure appeared quite distinct as they came forward, the air forming the background, for the islands are so low, and the extent even of the greatest so insignificant. Here is not a tree, not a bush, — a gooseberry excepted, which shot forth sickly in a corner of the parson's grounds.

All the houses of the town are built on layers of beams, and are placed close to each other with small openings between them; it is as if wind and stream had driven them near together, and close to the church, as the sheep to the ram. The small windows are placed high up, painted blue and green: they shine and look as if they belonged to the cabin of a ship.

The vessel ran in on the side of the island where the sea had made a creek. A number of the women who were waiting on shore, all dressed in black — as the females are on these islands — immediately fastened their skirts up around them, sprang into the water, and bore Madame Leyson and Hedevig on land. To the Commander and Moritz they only gave a hand; they received the travellers on their return home with great pleasure, and the heartiest congratulations.

The happiest among them was a middle-aged servant-maid, Keike, or, as she was called, the parson's Keike, for she was in his service. She, as well as all the others, knew that Moritz would bring his young bride with him, and regarded Hedevig as his wife, although she did not look exactly as Keike had imagined her: she was in fact an older woman, and her face was sorrowful.

She was, however, greeted as the parson's wife by Keike and all the women — for of men there were none just then on the island. They are seamen, and were with the vessels in Holland and Greenland, or in the fisheries.

Moritz told them in a few words his grief and his loss, and the circle that had so lately stood glad and laughing, with a pleased "welcome home," now became still and sorrowful, and they went towards the town with a silence and gravity that accorded with their mourning-dresses, with the gray air above them, with the black color which the sea had at that moment, and with the still, dark island. They went over the short stiff grass, which, from the sea often washing over it, has a peculiar crispness. Some large muddy spots, some heaps of sea-weed, and a few groups of sheep were the only objects that gave variety to the scene.

Keike, who had hurried on before the others, came out of the parsonage again with the greatest haste as Moritz entered. She had assembled the whole flock of children in the parish: not one had remained at home, except one in a fever, and a couple that were asleep: they stopped at the door, and Keike, who had something concealed under her apron, looked perplexed: it was something heavy that she was carrying away — and where to? — she shook her head.

Two letters, M. and C., the initials of Moritz and Caroline, she had bound together of grass, for she had no other green plant or leaf: these two letters were bound and hung up on the wall, as a festal greeting to the young couple, and as she had renewed them but a couple of days before, they were quite fresh; a single aster, brought from Föhr, was stuck between the two letters.

This ornament it was that she now hastened to carry away.

The door to the parlor stood open, and the blue newly painted wainscot gave it a lively appearance. Here stood the piano which Moritz had bought for Caroline; it was to have been her first surprise when she came; above it hung her portrait, young and sprightly as she was. Moritz remained standing before it; no tears came into his eyes, but he became deadly pale; he then turned round to his silent congregation, who, as we have said, had accompanied him home. Even the Commander and his wife were there: both the room and passage were filled with persons.

"So glad, so happy did she look!" said he. "She was my best treasure on this earth, and our Lord took her away from me. His will is the most just, even where we cannot comprehend it. God has tried me severely, taken from me what my mind and heart leaned to, that I might hold myself faster to Him, and that I, in *my* sorrow, should understand that of others. Sorrow and misfortune come to us, as to Job, that we may understand God, ourselves, this and yonder world."

And he spoke to them of his sister's little lively boy, whom

7

our Lord had taken unto Himself. He touched on the events
of the morning — his apprehensions, and fear for little Elizabeth.

"I can say with Job, '*my stroke is heavier than my groan-
ing*,' but I know that that hand will again lift me up, that
hand will again lead me to a better life. '*The needy shall not
always be forgotten; the expectation of the poor shall not perish
forever!*'"

And his speech, which flowed forth from his inwardly moved
soul, became more and more as the voice of God; the little
room became a holy church, the congregation stood in pious
devotion, and when Moritz concluded with the words of the
psalmist, "Our Lord he is so firm a rock," all the voices
joined in the hymn.

This was the entrance to his new home.

CHAPTER XII.

A COUPLE of days had passed, and as yet they had heard nothing about little Elizabeth, though she was in the best health. We shall soon see her, and hear her adventures; but in order to do so, and to see her safe within four walls — as one says — we must visit the Commander: here we find Moritz and Hedevig as guests.

The dinner is ended; the large, bright, polished coffee-can stands on the old carved table.

No *genre* painter could find a better subject for a wealthy Halligers' comfortable parlor than this was; a model of *The Wild Duck*, the name of the Commander's former vessel, with its whole rigging, hung under the ceiling. On each side of the vessel two large glass balls were suspended in silk ribbons, now somewhat faded: in these balls the whole room was reflected in miniature, and even a part of the kitchen too, for the door leading to it stood open, and the copper utensils shone bright on the shelves. One side of the room was ornamented with pictures, but of ships solely; one also saw the large painting with the mother of the family, Osa, — it was as good as a whole covering of tapestry. Then all the *rococo* furniture, and particularly the great pedestal that looked like a pulpit; not to mention the company, — the Commander in his arm-chair, with his long pipe, Moritz on the sofa, which was covered with gilt leather, and both the women on chairs, the stiff high backs whereof invited them to sit upright.

Geraniums and house-leek flowered in the small windows; books were in the long book-case, which stretched along the whole breadth of the room; a jackdaw hopped about on the floor; its name was Claus, and it kept continually crying out, "Claus goes in the loft with Piltitz!" This was all that it knew, but it was its every-day story. Piltitz was. an old cat with whom it lived on terms of the greatest friendship, and went out with daily, sometimes into the street, sometimes into the loft, — the latter appeared to be the more interesting place of the two.

In the two glass balls one had thus at once reflected, besides the Commander and his wife, the whole of their domestic associates and intercourse.

Everything was shown, both above and below: the Commander had shown them his coffin which he had ordered, and had had ready long since.

"Large and roomy," as he said, "with mattress filled with shavings." He took his regular nap in it every day after dinner, and assured them that the hammock was good and well tarred; "and then it will last longer than I !" said he.

Madame Leyson had shown them her Elimar's picture, or rather profile, cut out as a silhouette, — a terrible square lump: it was said to be a good likeness, only that he was much prettier.

"And then he is so amusing," said she; "he calls me ' old cruiser,' that is because I pet him. O, he is so amiable !"

Of all that was shown, however, that which interested most was the great wooden pedestal-looking thing, with the carved angels, and the Virgin Mary in a cloud, whence descended long rays; it was called "the pulpit," and it had been one. The Commander had been christened under it when an infant, and he and his now old wife had sat under it as a young bridal couple. It was from Rantum Church, on Sylt Island, which had been destroyed by quicksands.

"Three times was the church moved further into the land," said the Commander, "and three times was the town moved further in, and it was so large a town that it once lost more than two hundred boats in a storm. The sand-storm drives inwards, and the sea follows it and carries away all in its course; it will take us altogether, when we are n our graves. But I have no objection to go to sea !"

"Don't talk so wickedly to his reverence," said the wife. "Our Lord will hold His hand over our little island; we have only the sea to fight against, but on Sylt Island they have the sand too. I shall never forget the last time we went to Rantum Church; it was in 1801, when the English lay before Copenhagen. The sand banks had increased terribly about the church, which lay as it were in a deep valley; the sand drifted up night and day against the walls; it forced its way through the closed windows and door; it stood in heaps on the church floor and in the pews; the last church service was then performed there, and we had to go in at the windows; the sand lay quite up to and round the altar table, where the great wax-lights burned."

" My father bought the church," said the Commander, " the altar and pulpit were set up in my cabin, and went with me over the German Ocean. I gave the altar to a church in Greenland, and the pulpit stands there ! "

Thus there was a story connected with every piece of furniture in the rooms; the most important perhaps was that appertaining to the grandmother Osa, whose portrait appeared to Moritz to resemble the old Baroness in Funen in a remarkable degree. Yes, it was she, feature for feature, but in a Frisian dress, red and white, with the large, roomy, fur cloak, for which seven sheep had yielded their skins. On her head she wore a cap of hollow oval ornaments, joined together like the scales on a fish.

The visitors, however, did not hear her story at that time, though it belongs to one of the finest sagas in that district. The soup was brought in, and with the soup followed other stories, — they went from Föhr to Greenland, and then to Varde and to China, as happens in a conversation, but with every article the story connected with it was touched on, except one. We have forgotten the most important piece of furniture in the house here — the most important in every dwelling that is at all well arranged on these islands; nay, more important than *Ovngröden*,[1] which, with its slow-burning fire, bakes of itself on Sundays whilst they all are at church, — and this is the house's telescope, which had its place by the door.

A telescope becomes a strange means of awakening the spirit; it is the telegraph from the life which moves on the

[1] O'enbras, " Ofenbrei," of milk and flour, with pieces of bacon.

sea. It is drawn forth in storm and shipwreck, and tells of death or rescue, during a long and continued east wind. When the sea is blown back for miles into an ebb, and the remains of sunken towns, the hulls of stranded vessels, and the skeletons of whales, harbors, church walls, and tomb-stones, protrude like ghosts from out the red sand, it is a rare and curious spectacle to draw the overwhelmed world nearer, by means of the telescope, and to make out what every object has been, not to speak of the daily pleasure of seeing to what nation the ship belongs, which now appears like a spot in the horizon, or to look at the small vessels crossing from Dageböl.

It was the telescope which, as they now sat around the coffee-table, was taken down.

"It can haul well!" said the Commander, as he laid it on the corner of a low closet and regulated it for Moritz. "One can see every man, one can know him, see every rope, and all that they have on board;" but neither the Commander nor Moritz saw what would have surprised and pleased them very much, a very little sailor-boy, who sat between some coils of rope. The little fellow had on a pair of thick yellow flannel trousers, a long jacket of the same stuff and color, and a worsted cap on his head. This little fellow was Elizabeth, whose adventures we are to hear, but as yet she is sailing: the telescope was again hung up over the door. Hedevig had the third cup of coffee pressed on her, Claus had hopped for the fourth time on to the Commander's shoulder and said, —

"Claus goes in the loft with Piltitz," when Keike rushed into the room with the little dressed-out sailor boy, and cried, — "The child has come, and here it is."

"The Lord be praised!" exclaimed Hedevig, and ran towards Elizabeth, who began to cry and shrink from her, as if more than a verbal lecture was in preparation for her. One of the seamen waited outside the door; his message, and what they drew from the child by degrees, we will separate from each other in a more comprehensible manner than it was stated by them, and help it out with subordinate circumstances.

It is said that magic gold and glittering jewels are, in human hands, transformed to withered leaves, pieces of glass, and coal : thus the gleaming star on the floor that allured little Elizabeth, proved to be nothing else but the neck of a glass bottle, which the moonlight fell on through a hole in the roof ; she took hold of the shining glass with the most anxious expectation, but the moment it was touched, it lost all its charm. But what was still worse, a dog started up close beside her with a loud bark, and had it not been bound to the wagon-wheel with a stout cord, it would have seized her. She screamed, and the dog barked still louder ; it stood right between her and the door to the bed-chamber ; its eyes shone in the dark like balls of fire, so that, terrified, she climbed into the nearest wagon ; it was Mr. Petters's, the horse-dealer's ; she crept down into the hay that was in it, just as the Commander's wife, awakened by the dog's barking, had got up, found the door open, and thought that that was the cause of the dog's noise. When she reached the door the dog turned towards her, and barked in that direction, and when it was fastened, and as Elizabeth kept quiet, it lay down again, with a lurking glance, and growling.

However much frightened Elizabeth was, yet she fell asleep, nay slept soundly — so soundly, down in the hay — that she did not even know that the man came and put the horses to, and that Mr. Petters got up on his seat and rolled away on the dike along the sea-side, southwards.

It was quite daylight when Mr. Petters stopped before an inn in Marskland ; he turned to lay his whip on the seat, when Elizabeth at the same moment stuck her head up out of the hay.

"What rogue are you ? was Mr. Petters's first exclamation, as he raised his whip and Elizabeth screamed with fear. "Who has put you into the wagon ?" he asked with his fine, screaming voice, and drew her out of the hay ; "no clothes on ! who has put you down there ? will you speak, hussy ? do you think that I am going to have such goods foisted on *me* ? "

She could not understand him at all, but she saw that he was angry.

The whip was raised again, but the woman of the inn now

interposed, and began an examination, which was still more incomprehensible to the child; the landlord laughed, clapped Mr. Petters on the shoulder, and assured him that, —

"One had got a bad bargain, and another a good one at night. You got a young one last night, and I got the other night a piece of high Marskland, that was driven up on my ground."

"Then I can have her put out to grass there?" said Mr. Petters, vexatiously, and then began to question her, first in low German, and then in Frisian. At last the woman, who now struck in with Danish, ascertained thus much: that the child, afraid of a great dog that was going to bite her as she was returning to the chamber where she had come from, had climbed up into the wagon. Mr. Petters now recollected that a little girl had come to Dagebòl with the parson, and at length they all understood how it was.

The child trembled with fear and cold; she was half dressed, and stood without shoes in the middle of a pool of water, where she had been placed. The mistress of the inn took her into the house, and looked after a few clothes for her, but as there were no little girls in the house, the fisherman's son had to give her a jacket and trousers, which they were obliged to let her wear until she could be better supplied. She was to be sent back to Dagebòl on the first opportunity. The mistress of the inn predicted that as Mr. Petters had thus unexpectedly got a little daughter, he would also soon, and as unexpectedly, get a great wife, for those two things always followed each other, sometimes one came first, and sometimes the other; and thus they jested and talked what they called amusing things, but the chorus always was: "You must see my piece of high Marskland; it comes straight from Scotland, or Iceland!"

This piece of land which the sea had given him, was his continual thought and pride. *Das hohe moor*, as it is called — two swimming islands were added to his land. According to the belief of the people there, they came from the coast of Iceland, or from Scotland; but it is more easily explained, and also more correctly, by supposing what is the only just opinion, that these pieces of land are parts of Friesland, which has sunk, and, lifted up by the sea itself from its bottom, where it lay, drives about and settles on the sand banks.

Mr. Petters, and every traveller that came to the inn for the first few days, were taken out to see it, and then they had to stop and look at some red bricks, and a piece of timber that stuck fast in the ground ; it had been a house and yard, said the landlord, who, perhaps, told no lie when he asserted it. Elizabeth was more than ten times on that " High Marsk-land," during the two days she stayed with them : the mistress explained to her what she saw, and it made a deeper impression on her than the episode of her being away from Moritz and Hedevig. This little event implanted a seed in her mind which we shall afterwards see shoot up to an important and luxuriant tree. Having said thus much, we will now let her depart from the inn, and that with the first eel-wagon that goes to Dageböl ; she came there in the fisher-boy's clothes, and went from there with the sailing-boat to Oland, where, as we know, she was received with glad surprise, even by Claus, who said what he could say, " Claus goes in the loft with Piltitz ; " the latter alone lay, without any apparent sympathy, in the arm-chair, blinked with his eyes once or twice, and moved one of his ears ; this was all the politeness he showed. Hedevig wept, yet she was lively and talkative, contrary to custom. Moritz also felt happier, and the Commander ordered punch to be made ; for the seaman who had come with Elizabeth — it was Jap Lidt Petters — should have his glass with them. The punch was prepared, and it must be drunk, and toasts too. The Commander's wife thought they ought not to forget little Elimar, her joy and comfort. "If he only be not sitting in the cask upon the mast ; I don't like that ! "

" But if he be there, there he must sit," said the Commander, "though you can well imagine that the fishery is now over, and that they are nearer to us than they are to Greenland. And if he has sat in the cask, he sat well. I have often sat on watch in it, up in the mast, and peeped through the holes after the whales. One sits comfortably sheltered from the wind and cold ; and amusing enough it is to see when the whales come and spout up the water like jets through their

nostrils, for they swim in ranks, he and she, side by side, the
young ones behind; and when the new-born little whale cannot keep up with them, then the mother takes him up on her
tail. See, that is what you would also do, mother; one
mother is just like another, even if she be only blubber and
train oil! and then they rub themselves on the ice-blocks, for
they have no combs; one must help oneself as well as one
can! If they lose the young one, they turn round directly,
even if they have the harpoon in their body, and then they
strike with their tails as if they were mad. You would also
do that, mother, ha! ha! But don't cruise too much about
the boy when he comes; he is quite right, when he calls
you 'a cruiser,' though it does not speak much for his education."

"He is the sweetest lad in the world," said the old woman,
"and you least of all deserve to be his grandfather!" With
that she pulled her old husband by the ear, and filled the
punch-glasses, whilst Moritz rose to break up the party,
and Keike appeared at the door with a lighted lantern to
show them the way home through the small pitch-dark alleys.

CHAPTER XIII.

ON Sunday all the people in the island were in church, also little Elizabeth, whose eyes, like those of an imprisoned bird, wandered unsteadily about, sometimes to the peculiar mourning costume of the women, and the long linen kerchief which half concealed their faces; sometimes to Saint Nicholas, the tutelary patron of ships, who, carved in wood, painted and gilt, was placed at the entrance of the choir; and at last to the two portraits of the King and Queen, in gilt frames, which hung one on each side of the half obliterated altar-piece.

When the prayer for them and the whole of the royal house was read from the pulpit, all eyes were turned towards these pictures, and every one, according to their power of imagination, now completed for themselves a King or a Queen after these miserable performances that Moritz's predecessor had hung up, and colored to the best of his abilities, as with the simple and ignorant, the natural color of the lithograph, black and white, would make "a bad appearance." Moritz read from the Gospel about "the widow's son in Nain," and transferred it, in a comprehensible sermon, to nature itself, which was now enshrined, wrapped in winter's shroud, whilst the storm sang of the grave and oblivion, but how the dead would again awake to life; and he transferred it to the congregation themselves, who, with their beloved dead, should herein hear God's voice, "Weep not!" The Resurrection he pronounced as certain and consoling. Here, as in every one of Moritz's sermons, there was a transmission, a coalescence of the Bible and nature: he borrowed his expressions from his congregation, images from their business and occupations; and as he knew their joys and sorrows, their mutual interests, he united these with his sermon, which was understood, and found an entrance into the spirit and thoughts of his flock.

He did not take his sermon from the Gospel itself, but gave intelligible living words to those thoughts, which, in the reading of them, must be awakened in the mind of every thinking listener. Nature around them, and the events of their own lives, were as if enlightened by the Gospel for the day, or transferred to that; and when this mental structure had been raised, he hung his own inspiring and consoling wreath upon it, and every one, even the poorest in thought, then returned home with some portion of the harvest.

Little Elizabeth's rescue had this day been alluded to, and it had moved Keike in particular, for in a few days these two had become as well acquainted with each other as if they were old friends.

"Now we shall go out this afternoon and amuse ourselves," said Keike, who promised Elizabeth that she would go with her, both to the new and the old church-yard: it was very pleasant indeed.

Hand in hand, they wandered through the village, and across the island, which is scarcely a mile broad. Some sheep were nibbling the stunted grass: they were patted and talked to, and then the two walked on towards the sea, where the old church-yard was, and where the surge, in every storm, had carried away parts of the low slope, and round about there stuck forth pieces of coffins and whole human bones. Keike crept down to the lowest point, and gathered up the bones in her apron, or they would otherwise have soon been washed away. These, she said, she would carry up to the new church-yard, and lay them in the ground there, so that they would at least rest in peace until the sea reached so far.

"Here we will not stay at night," said she, "for the mourning widow, as she is called, often sits here;" and then Keike stated that it was not the ghost of a dead person, but the figure of the living wife, whose husband was drowned at sea. Many a seaman's wife had seen herself sitting here by the strand, dressed in mourning, and wringing her hands, and then she knew that her husband was dead; she — Keike — had seen herself as "the mourning widow."

Such stories as these and others did Keike relate, in order to make their walk *pleasant*, and then turned towards the new church-yard, where she took a spade and buried the bones of the dead that she had found by the strand, and then said the Lord's prayer over them.

She led little Elizabeth from grave to grave, for Keike could read the inscriptions and knew all the graves; on some of them there was raised a large and somewhat flat stone, on which was cut, besides the inscription, the deceased person himself, hovering in the clouds, and received by those previously departed. There were many touching and many very short inscriptions : many appeared very curious, but this never came into Keike's mind. Here on one grave-stone one might read that besides the husband himself, here also rested the bones of his still living wife. She herself had had this inscription put on the stone, so that it must be true. Another stone was put up for a steersman, who had perished at sea, but whose body had never been found, and for the children he had left behind; the date of the year was wanting, but there was a place left for it to be inserted.

All the grave-stones were covered with a damp, green growth; not a flower was to be found here; a few box-trees were the only plants one saw, and these were half withered; whereas a few children's graves had pretty mosaic-like borders of shells and round stones, washed up by the sea.

"There lie Jap Lidt Petters's seven children," said Keike.

But who was Jap Lidt Petters ? Well, he was the seaman who had brought Elizabeth here from Dageböl, and who got his glass of punch at the Commander's, as good as Madame Leyson could make it.

When they returned to the parsonage, Keike told them how well they had amused themselves, and that they had been at both church-yards.

The words Elizabeth had heard, "that the buried bones would now rest in peace in the new church-yard, until the sea reached there," had made a deep impression on her. Then the sea could come there, come right up to the parsonage, nay, even run into the room. She asked Keike about it, and she replied with the greatest calmness, that it *might* happen at any time; and then she told — what she knew well — about old days; that many hundred years since, all the islands about here had been one, but the sea had come and swallowed up towns and churches; people had swam about on beams and rafters; cradles, with little children in them, were driven out to sea; then the land had become many islands, but afterwards, one island after the other had been washed away, or become less and less, from the inroads of the sea.

Föhr and Sylt had, however, then been one land, and there was a large town, Rungholt, where the people were very wicked. Some bad persons there had made a sow drunk, laid it in a bed, and then sent for the parson to administer the Sacrament to a sick person, and if he refused, he would be thrown into the water. He came, and whilst they were debating, he escaped; but on his way home, two wicked fellows met him near a public house, and forced him to accompany them into the tap-room, and tell them where he had been; and when he told them how he had been made a mockery of, they laughed, took the box from him, in which he carried the Sacramental cup and wine, and poured ale into it; "For our god there," said they, "as he should have a little to drink." When the parson got it back again, and made his escape, he carried it to the church, and prayed to God to punish those wicked wretches, and at night, as he lay in his bed, he was warned by God to leave the land in all haste, and then the storm began, and the water rose — all Rungholt and seven church-villages sank; the parson, his servant-maid, and two young girls who had been in the church, alone escaped. "That race still lives," added Keike; "they are called Boyesen; and it is sure, that before the day of judgment, Rungholt will rise again from the sea with all that were in it. When the water is still and clear, one can yet see houses, church-towers, and mills; I have not seen them myself, for I shut my eyes, but there was such a ringing in my ears, — it was the church-bells that rung!"

Little Elizabeth sat quite pale, looked at Keike, and swallowed every word, as she had swallowed the stories she had heard at Katrineson's, the clerk's, in Funen.

"But can the sea come up to this house and wash us away?" she asked.

"It can wash the house, and us, and all the islands away; and that will happen one day, but it may be in a hundred years to come, and then we shall be dead; it might also happen to-night, but it will not. O, the sea is terrible! I have seen it, and I have the proofs of it in my time. It was in the year 1824 that there was a flood; the sea went over all these islands; we had to drive the sheep up into the lofts, and were obliged to go up there ourselves, and the sea beat against the walls so that the stones were loosened, and the walls fell down, and the sea rushed through the rooms: where the beams had not fallen down, the people sat on the roofs, — we sat there for two nights, and not a boat could come to us from Föhr, nor from the Marskland. O! when the first boat came with bread and water, fresh, drinkable water, it was as if our Lord himself came and said, 'Now everything is well!'"

And tears stood in Keike's eyes, and also in little Elizabeth's, but in the latter's it was from fear and dread, for she saw it just as vividly as it was in Keike's thoughts.

We should, however, do great injustice to Keike, if we supposed she filled Elizabeth's imagination only with pictures of dread and terror. She told also the prettiest stories she could think of, and which she knew from printed books. Yes, one of them — it was about Priest John, who was a Frisian king's son — she had retained in her memory, and repeated it word for word as in the book. She knew also that about "Mr. Peter with the silver key;" about "Malusine;" and about "Whittington and his Cat;" so that every evening went on charmingly.

It was bed-time, when there was a knocking at the door; Madame Leyson herself had come to say that there was a ship at anchor out by Seesand, and that she and the Commander himself had seen through the telescope that it was "The Three Sisters," and therefore the vessel that Elimar was on board of; he, the sweetest and cleverest boy the world possessed. Madame Leyson laughed, and yet she was almost in tears.

"If this night were only gone!" said she; "for now I cannot sleep before I have him in the room!"

There was a pecking at the door.

" It cannot possibly be him ! " she exclaimed ; " he cannot
come before to-morrow ! "

Nor was it he.

The door was opened, and the tame jackdaw that had followed Madame Leyson to the house now hopped in ; he had
been tired of waiting outside, and therefore pecked at the
door for admittance ; he said all he could say, " Claus goes
in the loft with Piltitz ! " and it was said with just such an expression as would lead one to think that he also was glad of
Elimar's arrival, which, however, was an event that he had the
least cause to be glad of, as the story will show.

CHAPTER XIV.

THE next day Elimar stood in the middle of the room, and it was not that square lump which the silhouette portrayed, but a pretty lad of fourteen years, with bright blue eyes and light curling hair, that contrasted with his cheeks, which were tanned brown, from exposure to the wind and weather. He seemed to be an active lad, and one might also call him somewhat mischievous-looking. He had now made his first great voyage, and grown on the way full two inches. The measure of his height, when he had set out, was marked on the door-post.

"He has made the voyage to Greenland," said Madame Leyson; "nay, one may also say the voyage to America: it amounts to the same thing. Greenland is close to it, my old man says, and as Greenland was first discovered by the Norwegians, so it is in fact we here in the north that discovered America, and not that Columbus; but let him have the honor, I have now my sweet boy. Come and kiss your grandmother."

"You kiss Piltitz, and let me go," said Elimar with a morose face. "It is just as if I were a baby!"

"O, you dear angel!" said Madame Leyson, with half-extended arms, and happy in regarding him; but Elimar went up to the window, where he wound the string of the window-blind round his finger, and when his grandmother came nearer to him he made a pull so that it sounded, "ritsch! ritsch!" and away went the blind,

"Then you might have kept away from me," said Elimar; "now you have got that to sew together, and then I shall be free so long." And he took up the jackdaw as it hopped

8

along the floor, and pinched it between his fingers, so that it screamed with terror, "Claus goes in the loft with Piltitz!" and as Piltitz chanced to be lying close by in the chair, Elimar sat the terrified Claus right on the head of Piltitz, and as Claus stretched out his legs and claws, he did not let them pass very lightly over the cat's fur. The whole was but the work of a moment, but during that moment that fine, lively face had an expression of ferocity. Madame Leyson knew it well; she herself had, one may almost say, fostered it. "Now you are like Jes Jappen," was all that she said, and Elimar understood her, but cared nothing about it; he was the very rudest of boys towards her, but this she tried to deny to every one and to herself, though she had done everything to spoil him by indulgence. When he, as a little one, deserved a good flogging with the birch, it was always, "The child is sick," or else, "He is the mildest and most obedient lamb."

When she begged him to take the greatest care not to spill his coffee over the new sofa and chair covers, it ran directly from the cup over chair and sofa; and then the sweet child was inattentive and heedless!

Keike could also tell about Elimar, and the deceased parson's wife knew it if she could get up out of her grave. They knew a story about him, a story of some consequence, and they had then said, "Now you are like Jes Jappen. It was during the time that Moritz's predecessor was alive, where Keike was in service. She, the parson's wife, and Madame Leyson, sat sewing round a little table; Elimar would have that table, and as the parson's wife refused it in the most positive manner, Elimar went home, took down the Commander's pistol, which was always loaded, then returned to the parsonage, and when the women least suspected it, he fired off the pistol right over their heads, so that the whole three fell down on the floor, and when they lay there, Elimar took the table, and bore it away in triumph. "Such a one was he."

This story had not only reached Föhr and Dageböl, but was known in the Duchies, though it had not yet come to the Commander's ears, as almost all these "indications of character," as Madame Leyson called them, were carefully concealed from him. The Commander himself, however fond he might be of his grandson, never entered into conversation with him, but was chary of his words towards him; in short he was a Commander, and Elimar was a ship-boy; and on these terms they went on best of all. Though this year, it was not to be concealed, he heard, with no small degree of pleasure, Elimar talk about Greenland and the Greenlanders, whom he himself knew so well; but yet Elimar told it best to Keike and little Elizabeth, in whom he had also the best listeners.

The swinish manners of the Greenlanders, which were depicted in all their filthiness, interested Keike in particular, who was cleanliness personified.

On the contrary, the description of the floating icebergs which resembled churches and palaces, the whales that spouted up jets of water through their nostrils, and their little carriages with ten or sixteen dogs before them, was the most interesting to Elizabeth. However, Keike complained that Elimar had become mischievous, and impudent in a new way, and that he already began to talk about sweethearts; *that* he had also learned of Jes Jappen.

And who was Jes Jappen?—the name was Frisian, and a very good one, but he who bore it was but ill regarded, particularly by Madame Leyson, and would have been still more so if Elimar had told his last story about him; but that was nothing to tell, he thought. Jes Jappen was caboose-boy on board "The Three Sisters," and had been punished there several times for his bad disposition and rude temper; at last they had put him into another vessel, so that they were quit of him. He and Elimar had shortly before been fighting, and Jes Jappen had then made use of his clasp knife; this Madame Leyson ought to have known, but Elimar said nothing.

"I beat him," thought he, "and if I had had my clasped knife, I should have stabbed again."

Jes Jappen's mother had been in service at the Commander's, but had been sent away as a useless person.

Jes had afterwards been rude to Madame Leyson, who had seen proof of his bad tricks, she said,—and an expression of the worst evil she knew, was, she insisted, to be seen in that boy's face; therefore her "You are like Jes Jappen," was the severest expression she could make use of.

That both the boys resembled each other in violence and mischievous tricks is certain, but in which of them it will sprout, be the greatest, or come to the most vigorous development, time will show. Jes Jappen was the servant girl's child, poor, without resources; Elimar was the wealthy Commander's indulged grandson.

Elizabeth and Elimar, however, agreed best together: the little strangely reserved girl attached him towards her; here he felt himself the superior, the protector. These two were often seen sitting in a boat, and he rowed over to the other Halligers, nay, even to Föhr and Amrom. There they walked together in the dikes, and he helped her to gather flowers, and collect stones. They played in miniature Ingomar and Parthenia;[1] they went together to the old and new church-yards, sat with the sheep in the pastures, and visited the fishermen.

On these wanderings, Elimar had sometimes his bad moments; violence burst forth, and then changed to slavish adoration, to the sincerest expression of affection, and desire to please his companion. She was regarded by most people as a rude, uncouth child, and they found that this coarseness increased every day: this Elimar did not notice; as children in general understand other children best, and are understood again by them.

She often sat, as they said, quite thoughtless, and scratched figures in the sand with a stick; it looked like an idle trick, and Hedevig would say, —

"Is that employment for a great girl to sit so, and scrape in the sand without thought or meaning?"

But thought was there. In those strokes, and that loose sand, lay the *fata-morgana building*, which, when described, became visible to Elimar; she explained to him the whole glorious structure. It was a sort of outline of the palace and garden she would erect if she became great and immensely rich. The palace and the garden should be placed by the sea, but not on Oland, where the place was too small, but over on Föhr. Trees should be brought from the woods in Funen; foliage, as at the Baroness's manor, should grow up the walls right to the chimney; silk and velvet hang on the

[1] Halm's *Sohn der Wildnis.*

walls, and gold and silver candlesticks, like those on the altar
table, stand with lighted candles the whole night. O, it was
so delightful to imagine, so easy to sketch, — it was the rooms
and the walks in the garden that she drew in the sand, and
saw completed, saw them in imagination so vivid and complete. As she was thus one day in the very best and most interesting part of her description, Elimar sprang into the sand
and scraped with his boot to the right and left, so that the
whole was rubbed out, and he shouted, —

"Now comes the sea! huss, buss!— and washes away the
whole!" and it was to Elizabeth as if he had overthrown the
reality, and the tears stood in her eyes; but Elimar laughed
and shouted, "The sea comes!" took the great girl on his
back, and ran off with her as fast as he could. She screamed,
and when he set her down again, and saw that the tears still
ran down her cheeks, he asked, —

"What are you crying for? you are a stupid child. There
was neither palace nor garden, it was nonsense altogether;"
and he ran and romped with her till the sorrow was forgotten.
They were down by the sea, just where the old church-yard
lay; they looked at the vessels at a distance, large and small,
and then Elimar told her how his ship should be equipped, —
there could be a private cabin and mainmast, and that was
something different to her palace, which she only imagined,
and which would never have existence.

"But no ship can be as large as a palace," said Elizabeth;
"there is no ship like the old Baroness's palace,"— and then
she told him about the room where the old portraits hung behind the living foliage; she depicted the manor-house as
larger than all Oland, and so large no ship could be.

"The giant-ship is still greater," said Elimar, and told her
about the phantom-ship, which the seaman here believes in.
"It sails out in the great ocean, and it is larger than any of
the islands here; the deck is so long that the Commander on
board is always on horseback to give his orders; the rigging
is so large that the young sailors climb up and roll about on
the maintop; then years pass away before they are ready to
sail, and they come down old men, with white hair!"

"But, where do they get food from?" asked Elizabeth.

"There are inns in all the cross-heads in the rigging, where they can go in. Jap Lidt Petters's father was once on board when he was a boy. They had got into that sea which they call the Channel, there by England, and as it is but a few miles broad, between land and land, the ship stuck fast, and they had to smear the coasts with soft soap, and since that time they have always shone."

And Elimar believed what had been told him.

"I shall meet sometime with the giant ship," said he, "and I am not afraid!"

Little Elizabeth, with tears in her eyes, then begged him not to go on board, and above all things "not to come home again as an old man with white hair and a white beard!"

"But then you will be an old woman, when I return," was his answer. "Can you not understand that just as many years will pass over your head; you will surely not have me for a sweetheart!"

And he looked at her with a laughing face, while at the same time he drew out a couple of loose human bones that projected above ground, and threw them far out into the water.

"You must not do that," said Elizabeth; "they must be buried over again there by the church."

"Must I not!" he repeated, and took up one of the largest he could find, which he was just about to fling into the sea; but he let it alone, saying, —

"Yes; will you be my sweetheart when you are grown up? it cannot be so long now, and a sailor must have a sweetheart! I shall soon be fourteen years old."

He then took Elizabeth round the neck and kissed her.

"You shall not say anything about this to the others, nor yet to Keike, for she would gladly have me for a sweetheart if I would, but she is too old; you, on the contrary, are just suitable. The men should always be older!"

Elizabeth listened to him as if he told her one of his stories; but to be sweethearts she thought was amusing, and she held him still faster by the hand.

One day passed quietly on like the other, and the autumn storm blew, and the sea rolled over the flat island: town and church lay like a wreck in the midst of the waters; the inhabitants were quite separated for many days from the continent and the other islands.

In flood-time and stormy weather it was quite strange to Hedevig, who was quite unaccustomed to these scenes: she could not sleep for the thundering sound of the sea and the waves, which, in long, broken surges, reached almost up to the house, against whose walls she expected that some ship would one day be dashed.

At the Commander's everything went on in its old way, except a few connubial disputes which Elimar was the occasion of.

"The wild cat becomes too mad," said the Commander. But the grandmother always knew how to find out something excellent in what the boy did, or to take away the blame from him, even when grandmother Osa's portrait was found with its eyes put out.

"It was the worms," she said, "that had gnawed two round holes so accurately in the eyes of the old portrait."

Between Claus and Piltitz there had become somewhat of a coolness, occasioned by Elimar's tricks, and which ended tragically. The old cat had not understanding enough to see that the whole blame was attributable to Elimar, and that not the least could be attached to the poor jackdaw; for it was in convulsive terror that Claus stretched out legs and claws, and it was Elimar who drew them like a comb over Piltitz's head and back. But Piltitz was no thinker, however much he had the appearance of one, — a peculiarity we often see in men. Piltitz discarded all feelings of friendship, and one day they all heard — but they were so accustomed to hear that story — "Claus goes into the loft with Piltitz!" It was uttered so loud, that it ought to have awakened attention to it, but it awoke none, although it was often repeated, and was so loud and strong. They heard it from the stairs, from the loft, but each time weaker; at last it was no longer heard, and that was not the worst.

In the course of an hour after they saw Piltitz stretch himself in his chair with a gloomy look. Claus did not appear; he was not to be found, neither in the house, nor at the neighbors'. Poor Claus! the friend of his youth had taken him by the back, dragged him into the loft, and devoured him: the feathers lay strewed about, so that the story really ended with " Claus going into the loft with Piltitz."

This was the first time that Madame Leyson was really angry with Elimar.

"You are the cause of it," she said, "you are still worse than Jes Jappen;" and that was the very worst she could say, and she burst into tears, perhaps because she had said it. "For shame of yourself!" she added in a milder tone; "Claus and Piltitz were always fond of each other, and lived so united and happily; you have set them by the ears, just as you do me and the Commander."

Elimar laughed, and assured her that the Commander would not drag her up into the loft and eat her; and then he took his grandmother round the waist, swung her round in a waltz, and she laughed.

"I cannot help it," said she, "for he has now that sweet, handsome face, and is, in fact, a good child; yes, that you are, my dear boy." Thus the reconciliation was concluded.

But there was not one on the whole island who did know that Claus was dead, and that Elimar was the cause of it.

The winter came with storms and sea-fogs. During the long evenings, Moritz and Hedevig read aloud, alternately, Walter Scott's novels, — those true pictures drawn from life and nature. They read "Waverley" and "Rob Boy."

The Commander and his wife were listeners, and as interested listeners as but few have; this reading was to them a part of their lives: they seemed to have lived with Fergus M'Ivor, Rose, and Flora; and thought they had seen and known M'Gregor and Diana Vernon.

The descriptions were transferred to what they themselves knew and had experienced: the connection between the Scotch and the Frisians was so close, not alone in the language, but in old habits and customs. The Frisians had, like the Scotch, their clans; two of the most powerful of these families are still amongst the inhabitants of Ditmarsk, the Boyers and Reventlows. Here, also, sanguinary revenge reigned almost as long as in the mountains of Scotland.

This was also spoken of: the living word proceeded from that which was read. The Scotchman's emblem is a flowering thistle, so significant of his mountain life. The Frisian's, on the contrary, is a soup-kettle over the fire; yet they found in this a connection: the emblem of home. The partial Scot sees it in the flower of his mountains; the Frisian in his hearth, to which the whole of these people's endeavors are turned; for their hearths they combated; their hearts are wedded to home.

History, legends, old customs, and usages, filled, as it were, the furrow more and more which the sea had made between Scotland and the Cimbric peninsula.

"But these lands, you know, were once united," said Madame Leyson; "at least, England was joined to Sleswick and Jutland. It is an old *saga*, that a whole chain of mountains united England with our land; and the English queen was to have been married to the Danish king, but he deceived her. Then, in her vexation, she ordered seven hundred men to dig through the green hills that restrained the sea on both sides, and the seas rushed through and joined, swallowed up all the islands, and overflowed the whole of Friesland, which became the island it now is."

Moritz then related about the immigration of the Angles from these districts to England and Scotland; and the Commander proved that even "The Wild Duck," which his vessel was called after, screamed good English and Scotch, as it cried, "Go-day! go-day!"

The many stories and *sagas* that exist among the Frisian people, the whole life on these coasts and islands, awakened regret that no Walter Scott had been born in these lands, and that the Frisians were almost without an author.

"Yes," said Moritz, "here are materials, but they still lie like the marble in the quarry, and await the sculptor. It is said there were many heroes before Homer's time, but the world knows nothing of them."

"What an excellent story might be made about grandmother Osa; that was a woman! And then it is all true that is told about her."

Moritz had only heard the story twice, Hedevig once, so

that it might very well be told again, and it was so, but we will not hear it yet, — we will wait for a better opportunity, convinced that Madame Leyson will relate it again if she lives, and we will hope that she may do so. During all these conversations and readings, not only Elimar and Elizabeth were present, but even Keike, who was perhaps the most enthusiastic for the Scottish poet. Elizabeth, however, understood but little of it: she was as yet not far advanced in German, and it was in that language that Walter Scott was read. Thus the winter passed.

The drift-ice had laid itself like a bulwark around the island; then came gray foggy days; at length the first beams of the sun broke forth, and spring came. The only tree on the island, the little gooseberry bush, which stood sheltered, shot forth fresh green shoots; the sunshine caused its fine leazes to unfold themselves: this renewed life brought tears into the eyes of Moritz; the green shoots of spring awakened more sadness than the falling leaves of autumn; the silent sunshine thawed, as it were, the pain. He looked at the full-blown buds of the gooseberry bush, and thought of Caroline, who had possessed life's freshness, just like it, and who was now but dust under the earth.

Elimar, who during the whole winter had shown himself an active sportsman, shot and caught wild ducks, and eider-ducks, nay even a swan, which Jap Lidt Petters had stuffed for Madame Leyson. He was also the most courageous in springing about on the floating sheets of ice, and the first to put his boat out to sea. He was to make a voyage to Holland this spring, and he made himself happy with the thought; he had been told that it was a splendid country, the very semblance of Marskland, and besides that, there were great cities, splendid and powerful. In consequence of this voyage Elimar was obliged to go for several days to Föhr, and this occasioned great regret to Elizabeth; even Keike's stories afforded her no consolation. The departure of the Halligers and the Föhringians takes place on a fixed day in the spring. The week before this Elimar was again with Commander Leyson, and it was there determined between the two families, the Commander's and the Parson's, that they would pay a visit to some friends in Amrom, and Elimar should also have the pleasure of accompanying them, for he must at all events bid farewell to their friends and acquaintances.

Amrom, with its white sand dikes, is a complete highland when compared with Halliger ; the children know well where the most rabbits hide themselves there, and where the prettiest heath-flowers bloom behind the dikes. The wind was favorable, so that it was but a short sailing tour ; both families were received with great pleasure and exultation. The best viands were brought forth, the great coffee-can made its appearance ; the men talked about their concerns, and the women about theirs. Elizabeth was out of the room, and Elimar sneaked away soon afterwards ; he passed through the kitchen, and as there was no one there he peeped into the soup-kettles and drawers. Some fishing-tackle lay in a corner, and he felt a great desire to try it ; the box in which it was and which is made to be carried on the back, he must also have with him ; therefore, without further ceremony, he threw it over his shoulder, and was out of the house in a moment.

Close by the house sat Elizabeth, looking at a hole in the declivity where the rabbits had burrowed deep under the heath ; she had seen a couple of them run into the opening. The most abundant game on Amrom are the rabbits, all of which are the descendants of one single couple that were stranded here on the island several years ago. Elizabeth pointed to the opening, and Elimar immediately laid down on his stomach, peeped into the dark passage, and threw stones in, but the rabbits kept themselves quiet. Three others, on the contrary, appeared on the top of the slope, but these, directly they saw him, immediately turned round with a comic spring, and took the way to the nearest dikes. Elimar started off after them, and Elizabeth followed him at a slower rate ; the rabbits stopped every moment, turned their heads, made a high jump, then ran close together, and again apart from each other, then suddenly disappeared in the foremost valley of the dikes.

Elimar stood still a long time, looked about on all sides, and then returned to Elizabeth. They were a considerable distance from home ; but here, where they stood, between the sand banks, it was delightfully warm. Elizabeth sat down, she was so tired, and he lay down in the sand beside her. But he did not lie long before he sprang up again, pulled the long roots of the lyme-grass, that hangs like ribbons from the slopes of the dikes, and whole shoals of sand rolled down. One must not imagine the dikes to be like a chain of mountains, — he would not have pulled up the wild plants from their sides — no, they present the most singular shapes! Where the sea can operate against them with much force, they are cut off at the bottom as if it were with a spade, — one fancies one sees a range of grayish-white, colossal walls, on the top of which the lyme-grass grows, and about whose sides the roots hang forth like creeping plants, whilst down in the gray damp soil appear strange, almost circular figures, impressed by the sea, as if it were its mysterious writing, left to announce what riches and horrors it conceals.

Elimar crawled up one of the high sand dikes, and Elizabeth, of course, attempted the same: it was one of the highest they were now on, and whence they saw the whole North Sea, which, during the ebb, had receded from the land for miles around; not a breeze was stirring.

They did not stand long, for they could not avoid the temptation of going out on the firm, wet sand, where there lay so many stones and shells about: there was also a whole bottle, well corked. Elimar held it up against the sun, and saw that there was a paper in it, and so they broke the bottle. The paper was written on, but in a language Elimar did not understand; yet this much he knew, and he explained it to Elizabeth, that the ship had struck, and that at the last moment they had written this paper on board, and put it in the bottle, that some one might be informed when and where they had perished, and the name of the ship.

Elizabeth found a curious yellow stone; it looked like candied sugar, but it was a fine large piece of amber; and when she rubbed it on her arm till it became warm, it attracted pieces of straw. This day was a real lucky day for finding things, so they continued their way further and further out. All around it was like a net of water stretched over the whole sandy bottom. At some distance out were some high stones, and between these they found pieces of a rudder, a glazed hat without a crown, also some variegated mussel-shells ; and, what was still finer, there were two large fishes sprawling about in a pool of water. Elimar would take them with his hands, but they glided from him again ; but caught they must be. Elizabeth stood on one of the large stones and looked on. The time went on pleasantly, it was quite calm, and the sun shone delightfully. Then Elimar remarked that the ground began to be more damp, that the net of water became fuller, and that it was therefore time to return, as the tide would soon be rising.

He looked towards Amrom, which might be about four hundred paces distant, but it was as if the island had suddenly sunk. A fog from the north rolled forward, and had quite enveloped the nearest sand hills, and in the next moment both the wanderers too ; the sunshine was hidden from them, the sun became redder and redder. Elimar seized Elizabeth by the hand, and hastened towards the island.

" I am so afraid," cried Elizabeth ; " where is Amrom ? and where are my shoes and stockings ? I must have them ! "

She had just taken them off, and was about to go into the pool to Elimar and the fishes, when the fog was observed. Elimar turned round ; the shoes must be on the great stone where she had sat ; they had glided down, but were found. The fog was icy cold and thick. Elimar now took Elizabeth on his back and hastened away ; but the different branches of what we have called the water-net, formed by the standing water-ripts and pools, increased ; they were obliged to go round, and when he thought they were close to the sand-dikes he stood by the same stones they had left. He struck his foot against some object ; it was the little wooden box in which the fishing-tackle lay, and which in his haste he had forgotten ; he took it up, but he was now quite at a loss to know in what direction the island lay. To shout and scream was of no use whatever ; but yet he shouted. The tide already rolling on, the first long wave struck over his feet. He then lifted little Elizabeth up to the highest stone, and sat down by her side ; the next sea came stronger, but as it rose higher and higher up over the sandy bottom, the motion became weaker, for it was a dead calm.

Elizabeth did not cry; it was as if she understood **the** whole danger; pale and with a strange look she regarded Elimar. The tide rose and rose, so that he was obliged to stand up on the stone beside her, though there was scarcely place for two. He again shouted with all the strength of despair that he possessed: now he fancied that he heard a dog bark, though it was certainly from a very different direction to that where he thought Amrom lay; perhaps some one was approaching in a boat. The fog became thinner for a moment, so that he knew by the lighter part of the sky where the sun was, and it became his compass. Amrom lay just in that direction whence he fancied he heard the bark of a dog, but that had quite ceased, and the sea rose higher and higher.

The water was now over their feet on the great stone. Elizabeth could not stand fast; she clung to Elimar, and they both fell down into the water, but he got her quickly up again on the stone: he himself stood below in the water, which reached to his breast, and held her with both his arms. The tide continued to increase, and he then hastily pushed the box with the fishing-tackle under his feet, so that he got a good way higher up, and his head was now almost on a level with Elizabeth's.

There was no motion of the waves; the surface of the water rose quite silently, as if it were not that which rose, but as if the two who stood there sank gently down to the bottom of the still water. Elimar uttered a despairing cry, but it was not answered; every minute that passed the watery mirror came higher, — it would soon be over their heads. Elimar was pale as death; the tears stood in his eyes, and he kissed little Elizabeth, who threw her arms round his neck. The water had now risen to their breasts, and began to buoy them up!

A voice then sounded close by; the plashing of oars was heard, and a boat, in which sat a man, was seen through the fog; it came nearer; it was Jap Lidt Petters, who had heard the scream, and had come just in time to their aid; he got them quickly into the boat, and then with rapid strokes made towards Oland.

Here he learned from them how it was that they had got

into the danger and peril in which he had found them, and that both the Commander and the Parson's family were on a visit on Amrom; accordingly, as soon as he had delivered Elizabeth over to Keike, who immediately put her to bed, and Elimar had gone home to do the same service to himself, Jap sailed over to Amrom to tell them, though without entering into minute particulars, that they were both at home and taken care of.

Elimar received no injury from the immersion, but Elizabeth, on the contrary, was obliged to keep her bed for some days, and could not go to Föhr on the day of the seamen's departure; but her thoughts were there, and foremost among them was the heroic Elimar, with vivid distinctness. In the few minutes, when the sea united them, they had become indissolubly bound together for all time. A feeling had been awakened like that which exercised its influence at equally as young an age in Ariosto, in Byron, and others, whose names irradiate our every-day life.

On the day of departure men and women had assembled in the village of Gothing, on Föhr, to bid farewell to their relatives and friends. The little vessels glided from the shore; the crowd of women in their black dresses stood on the highest point of land, an old tumulus, and from thence they waved to their beloved ones the last farewell.

CHAPTER XV.

NOT before seven or eight months could Elimar be expected to return; this appeared to Elizabeth to be a
long, long time, and she was quite dejected; but how would
she have borne it, had she known that months of hope often
in reality become years; that the day of his return would
be still more distant than the one she now least thought of,
her confirmation day?

On that day, "the child is shaken off the arm," says the
phrase; on that day, the voyage begins on life's open sea:
it is a serious, solemn day, and we will now hasten to it, and
to those singular events which then unfolded themselves, but
not before we have collected, as in one great frame, the inter-
vening years, and presented to view, what may, in Elizabeth's
life, be called "Home on the Halligers."

As a fortunate counterbalance to that imaginative and
superstitious world into which Keike's stories betrayed Elizabeth, was that healthy nature and sensible industry which
Hedevig always sought to lead her into. She had to learn to
sew and knit, she knew a little music — and Elizabeth was
singularly quick at learning, comprehended all that she was
taught, and disclosed unusual talents; it was Hedevig's
delight to direct her intelligent observations to nature; that
and the Bible were the two books that always lay opened, the
first around them, and the last within the house. Both were
read, both reflected a lustre on that home, and penetrated
those who dwelt there. Hedevig, with her still affectionate
manner, was a blessing. She lived entirely for her brother
and the child she had adopted; there was poetry in her soul,
although she herself knew it not, and by the aid of that, she

comprehended everything, and her eye would then beam strangely, as that of a crying child will sparkle when sorrow suddenly gives place to joy.

"How poor," she thought, "are great cities, with their societies, parties, and plays, compared with that affectionate family life here in solitude, — or that grand spectacle which the sea and sky present to us every morning and evening!"

Nevertheless, how the rest of the world went on, they knew; the newspapers were sent round from one to the other, even if a week old, and books came every month. The newer productions of modern literature found their way to this remote corner of the world. Before that small public, as if before a second judgment-seat, many a book, well-advertised and flourishingly announced, sank before nature's criticism; the admired but meretricious art, in which there was no inward truth, here found its level.

Here, where those two books, Nature and the Bible, were the chief and exemplars of all writings, a different measure of excellence from that which fashion prescribes was exacted.

This intimacy with the Book of books, and the opportunity of reading aloud therefrom to his private circle and his congregation, just as Moritz's heart dictated, led him, not alone from the pulpit to point to God, but from the low shores of the strand, from the dikes of the neighbor islands — and men in all ages have understood such significant lessons.

He regarded nothing as accidental, but, on the contrary, as a link in the great chain; in the most insignificant things he often found the germ of something great and important, and he led the thoughts and attention of others to it. He taught them how a single weed which the wind drives up on the coast, and which takes root there, may perhaps in centuries become a safeguard for the country against the encroachments of the sea. The insignificant weed gathers the loose sand around it; it grows and grows, and at last stands like a protecting sand-dike. Yet do not depend on such! — in them behold the fall of power and greatness! — nothing in the world is durable. Yonder, where the sea breaks against the shoals, there stood, not many years ago, a mighty sand bank; the rabbits came there and dug their holes, the wind blew

9

in there, and forced its onward way incessantly the sea struck
against the loose ground, and the sand bank fell and was en-
gulphed by the ocean.

This intimacy with nature, the evening readings, which
were always sound and entertaining, the novels of Walter
Scott, which, to Elizabeth, were embodied realities, filled her
mind, as the sunlight fills the plant, and gave a freshness and
expansion to her thoughts. "The Heart of Mid-Lothian"
was the one which above all others addressed itself to her
feelings ; in it she found her heroine, her *idéal*, and that was
"Jeannie Deans." The journey from Edinburgh to London
often filled and occupied her mind ; she was far more at home
in the scenes and manners of Scotland, than in the land she
herself belonged to.

Of late years a great intimacy had sprung up between the
world and the inhabitants of the islands here. The bathing
guests who frequented the little town of Wieck, on Föhr, situated only four miles' distance from the Halligers, had increased considerably in number. The bathing establishment
founded here in 1819 was greatly enlarged, as visitors came
not only from Slesvig and Holstein, but also from the interior
of Germany. A sort of hotel, conducted by a person from
Hamburg, was established here, and here a band of itinerant
German musicians performed every Sunday. When the wind
blew in the direction of Oland they could hear from thence,
quite distinctly, what was played, and the music thus borne
over the water sounded sweetly. They could see, too, through
the Commander's excellent telescope, the lengthened row of
promenaders in the long avenue of young trees along the sea-
side, and in the dark evenings it was a pleasure to see the
rockets mounting in the air, or to view a slight display of fire-
works. Some of the strangers came regularly on a visit to
Oland ; some of them were recommended to the Commander's
or to the Parson's. When the bathing season ended — in
September — every one returned to his home, and once more
the still monotonous life began.

Amongst those who had been recommended to Moritz was
a Scotchman named Knox, who stated himself to be a de-
scendant of the family of Scotland's reformer, whose name he

bore. He had in his youth travelled through the whole of Europe, but of late years it was Germany, Holland, and the Scandinavian north that had especially interested him ; the relationship between these nations and their family ties were his study ; he expressed himself clearly and thoughtfully on these subjects, and was, besides, the most excellent living commentary on the novels of Walter Scott. As a boy he had travelled over that, his native country, which the poet has celebrated as the —

> " Land of brown heath and shaggy wood,
> Land of the mountain and the flood ! "

His family residence was in Kilburn, and therefore not far from Abbotsford, where he had often visited the great poet, of whom he gave many characteristic traits. He knew, too, Scott's faithful dog Maida so well, had passed many evenings in the family circle, and had carried Scott's grandchild in his arms — Lockhart's sweet child, the ennobled image of Walter Scott. All these narratives, explanations, and traits, arising out of these novels, now presented themselves still more vividly to Elizabeth, so that in the living reality of the moment, the whole received such a romantic lustre, such a charm, as made her life appear one of entire happiness.

The personal character of Moritz and his sister pleased the Scotchman ; their purely religious manners, which naturally disclosed themselves even in the customs and diurnal duties of the house, accorded with the Scotchman's education ; at the Parson's or the Halligers, he likewise found the usages of his home ; here grace was said at table before the family sat down to their meals ; here Sunday was observed with quiet holiness, the evening hours were passed in devotion. There was no effort at display, no attempt at effect ; everything sprang from the natural feeling, and a tranquil mind.

It was the second summer that Knox had visited Föhr : one day he brought with him a new guest to the Halligers. He was a Dane, who, however, had not been in Denmark for many years, but, on the contrary, in Paris, where he had caused much sensation by his musical compositions. The newspapers foretold that he would open a career for himself ;

that never before had tones such as those he produced become living words. He, however, had always been called a Swede in the papers, because Sweden was that land in the north which the French knew best, for there one of their generals, one of Napoleon's marshals, Bernadotte, had become king.

The Dane, who, at that moment, was the lion of the bathing season, — for what does not a name do when French renown is attached to it? — was a slenderly built man, between thirty and forty years of age. There was a strange movement in his face, a mixture of good nature and pride, which vibrated about the mouth in particular. Perhaps, from the fine features around it, more than from the eye itself, a physiognomist would have tried to discover his character. His talk had a good deal of the liveliness of the Frenchman, with no small share of his vivacity of expression. He intended to return to Paris again, after the bathing season, but would first pay a few short visits in Denmark.

He appeared to know most of the families of the nobility, and was well acquainted with both summer and winter life in the north, and praised much of it ; but he mixed a great deal of irony with his praise, nay, even bitterness at times. It was his matchless skill on the piano — in particular, his performance with one hand — that had bound the Scotchman to him. It was this wonderfully clever performance that the former wished Moritz and Hedevig to hear ; for there was, as we know, a good piano at the parsonage. Elizabeth sang to its accompaniment all the songs which Caroline had sung — Sohnbarth's splendid compositions to Goethe's poems.

Knox had, a few days previously, mentioned this new guest, in a letter to Moritz, and he now stood in the parlor at the parsonage, where he was received in the most cordial manner.

Moritz started on seeing the face of the new-comer. His person — there was something in it that appeared as if almost familiar to him ; they must have seen each other before, and not transiently ; there must be some remembrances bound up with their meeting.

" We are scarcely strangers to each other," said Moritz ; " I must have known you before, but where I cannot remember at this moment: where can I have enjoyed the honor of being in your company?"

"Perhaps in Paris," he replied, "or in Denmark; I passed my whole youth there, though it was not my happiest time. However, I found my advantage in it."

Hedevig was requested by her brother to assist him in recollecting where it was that he had known the stranger, but she could not ; and it was quite certain that she saw him for the first time. They conversed, promenaded, and were shown about ; they had seen the church, visited the old church-yard, been at the Commander's house, and taken dinner. The Dane was so entertaining ; he related a hundred little anecdotes, which sparkled like rockets, and illumined the conversation. The library was seen, and so was the music-shelf, but the latter looked rather bare.

"Weyse !" he exclaimed; "my dear, excellent Weyse! Denmark has in him a clever and national composer, greater than she knows. No one has heard of him abroad, and at home it is only real musicians who are aware of his value."

It was Weyse's music to "Macbeth" that lay on the shelf, and which he had taken up, that called forth this deserved eulogium.

"*That* has, however, been generally appreciated," said Moritz ; "what beautiful chamber-music there is in it ! — the watchman's song, and the scene with the witches."

"I value and admire Weyse," he answered ; "and I think I dare call myself his most zealous admirer ; yet, in this composition I am, perhaps, on account of my musical peculiarity, of a different opinion to my countrymen — ay, even the most able musicians. I demand from him something else than what he has given us. I miss here just what Weyse knew so well how to impress on his compositions — the characteristic. The chamber-music in Macbeth's castle is, I will acknowledge, even to be genial, but it is not characteristic of the time and place. Such a piece of music does not carry us to Macbeth's castle in Inverness-shire. Old Scotch ballads, or songs like these, should be heard ; those instruments must predominate which lead us to think of the bagpipes. The witches' scene in music I can only imagine, from music depicting the situation. I would give the hideous and the unearthly, the mysterious, the night-storm on the heath ; and the singing voices of the witches I would confine to a monotonous song that should only change with the sinking and rising of the voice."

On Hedevig's stating that the chamber-music sounded, at least to her, like real Scotch, he sat down to the piano, saying :

"I cannot, however, play it, for ten fingers are wanted, and I have, properly speaking, only as good as five !" And he showed them his stiff hand. "This is a remembrance of a forest drive in Denmark."

Then with his sound hand he played with such expression, and with such consummate mastery of the instrument, that one would really have thought he had four hands. There was a life, a soul, in that delicately formed face : his eyes shone, his lips quivered, and it was then clear to Moritz where he had seen him, and who he was. And yet, how was it possible? He whom Moritz remembered was poor, neglected, treated with rudeness ; and this was a celebrated man, whose name resounded from France with a thrill through the world of art.

"I saw you in Funen, many years ago," said Moritz.

"It is possible," he replied : "it was certainly at my old friend's, the Baroness's. In the bird-cage, as they so wittily call the manor, for where are they so witty as in my dear country ? "

"No, it was at the estate where one of my old pupils resides, Count Frederick's."

"There," said the stranger, and the blood mounted for a moment to his cheeks ; "it is probable, for I have often been there for several weeks together."

"And you are, or were at that time, a Gentleman of the Bed-chamber," said Moritz.

"I am that person," he answered ; "and I have not advanced in title since then. Then you certainly know the old Baroness at the adjoining estate? An excellent woman she is, notwithstanding all her strange ways. I am as fond of her as if she were my mother ; and this I tell you beforehand, that next to Providence I owe to her that which I now am —

to her I owe my independent situation, and the maturity of my talent."

Moritz reminded him of the evening at the Count's when they got — he still remembered the expression — " a musical lecture."

"You extemporized one of the ancient ballads for us on the piano," he added; "the present Countess had just then come with her mother on a visit, and was charmed with your playing."

"Clara!" exclaimed the Gentleman, — for we must let him retain this appellation; "Clara! how handsome she was! she also paid me compliments, such as I was at that time unaccustomed to hear: she was delighted, but yet she preferred my playing dances."

"We were all delighted to hear you!"

"'Only nothing of your own, if we may beg,' was Count Frederick's request. O, I remember that evening so well — there are certain moments in our lives that we retain in memory whilst whole months are forgotten, and are never brought again to mind."

"That is surely not the result of that unfortunate upsetting of the carriage," said Moritz, as he pointed to the Gentleman's stiff hand.

"Yes, I got that because the young gentleman had not learned to drive, and yet he would handle the reins: but I must not complain of that event, for it has been to my advantage, not to my injury. With two sound hands I might, perhaps, have become a clever pianist, and continued in straitened circumstances, to be *maître de plaisir* for some vulgar persons to whom birth and fortune had given this world's favors; but as my hand became stiff and useless for playing the piano, other talents had to be developed, and, thank God, I had some left, — for instance, my talent as a composer. My misfortune, or, if you choose, my accident, and the manner in which it happened, came to the ears of the old Baroness: she had twice before heard me play, and was pleased with my skill, and her compassion was now awakened. Some few injurious mortifications, — I may venture to say undeserved on my part, but which I suffered from the haughty Count Fred-

erick, — induced her to become my protectress, and strangely
clever she showed herself to be. I am not ashamed to confess
that she supported me in Paris, and she, like a mother, spent
large sums of money on me. At first it was but a notion of
hers, a willful determination that she would carry through.
They laughed at her as they have laughed at her best actions ;
but at last she became fond of me, and understood that talent
which God has given me, so that she held still faster to her
will ; and I am glad that she has derived some honor from her
patronage of me."

Elizabeth listened with astonishment ; and now she remembered the pale musical man who, with one arm bandaged and
in a sling, had been for a short time at the manor-house, and
had played with one hand — he was so still and sorrowful.
But how very differently did he appear here ! free, conscious
of his own abilities, and lively in conversation ; never before had she heard any one speak with such cordiality and
warmth about the old lady as he now spoke of her.

"I always thought that there was something particularly
good in the old Baroness," said Moritz. "I have known her
myself — nay, I once had a sort of correspondence with her ;
she is, however, very singular in many things, and one cannot
in truth blame the world for forming the estimate of her which
it does."

"The Gentleman " spoke about her life in childhood, which
we know ; about her father, " long Rasmus," who rode on the
wooden horse in the court-yard, where she now, as an old
woman, lived, and was the mistress ; he knew, too, how, under
the circumstances she grew up in, and was subjected to, she
must have become the singular character she was ; that in her
ill-regulated individuality there lay the best and noblest elements ; but that the world now only spoke of, and expatiated
upon her oddities, and what would raise a laugh against
her.

"I do not wish to subvert your faith in your essentially generous and correct conception of the old lady's character," said
Moritz ; " but in some few instances I cannot, nor will you be
able to excuse her unreasonable conduct. For example," and
he pointed to Elizabeth, " this child was her avowed favorite ;

but for an act which a child of her age would at most deserve a flogging for having committed, she cast her out into the wide world. It is true she did not allow her to starve, but she dismissed her, without caring into whose hands she fell, or what might become of her. She has never even once asked about her since. And then, there is her own flesh and blood, her own grandson, whom she would never see, and whom she allows to go about in the world like one that is an entire stranger to her."

"It is unjust!" answered the Gentleman: "in this case she cannot be excused, but her personal character may explain and qualify her manner of acting: with respect to her grandson, who is said to be an excellent young man, the Baroness has a motive, perhaps it is a fixed idea, as to her relationship to him. I know it, but have no right to divulge it, even in her defense, or even to explain her actions, but in this unfortunate idea lies the whole mystery of her conduct. He has lived many years in Italy."

"I have only heard from him twice during several years," answered Moritz; "the first time was directly after his arrival there, when he devoted himself, heart and soul, to the profession of a painter; the second time he wrote, — it was a year afterwards, — he had laid the palette aside and turned sculptor.

"Now, I believe, he is neither of the two, at least, if he be, he carries on his profession very privately; I however know very little about him."

During the course of conversation concerning friends and acquaintances in Funen, it appeared that it was the Gentleman who was best informed of the state of matters. Baron Holger had been in Paris the previous winter, and during a visit one day he had assured him that when in Denmark he had regarded Paul de Kock's novels as the first in the world, but that in Paris he had found that to enact his scenes in real life was, strictly speaking, the greatest exploit. At the same time he reproached himself for his volatility, and excused himself by saying, that if he had got Clara for his wife he would have been a pattern for husbands; but as Heaven paid no regard to virtuous wishes, so he had no obligations towards Heaven.

As to Count Frederick, he had succeeded to the estate on the death of his father, and was an aristocrat of the haughtiest stamp. The winter months he passed in Copenhagen, where all the great and fashionable were invited to his house — princes and diplomatists, yet artists also, because Clara was a patroness of the fine arts. She painted, and wrote beautiful small poems, as it was said, and had not only herself given, but had also collected and forced persons to contribute money towards the erection of Thorvaldsen's Museum.

This was about the result of the Gentleman's first visit to the Halligers; on a renewed visit, his interest for Elizabeth was particularly awakened; he was made acquainted with her whole history, and discovered in her great musical talents, and a voice of surprisingly sweet expression; but it awakened no little surprise in the quiet, pious parsonage, when he proposed to them to let her voice be cultivated and perfected for the opera; and on that occasion he set forth a Grisi's and Albertazzi's merits, honor, and riches. Moritz smiled and shook his head, and said how dear his foster-daughter was to him — that it would be painful to him to be separated from her, even if it were only as far as Copenhagen to Heimerant.

That worthy old man, in one of his last letters, had just proposed that Elizabeth should pass a winter in Copenhagen with him, there to see a little more of the world, and receive that beneficial influence which a large city can always impart to a young girl. This, however, he could not permit until after her confirmation, and to that time there was still a year and a half wanting.

At the end of the bathing season, in September, the Gentleman and the Scotchman left Föhr, but we shall afterwards meet them in another place. Now we must hasten towards an event which, like a thunder-clap from a clear sky, awakened the terror of the Commander's and clergyman's families, and became a point of transition in Elizabeth's life.

CHAPTER XVI.

DESPAIR. — HELP FROM THE "HEART OF MID-LOTHIAN."

BETWEEN Elimar's departure and his return home only a few months were to intervene, but we know that these sometimes seem to be years. The Commander had made an arrangement that Elimar should acquire a good theoretical knowledge as a seaman in Holland, where he would be amongst friends and acquaintances, and in a good house; thus the first winter passed, and he appeared to be cheerful and satisfied. Elizabeth heard the letters read, and always had a greeting from him. She knew all the rare and splendid things he saw, the large palaces and churches, the deep canals in the streets, where large vessels lie directly under tall trees; she knew that the high-roads throughout the whole country were paved like the stone floors in the Marsk dairies. O, how one could drive on them without being upset, as on the Slesvig dikes ! Elimar, too, had been to the theatre, where they performed whole stories with song and music, and he and all who saw them sat there with long pipes in their mouths, and puffed away, so that there was a dense cloud of smoke in the house; but the play went on charmingly, and they drank tea and read the newspapers. And in the course of the winter, when the canals and seas were frozen, and bright as a mirror, they lighted pitch garlands there; torches burnt, and whole crowds of men and women, all dressed for the season, and all on skates, a complete masquerade, darted over the ice, and some carried torches, which they swung about and struck against the bright ice, which shone again : *that* had been a still finer comedy than the one in the theatre where they drank tea and smoked tobacco.

Elimar was inexpressibly happy in Holland, and liked the country and the people; a year afterwards he went to sea,

and in the autumn returned to Haarlem, where the organ in
the church was the largest to be found in all the countries of
the world, and sounded as if a hundred musicians sat at it ;
and then how the tulips bloomed with colors, such as were not
to be found in Madame Leyson's bridal gown, which, however, shone brighter than any other gown on the Halligers.
Now and then there certainly came a stray complaint about
"the Scapegrace," as the Commander called Elimar, but only
once was there real cause for a serious reprimand, and this
was touching Elimar's indomitable impetuosity, which might
one time or another easily bring him into trouble, as the letter
said. At the beginning of the third year, however, he went
as second mate on board a large vessel to North America.
He did not come home on a visit before his departure, as had
been previously determined, but in his greeting to Elizabeth
he called her — and that was for the first time in writing —
"my little sweetheart."

He sent her a couple of amusing dolls, from a fishing village near the Hague : they were man and wife. made of small
shells gathered on the beach, and put together, so that they
showed the whole costume and appearance of the fishermen
and their wives at that place.

But Elimar did not come to the Halligers the next autumn,
nor yet the following one ; he was continually absent on long
voyages ; and America was always the country they were
bound to.

If Elimar had returned, and remained on the Halligers for
a longer time in Elizabeth's society, perhaps that halo which
now encompassed him in her thoughts would have been dispersed ; perhaps that precocious girl would have seen him
otherwise than her imagination now pictured him.

Her mind had developed itself in a remarkable degree during the last few years, and with respect to her physical growth,
that also was forward for her age ; one might almost have
supposed she was sixteen, and yet she was but fourteen years
of age.

Her confirmation was fixed for the coming spring ; but she
fell ill at Christmas with a form of the typhus fever ; Moritz
himself sat up and watched by her bed for a couple of nights :

and during that time it was to him as if he again underwent those sorrowful hours by the sick-bed of his deceased Caroline.

Elizabeth, however, recovered, though but slowly; and whilst that weak body lay helpless, the spirit had raised itself wondrously towards God, and now returned as with greater strength and expansion. The body vibrated under the fullness of a nervous enthusiasm and zeal that were almost alarming. She could not bear any kind of exertion; they durst not let her read; her confirmation was put off until the autumn; and secretly this pleased Elizabeth, for just at that time they expected Elimar.

The confirmation Sunday came; the little church was ornamented with long ribbons, on which hung variegated flowers of paper; Madame Leyson herself had clipped them all, and they now hung in garlands around the choir. The lights burnt on the altar, and the song of the congregation arose melodiously to the vaulted roof. Moritz, who was deeply moved, spoke of the wonderful vicissitudes of life, of its shortness, uncertainty, and sorrows; and in the peculiar manner he had of making himself understood by his congregation, he spoke to them words of consolation; and of these words one image seized on and filled Elizabeth's thoughts, and fixed itself firmly in them forever.

"In the British navy," said Moritz, "there is a red thread that goes through all the cordage, great and small, which shows that it belongs to the crown, and there is an invisible thread that goes through every person's life, which shows that we belong to God!" And Elizabeth felt the truth of what he said, by reflecting on her past life: her eyes shone with a kind of exultation; the blood mounted to her cheeks; she thought of her deserted situation as an infant in her dying mother's arms. Trina had once told her about it, Moritz never. She remembered vividly the scene with the old Baroness, who thrust her out of the mysterious chamber; she remembered those dreadful moments when she stood with Elimar in the rising sea, near Amrom. She felt that God had kindly and graciously protected her, and with all the heartfelt devotion of a child she clung, in thought, to *Him*, the Eternally Almighty Father and Friend.

It was a happy festival in Elizabeth's home that evening. All who had been confirmed with her, five in number, the children of poor fishermen, were, with their parents, invited to the clergyman's. The Commander and his wife and friends from Föhr and Amrom also came.

" O, if Elimar were but here too ! " said Madame Leyson, "that dear sweet lad ! but there is always something wanting to complete our happiness ! but wait only until he comes, then I will give a grand party, and then see how you shall dance ! O my God ! I now remember you have not learnt to dance " — she suddenly stopped. " It was stupid of me to speak to you about dancing on such a holy day as this ! The Lord surely will not punish me for it ! I am in fact so glad, so happy ! and perhaps it may not be eight days longer before I am still happier ! the happiest old Grandmother " — and tears stood in her eyes.

On the following Sunday, Elizabeth was to have gone to Communion for the first time, but between that day and the one we are now speaking of — the taking of the vow and receiving the Sacrament — there interposed a dark cloud ; the heaviest day during many years for the Commander's family and those persons who had attached themselves to them by ties of friendship and affection.

On the Friday morning a letter came to the Commander's from Föhr. How much sunshine, and how much joy may not lie in a letter ; but also how much darkness and sorrow ! If this news had come, that " Elimar was dead," it would certainly, for a moment, have weighed down the old couple with sorrow, as heavily as the blow which now fell on them ; but this struck so deep a wound that it must bleed during their whole lives ; there was a despair, a dread, in the midst of which thought became, as it were, paralyzed. When a dear wife or beloved child dies unexpectedly, then the husband and father, during the first few nights after the death, can awaken from a sleep that the body required, and in awakening forget for a while the great loss he has suffered, the depressing misfortune that has fallen upon him ; but anon there supervenes a dread, a fear in his blood and thoughts, and he asks himself **What has happened ?** and that which has happened appears before him in all its terrible reality — it is the harrowing return from the world of dreams to reality. And in such a state of mind as this were the old couple.

"What is it? Is there possibility in it?" Yes, they must themselves acknowledge that there is: it was stated in that letter, it was within the bounds of probability; and now dark images obtruded themselves in connection with the remembrance of Elimar, with recollections of what people had called *his evil mind* — that which the old couple could not bring themselves to believe.

Elimar had returned to Copenhagen, but how? in fetters. The ship in which he had been mate, had stranded on the coast of America, and he had been obliged to take service in another vessel, the "Susanna," and there, in a dispute, had killed the mate. He lay in prison in Copenhagen, and as he possessed no papers, — for they were lost with the wrecked ship, — the police had written to the principal judicial authority on Fohr, in order to obtain all particulars relative to Elimar; from this person a letter had come to Moritz, requesting him to prepare the Commander's family in the best manner for their great misfortune, and to tell them how matters stood.

" No, no," said the old woman, "he cannot have done it — and yet his wild temper! — O that the Lord had closed our eyes before we heard this ! No, no, it would not have saved or helped him! and who can feel for him as we do ! He is so young, there is so much that is good in him !" — and in her thoughts she recalled every trait, every smile, that she had rejoiced over, and it became so rich a sum that it must have purchased the freedom of the greatest criminal.

The Commander wrote to his son, the town magistrate of Husum, to do all in his power for Elimar.

" Life for life," says the law ; and the old man sat in deep thought and murmured to himself, " My blood will flow under the axe of the executioner, and if he should even be spared his life, what is life in eternal imprisonment, in constant intercourse with wretched felons ! — and the poor old man wandered about in disquiet, from his home to Moritz's, and again home, again to wander forth.

Madame Leyson sat in a corner and wept ; she looked at the portrait of their grandmother Osa.

"Yes, yes," she exclaimed, "had she but lived, or had I her strength, I would go to Copenhagen to save him!"

Elizabeth also stood there, crying, with her heart still full of love for Elimar.

And what had Osa done? Was her history really so affecting?

"Elimar resembles his forefather," said the old woman ; "it is Frisian blood that is in him. His forefather would also fly out in a passion, and like the sea, rage fearfully in his wrath ; but yet, like the sea, he was deep and clear. He killed another Frisian ; *he* also shed blood ;" and the old woman wept, and then began again, — "He was then filled with remorse at the deed! O, what must not Elimar suffer! My forefather fled from house and home ; his wife, Osa, she whose portrait hangs there!"—and she pointed to the likeness, where she had been drawn with the sheepskin cloak and silver cap, — "she had to pay compensation for manslaughter ; that was the law in those times ; and she had to sell her house and clothes, and provide for herself and children, and she did it, for she could do it. She spun wool, night and day, and gained bread for herself and her family ; and years passed away, and her husband and his deed were forgotten. No one was more respected than Osa : her conduct was truly Christian-like, her industry and care for her children unexampled ; she was truly a pattern for all ; a pattern of good morals. But then in time it was seen that she, whom all respected and honored, she, the lonely woman, was again about to become a mother, and they now began to watch and lurk around her dwelling. They watched her with evil eyes, and it was discovered that she went regularly every week to a solitary dell in the dikes, to a place that was reputed haunted, where a bloody hand often appeared above the sand, and where dreadful howlings were heard. There it was, then, that she had her rendezvous, she, the godly, honest Osa ; yes, there her lover must be concealed, and they found him there, in a great sand-pit. It was her husband, who, during all the years they had thought he was far thence, had lived in this spot, where she had visited him every week, brought him provisions, comforted him, and supported him in his trouble.

"His long penance, and her fidelity, brought the judges, and even his enemies, to grant him a pardon, and they afterwards prospered well, lived happily, and became rich, honored, and honorable; but such things will never happen more! O my poor Elimar!"

"Elimar would likewise become happy and good," said Elizabeth; "is there then no one on earth who can save him — no one?"

"Yes, the King," said Madame Leyson. "The King is above the laws, and he knows my husband, the Commander. King Frederick VI. has the kindest heart!"

"Let us pray to him — let us not cease our petition until Elimar is at liberty. We can write at all events, and the King hears all; the Commander will surely go to Copenhagen."

"No, no!" interrupted Madame Leyson; "he says that the law must take its course — and to suffer as I do! He will not go there — will not write, except to our son, the town magistrate, and he also is a man who obeys the laws. But *I* will write; as the grandmother of the unfortunate I will appeal to my King's warm heart, and plead for the misled one, who may yet be saved."

"But my old man will not allow the letter to be sent," said she after a short pause, and bethought herself; you must get it conveyed for me over to Föhr, or else I shall not get it sent off. And *you* I can depend on; you are careful and silent; not even at home must you speak about it."

The old woman trembled.

"I will write in my anguish; the Lord will guide my pen, and He will direct everything for the best."

She then wrote, and then tore in pieces what she had written, and wrote again; at length the petition was ready. Particular expressions in it might well have caused a stranger to smile; yet on the whole it might perforce have called forth more tears than smiles. The petition was, like him it prayed for, brought forth in pain and dread.

On the Sunday there was to be communion: Elizabeth was

to go over to Föhr the day before to make some purchases ; she was accompanied by Keike, and they went across in a fishing boat. Madame Leyson had secretly given her the letter she had written to the King, in all simplicity and loyal affection ; she had also one from the Commander to the chief judicial authority on Föhr ; and whilst Keike visited a relation, she went to deliver the letters.

Elizabeth stopped in one of those narrow lanes between the sea and the backs of houses, took Madame Leyson's letter from her bosom, where she had placed it, and read the address : "To the mighty Monarch, the land's father, King Frederick VI., Copenhagen."

These words of themselves gave the letter an importance, a sacredness ; she fancied that she saw therein a part of majesty itself. Now, she thought, if the postmaster asks from whom the letter comes, he will not perhaps receive a letter for the King. This thought made her tremble ; she approached the house — went past it ; what should she do ? Involuntarily she approached nearer to it ; a small book-case hung outside, for it was also a circulating library ; several books lay there with the title-pages disclosed, and the first she accidentally saw was, "The Heart of Mid-Lothian," by Walter Scott.

An idea came into her mind by being thus accidentally brought to think of Jeannie Deans. She stood still for a moment — her resolution was formed — she turned round — placed the letter in security on her person — went to look for Keike, and after every errand was executed, they again entered the boat, and reached Oland.

The agitation of Elizabeth was partly attributed to her grief for Elimar, partly to her nervous constitution and expectation of the holy act of which she should next day be a partaker. Madame Leyson looked at her with an inquiring look, as if to say, " Is the letter delivered ? " and Elizabeth nodded, whilst the paper burnt in her bosom.

Elizabeth told them at home, in the evening, that Madame Leyson had first thought of going to Copenhagen, where she had never been, but that she had afterwards given up the intention. It would have been too toilsome a voyage for her to undertake ; and Elizabeth inquired about the way, and how long it was, and how it was to be accomplished. Speaking about this appeared to interest and divert her thoughts, and therefore Hedevig continued to answer her, and give her particulars.

"It would have been an impossibility at that bad season of the year," said she ; "and the old woman would have been obliged to pass over the islands, unless there had chanced to be a vessel from Flensborg.

It was Sunday morning, and the day of communion. Elizabeth looked at the portraits of the King and Queen, and her eyes filled with tears. Alas ! she felt most courage to speak with the Queen, but it was to the King that the letter was addressed ; it was the King who was above the laws. Elizabeth's determination was fixed ; as Jeannie Deans went from Edinburgh to London, she would also go from Föhr to Copenhagen ; go to the King, deliver the letter to him, and plead for Elimar in the perfect fullness of her heart. There was nothing overstrained in her course of thought, and the determination to which it led ; and we shall understand this, when we remember how entirely she lived in the realm of illusion — how she knew the world only through the medium of books. Walter Scott's novels were declared to be reality itself — historically true ; she would be able to do what, it was there related, had been done before. This was a kind of simplicity united with the warmest confidence in the Almighty ; and yet what a combat had she not with herself ! To go to Copenhagen or to remain, that was no longer the question here, or if she should previously tell her design to Moritz or Hedevig ; she feared that they would not permit her. And what fear and anxiety would not her absence create in their minds ! It was a sin, an injustice ! Yet the letter, which she had retained, burnt on her bosom ; O ! if she only durst confide in Keike — once she had nearly done so, but yet she did not. The tears gushed from her eyes ; they eased her mind, and her emotion in no way surprised the rest, as they all knew how fondly she was attached to Elimar.

The ferry-boat to Dagebøl always starts with the tide, which would, next morning, serve at three o'clock; consequently, at a time when every one, not going with it, would be sound asleep. Elizabeth could not rest; she went several times to the window; the air was clear, and Charles's wain still shone. This constellation is regarded by the islanders here as the car in which Elias the prophet ascended to heaven; and it came into her mind what Moritz had said about the prophet, that for other persons life was also often a glowing car, on which the way led to heavenly peace. She had already felt how life could glow; she felt that seriousness which disclosed itself behind the years of childhood, but she also remembered the invisible thread which showed that we belong to God; and there came consolation to her soul.

She had written a few words, which she would leave in her chamber; and, with suppressed sobs, she read her own writing: —

"May the Lord our God assist me, and let us meet again happily! Believe nothing bad of

"Your affectionate ELIZABETH."

At half-past two she stood ready, with her little bundle in her hand, and with all her money from her savings' box, which amounted to about ten shillings. She had wrapped her gold rings up in paper, and taken them also, as she could sell them in case of need; and she now thought herself rich enough for the journey. She knelt down once more, prayed to the Lord, and then hastened out of the house, where all were still asleep, and down to the boat.

"Is Miss going with us, and alone, too?" asked Jap Lidt Petters.

"Yes, to Dageböl," she replied. "Take me with you, Jap; but," added she, as with a perception that he might suspect she was going out into the wide world, "I must return with you in the afternoon. So don't forget me. I shall remember the time well enough myself; but you must by all means let me return with you."

There was an anxiety in the expression with which she said this which caused Jap to laugh.

"Yes, it is bad enough on land for a young lady," said he, smiling; "they run away with them when they are pretty."

The wind was fair, the sails were hoisted, and the boat darted away from Oland towards Dagebol.

Elizabeth looked towards heaven, and repeated the Lord's prayer; He above was now her only guide and supporter.

They arrived at Dageböl in less than an hour, so that it was still quite dark.

"There is the inn — there, where the light is burning," said Jap; "can you find the way alone?"

"Yes, I think so," answered Elizabeth; "farewell, Jap, till we see each other again." And she went in the direction he had pointed out, but soon turned off over the dikes, where, eight years before, she had been driven away in Mr. Petters's wagon, and had come back again with the eel-man; she knew every turning she had to take in order to get to Flensborg, and followed the right road.

It was just at the same season of the year as when she had been here for the first time with Moritz and Hedevig; everything was unchanged: the rain had made the meadows below like great lakes; the dikes were almost impassable; she lost her shoes two or three times, found them again, and walked forward without delay on her bare feet. The wind blew stronger and stronger, and before the sun rose it had become a perfect storm. O, how slowly could she proceed! She stood still a few times, and was not able to go further: she then folded her hands and lifted them towards heaven, and it so happened that the gusts of wind came less frequently. She had the wind now at her back, and it helped her forward. Now some large drops of rain fell; then came a drenching shower, which passed over, as the storm drove it onward; thus the forenoon wore away, and towards noon Elizabeth was so fatigued, and the roads and weather were so bad, that she was obliged to remain at the inn which lies between the Marsk and Geestland.

"I am going to Flensborg," said she at the inn, and that was enough. There were many guests, but no one took any notice of her; they were all obliged to stay; it was such dreadful weather, with rain and storm, and much damage must have been done at sea.

Elizabeth got a bed for the night here, only a few miles from home, and they must have missed her long already, and read her letter; but in this weather she knew that no one could come to Dageböl, and Jap Lidt Petters could scarcely have been able to return to Oland.

Tired and weary, she threw herself on the bed, and slept until it was broad daylight. She started up quite frightened; the air was clear, but the wind still blew strong, so that the sea must be in a terrible ferment, and she thought that she could hear it roar. The way was closed against her, even if she desired to return, but that she would not — she could not do. It was now clear sunshine, and she went forward, almost borne on by the wind; the roads, however, were heavy and wearying, and it was late in the afternoon before she reached the bank whence one sees Flensborg beneath.

Taken by surprise, she stood still on beholding this prospect; she saw the great town, the fiord, and the wood-grown banks! How many trees! She had not seen such a sight for many years: leaf-covered trees were to her like fantastic images from her childhood's dawning remembrance.

She fell on her knees and prayed to the Almighty: "O, give me help, Thou, my only help!" The sun shone so enlivening on the whole of the high and picturesque coast on the opposite side of the fiord that it was a delight to behold. While she knelt here an elderly female and a younger, certainly her daughter, came up. They were passing close by Elizabeth, and looked her in the face; and as they saw that she wept, stopped for a moment, bade her good-day, and walked on. Elizabeth, who thought that she saw a familiar face, sprang up, walked involuntarily some paces after them, and the woman stopped. Elizabeth inquired of her the way to Copenhagen.

"Copenhagen!" repeated the woman; "well, there are many ways to it, both by sea and by land. Copenhagen! it is further than to Hamburg. But have I not seen you somewhere before? have you not been on Föhr?" Elizabeth replied in the affirmative, and told her who she was.

"Now see, did I not think so?" said the woman; "and do you not remember me, Widow Tredemann? I have been over on Föhr, and over at the parson's, too. But where are you going, and alone? Would you go to Copenhagen?"

Elizabeth could not speak — her excitement of mind dissolved itself in tears. The widow let her accompany them home, and on the way extracted from her that her journey concerned a human life, and that a letter was to be delivered to the king. This gave occasion to a hundred questions, but not to that one which would have been the most important — If they at home knew anything about this undertaking? This the widow naturally concluded they did: she listened with deep emotion to Elizabeth, who described the Commander's and his wife's trouble in a vivid and touching manner.

"But whom shall you go to in Copenhagen?" she asked; "whom do you know there?"

This Elizabeth had not thought of before; she, however, suddenly recollected Councilor Heimerant, Caroline's father, whom Moritz corresponded with, and who had once written that Elizabeth should come and pass a winter with him in the capital. She therefore mentioned his name — yet without adding that she had no letter to him, nor yet that she knew not where he lived in that great and, to her, strange city.

"Well — it is well — that you have the Councilor to go to! or else your journey would be of no use: but they ought to have provided better for you at home, and thought well over matters; but they live there on their island in such ignorance of the world that it's no wonder. Now hear me. I shall drive you over to Holnis, where it is most likely you will find a conveyance to Copenhagen; our vessel, which should have gone this morning, is certainly there still, for it has been a dreadful storm; it was to sail with a cargo of bricks to Karrebæks-Minde, and if you get there, then you are in Sealand: But true! I must also get your passport undersigned, or else the skipper will not take you with him, so give me the passport."

Elizabeth had no idea that such a thing was necessary;

she was, therefore, greatly terrified, and said, " Passport ? — I don't know, I have none — they did not give me one with me ! is it necessary ? "

" Good Heaven ! " said the widow, " one cannot travel in Denmark without having a passport for every bit of water one must cross, and now, into the bargain, from the Duchies ! nay, this is too bad."

The widow was, however, a practical woman, and there was no time to be lost; as an inhabitant and householder, she got a passport made out, and Elizabeth arrived at Holnis by the wagon, and fortunately found the vessel still lying there.

Skipper Thömming read the letter from the widow, and took Elizabeth on board. Next morning early they sailed out of the fiord, which, at every bend and curve, unfolded such charming views and magnificent wood scenery, that Elizabeth, on seeing all this, so new to her, forgot everything else.

The wind was fair, and they were soon out of the fiord ; to the right lay the open Baltic, to the left the island of Als ; with Sönderborg, whose red-roofed houses and windmills rose behind the gloomy palace where Denmark's king, Christian II., had suffered and lived in the tower eighteen long years.

CHAPTER XVII

WHILE Elizabeth is sailing towards Sealand, we will return to the Halligers, where she was missed directly after daylight. Moritz and Hedevig thought she was at the Commander's, but as she did not return home in the course of the forenoon, they sent Keike over to look for her; she was not there, nor in any of the houses in the neighborhood. Hedevig now found the letter Elizabeth had left, and their consternation and anxiety were great. Out-of-doors it blew a terrible storm, which increased so, that by the next tide not a vessel was able to set out to Dagebòl, nor could Jap Lidt Petters be expected to return. A fisher-boy, who had been at the ferry early in the morning, said that Elizabeth had actually gone with the boat.

"Gracious God!" said Hedevig; "I cannot conceive what has driven her to do such a thing!—unfortunate child!— why will she?—what is her intention? Moritz, what have you said to her?—what has happened?"

"The poor, dear, blessed girl!" sighed Madame Leyson; "I have an idea!—yes, she would do it!"—and the old woman covered her face with her hands. "O, my God! she has certainly not delivered the letter at Weick! she has gone with it herself direct to the King! she has gone straight to Copenhagen!" and then she confessed everything; but added, that Elizabeth, on her arrival at home the day before, had nodded to her question, "If the letter was delivered?"

The storm continued to increase; it was just at that time of the day when, as we know, Elizabeth was obliged to seek shelter in the inn near Geestland. A ship was in sight; the storm drove it in towards the land; large waves rolled in on Oland, so that one could no longer stand firm out-of-doors;

the sea and storm rose with a deep rumbling noise, with a whining and whistling that took such a violent hold of the houses, that the doors and windows rattled ; the loose ground seemed to shake ; they were as if on board a ship ; the long, heavy seas rolled on over the island, and reached in their last strength, as they died away, the lowest situated houses.

"O, that poor child!" sighed Hedevig ; "where is she at this hour?" for her she felt anxiety and fear, more than for the unfortunate men whose ship at that moment drove against the shoals near Seesand. This is a large white sand bank stretching out from the island of Amrom ; at half-tide it is dry, being only washed over in a storm-flood ; about the middle of it is built a pyramidically formed beacon, of strong beams, with a large globular-shaped erection fifty-five feet high, and visible at a distance of forty or fifty miles in clear weather. This tower of beams is the only sure landmark on the outer side of the land between Amrom and Eidersted, and of particular importance, partly to the vessels that are accidentally driven on this part of the coast, and partly as a guide when sailing into the entrance of the channel west and south of Amrom. Near this beacon the vessel now lay stranded. The inhabitants of Oland had seen them in the morning, before the storm had set in, steer for the entrance ; but acquainted with the danger, they had, when the weather became so violent, again endeavored to gain the open sea, but too late, as the heavy seas and the sea-wind drove the vessel against the shoals, and soon set it fast in the sandy ground. It was impossible to send out help to them, but in their distress it was fortunate that they stranded directly opposite the "beacon," which is not only a landmark, but a refuge for those who reach Seesand, and are not washed away there by the rolling waves.

Up this gobular-shaped building there is a sort of chamber, in which are placed a cask of fresh water, some sea-biscuits, and a bottle of spirits, so that the stranded mariners may sustain life here for a few days, until the sea has become so calm that help may be sent from the islands.

Towards evening they thought they saw a yellow handkerchief wave from the beacon; the stranded ship was thrown on its side; it parted its timbers in the sand, and lay in the foam and surge; not a soul seemed to be on board. The ship's name was "Kalver Street," called after the first street in Amsterdam.

Up in the chamber of the wooden building sat three of those who had been saved — nay, we may say four — for the ship's dog was also saved. It crept into a corner, and without shaking its wet skin, lay down and looked with its large, honest eyes at the old steersman, who went directly to the ship's biscuits, broke a piece off, took a dram of spirits, and left the two others to follow his example. The dog was not forgotten; he also got a whole biscuit; and then the old fellow folded his hands and thanked the Lord that their lives had been spared. The only thing now to be done was to pull off his boots and pour the water out, strip himself naked, wring the water out of everything he had worn, and then put them on again just as they were. The sailor did just the same as he, but the third person, who was dressed in a black, tight dress, and with a large, gray cape over him, only loosened it, poured the water out of his boots, and then went to the spirits and the ship's biscuits.

"Do as we do," said the sailor; "then the togs will dry better."

But the pale, thin man, whose wet clothes made him look still thinner, only shook his head.

"I am afraid I shall get a cold," said he, "but now I am warm, delightfully warm, and I shall be more so with another dram."

"Yes; but only one," said the steersman; "we may be obliged to lie at anchor here for several days yet, and you see all that we have to live on. Unship your toggery, like us, and squeeze it dry."

The pale man shook his head again; a cold shivering passed through him, but he said he was delightfully warm; what was the reason that he refused to undress himself? Therein was a characteristic trait, by which we may perhaps know the man of former years again.

There is a story about a king who suffered from a severe

and mortal sickness, and could only be cured by putting on a shirt which had been used and worn by one who regarded himself as being perfectly happy. They sought everywhere for such a person, but not one was to be found. At last they met with a shepherd ; he sang and was merry ; he was perfectly happy ; he wanted nothing ; he wished for nothing, and they therefore begged his shirt of him for the king, but he had none ! — the perfectly happy man had no shirt ; and in this chapter our shipwrecked voyager resembled the perfectly happy man, and on that account it was that he could not take it off and wring it, that he would not take off his clothes, lest they should see what he wanted. The wet clothes, with the exception of boots and stockings, therefore, dried on his body.

None of the three who sat in the beacon had any desire to talk ; tired and exhausted with the difficulties they had undergone, they each sat down in a corner ; the ship's dog, " Nibble," lay in the fourth corner. The floor flowed with water from their clothes, and from the spray which beat against the trap-door.

" There are two things in the universe," says Walter Scott, " whose like it would be difficult to find ; namely, the sun in heaven, and the German Ocean on earth." One of these incomparable things the men who sat here knew only too well, and during its continually rolling thunder, they bent their heads and slept.

When the storm had abated, some fishermen ventured out at high-water towards the beacon, and took the stranded men off ; the steersman and sailor were taken to the Commander's, and the pale thin man, who seemed to be somewhat more than forty years of age, was removed to the parsonage.

" Excuse my very wretched appearance," said he with a voice that, under the circumstances, denoted an uncommon liveliness ; "I always travel with the worst clothes I have ; the best I put in my portmanteau. 'Clean and decent,' that is my motto."

Hedevig was already standing with an old dressing-gown of her brother's, and opened a chamber door for their new guest.

"I was going to Föhr for the benefit of my health," said he, "and to use sea-bathing; I have not got it from the first hand."

"Your life has been spared — the Lord be praised! now rest with us awhile, and write to your family as soon as possible, that they may be in no anxiety about you. What may one not suffer — what may one not think!"

And Hedevig sighed deeply, for she thought of Elizabeth.

The man, who was now thoroughly warmed, completely rested, and strengthened with food and drink, related his story to Moritz; stating that he was a Hungarian actor of considerable fame, and assured him that he, particularly in Comora and Gran, had made a sensation as *Max*, in "Wallenstein," but that the too great interest a lady of rank had taken in him had brought his sense of duty in collision with his fortune, and that he had resigned it.

"I gave dramatic readings in St. Petersburg, which quite astonished them; but I could not bear the severity of the climate, and was obliged to go to Norway. There, where they had not seen a Laroche, a Lowe, an Anschutz play, not known those heroes of the Burg Theatre in Vienna, my scenic performances were new revelations in the realm of art. All were affected; but there was one young girl — Stella was her name, and a Stella she was. She looked towards the ceiling — my performance enchanted her — she loved me, and was cast off by her family; we were married; and then came cabals in the theatre. A party arose and hissed, I say hissed, but the whole fashionable and enlightened world in Norway drew their boots off in the theatre, and beat the hissers out of it. That was my triumph; so I left the country, and then it was, that on my return home, over one of the small Danish islands, my Stella gave birth to a daughter; the little angel came so unexpectedly that we had to leave the high-road and seek refuge in a manor-house near at hand.

"The mother and child were well nursed and honorably treated, but Stella's heart burst." Here he wiped his eyes with his fore-finger, made a little pause, and continued: "They kept the little one, for she was, I will not say mine, but the express image of her mother. She is now educated with the young Counts, and must be about fourteen years of age. She will probably, in the course of time, appear as a wife in that high and polished circle in which she moves. The young Counts are excellent persons ; they adore her, but I shall not see her ; I will not appear before her until I can do so in a manner worthy of her associates. There is something, reverend sir, that one calls a noble shame, and that the poor, worthy man feels — he whom accident, or the moment, places on the dark steps of life's trials."

Moritz fixed his gaze on him, and exclaimed, —

" I have heard another story that resembles this very much, if I except the conclusion. There it was that an unfortunate organ-player's wife gave birth to her child in an old ruinous manor-house, where by accident came some young noblemen, friends of each other : they interested themselves for the child, and as there was afterwards an examination of the father before the magistrate, the child was taken into the house of an old Baroness. I was present myself ; I was a guest, and you were also present ; you were the organ-man."

" Yes, so you see that my story was correct," said he, without any embarrassment.

The man was so accustomed to " group " his events, that when he had related them he thought they were true, or at least that they deserved to be so.

The steersman and the sailor, who had both been taken into the Commander's house, were from Föhr ; the vessel, although it bore a Dutch name, belonged to Föhr, as well as the ship's dog Nibble, called after its native place, Niblum on Föhr.

" I have a letter for you, Commander," said the sailor ; "it has got a little wet in my pocket, and spoiled about the edges, but I dare say it's readable. I was very near not bringing it. But you see, Commander, I should have been lawfully excused."

" From whom have you a letter to me, Nichols ; from Van Groote in Holland ? "

" No, from your own grandson. I fancy you would not have been glad if it had been lost with me."

" From Elimar ! " exclaimed the Commander.

"Yes," answered the sailor; "he wants so much to have the papers he writes about. Now they are of use."

"They are sent in another direction," said the Commander, who could not restrain a deep sigh. The deepest sorrow was depicted in the old man's face.

"How did you know it before?" asked the sailor, with a sly smile, which did not seem suitable just then. "We have had a quick voyage from there; but of what use is all that after the last disaster we had?"

"Tell me all you know about the unfortunate lad," said the Commander.

"So very unfortunate one can't call him," answered the sailor; "he would, however, have got into that scrape sooner or later. It always follows after."

"Shame!" said the Commander. "Can you speak so to me in my own house, and in such a time of trouble?"

The sailor looked at him.

"It is, however, a good match, as they say; why shouldn't he take her, even if she is old enough to be his mother? Would not you, Commander, have done the same?"

"Whom do you speak of?" asked the Commander.

"Of Elimar Leyson, your grandson," replied Nichols: "he is to marry the widow over there, and have the command of his own vessel. Don't you see it in the letter?"

"Your head is turned, man," said the Commander. "You have not recovered from what you have suffered out there; your thoughts wander. Yes, yes, one can also make seas on land, which break up our hearts within us."

"Elimar Leyson is in the widow's favor," said Nichols. "It is surely not so incredible; he has a bold, active way with him, he is good looking, and that the women are fond of; and so the rich widow, whom he trades for in America, has made him, from steersman, her own captain. I spoke with him myself there; their engagement had just been brought to bear when I had to come home, and so he wrote the letter I have here, and which he gave me to bring, for he knew that, from Holland, I should steer home directly with one of our Fohr folks."

"Elimar is in Copenhagen," said the Commander. "Do you not know that? He is there in prison, and in fetters."

"How should he get there?" said Nichols, and stared with the greatest astonishment. "Then I must be a strange, goose-headed fellow, but that I am not; and here is the letter, his own hand-writing, wet at the edges, but yet the driest in the whole pocket-book."

The old man seized it; his hand shook — it was Elimar's writing. He opened it and spread it out on the table, for it had parted in the folds.

"It is a little leaky in the seams," said Nichols.

The Commander read, began to tremble, sat down, stood up again, and went to the drawer where the letter from the authority in Weick had been placed. Yes, there it was, written clearly enough, — that Elimar had come to Copenhagen, that he was a prisoner, a criminal, and that he had killed the second mate of the vessel he was on board of. But now this letter from America, which Nichols had brought, was certainly of a later date; it was Elimar's writing; and everything in it spoke of happiness and pleasure; he spoke of successful voyages he had made, of the rich widow he had traded for there, and that she was pleased with his person; that they were to be married; that he was extremely glad and happy, and he requested the certificate of his baptism and other papers to be sent before the marriage. In a postscript was added a greeting to his little sweetheart Elizabeth, whom, he said, he could not wait for, but promised to marry her if he should become a widower.

"He has killed no one," said the old man, and sank back in his chair, weeping.

Madame Leyson's joy and happiness were immeasurably great; she kissed Nichols, ran over to Moritz and Hedevig, and laughed and cried in a breath. Their thoughts, however, were continually fixed on Elizabeth: what had become of her, where had she got to? Moritz had already finished several letters, which he was going to send to the different ferry-places, where he thought she must have stopped, as she had no passport with her, and was writing one to Councilor Heimerant, for him to make all possible inquiries about her in Copenhagen, if she should have reached there. Not even to Hedevig had he said one word about the shipwrecked man

they had in their house being Elizabeth's father, nor did
he himself know that his child had the morning before been
in the same house in which he now was — that it was on her
account they were in so much trouble and anxiety. It was un-
necessary to say anything about it, as neither advantage nor
pleasure could arise from the communication.

Now came the Commander, but not so well pleased as his
wife, who, in her joy and rapture, had directly run over to
Moritz's : the Commander himself had been for the moment
glad, but this sorrowful and probable doubt had soon arisen
in him : " All was well and good when this letter was written ;
so stood matters at that time ; but can this evil deed not have
happened ? — yes, perhaps the same day that Nichols sailed
away with the letter. The match may have been broken off ;
Elimar may have done some stupid trick, given up everything,
and gone on board another vessel : everything that we fear,
and must fear, *may* have happened. There it is exactly described, with all particulars from the police in Copenhagen.
It is madness to be glad, and think and believe in such in-
credibly good fortune ! "

Madame Leyson grew pale with terror, wrung her hands,
and was just as ready to fear the worst again, as she had been
to seize the joyous message that had been brought them.

Moritz, on consideration, was obliged to allow that the
Commander's opinion was right. "Yet, one hope there is,
however," said he, — "a hope which ought not to be aban-
doned." He opened the letter again which he had written to
Councilor Heimerant, and added the accounts given in Elimar's letter, also Nichols's communication, requesting him to
use his best endeavors to obtain all particulars relative to the
prisoner, and to write to them with the least possible delay.
Jap Lidt Petters, who had returned from Dagebôl, told them
that Elizabeth had, sure enough, gone over with him, but had
not gone to the inn at all, as he supposed ; no one on the isl-
and had seen anything of her, so that she must — as was actually the case — have gone directly onward.

We will now see how far she got. She sailed in the Great
Belt, opposite Langeland, in the same place where we, the
evening she was born, saw Moritz with his young and noble

pupils in an open boat steer towards Funen ; the wind now, as then, was contrary ; the skipper was obliged to tack about, and it was late on the following afternoon before he reached Karrebæks-Minde, where Elizabeth went on shore, thence to proceed to Copenhagen and seek the King and Elimar.

CHAPTER XVIII.

THE WIDOW LADY.

ELIZABETH had landed at Karrebæks-Minde.[1] Skipper Thönning had shown her the way she should take to Nestved, and had advised her to sleep there that night, and next morning early set out for Copenhagen with the fly-wagon, as it was one of those days on which it went to Copenhagen, and in this way she would, for a trifling sum, be able to reach the city before evening. It was, besides, the safest and most advisable manner of travelling. At Nestved she was to stay at the wine-seller's, at the corner of Holy Ghost Street and Catechism Lane : it was a good inn, and it was from there that the fly-wagon set out. Everything, he added, would be all right. It was not without a feeling of sadness that she bade farewell to the kind skipper, and set out on her way through the wood to Nestved.

It was in October; the trees were still full of leaf, and in their rich autumnal colors, though it was unusual at this late season. The air was so clear and rare after the storm ! It was the large trees, the whole woodland nature in its declining magnificence, so strange and yet so familiar, that seized her pure poetical mind ; there was something churchlike in the wood, and the sun shone like one of God's words — like one of God's sermons.

She did not take the shortest way, but not knowing, she did not remark it. She suddenly heard the tones of an organ, the sounds of which came towards her from within the wood. She was close by old Herlufsholm, and some of the pupils from the school were playing on the green plain before the antique red mansion. The sun shone, the organ pealed, and

[1] Karrebæks-Minde is a harbor in Sealand, for the provincial town Nestved, situated four miles distant inland, by Suse-beck.

it looked so homely and cheerful : one of the boys nodded to her so kindly, so friendly, that it did her good. She ventured to ask the way to Nestved, and he showed her the path along by the rivulet, past the water-mill, where Bergitte Gjon had dwelt, and where that pious, chivalric lady's state-drawing-room is now transformed into a pig-sty.

She soon saw the town before her, under the great sand bank which reaches to the height of the church tower. She found the inn and got a little chamber there ; she had bought some bread at the baker's in the street. This she ate, and drank water with it, that she might not have too great a score to pay.

Elimar occupied her thoughts continually. She should soon see him, perhaps on the following evening, but how should she get to him ? What must he not suffer ? and she thought of her foster-parents, to whom she had caused such bitter sorrow by leaving without bidding them farewell, which she could not, which they would not have permitted her to do ! And what will the monarch say ? will she have courage to speak to him, to make her petition to him ? "I will kneel at his feet and cry," thought she ; "he will read the old grandmother's letter, and be touched by so much misery !" The tears trickled down Elizabeth's cheeks. Music was heard from the street ; it was the trumpeters and drummers beating the *reveille;* her thoughts were raised, and her spirit was lightened ; she said her evening prayer in silence and slept.

Early in the morning she was awakened by the servant, who told her that she must now get up if she meant to go by the fly-wagon. Two large spring-wagons, with four seats in each, stood in the yard below ; several women and gentlemen, all fine persons, as Elizabeth thought, got into them. The wagons were very high ; she got a place in the middle ; the driver blew his horn, and they rattled quickly through the streets, where the people came to the windows, and there was such nodding and greeting, such a shouting hither and thither, and they went briskly on, but only till they got out of the town ; they then went very slowly indeed. It was the fly-wagon pace ; the fly-wagon conversation began, the fly-wagon acquaintances were made. They all were, as we have said, fine persons.

The heavens were clouded, and it blew hard ; but with Danish equanimity, as regards the climate, they mutually consoled themselves, saying that they ought to be glad of the wind, otherwise they would have had a drenching rain. Two women told each other the most frightful stories about the fly-wagon, which had been upset the day before. It had once, the year previously, run over a child ; nay, they were never safe. Then they began to talk about misery ; and from the fly-wagon they directed their discourse to an air-balloon that had fallen from a terrible height in England. There was a middle-aged man who spoke æsthetically, and was encouraged in it by a young student, who seemed to be shrewdness itself.

" I say with Shakespeare, ' no, no,' " said the elder of the two, for he could quote.

"Where does Shakespeare say that ? " inquired the student.

" He says so in many places. It is a well-known reply."

" Yes, but then he says something more, surely ? " said the student.

" Indeed, do you think so ? " answered the old man, a little offended.

One woman spoke continually about cookery, and what they now dared to write in America.

An old and sickly gentleman sat with his very young wife, and a friend he met with in the wagon approved of his marriage, and spoke very consolingly to the wedded couple, saying, that it was very prudent of him to take a wife that was young and active, as she could nurse him in his old age and sickness, and to whom he could leave means, so that, after his death, she would be able to live in comfort.

The young wife was an enthusiastic admirer of two things, — her old husband, whose fingers she sat and played with, and the theatre in Copenhagen. Her calculations of time were always based upon the opening and closing season of the theatre. When she read in the newspapers that the boxes in the theatre were to be let for the coming season, it was to her, as it is to us to read about the storks having appeared, or that ripe strawberries have already come into the market. The travellers by the fly-wagon became more and more acquainted, and it was soon discovered that Eliza beth was "a stranger"—from Holstein, as they said—and that she was quite alone. Where the Halligers lay, no one knew, not even the student, who stated that it was a wrong pronunciation of the name, or else he should have known it. Halligers he made out to be Heligoland, and then it was soon Helgoland. Elizabeth shook her head, but did not enter into any further explanation. They then drove over the highly situated and hilly heath-land, with its wide prospect, past the Gisselfeldt and Bregentved woods.

She did not see them in their freshness; she did not see into the summer's forest solitude, where the game springs in the high grass, where the stork strides in the meadows. She saw the coming death of nature, saw it in its decay, saw it from the fly-wagon; and yet, like a beautiful picture, it seized on her soul uncontrollably, during all the empty chatter around her. At length they reached Kjoge. The invalid exhibited the greatest desire during the whole journey to tell Elizabeth every particular about the country and houses—about everything—but she did not understand him, so peculiar were the remarkable things he pointed out.

"That now is Red House," said he, about a house they passed on the road. In Kjoge he pointed to another house. "There lives my brother-in-law," but Elizabeth turned her head to the opposite side. There stood the church, separated from the street by a low wall: a whole carpet of evergreens grew up the sides of the church walls, which reminded her of the old lady's manor-house in Funen. Since Elizabeth was a child she had not seen such verdure. Thus poor Kjoge had the best flower of remembrance to show. After passing through the town they arrived at the inn; here a change of wagons having taken place, Elizabeth got a place with the two women who had spoken so much about accidents. They must know, they said, who the little "Holsteiner" was, and she, with childish inexperience, told them the purport of her journey—that she had never been to Copenhagen, and that she knew no one. And now both the women—the one was the widow lady — had a new and true misfortune, which they might add to the fly-wagon accidents.

"But whom will you go to when you get to the city?" asked the widow lady.

Elizabeth named Councilor Heimerant, whom she did not know, but who knew her foster-father. The Councilor was, next to the king, her hope and support.

"Yes, but where will you find the Councilor this evening? Copenhagen is a large, terrible city, with bad men in it. Such a poor young child as you are cannot go alone through the streets; there are the vilest young men! O! it is shocking." And she made Elizabeth still more afraid.

"I don't know what I shall do with her!" said the widow lady.

They now approached Copenhagen: it was, as we have said, in October; it was quarter-day, and wet and raw. There is at every season of the year something oppressive in coming from the country into a fortified city like Copenhagen; to drive for the first time through narrow, dark fortifications, over small bridges, and through a long tunnel-like gateway under the ramparts into the narrow streets, with high houses on both sides; and this Elizabeth now did in the autumn season, in rain and drizzle, in an open wagon, just in the twilight of the evening of a removing-day.

In other countries they do not know this day, which with us occurs once in the spring, and once in the autumn, when those families who change their dwellings, remove with all their goods from their old house to the new one. There is a bustle and a rummaging, such as might form a capital subject for a *genre* painter to study; but is not so agreeable to the parties concerned.

The stranger who does not know a Copenhagen removing-day, and comes into the city on that occasion, would imagine that he had got into a street where that quarter of the town was in flames, and that every one was dragging away bedding and furniture on wagons and hand-barrows in order to save them. Whole streets are heaped up with straw and dirt, and everything that is not worth keeping — an endless dung-hill, What a picture of perishableness! There lies a shocking old

silk hat, which once awakened envy in the whole neighborhood, and yet surmounted an ugly phiz; here lies a gray
glove; it was once white; the bridegroom wore it on his wed-
ding-day. Through this chaos drove Elizabeth. She felt
oppressed, dispirited, and fearful.

They all descended to the inn-yard where the fly-wagon
stopped; most of them found acquaintances waiting, and
there was much joy and much chattering, inspection of boxes,
crowding, and cab-driving. Elizabeth felt herself more desolate than she had ever done before. Here she stood with her
little bundle, and knew not which way to go.

The widow was seeking after some one; all at once she
screamed out, — "Sanne!" when, quite a little girl, thin and
dirty, her hair hanging like rats' tails about her face, struggled
her way forward, kissed the widow lady's hand, and took a
little box that had lain on the lady's lap during the whole
journey. The little girl chattered away without ceasing,
turned and screwed herself about, bored her way through the
crowd, and screamed with her sharp voice to a country soldier
who was to carry the trunk. The widow lady nodded to Elizabeth, looked at her again, and was going away, when Elizabeth in her fear seized hold of her cloak and asked, whilst
the tears ran down her cheeks, —

"Good God!" where shall I go to?"

"Poor child!" said the widow lady, "it is almost pitch
dark; come with me; for a night or two I can surely find
room for you. You might get into bad hands, poor child!
it is a dangerous town, and there are many wicked persons!"

The soldier walked on with the trunk on his back, and
Sanne ran on before with the little box.

"We are going to Laxegaden" (Salmon Street), said the
widow lady; "you have certainly heard speak of that street;
it lies in a good direction, between the theatre and the exchange. It was in that street that the devil appeared a few
years back, and which there was so much talk about; but the
police could never find him out."

They made their way in rain and drizzle, through all the
removing-day's rubbish; the many persons in the streets, the
great bustle everywhere — everything had in it something

alarming to Elizabeth. "So many persons about, and not one knows me or cares about me!" this was the thought that forced itself on her. At length they reached Salmon Street. Like the other streets, it was filled with straw and heaps of dirt. A coppersmith stood with his three apprentices, and hammered away, blow for blow, on a large boiler near the house, which they entered, ascending many stairs, certainly more than there were in the church tower at Oland. The room they walked into was not the most orderly in appearance; the place did not quite answer to the fine clothes which the lady had on, in such bad weather, during the journey by the fly-wagon. Everything was thrown about in beautiful disorder. Sanne ran hastily out to make a fire in the kitchen, then came for some money to buy wood, cream, and extract of punch.

"That's a little wild, giddy thing," said the lady. "Sanne comes in the morning and evening to do the few house jobs for me. The last one I had was a good-for-nothing; I was forced to send her away. By and by you shall see a young lady, Adelgunde, a clever, accomplished girl; she goes to the best families, and assists them in dress-making and ornamental work — she is perfect in that. She will certainly one of these days make a match in the higher ranks; she is in fact born to be a princess."

Elizabeth knew not what to answer; she sat there quite dispirited, and pressed the lady's hand to her lips. The lady then gave her a drawer to herself, and a key, that she might put away her clothes and what money she had; "for some she must have, and then they would not grieve any more that night," said she. Adelgunde would be there directly, and then they would each have a glass of punch; in the morning they could think matters over, and then Elizabeth should go to Councilor Heimerant, who must take care of her, and would certainly do so.

The lady put on a very good shawl; the table was well spread, and then came Adelgunde, in a silk cloak and velvet bonnet. She was scarcely twenty years of age: her figure was slender, and her eyes sparkling; she was an excellent talker, and by profession a seamstress.

The seamstresses in Copenhagen are a distinct class, and highly respectable girls — with exceptions. Their condition is usually very laborious and painful; their gains are very trifling, and their life is often a prison life. From early morning until late in the evening they must work indefatigably at the houses of families, often entire strangers to them, from whom they receive various treatment. In the houses of the citizens they are generally reckoned of the family, and even take their meals with them, or in the children's bed-rooms; but with persons of a higher rank, they are under a sort of arrest; they are shut up in a room with their sewing, and there does not come a living being to them, except, as in prison, when their food is brought to them.

There are many instances of these poor seamstresses utterly avoiding and detesting those houses, where, if even their gains are greater than in other places, they are not able to bear this separation from all society — this eternal silence.

Adelgunde had long since made her own connection; she only went where she amused herself, and that was not in many places, yet she was nevertheless like the lilies of the valley, well arrayed.

The families she plied her needle for, she knew excellently how to take off, and she could, when she came home, represent their foibles or peculiarities with genuine dramatic talent. She was at home at all places; she knew her families from beginning to end, from top to bottom.

The widow lady made her directly acquainted with Elizabeth's story, and Adelgunde was so affected by her friend's conduct, that she fell on her neck, and called her, "her sweet lady!" What Elizabeth had done, she also pronounced charming.

"I hope the fellow will not come to be a convict," said she, "it is so mean! He is your sweetheart, then? O yes! one so easily thinks of such things at your age; I should do the same — it is in us. Ah! see, she blushes! I like that," exclaimed Adelgunde. "She is, in truth, not so bad, that little thing yonder; there is something out of the common, something clever about her; but her gown is from the country" —

and she laughed, and told her own stories the whole evening ; she knew so many, and had so much to tell. And they drank punch, and struck their glasses together, and drank a toast, which the lady whispered to Adelgunde, who then laughed and threw herself back on the sofa. It was strange to see the two merry women there, and the timid, afflicted girl.

It was late when she got to bed : a pantry, separated by a wooden partition from the kitchen, into which the door opened, with two hearts cut out to admit air and light, was her bed-chamber. She said her evening prayer, and thanked the Lord that there were good persons in the world, and that she had found them in that great and terrible city.

It was late in the day when she was called ; she had slept long. Adelgunde herself brought her coffee to bed to her, and when she got up and looked out of the kitchen window, the air was clear, the sun shone over the neighboring houses, a window stood open at a garret, and a little bird in a cage sang there so loud and merrily that it was a good omen of what the day would bring forth. She was soon dressed, and ready to go to Elimar directly. To see him, to console him, was her first thought; but the widow lady said that she could not hurry in that way to him ; she must first have permission from the police office. There was much to be done before one could get to see the prisoners, and particularly prisoners under sentence of death. She would, however, make all inquiries herself that day, and then have matters so arranged that Elizabeth might get to see him as soon as possible ; but that she must go directly, that very forenoon, to Councilor Heimerant ; Sanne could accompany her. They must, however, go first to the grocer's opposite, borrow the Directory, and see where the Councilor lived.

His house was in Christianshaven, and thither they must bend their steps. Sanne knew the way through the exchange, for there was something to be seen ; shops and passages, two whole long streets under cover, and outside lay vessels of all kinds, from the small barks with apples and pots, to the large coal-vessels. There was such a crowding with wagons and hand-barrows, girls with market-baskets, school-boys with their books, and the whole street was one sheet of mud.

The girls from Amack with vegetables, and the fish-women shouted and bawled, the one hoarser than the other.

Sanne skipped sometimes before, sometimes at the side of Elizabeth; she was extremely nimble, and *she* also knew how to talk.

Her eldest sister, she said, had just been married to a man whose employment it was to carry out newspapers; the wedding was celebrated at her parents', and the sister had got five dollars given her by her mistress for the wedding; two of them she had paid for a myrtle bouquet, — for the bride must have that, — and then they danced the whole night in their little room, where the bedstead and drawers were put into the passage. They had sat on the window-sills and had stock-fish and punch, and little Sanne laughed over all her little dirty face, and lost her slippers twice, which she had danced in and trod down, but she got them again, and so they arrived at the Councilor's.

George opened the door — honest old George — whom Caroline had so often jested with. Elizabeth knew him from the descriptions she had heard of him at home; nay, she even knew the furniture itself, so often had she heard about everything in that house.

She said that she came from the Halligers, from Moritz, and George put on his very best face, but at the same time said that the Councilor had that very day gone into the country and would not return for five or six days. Elizabeth was astounded; she was nearly bursting into tears; and when George asked her where she lived, Sanne was obliged to answer for her. They then returned home. When they arrived, Adelgunde was reading a novel by Johannes Wildt. It was so exciting, she said; it was something different to those of Walter Scott, who did not understand the passion of love. As to Elizabeth's disappointment, she consoled her by saying that five or six days were not an eternity, and that the Councilor would then return; she would meantime talk the widow lady over.

The latter, however, did not listen with a very satisfied air, but Adelgunde knew how to talk, and pleaded that her friend had now become the little girl's protector, and that her kind-ness would assuredly be repaid.

"My good-nature costs me much!" said the widow lady; "it always gets the mastery of me. If I were a rich woman, it would be nothing; then I might do as I pleased, and it would signify nothing; but now I must think of the future. Well, then, you will remain here till the Councilor returns; but then you must tell him what I have done; I must have some recompense," — and then she called Elizabeth aside, and begged her to let her have three dollars beforehand, by way of loan, from those she had. The widow lady was in a momentary pecuniary embarrassment. As to Elimar, the police officer had been spoken with, and she would probably get permission to speak with him the following afternoon. That day was also an audience day, and so she could take the forenoon, and try her fortune with the king; but she must hit her time well.

Still another whole day before she could see Elimar! Her heart throbbed with grief and impatience; her head was as if it would burst, but she was obliged to reconcile herself to the conviction that what the others said was just and probable. Adelgunde read aloud, for her, out of "The Death-finger," from one of the most charming places in it, as she assured her; in the evening there were two ladies on a visit, and they were treated handsomely, probably out of the three dollars that Elizabeth had lent; but she found no comfort, felt no joy, not even in the widow lady's love story — an intrigue, as she called it — by which she had got her husband.

She had loved him from her earliest youth, but he had not observed it, for he was a man of business; they then came to live in the same town — it was in Elsinore — and then began the intrigue. One day when she was in Copenhagen, she read in the newspaper that a man in Slagelse had advertised for his dog that had run away. She then lighted on a thought and wrote directly, and without more ado, that the dog had been seen in Copenhagen, though there was not a word of truth in what she wrote; but within this letter she inclosed another, which she begged the man in Slagelse to forward to Elsinore, and this letter was to him she loved, which love she confessed to him without reserve, "for it is always the best." She did not write her name, and she thought that the circuit which the letter made would lead him on a wrong scent. And then she had written, " that if now, after knowing the feelings of her heart, he wished to know her person, he could on Saturday at noon find her likeness in four different girls in Elsinore. One was the woollen-draper's daughter at the corner ; there he might go in and ask for some patterns of fine cloth ; the second was at the iron-monger's ; there he could buy a few nails ; the third place, he was to go into the passage and ask for some one who did not live there ; and at the fourth place, it was at the consul's, he could do the same ; and when he had seen them all four, he could think over it. After this, on Sunday, he was to go to church, where he would find all the girls in the last pew ; and when they went out, he was to speak to the one that pleased him most. If he chose the right one, he would receive a little note from her, and their engagement was then settled. And the letter came to its destination, and everything went right. He went to all four houses and to church on Sunday, and met with the right one : "and so it was, as you see, mutual affection." They became husband and wife, and now she was a widow lady.

Adelgunde looked at her with all her eyes, laughed, and assured them that it might be the most charming novel, if it were only properly put together ; and the ladies admired what she had said, and told stories that might have placed them just as high in the fields of invention as in the records of love. Elizabeth knew not at last what they talked about ; she was absorbed in her own grief and the dark thoughts it gave rise to. Next morning she was to seek an audience of the King, and to see Elimar the same day. She felt that it was the most important day in her life ; how would it end ; with what peace and consolation should she go to bed on the morrow ? She was so young, and already so old in sorrow and anxiety.

CHAPTER XIX.

LITTLE SANNE was to show Elizabeth the way to Amalienborg, where King Frederick VI. resided, and that day gave audience to all.

There was such nimbleness in Sanne that neither her hair nor her slippers would keep their places. She had again a story to tell: her brother-in-law, who carried out the newspapers, on the strength of which occupation he had married, was now to have his name printed on the paper as the responsible party for what was published in it! And Elizabeth, that she might say something, though the whole was quite indifferent to her, asked "if he wrote the paper?"

"He neither writes nor reads," said Sanne; "he only carries them out, and is responsible."

They had now arrived at the palace. There stood soldiers in the colonnade, and a porter in red, with a silver stick. Elizabeth courtesied quite low, and remained immovable; she expected that he would send her away, but he pointed upwards to a passage where the life-guards stood with drawn swords, and she trembled. She, however, went the way she was to go, and stopped in the chamber where the lackeys sit. Here she courtesied and courtesied again, until, with a smile, they opened the door for her, and she stood in the anteroom to the audience chamber.

Here was an immense number of persons, gentlemen and ladies; they stood together in silent expectation; further on several gentlemen in gold and silver lace walked to and fro; they might very well have been all kings, from their appearance; some of them also had stars on their breasts, and all were decorated with an order. They talked much, but not in a loud voice, and they looked proud. They did not speak to those who were dressed in black, except it was the clergyman, with velvet on his coat, and the badge of an order: if they had not *that*, Elizabeth thought they were not wanted there. Some old embroidered flags hung against the wall over two kettle-drums, and these were the only remarkable things in the room.

Here, then, lived the King. She knew that he did not bear the crown and sceptre every day, and she had formed a sort of idea of his person from the portrait that hung by the altar in the church at home on Oland. How would he listen to her? how would God dispose her speech? She endeavored to arrange it in her mind, and she thought she had words that would plead her cause. One of the gentlemen in waiting went about in the crowd where she stood, asked every one their business with the King, and wrote it down. He came also to Elizabeth; he must know her name, and whence she came from. Her voice trembled when she answered him. An hour passed away, and a second, too; many persons were admitted to the King and went away again, but there were still many remaining. Half an hour more elapsed when the officer nodded to Elizabeth, she was so far from him. On her approach he called on her to enter, and she stepped up to the side of the door of the royal chamber, as she had seen the others do. Now then was the moment! She closed her eyes, folded her hands, and collected her thoughts. Just then a lackey came and whispered to the officer in attend- ance, who went in to the King, and came out again directly with this intimation, " The King will see no more to-day ! "

" Give me your petition," said he to Elizabeth, " and I will take care that the King gets it."

"I must speak with him," she stammered out. "O, my God!" and she was nearly fainting.

" Come on Monday," said he, " and you will then get an audience."

All present departed; Elizabeth was also obliged to go at the moment she stood so near the door of grace — at the mo ment she had vividly collected all that she would say.

She returned home deeply dispirited, but the widow lady who knew the custom of the antechamber, had foreseen this

She would herself go with Elizabeth in the afternoon to "the sinner," as she called Elimar.

"I will go with you to the council hall," said she; "though it is a detestable place, where I have never been before; but now, as I have once taken you under my charge, I must go through with it."

They went to the "council and judgment house." It was to Elizabeth a heavier and still more terrible road than to the King's palace. In a few moments, then, she should see Elimar, her childhood's friend, him who held her fast in the rising waters, him, her constant thought.

The high columns of the council hall, the large grated windows, the broad steps, the difference of the whole building from the other houses in the square, contributed to heighten her feelings. They went up the broad stairs, down long passages, and over a gallery whence they looked down into a large hall; everything was so vast, and different from the representation which Elizabeth had made to herself of the way to a prison! Here it was not dark, gloomy, and old, as in the Edinburgh Tolbooth; and yet the widow lady kept on chattering about its being so terrible,—that the air was quite oppressive, and that her legs trembled under her.

They now entered a chamber fitted up as a sort of office or counting-house; and the officer sent one of the policemen to fetch Elimar Leyson. A deadly paleness overspread Elizabeth's brow; she was obliged to hold fast by the chair, for it seemed as if everything in the chamber turned round. The officer returned with the prisoner, who was dressed in a dreadnought seaman's suit. He looked boldly around him: Elizabeth had made a step forward, but stopped.

"You may now speak together," said the chief officer.

"It is not he," exclaimed Elizabeth; "it is not Elimar Leyson, he whom I seek,—I don't know the man who stands there."

"That is Elimar Leyson."

"No, no, it is not! I seek Elimar, over from Oland, the Commander's grandson, who"—she could not pronounce it—"has murdered—they said—who has come home from America as a prisoner."

12

"That is you," said the chief officer to the prisoner; "is not your name Elimar Leyson?"

"That is my name," he answered with a peculiar smile; "I am the grandson of the Commander on Oland."

"No, it is not possible," said Eliabeth, with singular vehemence. "Elimar did not look like him; he could never look so; they are not his eyes — not his face — nothing is like him!"

The chief officer listened with attention to Elizabeth, regarded her and the prisoner; and a sort of examination took place, during which Elizabeth naturally and innocently described all the grief and trouble that had fallen on the old folks at home; that Madame Leyson had written a letter to the King, and that she had come with it to Copenhagen, and that she had sought an audience that very day.

"So, the Commander and Mother Leyson take it so terribly near to heart, eh!" said the prisoner. "I thought as much; it will do them good. They will remember Jes Jappen!"

"Jes Jappen!" cried Elizabeth.

Yes, it was he — Jes Jappen, the servant-girl's son. He had actually been shipwrecked in America, had lost his passport and papers, and without any fixed purpose, but for a momentary whim, had called himself Elimar Leyson when he entered into service on board another vessel. In a dispute he had stabbed the mate with his knife, and when he was brought to Copenhagen in fetters it was a pleasure to him to think what anxiety and terror it would place them in at the Commander's, when they heard that "the old dame's brat," as he called Elimar, had come to such disgrace. "Such a little touch would do them good," he said, "for they would soon know that it was a lie, and so they would have double pleasure."

All this he confessed voluntarily, and when he saw how Elizabeth's eyes glistened, how her whole face expressed a feeling of delight, a grin overspread his face, and he said, "it was a sin if he took the rich widow over there, when he had such a sweetheart!"

Elizabeth crimsoned, and the prisoner was led away to be afterwards reëxamined. The chief officer told Elizabeth that it was probable she might be summoned there again, yet it would not happen unless Jes Jappen came forward with fresh lies, in which case her statement would be required. He then got the widow lady's address, and when he congratulated Elizabeth on the fortunate result to her, she seized his hand and kissed it with as much feeling and emotion as if a human life had been given to her at that moment. The whole building, with its stairs and passages, was now as beautiful in her eyes as a fairy palace. She laughed, she cried, and kissed the widow lady's hand and cloak.

"But God save us, child!" said the widow lady; "it is charming; it is beyond all expectation, is it not? — but be reasonable; let us only get home! let us get out of this thieves' hole! Ugh! the air will cling to our clothes: there is something in the air of the council hall like the air in the hospital; it gets right into the clothes," and she puffed and fanned herself with her embroidered handkerchief.

Elizabeth was glad and happy as she had never been before. She must write home directly to say that it was not Elimar who was in prison and in fetters, and that she herself was in good hands, with a kind, dear lady, whom she had met with in the fly-wagon; and that in two days the Councilor was expected home, and that she would pray him to assist her to Oland. And she now remembered that she had another acquaintance in Copenhagen, the dear Trina, who was married to shoemaker Hansen — Trina, who once, as a child, had been in the theatre and danced with wings on, and with spangles on her shoes. Elizabeth asked the widow lady if she knew her; if she knew where she lived, if they could not find her out from that book where they had found the Councilor's dwelling.

"He is assuredly too common a shoemaker to have his name in the Directory," said the lady, "and there are swarms of people called Hansen; most of them change their dwellings every half-year. They have only an awl and a strap, and a whole flock of children."

"Oh, yes, it must be she!" said Adelgunde. "I know her; they have no children, and they live over the way in the cellar. She is still at the theatre, and sings in the choruses;

her name is Trina Hansen. It is true I have never spoken with her, but it is she sure enough; she has been in service in Funen at the Baroness's with the turban!"

"With the mad Baroness!" said the widow lady. Do you not know that she came here from Funen a week ago, and her grandson is with her; but he stays at the Hotel Royal. He is a handsome young man; he looks like an Italian. You would like him much, I'm sure, Adelgunde."

Sanne now came in from the grocer's with half a sheet of letter paper. The little bit of silver paper which the shop-boy had laid between it and Sanne's small fingers, was the cause of its coming shining white into the house. Pen and ink were brought out, and Elizabeth was soon occupied in committing all the late important events to paper. "It was a sin if he took the rich widow over there, when he had such a sweetheart," were Jes Jappen's last words; they were ever coming into Elizabeth's thoughts; they remained there at least for a moment, so powerful, so disturbing, however insignificant they might be; yet they had an effect like a fine hair in the telescope, which seems like a cable, and prevents one from properly regarding the object that is to be seen. But as we have said, it was only for a moment. As she wrote, the light shone more and more into her soul. Elimar was free and innocent— the whole had been like a horrible dream. She thought of the old couple's joy and happiness when they came to know all this; and her next fear, which she expressed to Adelgunde and the widow lady, was, if the letter would go safe, if they would take good care of it, and how many days it would be before it reached Oland? To the last question they could give no answer; they, however, consoled her, so far as concerned its safety. All letters, they told her, were registered in a book at the post-office, and then they were quite safe.

Sanne was to go with the letter; but Elizabeth was so afraid that she might lose it, or deliver it to any other than the postmaster himself, that she would rather go with it herself, and begged them at the post-office, that it might go safe, as it was so important; and they promised her that it should be safely delivered.

Now therefore that it was no longer necessary to go to the

King, she had no one to see except Councilor Heimerant and Trina — yes, she must visit her honest, affectionate Trina. Would they know each other again ?

Gay, and unusually talkative, which she had not been before, she now came home with Sanne, with a pleased face, and Adelgunde said " that that lively manner suited her ! she might be quite *piquant* if she had clothes that were somewhat *en mode !*" and they laughed and talked, and drank punch, and an arrangement was made that Elizabeth should go out next day with the widow lady, and see a little of the town.

Their observations during the walk were not the most profound ; *we* may, perhaps, be led into others, however, during the tour, which, if they be not profound, may yet serve as a bridge of communication to what is further to be related. Fishing and begging have something in them nearly akin. The angler can sit the whole day on the same spot, and wait and wait, and often only get a miserable little bleak, or a gudgeon, after all. The beggar also sits the whole day in the same spot, and waits and waits, for a miserable copper coin. There is, however, this difference, that the one says he does it " to amuse himself," the other, " to support life." The one who amuses himself often tears the innocent fish off the hook, so that its mouth, gills, and eyes are rent asunder, and if the fish be too small it is thrown bleeding into the water again, or on the grass to die there. The beggar — at least he who sits in his fixed place like the angler — does not commit such barbarous mischief — that sort of beggar at least does not ; but there is another sort, not the worthy, but the well-dressed, itinerant beggar, who often rends mouth, gills, and eyes in a spiritual sense ; one of these well-dressed, itinerant beggars — nay, it is not to be concealed — we are in her company when we are with the widow lady.

" You must do me a service," said she to Elizabeth, as they walked along. " Here in this street lives a man of whom I ought to have some money. Go up with this letter, on the second floor to the left : he is a man well to do, and if he asks you who it is from, you can — not to make a long explanation — say, that it is from your mother ! I don't like to dun him verbally, for then he talks so piteously that I am affected by it; but now that I have written to him I shall not get much, I dare say, and it is cruel not to be able to get one's own hard-earned gains! But do not say a word about what I have said; not a single word; it would trouble him, and that I cannot find in my heart to do!"

Elizabeth went into the house with the letter. The person to whom it was addressed opened the door himself. He was in his dressing-gown, and appeared a friendly old man. He read the letter with something of a piteous face, shook his head, walked about a little and said: "Yes I would, willingly; but it is impossible. I have, of late, had so many expenses. Every one flocks to me! Hm! hm! poor woman!" and then he went to his desk, took out a dollar, and gave it to Elizabeth. "Tell your mother," said he, "that it is all I can do for her at present," and he looked quite kindly, and opened the door for her.

The widow lady, who stood in the next door-way, came forward and asked what he had said.

Elizabeth told her every word, and gave her the dollar.

"Is that all that you got?" asked the widow lady; "it is shameful! I ought to have a good deal of money from that fellow, and he gives me a dollar! it is almost an insult! he deserves that I should go up and talk to him. He must have been in liquor when he did it — for you must know that he drinks! Did he not run on strangely! did he not say anything that you thought strange, respecting my dunning him for my money?"

Elizabeth repeated every word he had said, and the lady was relieved. There was nothing that could lead the old gentleman to suppose that he had received a common begging letter.

"He is a miserable fellow," said the widow lady.

That was the character the worthy old gentleman got, who thought that "the highly necessitous widow, who had known better days," at that moment blessed him.

"It is not enough for a pair of French gloves, which I am so much in want of!" said she; "I must add something to it to get them;" and she did so.

When they got home Elizabeth had at least seen and been in most of the shops in East Street.

"We have not been idle," said the widow lady.

"And now I shall give her a treat," said Adelgunde.

"You have certainly no theatre in Holstein, on your islands. Good Heavens!" she added; "well, I never thought before that there were islands in Holstein. How remarkably large the world is! You shall go with me to the theatre this evening. I have got two tickets from my sweetheart to the boxes, in the second tier. But we must go early, to get a place on the front seat; and you must be dressed a little, child. You will lend her your shawl — the old one," she said, turning to the widow lady, "and I shall arrange her hair."

They set about it directly: Elizabeth had to sit in the middle of the room.

"She has no holes in her ears," exclaimed Adelgunde; "she has never worn ear-rings. How neglected she has been! She must have my *bandeau* on; it improves the complexion. Nay, but she is charming! she will make a sensation; a little innocent face like hers looks so well!"

The two then set off to the theatre.

"We must go round by that little street there," said Adelgunde; "I must see the lottery numbers at the collector's, for I have a ticket with three marks[1] on the numbers I have dreamt of. If I get three out of the five,[2] you shall have a present."

They went past the collector's, but the numbers were not there.

"It is down there in the cellar that Trina Hansen lives, whom you know. Did you not see the name and the sign; but you cannot run down there now; there is not time for it, if we would get a place on the front bench."

And away she walked with Elizabeth, who noticed the house where the collector lived, close by the corner. They arrived at the theatre just as it was opened; and with a singular adroitness in using her elbows and pushing aside others, Adelgunde led her through the crowd in at the door, and up the stairs, and they got a seat on the front bench.

Adelgunde knew almost every one there, particularly the

[1] About eighteen-pence, English.
[2] Ninety numbers are placed in the wheel, out of which five are drawn.

gentlemen, whom she mentioned by name; but, amongst all these names, there was only one that sounded like a well-known name — it was Thorvaldsen. The hale old man, with that friendly face, and long white hair, stood down in the pit. He seemed to look straight up at her: her heart beat quicker, as if it were the King she saw. How often had she not heard Thorvaldsen named during the last year! The description of his splendid reception in Copenhagen had brought tears into Moritz's eyes. Here he now stood; here in the same house, under the same roof; she thought that all the rest were only here to see him, to be in the same house with him.

But such were not Adelgunde's thoughts. The music began; the curtain rolled up, and they performed the *vaudeville* — "Kjoge-House Cross." The scene was laid in Kjoge, that town which Elizabeth had passed through three days before in the fly-wagon; there, where she had made acquaintance with the widow lady. It is true she did not recognize the houses, but she knew the green trees and the sea. Yes, it was Kjoge, but the "House Cross" was not taken from the dreadful ghost and witch story. Elizabeth understood well that the honest brick-layer, who from his scaffolding before the house looked in like the swallow, and saw what passed, was the supernatural being — was the House Cross that helped the lovers. It was an entire story, so real, and yet not quite reality, for they sang so much; but it was charming, and Adelgunde explained to her throughout the whole piece.

"That is Fru Heiberg," said she, "but it is a poor part she has. She is in her own clothes, and what she has to say here is so commonplace; but now you can imagine her in gold and silk, and when she speaks in verse. I am not over fond of *vaudevilles*, that I must say." That was Adelgunde's opinion, and it was just as shrewd as that of many others.

The empty places in the court part of the pit, the numbered seats in the "lion's row," as the bench nearest the stage is called, and which is usually frequented by the Copenhagen lions, was filled, for the real play now began — the ballet. Amongst those who had entered was a young man in a rich fur-lined surtout. He had kept it on, for it looked well on him. His well-arranged hair was somewhat thin, but his beard, on the contrary, thick and handsome.

"Do you see him who came in just now?" said Adelgunde, "that handsome young man — him in the fur surtout? It is a valuable skin. Is he not handsome? Did you see that he saw us — he smiles! — look through my glass : he winks with one eye! — do you see? That is my sweetheart!" And Adelgunde blushed like crimson, laughed and talked, rose up and sat down, put the shawl round her shoulders and off her shoulders ; there was just such an uneasiness and agitation in her as if she herself were going to take part in the ballet.

The music began again, and the curtain rolled up. The ballet was "The Festival in Albano." The soft melodies, the southern scenery, the Italian dresses, the whole life and motion on the stage were like sunlight to Elizabeth's fancy ; the Campagna with Rome lay before her ; she was there herself ; the dancers ascended the mountain ; children with waving flags, and the whole nuptial procession followed.

"They come up out of a hole in the floor," said Adelgunde ; "do you see that great lamb right down in the cellar?"

But Elizabeth saw the mountains and valley, the clear blue air, the artists' festival ; she understood all, except wherefore the two pilgrims became Greek gods, and accordingly asked what it meant.

"It is the ballet-master himself," said Adelgunde, who had an answer for everything.

The music continued, and the varied dresses dazzled the eye. The roseate hues of eve shone on Rome, the night broke forth, and the torches were lighted during the exulting dance. Elizabeth during the whole time had collected all this as in one sum of thought ; all that she had read and heard spoken of at home, about beautiful Italy, stood before her, and the tears came into her eyes.

"It is over! come now," whispered Adelgunde. The curtain had not yet fallen, but she drew her away with her. The crowd streamed out after them. When they reached the furthest door which stood open to the street, the rain poured down : it was terrible weather, and there was a crowding and pushing with wet umbrellas. In the midst of the crowd stood the gentleman in the fur-lined surtout. He was looking for

some one — it was Adelgunde.   She followed him with Elizabeth, and before she knew where she was, they had all three
entered a hackney-coach.   It was particularly fortunate in
such weather, and away they drove.   Elizabeth neither knew
the right nor the wrong of the matter, but when they stopped
it was not before the house where the widow lady lived.

"But where are we now?" asked Elizabeth.

"We shall take tea with my sweetheart," said Adelgunde;
"it is a sort of amusement that is quite common in Copenhagen."

"Yes, you will do us the pleasure," said the gentleman, in
a very friendly manner, and she accompanied them, for where
could she go to?   And there is nothing wrong in taking tea
with one's betrothed.

When they reached the first room the servant said that
there was some one in the parlor— the gentleman who had
breakfasted with the Baron the day before, and as he saw the
table laid, and the tea-urn, he had walked into the room and
said that he would wait.

"Him! O, that's nothing," said he to Adelgunde, who
seemed as if she would turn back; "he is one of my most
intimate friends; he is no Copenhagener, and he is half a for-
eigner."

Orders were given to bring in champagne, as well as tea.
The door was opened at the same time, and a handsome man,
probably a little more than thirty years of age, with a perfect
Italian face, received the Baron with a smile, for Adelgunde's
companion — or, if you will, her betrothed — was no less than
a baron.

The friend began with an excuse for having forced his way
in, but stopped. . . . . "Ladies!" he exclaimed — "I
beg you a thousand pardons, my friend!"

"Don't trouble yourself about it," answered the Baron;
"I shall present you to each other directly.   Know my
charming little Baroness, and here is her younger sister and
true friend.   You present her," said he apart to Adelgunde.

The strange, handsome man laughed, showed the finest set
of white teeth, and looked with a piercing eye at Elizabeth,
who became still more perplexed.

"This is my friend, the Baron of Montefiertone, etc., etc., etc., and other lands," said the Baron. "He is, as you see, ladies, an extremely handsome man, and, I may add, a great connoisseur of the beautiful; and now we will have tea. How captivating you are, you little witch!" said he to Adelgunde, as he swung her round.

Adelgunde laughed, threw herself into a rocking-chair, and was up again at the same moment. She must be mistress, and pour out the tea.

While all this passed Elizabeth stood still, and fumbled with her large shawl; she knew not whether she should go or stay.

"You are not afraid of me, are you?" said the stranger, and looked at her so steadfastly and strangely with his dark, lively eyes, that she cast hers down. She felt a fear at her heart, as if that man would do her some injury.

"It is a charming little face," said he, and he took hold of her hand; involuntarily she screamed aloud, and darted towards the door.

Adelgunde looked angrily at her.

"Don't be a child; one would think you had never been in men's company before. This is the way in Copenhagen, child!"

"O God, I am indeed a child!" exclaimed Elizabeth: "let me go home!" and she looked with such a strangely piteous expression at the Baron, who was the one she had most confidence in of the three.

"O you little fool!" said he; "why, you *are* at home, you are with your friend," and he laughed and nodded to Adelgunde.

The stranger again looked with a singularly scrutinizing look at Elizabeth, who was deadly pale, and had made her way close to the door.

"Is it your serious intention to go?" he asked. "You ought to have your will, but you cannot go alone, so permit me to accompany you."

"No, no," cried Elizabeth, as she threw the door open and ran out of the room, down the stairs, and, as she did not know the way, right into a sand-hole, where she fell on the soft sand

" She will not run away," said Adelgunde ; " she knows no place to go to : she is just from the country."

The stranger, who had remained behind, looked at Adelgunde, then sprang out of the room, threw his cloak around him, took his hat in the greatest haste, and was at the street-door as soon as Elizabeth, who, by falling into the sand-hole, had been detained some seconds.

" O, let me go ! " she said ; " do me no harm ! I am so afraid ! "

" But, my dear child," said the stranger, " I will do you no harm ; I will help you ; I will accompany you. I have not said a word that could terrify you. You don't know any place to go to : your friend up there said you were just from the country."

Elizabeth was silent, but walked on quicker, though she knew not whither. The stranger walked by her side.

" I assure you that you may place confidence in me," said he again ; " and if you have quite innocently got into bad company, as I believe, then I will help you out of it, and conduct you where you desire. If I have shown myself a little too familiar, then you shall see that I may be excused, and that, on my part it was quite natural. Give me your arm, and tell me where I shall accompany you ? "

There was something so frank and honest in his voice, that a natural and innocent child like Elizabeth must have believed it ; yet she did not take his arm, but said, with a trembling voice, " Do not be angry with me ! I know nothing ; I am a perfect stranger here in this great city. O ! how afflicted they would be at home for me, if they knew how I am situated."

The stranger then questioned her again with cordiality and compassion, and he then learned that she had come to town to seek an audience of the King ; that she knew no one ; that the widow lady had allowed her to stay with her, and that she had there become acquainted with Adelgunde, who had taken her to the theatre that evening, and that on leaving it, they had entered a carriage which she thought would have carried them home ; but, on the contrary, it had brought them to the house they now came from.

"But, my dear girl," said he, "that widow lady and this Adelgunde, are no fit company for you. It would be a sin to take you there. But what shall I do for you? Do you know no other person?"

"No," said Elizabeth, "no one but a Councilor, who lives in Christianshaven, and him I have never seen, nor is he at home!"

"Well, that is just the same as knowing no one," answered the stranger. "What shall we do? we cannot stay here in the street; it rains so terribly!"

"The widow lady is so good to me," said Elizabeth; "she is a very decent, honest woman!"

"No, no, said the stranger, "that she certainly is not; but that you don't understand, and it is very well you do not. If I only knew a decent person; but I am myself almost an entire stranger here. Where does that widow lady then live, for we must perforce go to her; and yet I cannot find it in my heart to take you there."

"If I had only spoken with Trina!" said Elizabeth; "she is good and honest."

"Who is Trina?" he inquired.

"She is a shoemaker's wife, whom I knew when I was a little child; she was very fond of me; she lives very near the widow lady's, but I have not spoken with her here in town, and not even seen her!"

"Let us go to Trina," said the stranger quickly, and with an expression of gayety; "I believe the shoemaker's wife is safer than the widow lady."

"Yes, yes, I thank you!" exclaimed Elizabeth. "O how frightened I am! what will become of me, if it be not Trina — not she I think it is! O God help me!"

"I will accompany you to the door; you go in, and if it be the wrong place, come back directly. I promise you that I will wait a quarter of an hour; if you do not return by that time, then I hope you are in good hands. But do you know the way we should go?"

"I think I know it, when I am at the theatre," answered Elizabeth.

He conducted her thither. but she did not know the building again directly — it was now so desolate. Instead of that mass of light which streamed out from it before, there now only shone a dull gleam from a window in the roof, where the watchman had a room. The large building, which a few hours before was the most lively place in the city, where the music pealed, where great thoughts and ideas were current, was now empty and ghost-like, a body deprived of its soul. Elizabeth looked around her, and on seeing the columns of the coffee-house, she remembered the side street she should go down in order to get to the house where Trina lived. Here, the lottery collector's sign was her guide. She pointed to the cellar where there was a light, and said in a singularly affecting manner, —

"May the Lord bless you for all your kindness towards me!"

"I shall wait a quarter of an hour," said he, and pressed some money into her hand. She looked at him once more with an expression of thanks and blessing, and darted down the steps into the cellar.

The stranger walked slowly away towards the street corner, stood still, went a few paces up and down, looked to the cellar steps, went on again and stood still, but no Elizabeth came.

"I am really out on an adventure!" said he to himself. "This is at least as innocent a one as can be! But what shall I do if she returns? Am I to be her knight again? — it is quite a peculiar situation!" and he continued to stand still by the street corner, where he received a "good-night" from the watchman.

CHAPTER XX.

THE SHOEMAKER'S CELLAR.

WHEN we think of Trina's maxim, "It is appearances one looks at, it is appearances, madame," and remember how severely her Hansen also thinks in this respect, then we may conceive what a surprise it was to the two honest folks to see a young girl, so late in the evening, with a long shawl over her shoulders, the *bandeau* on her forehead, and her hair wet and in disorder, enter the door, and in perplexity and great emotion inquire for Trina from Funen, where Trina had not been during the last seven years.

"Who are you? what do you want?" asked Hansen, who sat in his fustian working-jacket by the supper-table, and rose half up from his chair; but Elizabeth did not answer him — she did not see him; she had only eyes for Trina, who sat on the other chair, quite clean and neatly dressed.

"Trina! yes, it is you!" cried Elizabeth. "Do you not know me, little Elizabeth, who lived with the Baroness? You were so fond of me, told me stories, and sang songs for me. You gave me a book, and wrote in it, 'To my little Elizabeth.'"

"O gracious me!" cried Trina, "who is she? Hansen, who is that woman?"

"What do you want?" said Hansen. "What is the matter?"

"O Trina, do not drive me away," said Elizabeth, so beseechingly, so downcast, and she stretched out both her hands towards her. "It is surely you! I think so; I was, it is true, so little then; you went with me to Katrineson's, where you gave me the song-book which you wrote in."

"Jesus save us!" exclaimed Trina; "is that little Elizabeth! But how did you come here? and" — She would have said, "such a figure," but she did not; she looked at her from head to foot, at the *bandeau*, the long shawl, and her feet, that were soaking wet and muddy from the street.

"Let me stay with you till the Councilor comes home," said Elizabeth; "don't let me go to the widow lady: I am so afraid of every one, but not of you. You were so kind towards me; I remember it, as I have not remembered it for a long time."

"Is it really you, Elizabeth?" said Trina, in a tone that had as much of doubt as confidence in it. "I cannot rightly know you again, and yet I think it is you! You are so grown!—you are so"— She stopped speaking, and looked doubtful, but with an expression of compassion.

"Let me speak!" said Hansen. "It is a strange time for you to come here, young lady. My wife thinks as I do, and I think as my wife does. Will you tell us in a few words what is the matter, and what you want with us?"

"I come from home—from the parsonage," replied Eliz abeth. "We thought there was a person's life at stake, and I was to go to the King, and so"— She stopped.

"O my God!" said Trina; "I believe her!—that fac cannot lie!—I believe her, strange as she looks, and strange ly as she comes! Sit down, my poor girl, and tell us all th story."

Elizabeth related the whole, and was questioned, an replied, and explained again and again.

The account about Elimar, about the old grandparent grief, and lastly, her own determination to go to Copenhage affected Trina deeply.

"But, is it true what you tell us?" said Hansen; "is not a made up story, Trina, she tells us?"

"No, no," said Trina, and clasped her round the necl "it is true every word she says, poor girl!—it is just li one in 'The Elves.' I saw her as a little child, and now s comes again as a grown woman. But is the gentleman star ing outside yet?—it is more than a quarter of an hour sir you came. But, Hansen, do peep out and see, for he has all events behaved very decently, though he is certainly immoral person."

More than three quarters of an hour had passed ; no one was to be seen outside, and then Elizabeth had to describe who the widow lady was, and where she lived.

" O Heaven ! is it she ? " exclaimed Trina ; " she is a regular cheating Jezebel. She lives by writing begging-letters, and gets people to take lottery numbers for embroidered cushions, which they never get. I know the Miss also ! O poor girl, what hands have you got into ! So the gentleman was after all the *honestest !* Perhaps they have also deceived him, and I take my words back again, when I said he was an immoral person ! One can never trust to appearances."

In order to make ends meet better in their little household, Trina had again taken to the stage, as a chorus singer ; for, as she said, that profession was now highly respectable, and there were the most respectable persons' children amongst them. Those who sing in the choruses have also to assist in the ballets. Trina had that evening been a peasant girl in "The Festival in Albano ; " and after changing her clothes had just returned home, where she now sat with her husband over their frugal evening meal. Elizabeth would have found them up even still later, for it was Hansen's custom to read aloud every evening some piece from an historical work, such as " Pontoppidan's Atlas," " A Description of Copenhagen," or an old Danish magazine ; for Hansen was, as Trina said, a man of education above his condition. This evening, however, there was no reading ; there was so much to ask about, so much to hear. The clock struck twelve before they thought of making a bed on some chairs for Elizabeth.

"Now sleep, in Heaven's name," said Trina. " I certainly did not think this morning when I got up that you would come here at night, and that I should hear such a story. The Lord, however, looks to us when we are in need ; " and she kissed Elizabeth, and then Hansen, saying, " He is a good man, an accomplished man, more so than any one believes ; and you will come to be fond of him, as I am."

Next morning, Elizabeth was awakened by the blows of the hammer on the wet leather which Hansen made pliable : everything in the workshop was so neatly arranged — twine, awls, lasts, and polishing stick.

The books stood on shelves opposite the glass ball ; the canary-bird sang, and the coffee-can steamed. Elizabeth was to go at once to the widow lady, fetch her few things, and take leave there.

"God preserve me! are you not ashamed of yourself?" said the lady, "to be away a whole night; where have you been? You have behaved yourself shockingly, as I hear from Miss Adelgunde; nay, you cannot stay here — not an hour longer within my doors. Honor is what I look to above all. What would my deceased husband say if he could look out of his grave?"

Elizabeth told her that she came to take leave, to thank her for the time she had stayed in her house, and that she had come to fetch her clothes and money.

"That is what I get for my good-nature," said the lady ; "ingratitude — that one may be at all times certain of. Well, take your clothes ; take what is yours ; but I will have what is mine. Hand over that shawl."

Elizabeth had it folded on her arm.

"Wherever it has been, it smells of cellar air. You shall have what is yours, but I will have what is mine. Here lie five dollars, the least that I ought to have for three days' board and lodging, and for all that I have done. Be so kind as to take your things ; and so each gets her own — here are your clothes. Adelgunde has told me everything ; that you ran away with the strange gentleman — you begin early on a bad road. Ungrateful!" and then the widow lady cried, threw her cloak around her, and told Elizabeth that she might go, for there was neither time nor place for her to remain ; but the lady, however, called little Sanne in, that she might see what was likely to be the end of bad people, and be warned accordingly.

And Sanne cried and wiped her face with her dirty hands, so that she was blacker than before, and looked as if she had played that noble game called "Black Peter," where he or she who loses the game is rubbed over the face with a burnt cork.

Elizabeth then returned to Trina who had to be at the singing-school in the theatre during the whole forenoon at a rehearsal ; but she took the shoes with her that were to be bound.

Norma's priestess in Irmensule's sacred forest, did not forget shoemaker Hansen in Pink Street (Nellikegaden).

That evening there was no performance, and Hansen read aloud from the Danish magazine. He read about Master Brockmann, King Christian II.'s secretary, who had studied in Germany in his youth, and had there become a *magister*, or, as he was called, *master*.

"From that one can see," said Hansen, who always made an edifying lecture on what he read, "that *master* properly signifies *magister*, and, therefore, that I, as *master*-shoemaker, am *magister*-shoemaker."

He then related how many remarkable persons had sprung from his own trade, and he named the Jerusalem shoemaker, Pasquino in Rome, and that master-singer, Hans Sachs ; and at the conclusion of this speech there was a peculiar smile about his mouth ; it might be jesting with his own words, but it might likewise be a pleased self-satisfaction. Whatever it might be, it was snug, neat, and cosy in that little room ; and it was always "instructive" to hear Hansen, as Trina said. And her eyes beamed when she looked at her clever husband, whom she alone knew thoroughly ; and Elizabeth also listened with devout attention.

But now there was a knock at the door ; it was Hansen's cousin, the diver, a true friend, who always visited them when he was in town. He had himself invented his own apparatus ; and he, too, could talk about his workshop, the deep and wonderful sea.

Well, this person's entrance caused a stop to be put to the reading, but then they talked so much the more. The conversation took a turn to the diver's occupation and gains ; and Elizabeth listened still more earnestly than to the history of Master Brockmann, of Pasquino, and Hans Sachs. A new source of thought and inquiry that evening sprang up in her mind in the shoemaker's homely room.

"It was well that our cousin came," said Trina ; "for you learned from him that Mr. Heimerant came home this evening ; therefore, the first thing in the morning you can seek his assistance and advice."

But this important news was almost forgotten on hearing the diver relate all about his pursuits, as coolly and straightforwardly as Hansen might speak about laying the strap over his knee and using his waxed thread.

Elizabeth had seen the sea in ebb and flood ; it had once even approached her mouth to give her its death-kiss ; she knew it in its rage and calm, but never as the cousin spoke of it ; and she thought it was indeed wondrous clever to descend fathoms deep, and, with death hanging over one's head, to wander about at the bottom of the sea without restraint. This must be much more clever than to sail over it.

Long after the diver had left, and all were in bed, it seemed to Elizabeth as if she still heard him describe it. She dwelt upon his words, forgot her own fate, the visit she had to pay in the morning to Councilor Heimerant, and even Elimar glided from her thoughts. It was the fancy which, in its boundless power, began to elevate itself for the first time with change of place, and with the contrast of surrounding scenes. How strange ! was it not ? in the depths of the sea, — *how* strange to stand there like the diver, and exercise his calling in mud and slime up to the neck, liable to be inextricably caught by the iron crooks of the vessel, or squeezed in between the copper sheathing and the quay.

"There I stand in the mud," he had said, "and large water-snakes — some may call them eels — creep about me ! Fishes are so very inquisitive : the flounders run right against one ; the cod-fishes come in whole crowds, close round in a circle, and stare ! If I make the slightest movement, they are off like gun-shot, but come again directly and stand in shoals and stare. The crabs are the worst : the great crabs place themselves in a posture of defense ; nay, they will even engage with me. They look like great spiders, and are as large as a plate : they scratch and scrape, and the fat water-snakes lick themselves every now and then. I, myself, must certainly appear to them a strange crab ! I have a helmet over my head, to which belong two leather tubes, into which they continually pump air from the boat at the top of the water, down to me. It comes in two streams over my face, and keeps up a regular bubbling in the water round my neck.

It will go up, it *will* ascend; and, if they did not pump, it would soon be over with me. I have often thought of that. I throw off the leaden weights from my legs that hold me down, and then I come up to the surface with the swiftness of an arrow."

It was as if Elizabeth had heard one of Walter Scott's novels. It ought surely to be written down, and a whole story made out of it so as to be printed — a story of the sea; and she remembered the sunken places near Sylt and Amrom, the swimming islands she had seen driven up on the innkeeper's land, when she, as a little girl, was carried away asleep in Mr. Petters's wagon: she remembered the many sagas that Keike had related, and Elimar's story about the phantom ship. A wondrously magnificent picture of the sea filled her thoughts, but as yet this, her first composition, was unknown to her.

Here, in the shoemaker's little workshop, in a Copenhagen cellar, a performance of boundless fancy was brought forth. She arranged what she had heard and seen; it was like a beautiful dream. She felt as if she had a whole novel in imagination, but had not words for it; just as she had no idea that this feeling could be rendered clear, could be strengthened, and converted into a great and glorious picture.

It was daybreak before Elizabeth slept.

Councilor Heimerant had read the letter from Moritz the evening before, and was now, this morning, about to write letters in order to trace out Elizabeth, and get further particulars relative to Elimar Leyson, when Trina and Elizabeth arrived. The old man received them with evident joy and compassion; his extremely good-natured disposition shone forth in his face and words; and when he heard that it was clear the prisoner was not Elimar, the smile expanded over his whole face. It was, therefore, all right with respect to the letter that had afterwards reached the Commander and about which Moritz had informed him.

All had turned out fortunate and well.

"And that is the little Elizabeth," said he. "Well, then, now I have you with me; and I can write to-day and comfort them at home. You have frightened them terribly; but you are a good girl, a blessed girl, and fortune has been better than reason."

Trina gave a concise account of the whole story, and it was soon decided that Elizabeth should remain with the Councilor until an opportunity offered to send her home to the Halligers, for she must see a little of the town now that she was here.

"Yes," said Trina, "accept the offer. I would gladly keep you with me; but it is better to be there than to sit with us in the cellar; and then think how much of the day I am at the theatre."

The Councilor read from Moritz's communication what it contained concerning Elimar's letter, namely, that he was to be married to a rich widow in America; and the tears ran down Elizabeth's cheeks and she sobbed aloud.

"It is only because she hears all this from home," said Trina.

Elizabeth had a pretty little chamber in the old gentleman's house, looking out upon the large open yard, where the trees grew; and the lofty spire of St. Saviour's Church rose above the neighboring house, with its gilt railings around the spiral staircase on the outside, up to the image of the Saviour, which forms the pinnacle, looking over town and sea.

Elizabeth was now, therefore, safe in port.

CHAPTER XXI.

THE BARONESS'S SALOON.

THE same afternoon Councilor Heimerant proceeded on a business visit to the old Baroness from Funen. He had the previous year become her trustee and agent, as the former one was dead.

"The brigand is here!" said she; "he has of course been to see you. I am quite pleased with him, though he is not yet quite a free slave. Now, I shall soon have dabbled enough in the world, and he must then, as my daughter's child, have the estate, for my daughter's child he is — that cannot be denied. So he ought to know a little about the folks and animals he has to deal with before he gets the sway. We are now allied powers; and that any two can very well be without loving each other."

The Councilor told her that Count Frederick intended to sell the pretty little property where his father had built a neat mansion for him, on the site where we saw a ruinous frame-work building, where Elizabeth was born, and where the friends passed her birth-night during storm and rain. Count Frederick, after the death of his father, had removed to the family seat, so that the little newly-built mansion, so comfortable and pretty, had stood empty above two years. Frederick, as we have said, wished to sell it, and Baron Herman had a great desire to be the purchaser, and pursue agriculture there.

"Yes, he knows well enough what he would like," said the old lady; "and you didn't bite his ear, eh, when you gave him that advice? But I shall not do it, because he will have it, and then make a jumble of the story. I have thought of it before myself, or else I would not have made it. But I say that a wife shall be there; I will not have any *bach·*

elorism ; you see that I have made that word myself, and it is a very good one ; a man must be honest and decent. He shall have the estate, but he must procure a wife, and not one who resembles the Countess Clara ; he had better take her from the milk-pail than from the court calendar ! " and the old lady laughed her strange ringing laugh, and threw her head back in her own peculiar manner.

She was evidently in good humor: the Councilor therefore thought he could tell her the events of that morning — how little Elizabeth had come to him, what letters he had got, in short the whole circumstances. He began with his story, and she started, but it was not quite a natural start, for Trina had been there a few hours before, and related the whole, from first to last, to Madame Krone, who had again related it to the Baroness in her own way. And Trina was called a gossip, but she nevertheless had coffee and sugar given to her for a whole month. Now, on the contrary, when the Councilor commenced, the old lady laid her finger on her mouth ; she would hear nothing.

" I don't know that 'Lizabeth," said she ; " I will not know her, and I can invent stories for myself. If, however, you have a foster-daughter, a little young lady, or Miss, who would see a little of the world amongst company, she is welcome with you ; but she is your Miss ; I don't acknowledge her. She comes as yours ; bring her with you on Monday, when there will be a great chuck-farthing of all coins, of silver and copper. There will also be counters."

" And what sort of coin am I ? " asked Heimerant, laughing.

" One from the coin cabinet," said the lady ; " one of those there are not two of, and therefore we must not lose sight of you," and she nodded and laughed, as she called out to him in the door-way, " Don't be so good-natured, Councilor ; wean yourself of it. Good-nature is like corns ; if persons observe one has them, we may be sure of having our feet trodden on every moment."

Next day Madame Krone went to Christianshaven to see Elizabeth, who immediately interested her with her intelligent face and natural manners. The Councilor was quite impressed with the singularly vivid manner in which Elizabeth could relate things. She had told him the evening before so much about the Halligers, Fohr, and Amrom, that he imagined he had been there; no book, no verbal description, had ever before given him such a clear representation. Elizabeth herself did not know her own powers; her eye had unconsciously conceived the most characteristic traits, and the living words came forth in all their simplicity.

In the evening she sat down to the piano. The Councilor requested her to let him hear a little song, for he knew that she had learned all the songs Caroline had once sung, and she began in a low voice with "Roslein Roth," but by degrees her voice rose clearer, and yet it was so melodious, so soft, so touching! Elizabeth thought of home, where she had sung it, thought of Elimar, who was now married, and would never more return to Europe, and a trembling, a sound as from the heart, came into the melody. Tears ran down the cheeks of old Heimerant, for he thought he heard his own dear lost child — his blessed Caroline. He went up to Elizabeth, and kissed her as he would have kissed Caroline, and said, "You will not leave me so soon! Now, remain here this winter, my dear child!"

On the Monday evening there was to be a great chuck-farthing, as the Baroness called it: the Councilor would take Elizabeth with him; she might, however, have looked rather strange, as far as concerned her dress, if she, whom the world called "the mad woman," had not thought a little about such matters.

Monday morning came, and with it a large parcel for Elizabeth; a morning greeting from an unknown, in which there was the finest linen, — upper and under clothes, — and what was another "god-send," a black silk gown, which fitted as if she had been measured for it. This was from the Baroness, who knew well that the Councilor, however practical he might be in other things, would not think of such necessaries, and that Elizabeth would hardly venture to speak of them. The carriage came rather late: they would not be amongst those who arrived first. The stairs and anterooms were brilliantly illuminated, but the room they passed into was, on the contrary, quite dark, and filled with company.

"Take care not to fall over a privy councilor, or a student, for he may also become a privy councilor!" said the Baroness. "We are playing at Christmas Eve: I don't like to have my Christmas-tree with others, and so I have made mine ready this evening. I prefer to be a couple of months in advance, like the German New-year's gifts, which are old when New-year comes."

Elizabeth's heart beat with fear on hearing this voice; it seemed to her as if it were yesterday she heard her cry: "I can believe all that is bad of you! out of my house you shall pack!" Those words, screamed out in the mysterious chamber, were awakened to life again. Elizabeth clung fast to the Councilor.

All kinds of persons were assembled: it was a miniature picture of Copenhagen. Here sat a decent couple belonging to the government-office class, whose knowledge of literature was confined to the "Daily Advertiser" and the "Corsair."[1] There stood a member of several learned societies, of that kind which are established in order to give persons a name who would otherwise have none at all. Here a young man of the world's nobility — that to which the potter's son, Themistocles, belonged, and amongst us Danes, the tailor's apprentice, Tordenskjold, and the dock-yard man's son, Albert Thorvaldsen. Here sat liberals, who would be tyrants, and here tyrants who were not yet ripe; persons who had too little an opinion of themselves, and persons who had too great; in short here was a motley company.

The Baroness said very justly, "My house is like the "General Advertiser," all sorts of decent persons enter it, both those who seek a place, and those who give one."

At this moment they all sat, as we have said, in the dark, either waiting for more guests, or because the forthcoming arrangements in the saloon were not yet completed.

"There is surely somebody here who can play a little on the piano for us," said the old lady; "one that can do so without being stared at."

No one answered and a pause ensued.

"Then I suppose I must, Grandmother," said a gentlemanly

---

[1] The Copenhagen *Punch* or *Charivari*.

voice, which sounded to Elizabeth as if it were not strange to her. The blood rose to her cheeks; who could he be? He sang boldly and with animation: it was the Neapolitan tarentella to Italian words.

"Bravo!" cried the old lady.

"Bravo!" resounded on all sides when the song was ended; and a new one succeeded, and again a new one — Italian and Spanish. There was a life and resonance that carried the listeners along with them. There was then a short pause, during which two more strangers came.

"What Nicodemus is that who comes now?" asked the old lady.

"It is we, Baroness," said Clara, who entered with her husband, Count Frederick. "Nay, how dark it is here!"

"Yes, I am malicious," said the Baroness. No one can see how handsome you are, my dear, nor how elegantly you are dressed. When one comes late at night, then the candles are burnt out. But now Madame Krone shall let the sun rise."

She laughed aloud, and the folding-doors to the saloon opened; three fine, large, richly decorated Christmas-trees stood in the middle of the saloon; candles of all colors burnt between the branches, and the most comical pasteboard figures peeped forth from the green branches, which were loaded with golden apples and grapes. At the foot of the trees was a border of the most beautiful flowers in pots, but the pots were not to be seen, for they were covered with fresh moss, on which were artificial glow-worms, whole flocks of lady-birds, and a couple of frogs, that leaped about when any one touched them, for they contained a piece of mechanism. Everything was very well and pleasantly arranged. But Elizabeth was surprised only for a moment by the new and varied entertainment she saw before her. Adelgunde's sweetheart, that fine, richly dressed gentleman, stood there, in the middle of the saloon. and regarded her with surprise and astonishment. He laid his hand on his neighbor's shoulder, who turned to him. The neighbor she now saw was he who had accompanied her to Trina's door that terrible evening. It was as if the whole room turned round — as if the lights and colors flowed into one another.

The two gentlemen were Barons Holger and Herman.

"Who is that young girl there?" they inquired of Madame Krone.

"What! you do not know her, then?" answered she with a smile, — an answer in which their consciences saw a meaning which that honest woman, of course, could not have dreamed of; her thoughts were, "It is your own foundling from Funen!" and she continued: "Have you forgotten your adventure?"

Herman blushed and looked at Holger.

"Is it to be a surprise?" whispered the latter.

Madame Krone was now busily occupied with the company, in causing each to draw a number for the Christmas-prizes, and with each of these followed what the Baroness called an "after-game," which was the most polite, and which involved a gift she herself presented to the prize-holder, and which she had previously appropriated to each. Count Frederick got a volume of "The Danish Provincial States' Gazette;" Clara, on the contrary, a large box, in which lay pieces of bricks in different partitions, and on each was pasted an inscription stating where they came from; there were Nineveh, Babylon, Carthage, Thebes, etc.

Clara was quite transported. "And I am to have all these treasures?" she exclaimed. "Where did you get them from?"

"From my old cow-stall," answered the old lady, with the kindest face imaginable. "The names are correct; I have copied them myself from my geography — a book which I derive the greatest benefit from!"

"Then the whole is false," cried Clara.

"Only imagine they are genuine, and then they are so," said the Baroness.

All that belonged to the "after-game" was of this kind.

Holger and Herman soon learned who Elizabeth was, and Herman, who had been partly informed by herself, understood the story soonest.

"It was that child!" thought he, — "that child we promised to be fathers and protectors to."

A serious feeling passed through his mind: he felt satisfaction at his conduct on that night. "Thanks to God who has protected her and me. I have not courage to speak to her!"

"Then I have," said Holger, and went boldly up to the Councilor, whom "he was extremely glad to see; the young lady had certainly drawn a lucky number," said he, and asked what she had got; if it were the first time she had been in Copenhagen? if she had been at many balls here already? what pieces she had seen at the theatre? in short, the usual talk on such occasions was gone through. Holger spoke so freely that Elizabeth almost began to doubt her own senses.

Herman, on the contrary, did not approach until the Councilor took leave, when he said a few words to him, and made a very polite bow to Elizabeth.

What an evening! The remembrance of the secret chamber had never been so vividly present in her thoughts as this first visit in the saloon world. The entrance into the presence of the old Baroness; the meeting here with the two men connected with the most terrible evening in her life; all this caused her to tremble in every limb until she was in the carriage.

"That was rather too much for once!" said the Councilor, "but you have now seen the show."

Elizabeth did not answer; there was a conflict in her mind. Should she, if she could, say to the Councilor, "I have seen those two men before; the one who stood so strangely, that he did not say a word to me, was my companion, my protector." There came a bashfulness over her; an indistinct notion that it could not be told; she wanted words — and who were those two men?

"Surely you are ill, my dear child, are you not?" inquired the Councilor.

"O no, only tired, very tired," she whispered.

"Yes, you see you knew no one but Madame Krone; but now I shall tell you the most remarkable persons who were there;" and the old man told her about them all; but not about Herman. He did not even say who he was, for he thought it was clear enough; he had besides been called grandson! Whilst he related these particulars, they drove home and the rain poured down. It was just such an evening as when Herman accompanied Elizabeth to the shoemaker's cellar.

The rain beat against the carriage windows, and the lamps burnt miserably: but amidst the gloom, in the wind and rain, the watchman chanted, "'Twas in the midnight hour, a Saviour was born!"

CHAPTER XXII.

WE have not seen or heard anything of Herman, from the time of Count Frederick's marriage with Clara, when he left Copenhagen, until we, together with Elizabeth, met him at Holger's. Nine years have elapsed, — nine years passed in foreign countries, where nature, art, and the world's busy life had been his preceptors; and it must be acknowledged that, however high one may place the learning of the schools, and all knowledge acquired by diligence and difficulties, yet life bestows more. He was not transformed, but developed; he had gained a clear view of himself and of the world. By seeing foreign lands he had been brought to value his own father-land, to acknowledge its best points, and to become a patriot without warring against the rights of others.

We shall soon renew our old acquaintanceship in Councilor Heimerant's parlor.

From Trina's door, where we left him that memorable evening, he did not return to Holger and Adelgunde, but to the hotel where he stayed. Elizabeth's terror, desertion, and innocent faith in God, occupied his thoughts. "That poor girl! how had she been received in the cellar? how had she got on afterwards?" The day following, he went through the street, half inclined to call at the shoemaker's, but he did not. His interest in her was, however, awakened, and it became more so after the meeting in his grandmother's saloon, where he learned that she was his and his friend's foundling. There, in that great circle, it was impossible for him to speak to her; but speak he would, and therefore he set out next morning to the Councilor's. It was on business, and from that he passed, in a half-jesting tone, to his adventure in Funen, and his share in "little Elizabeth," but the meeting at Holger's was not touched upon.

"I know, from Madame Krone," said he, "that it is quite in a romantic way this young girl has come to town; I am afraid she is rather nervously sensitive, and *that* she has not from our good friend, Moritz Nemmesen, whom you know better than I. He is of a good, healthy nature."

"And so is she too," replied the Councilor; "it is entirely from innocence and the kindest heart that she made this strange flight forth into the world."

And the old man spoke so warmly and well of her; and also said what a pretty voice she had, and what a singularly endowed girl she was.

Herman stayed there to dinner. He stayed until the evening; but during all this time Elizabeth did not speak much; but she received him gladly and naturally, pressed his hand and looked at him with her intelligent, honest eyes, which shone with gratitude and confidence. She listened to his narrations — and he related much — with a lively attention, that several times brought a blush into her face. The Councilor knew little of Herman's life abroad, and he wished very much to hear it, and about foreign lands. Of these it was Italy and England that particularly engaged Herman's attention. The Baron spoke with enthusiasm of Rome and London, the cities of all cities, as he called them, so different and yet so alike, from the very force of contrast. Rome was night, the great, glorious night, rich and elevating to thought and fancy. London was day, the busy, active day, which carries all along with it to life and action; but it was Rome that Herman had first seen, it was there he had lived longest, and passed through his mental development. We shall only hear what he tells us from there, or else the evening's conversation would fill up a whole volume. The world's city, Rome, had at once made on him, as on most strangers, a deep impression. It was a city to learn and to live in, so that he had become domesticated there.

"There is an indescribable charm in that air, in that soil," said he; "would that I could unfold Rome to you, unfold it with its palaces, churches, and ruins, and give you an idea of social life with the great artists. Their naturalness and humor had the best effect on me: the varied manners and customs of the people filled my mind and gave me occupation. In Denmark I had, as a young student, a talent for catching and depicting whims and vagaries. My stay in Italy elevated this quality to a conception of the characteristic; my mind's eye was sharpened to a sense of the poetical and picturesque in every-day life, so that I at last actually fancied myself another Pignelle."

"And yet you gave up being a painter?" said the Councilor.

"Yes, after the first year I laid aside the pencil and took to the model-stick. I had brought myself to acknowledge that sculpture stood yet one step higher than painting. The sculptor is, more than the painter, obliged to restrain his ideas, to simplify his thoughts, and to approach as near as possible to nature; which is, however, our ideal. I studied the antiques in Rome, and the bronzes in Naples so long, that I came to the conviction that I had not genius to produce anything similar. This is a bitter acknowledgment for the young to make; but this bitterness gives health to the soul. It is also something to comprehend what is beautiful in the world — to be able to understand it. The third year I was in Rome I had advanced just so far in my judgment of myself."

To all that Herman related he had not a more attentive listener than Elizabeth; but she listened silently and with interest. It was only when he spoke of life in the mountains that she ventured a question — the usual one put by the stranger in the North — an inquiry about the brigands; and it was this, or perhaps it was on hearing the first words from the young girl's lips, that caused a slight blush to appear on Herman's cheeks. He repeated the word "brigands," and he almost started, but continued, saying that he had in fact seen but one brigand, and that was when the man was taken to the place of execution.

"He was not young, but still handsome and vigorous. He had, it was said, committed ravages for many years in the Sabine mountains, and it was also said that much money had been paid to him, at different times, as ransoms for imprisoned ladies. I saw him driven to the place of execution. He was bound with his back to the car, and was drawn by

14

two white oxen; it was if he were driving to a festival. He sat quite dignified but smiling, and was dressed in black vel-vet clothes with silver buttons on his jacket; a carnation was stuck in his button-hole, and ribbons were fluttering from his hat. Yes, everything is picturesque in that country!" — and Herman paused for a moment. He did not communicate the thought which made him shudder on seeing the robber — the thought that was awakened in him when he saw this man. If we had heard what his grandmother once whispered in his ear, when he visited her in Funen, when Elizabeth, then an infant, slept in the chamber close by, we should have under-stood him.

"It has been a rare and agreeable evening!" said Heim-erant, after Herman had taken leave near midnight. I could sit and listen to him much longer yet: I hope he will soon come again."

"What a world this is!" exclaimed Elizabeth, and her eyes sparkled. She had no other words to express her sense of the new information that had been conveyed to her. Her-man's relations had opened up a new world to her The spirit which had selected and enlightened them, filled her with admiration. At home in the Halligers, she had heard the Scotchman tell about his mountains, about Abbotsford and Walter Scott, and then her thoughts were filled with images. The novels of Walter Scott were now still more united with the reality in which she lived; but yet Knox had not spoken like Baron Herman, who was just as noble and good as he was wise and gifted. She remembered every word he had said that evening. He had compassionately and honestly accompanied her in the rain and storm. A thousand thoughts passed through her brain: she sat long by the bedside in her little chamber before she could go to rest, and if she did not say like Heimerant, "I hope he will soon come again," she meant it.

And Herman came again — was a constant guest. And "it was kind of him!" said the Councilor, for *we* cannot amuse *him!* Yet he likes your singing, I have observed. You also sing prettier and prettier; it is as if I heard Caro-line again; and he knew her: she was very fond of him, and was much grieved, in her way, when he went on his travels."

It soon appeared to Elizabeth as if she had been in all the places Herman spoke of. She saw them in imagination, and thought and said that Denmark, Copenhagen, and all here must appear to him quite poor and insignificant.

"Do not think so," answered Herman; "by travelling in foreign lands, and seeing what the world calls the greatest and best, a man gets rid of the illusion of perfectibility; his eyes are thoroughly opened, and it is then that the love of his country becomes stronger. We feel that we have taken root in the home soil, and we learn to value what we have ourselves. I know nothing that contains within itself a picture of Italy more than a Sicilian cloister garden. There is a peculiarly luxurious feeling in stretching oneself in one, on a very hot day, in the shady but open colonnade, where the walls are painted with sacred pictures; to look from there under the palm-trees, and between the tall poplar-like cypresses, and to see the fountains splash in the marble basin. One fancies oneself placed in the land of romance; and it was just there that a natural beauty came into my memory, which Denmark has in preference to any other country, and which is just as lovely to us, with our "*green islands*," as a Sicilian cloister garden is to Italy — it is our beech-woods! Where is there a cloister garden that invites to greater tranquillity, to greater peace, than they do in their extended greatness, with their depending and fragrant branches? Verdure in the South is not more exuberant! Remember our tall mighty beeches, where thousands of small shoots germinate all the way up the trunk, as if the bark could not retain that effulgence of foliage which forces itself towards the top, and there shoots out in a living roof of leaves. Remember the fresh grassy carpet below, with woodruffs, anemones, and violets, which the sun here and there illumines! The delight which the swan feels on diving into the fresh clear sea, I have felt to excess, by diving, as it were, into the Danish beech-woods. They compose a gorgeous prodigality of nature, that may compare with all that the South possesses! Even their perishable beauty, the falling

of the leaf, and winter-time are but new revelations. Remember the woods in a rime frost; the endless shades of color
they present, the splendor every tree, every branch, puts forth
in the sunlight!"

"Yes, yes," answered Elizabeth, and she embraced with all
the force of her imagination the Danish beech-woods, as she
had preserved them in her memory.

"And besides the woods, we have the sea," continued Herman; "if not that silk-like, transparent Mediterranean, yet
the living water, that ever-changing sea! When I sailed up the
Thames, the commercial world's great high-road, for the first
time, every eye on the vessel was overwhelmed with the sight
of those hosts of vessels. One could see and understand that
England is the queen of the sea; fishing-boats in full sail
drove on by hundreds, like swans in flocks; then sped past
vessel after vessel. One became tired of counting them;
steamer followed steamer all around me were astonished;—
enchanted; I alone was not astonished, I had seen something similar in Denmark; had seen it at different times in the
Sound, near Elsinore — certainly the only place where a similar
sight presents itself, and that too for a moment when a Rus-
sian fleet passes Cronborg, and merchant-ships by hundreds
scud along under full sail."

"What good it does one to hear this!" said Heimerant, inwardly proud. "Yes, our little land is a blessed land; one
does not know it oneself. Elizabeth has told me about Oland
and Amrom, about those islands near Sleswick, and it was as
if I heard her tell about lands in other parts of the world; for
she can tell a good story very well."

Herman looked with inexpressible mildness at Elizabeth,
who blushed at the value the old man set on her powers of
description.

"It is wild and bare in that part," continued Heimerant;
"and so it is also on the Jutland heaths, for those I have
seen."

"I have not yet seen them," said Herman; "but an enthusiastic Scotchman told me that they were as if cut out of
his native land. He had on the Jutland heaths found the so-
lemnity and solitude of his home, where the damp fogs are

driven by the blast over the dark-brown heathy hills. He showed me two flowering heath branches, between the leaves of a book. One was from 'Ben Lomond,' in Scotland, Rob Roy's land ; the other was from Viborg, in Jutland ; and these flowering heath branches were not to be distinguished from each other — they looked as if they had shot up from the same root. The resemblance between the flowers was also in their soil."

On mentioning Scotland, and Rob Roy's land, Elizabeth was reminded of her favorite poet, and in their admiration of his works all were agreed ; but because Walter Scott never laid his scenes in our days, she expressed her opinion that our times had no poetry in them. Herman asserted the contrary.

"It would otherwise," said he, "be a grievous thing for future poets. I regard even the events of our times as offering the richest gold mines for poetry. Has not even our little Denmark, where everything appears to go on in its quiet course, a whole series of events for poetic treatment? Here we have the stay of the Spaniards in Denmark in 1808. Imagine the southern life that discloses itself in our Danish nature ; here we have Catholic church service performed in the open fields near a tumulus ; Spanish dances amongst hazel-bushes and willows ; the night quarters under ammunition wagons, and cannons in the small streets of provincial towns ; the marches and flight. We will go back to 1801, and see the battle in the roads ; the burning ships, our cannon boats, and the hero of Aboukir and Trafalgar. But you will not go back ; you will come nearer to our time than 1801 and 1808 ? Well then, in our own days we have Thorvaldsen's arrival, the national exultation, the whole people's festivity."

It was such conversations, such hours, that shed their sunny warmth over every slumbering seed in Elizabeth's soul. The visits to the theatre had a similar effect and these were two weekly ; for the old Baroness had a box twice a week, where she had given Elizabeth a seat, that, as the Baroness expressed herself, "she might, like the grocer's boy, get plenty of the prunes when the drawer stood open every day." Many an opera-glass, and many a smiling face were turned towards the box between the acts, and the young girl was soon observed, who had now been taken into "the mad-house," as some persons called the Baroness's box; and yet there was a little more wisdom in it than in most of the other boxes, although the geography had of late never been seen there, as Madame Krone was tired of dragging that great book with her, "which they now knew by heart."

Elizabeth saw every performance with devout admiration, and expressed her opinion of each, when at home, to the Councilor and Herman, and her judgment was sound, because it was natural. Copenhagen was a dangerous city, the greatest, — the only great one she knew. "Here is so much for thought," said she; "one becomes wiser; one learns quickly, more than on our quiet Oland; yet there also it was good. There it was otherwise; every one knew each other; one thought more of" — she stopped, as if perplexed to express her thoughts, but began again with a peculiarly mild expression, as if to soften the words, — "one thought more there of the Almighty! I believe that persons here in Copenhagen are as religious at heart as those over there; but they have not time here to practice it, on account of the bustle and business. I miss — nay, I know not, but I was so accustomed to it; every day at dinner there was a prayer said. God came there more into the words and speech. Here I only hear him named on Sundays in the church."

Herman was a witness of her happiness on receiving the first letters from home. She laughed and cried by turns, and spoke of her arrival at home as if it were to be the very next day — there was so much she had to tell them. But the day of her arrival at home was far distant; Heimerant had said that she should first see the woods put forth their leaves. It was impossible to be otherwise than fond of her; she won all hearts; even Clara paid her attention, and invited her to her brilliant circle, where, at Clara's instigation and "amiable command," she was induced to sing a few of her simple songs. All were enchanted. Herman alone was not — he was still and serious, as if dissatisfied.

CHAPTER XXIII.

OCTOBER and November had passed away with parties and theatricals : Christmas was about to come with all its joys and pleasures, when all was suddenly wrapped in gloom. It was rumored that King Frederick VI. was ill, yet he was not confined to his bed, and every morning gave audiences in full uniform, but on the last two occasions he had looked like a dead man ; his usually erect figure was bent, and he had supported himself by the table with evident exertion. Early on the morning of the third of December, 1839, this news was spread like wild-fire through the city : " The king is dead ! " All the gates of the city were closed, in obedience to an old custom, whilst the troops were taking the oath of allegiance to the new monarch. From the balcony of the palace at Amalienborg it was proclaimed, " Frederick VI. is dead ! — long live Christian VIII. ! " — and all the church-bells rang.

A long reign was ended : a whole generation had grown up under it. There had been something patriarchal between the King and the people. The multitude looked upon his acts with submissive reverence : the royal purple concealed every human weakness. It was a great event for Denmark. There was sadness amongst the people ; all, even menial servants, clothed themselves in mourning ; effusions of genuine loyalty were published in prose and verse. Frederick VI., himself a stranger to poetry, had passages in his life of which the poet might have availed himself. It was in his labors for the oppressed Danish peasants that the King's good and generous heart particularly shone forth. That praise resounded in all the funeral songs ; it arose from the heart of the Danish peasants, who prayed that they might bear his corpse, sixteen long miles, from Copenhagen to Roeskilde Cathedral.

It was the lately deceased King's affection for the peasant, his noble humanity, that touched the deepest string in the old Baroness's heart; she was singularly affected. At every concession to the claims of the peasants, her heart had grown more devoted to King Frederick. She placed his bust upon her table, and arranged the loveliest flowers around it; with her eyes steadily fixed on it, her hands folded on her lap, she sat, and in this position Herman found her.

"A brave man has died this day!" said she. "Now the age to which I belonged has run out! They all leave us; but there will be an end of all." And she sat still and afflicted.

Herman spoke of the King's last hours, of what they knew he had said when the coldness of death chilled him: "It is cold!—we must think of wood for the poor!"

"Yes, he thought of the poor man," said the old lady; "he understood the meaning of hard times; he himself had experienced hard days, experienced them as a child, and as a grown man. You, surely, know something about it, Herman, but you do not know it so well as I do. They made his father believe that the sun and moon stood still; his mother was taken as a prisoner out of the country! Poor Matilda!—she knew not the customs of the country; she was so young and so alone!—King Frederick had a beautiful bride! I remember her entry into the city: eight splendid white horses drew the gilded state-carriage. I saw it—how his fine blue eyes shone—now they are closed! How mild and beautiful was Maria Sophia Frederikha! She now sits in her palace in widow's weeds. We may speak plainly of him now that he is in his coffin. He caused us to lose Norway: he would have his own will, and thought that the first man in the country had also the most knowledge. But I am not going to write his history. I would speak only of his heart; I would speak of that for which the country must bless him. He thought of the poor man; he was generous towards the peasant. I have lived too. I remember other days, when the honest man was put into the dog's-hole; when good conduct rode on the wooden horse, and an innocent child was beaten with the squire's whip!" The old lady stopped, bit her lips, and the color mounted into her cheeks.

" But that time is passed. The peasant lives like a decent man ; sits by the squire's side, and has a word to say with the others in Roeskilde.[1] I have seen good days ; I will forget the bad, and forgive the wicked. However, Herman, I shall give you something that will remind you of this day, and of what I have said to you. You shall have the new manor. Count Frederick will sell it, though I don't think you have learned to be a farmer ; but there are others that understand it, and so you can avail yourself of their skill ; but only let alone dabbling with the ground yourself until you understand it. The poor man can teach you something. Remember that, when I am on my journey after King Frederick."

Everything in Copenhagen wore a deathlike stillness ; all music was mute : crape hung from the instruments and flags. People went in crowds to Amalienborg to see King Frederick VI. on *lit de parade*, as it is still called, from old times, when they *ornamented* the language with foreign words. Ten days had passed since his death. People of all classes went to see the deceased once more : in the forenoon, the different ranks of civil and military ; in the afternoon the mixed multitude, and there was then a terrible crowding and crushing. The streets were lined with hussars and policemen to keep order.

The Baroness would also see King Frederick once more , but Madame Krone, who feared that it would shock the old lady, opposed it in the most determined manner.

" It is not the King that lies there," said she ; " it is rather like a doll. They have embalmed him, enameled him white, and dressed him out ; remember his living, friendly face ; that is better — you shall not have my permission to see him."

" Well, my dear," said the old lady ; " then I must leave it alone, and we will not quarrel. ' Peace at home is good,' said the man when he beat his wife."

But it was destined to be otherwise than Madame Krone and the old lady had determined.

They dined that day at Councilor Heimerant's, where they spoke about the many beautiful verses on the occasion of the King's death. Ingemann's poem, beginning : —

[1] In the provincial parliament.

"On his death-bed pale King Frederick lies;
  E'en from his cradle his pillow was hard;"

composed to the air of "Queen Dagmar's song," could be
sung, and Elizabeth sang it. It was the first time the old
lady had heard her sing; she had seemed not to care to hear
her. Every word was pronounced distinctly, and executed
with simplicity and feeling: her voice was so soft and touching! Tears came into the eyes of the old Baroness; she
kissed Elizabeth, begged her to sing it again, and requested
that she would accompany them home to get a fine present,
drink tea with her, and then sing it once more.

They were all three soon in the carriage. It was a dark
evening; just at the time when the doors to the Knights'
Saloon, where the King lay, were to be closed, and people
issued thence in crowds.

"Should we not drive round about by the street home?"
said Madame Krone; "then Elizabeth can see the illumina-
tion, for the torches are scarcely put out yet."

And the coachman had orders to drive that little way
round; but he had scarcely got through a great crowd and
into the street, where he was driving quickly past the row of
carriages that were still waiting, before a policeman shouted
to him, "Into the rank!"

The Saloon was not yet closed, and a great number expected to gain admission.

"Will you keep in the rank?" shouted the police.

The coachman began to explain that he was to drive home
with his company.

"No nonsense!" said the police. They did not understand what he said, and so — "no nonsense!" into the rank
he was obliged to go.

"What is the matter?" they inquired of each other in the
carriage, which now went slowly on, then stopped, drove on
again, stopped, and again drove on. It was not possible for
the coachman to escape; every time he attempted to get out
of the rank, there came a policeman or a hussar, who threatened and shouted. At length they stopped under the colonnade, and the carriage-door was opened.

"Make haste!" said the man who let down the steps; "it
is much past the time, and there are several carriages yet."

"We shall not go up at all," said Madame Krone, who sat nearest the door.

"You have certainly not driven here without intending to go up," said the policeman; "make haste"—and he drew her out.

"Quick, quick!" said the old lady, and nudged Madame Krone in the side, who was obliged to get out. The old Baroness and Elizabeth followed; the one held by the other in the crowd.

"Now I shall have my will yet," said the old Baroness, "and *you* have led us on, Madame Krone."

"I, who look such a figure!" said Madame Krone. "I have my very worst bonnet on: and now in all that light up there!"

But there was no time to make things better; those behind pressed forward; to turn back was impossible. The stairs, walls, and ceiling were covered with black cloth; here and there hung a ground-glass lamp, the faint light from which scarcely showed against the black ground where some of the national guard were standing like statues, or a picture from a magic lantern; the air was close, and difficult to breathe, from the great mass of persons. It was fatiguing to the old Baroness to ascend the stairs; Madame Krone supported her in the best way she could; Elizabeth followed. She was strangely touched by the sight of this passage to the hall of death: the silence was something to be felt; they went forward step by step through a suite of chambers, all covered with black—wall, ceiling, and floor. Officers, pages, lackeys in mourning, with variously colored shoulder-ribbons, all stood there like statues. The slow pace, the monotony of the chambers, and the expectation, made the way doubly long. No one said a word; Elizabeth experienced a singularly nervous sensation; it was as if the floor moved under her. At length they entered the Knights' Saloon. Sixteen high silver candelabra with lights stood in the chamber of death. The arms of the kingdom, and the provinces, shone from the black walls; yeomen with halberds stood in a long row against the walls, and in the middle of the chamber King Frederick's oldest courtiers, in full dress. Raised on a platform, under the canopy of black velvet and white silk, lay King Frederick the Sixth in his coronation robes.[1]

A trembling sensation passed through Elizabeth. This was the King, of whom she would have sought pardon for Elimar! this was the ruler! here lay his sceptre and crown; here were all his rich valuable jewels and ornaments, — the King, the dead King!

The Knights' Saloon was a vast temple of mourning, the same where, fourteen years before, we were at a court ball; where Clara danced with Holger, and where, the day after, the woman's brush swept away a button, whose fall to earth had great results.

Elizabeth felt a weakness — a giddiness, and if she had not suddenly entered an airy passage, on leaving the hall of mourning, she must have fainted. Her feet trembled; and, as the old Baroness, to support herself better, took hold of her shoulder, she fell down a couple of steps, but recovered herself directly. The old lady, on the contrary, had swooned: she was carried into the porters' room, where she soon came to; and when she was again in the carriage, and the smile reappeared upon her face, Madame Krone began to reproach her.

"I really thought as much," said she; "you ought never to have been there, my lady."

"I had my way; and then one is always glad," said she, but her cheeks burned as with fever. "I shall have a good dose of 'kinderpulver,'[2] when I get home; that is my apothecary's shop, and my doctor."

Next morning, when Elizabeth got up, she felt a stiffness of her knee. It pained her a little, but she did not think of keeping herself still, and the Countess Clara had promised to call that morning and take her to Thorvaldsen's *atelier;* she was to see the great artist himself and speak with him.

Elizabeth, however, went to the Countess, and they drove to Charlottenburg, Thorvaldsen's dwelling.

The friendly old artist received them cordially, took them about himself, and when the Countess expressed herself in

---

[1] Christian VIII. was also buried in his coronation robes.
[2] A quieting medicine for children, generally of rhubarb and magnesia.

rather too exalted a strain, which vexed him, he looked at her face, her speaking eyes, and was in good humor again, for she was still handsome. They were shown everything : the *atelier*, the rooms with the bronzes, and the paintings.

" Ay, but I must also see the most sacred chamber of all," said Clara — " your bedchamber ! "

" There are only my old boots and slippers ! " said Thorvaldsen.

" They, too, one of these days, will get a place in our museum," said she.

And she could say *ours*, for she had taken great interest, and had a good part therein.

" Then I suppose a cobbler will come to live in the cellar," said Thorvaldsen, and an expression of weariness passed over his face.

Clara would go again into the *atelier ;* see every statue again, every bass-relief.

" And where do these doors lead to ? " she inquired, and pointed to two in the chamber.

" To the botanical garden ; we can also go out that way," he added involuntarily, for he was tired, and opened the door.

There had been a heavy frost during the night ; it was now frosty and bright sunshine ; all the bushes and trees were as if crystallized by the rime frost, so that the garden looked quite fairy-like.

Elizabeth, who had regarded all the works of art with a still and solemn feeling, now cried out with surprise, —

" Good Heavens ! how beautiful ! "

Thorvaldsen turned towards her with a smile and saw her animated face, which he had not before taken particular notice of.

" It is a fine sight," said he.

" But there is too much rime frost on every branch," said Clara ; " a little less, and it would have been more picturesque."

" Yet it is very well done, considering that it is the Almighty who has done it," said Thorvaldsen with an ironical smile.

Now they were to see the hot-houses, then to visit again the *atelier* and the chambers. When Elizabeth was once more in the carriage she felt fatigue in all her limbs ; her knee pained her; and when she got home to Christianshavn, she was obliged to lie down from over-exertion; the next day the doctor ordered leeches and a poultice, and directed that she was to keep her bed.

This continued for days, for weeks. The old Baroness was as much concerned as though she had been the cause; she sent every day to inquire after her, and with the inquiry always came presents, such as Italian grapes, silk handkerchiefs, books, etc. Herman brought the best modern productions; the Councilor was like a father to her, and Trina came with a hundred anecdotes from the town and theatre. Many hours she was of course quite alone, but she felt the delight of being entirely so. She could commune with her own heart, where remembrance was awakened within her like an old melody. She saw what uncertainty prevails in this shifting scene, and was entirely herself.

" I collect my thoughts so well," said she, " it is a complete rest for body and mind ! " It was a dear occupation to her to commit to paper all the impressions that Copenhagen had made on her, with her conceptions of all that was new to her, and her remarks thereon ; but no one saw, no one suspected her employment. She still kept her bed when all the churchbells tolled throughout the kingdom for the funeral of King Frederick VI. She heard the bells of the nearer churches ; she knew that the mournful procession now passed through the illuminated streets, where the military lined the road ; she heard the cannons fired from the ramparts. She was almost alone in the house ; all were out to see the procession ; her thoughts followed them as they had once followed Elimar when she also lay ill in bed, and when he departed from Föhr with the seamen, and went to Holland.

The remembrance of Elimar supplanted the thought of King Frederick ; tears came into her eyes, she bent her head and slept and dreamt, as one can dream at times ; that slumber when one seems not to have fallen asleep, but to see everything in the chamber. She saw it all ; saw the air lighted up with every shot of the cannon, and she heard the bells ring. Elimar stood by the bedside, and it appeared to her neither unexpected nor strange that he should do so

They spoke as before, and read their whole future life together in a book. " Now remember it well when you awake ! " said he, and then it was no longer Elimar, but another, whom Elizabeth, as she started up from her sleep, could not remember, nor yet what she had read in her dream. It was as if it had been blotted out, and yet it had been so distinct, so natural. But she knew in the morning that she had dreamt something remarkable on the night that King Frederick's corpse was carried to Roeskilde Cathedral.

Later in the day came Trina, who, with the singers at the theatre, had been in the cathedral and seen all.

" The peasants were the best," said she ; " yes, the peasants in their long jackets with silver buttons. They bore the coffin in at the middle door of the church ; the organ played, and all the bells tolled, and King Christian VIII dressed in black, and the bishop in his cloak, and with his crosier, went to meet them. It was solemn to see, but I did not like it last night in Copenhagen ; they went at such a hurry, at a gallop ; the foremost rode too fast, and the others were obliged to follow ; the funeral car was driven so fast that the coffin danced on it. The poor old men, the commanders, and the councilors had to run, and that I don't think was right. There must be appearance in everything ; one of the old men nearly fainted from fatigue, and I was told that when he got to the west gate, he was obliged to get up behind the funeral car, and now he is dead ; now he lies like King Frederick. They sang, too, from the ramparts ; it was a ' farewell ; ' and the peasants sang by the ' Pillar of Liberty ; ' and then came soldiers and cannon ; they, too, went with the procession from the ' iron gate.' They drove slowly ; I was far behind, and it was not pleasant. Near the town there was a crowd of wild fellows ; they sang and shouted ' Hurrah ! ' and threw snowballs, and ends of torches after us. The soldiers with the hearse stopped at every inn on the road ; they drove up to the door and went in to drink ; it did not look well ; but it was, however, a cold night for the poor fellows. The torches shone so red ! wherever I came up with the procession, there stood a whole crowd of peasants round the hearse, and they sang a psalm, and the bells tolled from all the village churches ; and

in every peasant's house a light shone from the window over
field and road, which were white with snow. I saw Baron
Herman also. I saw him in the church, and he knew me ;
and when the whole was over, and we came away, he greeted
me ; he does so always ; he is a nice and polite gentleman.
He is to have a little estate, so the Baroness has said, and is
to be married this very year."

To whom he was to be married Trina knew not, nor did
Herman himself at that time.

CHAPTER XXIV.

THE COMPOSER.

NOW, Herman is going," said the old Baroness, "but I shall put a man in his place directly. You shall see him. Don't fear, Councilor; it cost a groat; but then he will be driven to your house free of expense."

This person was the Gentleman of the Bed-chamber, who was expected in Copenhagen by the first steamer, and was to complete a new musical work during the summer months, at the Baroness's country seat.

The Councilor said he regretted that he was to lose Herman, whom he was now so accustomed to, who had such a knowledge of books and men, and who spoke so well about his travels.

" Yes," said the Baroness, " so could Gert Westphaler[1] also, and do you not think that I can too when I like? I have travelled quicker than others : have you heard of my Berlin tour? I was in Hamburg, and intended to return home by way of Lubeck, but then I would first see Eulenspiegel's grave in Möln, and so we got into a broad high-road. ' How far does this go ?' I asked. ' To Berlin,' they said. ' What ! are we on the road to Berlin?' said I; 'then let us drive to Berlin.' And so we drove to Berlin, and saw the soldiers, and walked ' unter den Linden,' and got sand in our eyes. I stopped at an inn opposite the post-office, where the landlord was a poet and a little mad after the theatres, but that I am also, and so we two agreed very well together. Has Herman told you anything better than that? I don't mean to say anything against him : he is almost good enough ; but he that I shall put in his place is the pearl: he has genius ; he has what Herman can chatter about, with his definitions and all that.

[1] A garrulous barber in one of Holberg's plays.

15

They must both be provided for. One has dabbled in paint and clay; now he can dabble with grass and potatoes the other, whom great folks would dabble with, but who was too good for them, and who can now snap his fingers at them, shall be indulged, and we must take care that he has a good time of it, both in town and country."

It was, therefore, important to her, as she said, to get her "good child" into honest hands during his stay in Copenhagen. The Councilor had two furnished rooms vacant, and these he was to have.

After the King's funeral everything fell into its course; parties and the theatre were attended as before; but Elizabeth recovered only slowly. It was the beginning of March before she could move about the rooms with the help of crutches, when Herman came to bid farewell before his departure to Funen.

"I shall certainly never see you more," said she; and it was only with the utmost exertion that she was able to restrain her tears.

"Do you, then, think I shall die?" said Herman.

"No, not so, but my home is in a remote corner of the world; and when I am well enough to be able to travel, then, you know, I shall start for Oland."

"But I can come over," said Herman; "I will visit my good friend Moritz Nemmesen. I will take the baths at Föhr —this summer it can hardly be; but who knows what the next may bring forth?"

"Your grandmother is old," said Elizabeth; "the Almighty might call her : you will then have a new and greater sphere of action."

"But then Moritz can come to visit me, and you will accompany him: you will not surely forget me entirely."

"Forget you!" she exclaimed with warmth, "you who have been so extremely kind towards *me*, who am so mean, so insignificant. I have heard and learned so much from your visits to us; and do you think I can forget the evening I saw you for the first time, that evening when," — she stopped, and the blood rose to her cheeks, and the tears gushed forth; "then I saw into your heart. You are good and noble."

"Speak not of that night," said Herman, "my conduct then, my speech — nay, I don't remember what I said to you at the first moment, but I cannot stand in any particularly good light; my behavior afterwards was not different to that in which every other honorable man would have acted. And now 'live well :' thanks for those pretty songs, for the pleasant evenings — God bless you, dear Elizabeth !"

He pressed her hand, and was hastening away, when the Councilor came in. Much more, and on indifferent subjects, was now said; and Elizabeth had time to recover herself. Herman was in good humor, and full of desire and longing after his new sphere of activity in the country — so they parted. Three weeks afterwards the steamer arrived with "the Gentleman."

The spring had also arrived. The air had become milder, or rather, we had begun to get rain instead of snow. The water stood in pools in the streets ; the gutters were choked, and stopped the course of the water, which overflowed on all sides, and every fresh shower threatened to inundate the cellars, and drown a few little children and infirm old folks.

Floating straw and cabbage-stalks drove along ; the harbingers of spring-time ; the worn-out curbstones on the footpath stood with their little cisterns filled ; people jostled each other with their wet umbrellas ; "it was," they said, "delightfully mild weather," and in this mild weather came "the Gentleman."

Still meagre, as when we last saw him, but more lively than of yore, and with that singular mobility in every feature, which, as it were, reflected his thoughts, he now stood before Elizabeth. He remembered her and her sweet voice well, and his visit to the parsonage in Oland.

The life and humor, the volubility, even the sarcasms of "the Gentleman," pleased the Councilor at once. He only objected that "the Gentleman" was not a true patriot, and he told him so.

"I love nature here," he replied, laughing, "but I do not like our generation, — that extremely frivolous, little-minded, trifling Copenhagen ; and, therefore, I live in Christianshavn. It is strange to return here after years of absence, after years so full of events that they seem an age, so changed as if one had stood outside of the world and seen it turn round. Everything here at home is in its old course. Everything alike, just as the shadows that fall from the houses. The same persons in the same places, and in the theatre the same cry of *charmant* in the wrong place, the same ' beating of false time,' the same ingenious remarks. I heard it to perfection yesterday evening during the performance of Mozart's ' Don Juan.' It was one of the gentlemen of the court who spoke; the name is of no consequence, stupidity is enough. He made the remark to me when the ghost appeared, 'that it was so unnatural—that ghost; one ought in these days to make it more probable. Why should it not be one of Don Juan's friends wno had disguised himself in order to warn him, instead of that ghost?' 'But the music does not at all refer to a friend,' said I; but he thought otherwise."

" But does one not meet with such fools in other countries?" inquired the Councilor. "Is Paris really so much before us?"

" Not at all," said "the Gentleman;" "but we are not speaking about Paris; I have a crow to pluck with Copenhagen;" and he laughed and jested at himself; and this was his usual way.

Elizabeth compared their new guest with Herman, to whom she looked up in everything, as many an eye in the wilderness looked up to the Baptist, and the former suffered by the comparison; yet it was only during the first few days. Afterwards, when she heard him play, and heard him expatiate upon music and poetry with that enthusiasm and originality which were peculiar to him, he rose considerably higher in her estimation.

With respect to Heimerant's weak side they however always disagreed, but in this dispute of theirs they approached nearer to each other, and became more confidential. It vas her execution of " Schubert's songs," and the Swedish and Danish ballads, that gave him, as he said, ideas for " Miranda."

" But who will sing it for me like you? I can get a more powerful, a more cultivated voice than yours; but the soul, the innocence — *that* I shall not get. Miranda's part must be simple, as one of Rossini's songs: it must posess all the melody that the heart can breathe forth : on the other hand, falsettos, roulades, trills, and artifices, when the human voice becomes like tones from the flute and violin, I shall give to A:iel's and Caliban's parts, to which they belong — there they will have truth and nature."

Whilst " the Gentleman " composed, Elizabeth sat in her little room and composed also — no one knew this. Often in her solitude would her work sink into her lap. The book she read would close, and she would cradle herself in her own thoughts. That shadowy picture of a poem which first appeared to her in Trina's cellar, came involuntarily forth, subsided, and again appeared every time with a clearer distinctness. She must commit it to paper. It was a little novel, and the matter for it, her first childhood's remembrance, that floating piece of Marsk-land which the sea had borne to land. She made a picture of it in few words. A half dilapidated house stood on the island, and in a corner sat two little children, a boy and a girl. They grew up: they were Elimar and Elizabeth. It represented their childhood's life, their distress and anxiety when the flood came and the water rose to their breasts. Everything was vividly depicted, their terror, their threatened death: but no Jap Lidt Petters came to their aid; the phantom-ship came, that immense phantom-ship, and took them up, and then directed its course to India, — that land of imagination which Keike had portrayed for her from the chronicle of Priest John, the land with the white and red bears, the bird phœnix, and men thirty feet high. And years passed before they reached this country ; the children had grown up and become old, with silvery white hair ; supporting each other, they landed by the well of rejuvenescence, drank of its waters, and became young again, as when they went on board the phantom-ship. Hand in hand they entered Priest John's palace, which was built of gold and ivory ; the gates were of cedar wood, the windows of crystal, and the beds of sapphire overhung with a precious stone which dispels all sickness : twenty thousand men kept watch within it ; they were all kings, dukes, and archbishops ;

and before the palace there was a pillar of crystal, with a mirror wherein could be seen whoever had good or bad intentions towards us, and that over the whole world.

No one had any suspicion of Elizabeth's occupation. She spoke of "the Gentleman's" new composition; it formed a part of their daily conversation together; and even as every thought, every increased emotion, shone forth from his face, so did his melody, spirit, and humor flow from him. He was as singularly susceptible of everything about him as the surface of the water is to receive the colors of the red morning dawn, or under a gray sky to drink in its leaden heaviness and cold.

There was in him an all-embracing sympathy with other natures. Holger was the friend he most usually associated with; this was something quite inexplicable to Elizabeth. These two could not have any points of sympathy, and yet they had "the Adelgunde theme," if we may so designate it. The Oriental elements which formed Holger's life's problem, and afforded him the richest matter for conversation, had in it something attractive for "the Gentleman," who lived purely in the world of sound; the butterfly rests sometimes on the marsh moss, flutters its wings and flies again towards the sun. Hours afterwards, in company with Elizabeth, he listened with a natural and pure mind to what she in her innocence related; he was then in his inmost heart perfectly pious and good: his heart overflowed with gratitude towards every one who had met him in a friendly spirit; but at the same time he showed a remarkable remembrance of every little mortification he had suffered in former years. Whilst, like a sensible man, he acknowledged the nobility of mind as the highest distinction, yet there were moments when "the Gentleman of the Bed-chamber" got the ascendency, and, to use the Baroness's expression, he ought to have "illumined the court calendar." With her he stood in the highest estimation; his most trivial speeches were excellent, and if, as sometimes he did, he advanced anything that was entirely opposed to her view of the matter, she said "It is not he who speaks; he is giving us other people's sayings; it is good enough for us, we don't deserve his own sensible and acute remarks."

He saw his own weaknesses with a clear eye, and from the study of himself he understood others; but by this dwelling on himself he was often led to speak too much about his own person; to make himself the subject of the conversation, on which account others became more free in their judgment of him as if it had been a third person that was spoken of. Thus Elizabeth became more intimate with him; the intercourse was more free than with Herman; "the Gentleman's" life was more like an open book to her. He told her reminiscences of his bitter youth; of his own proud dreams, like Joseph's, and the superciliousness and indignities of others, because he was poor. He played to her his first written compositions, and told her the origin of several others. During one of these conversations, he asked her if she never felt similar musical inclinations, if the tones did not, as it were, well forth in the soul, there, where thought had not words. And she said that she never wanted words; she thought she had an expression for every thought, only that her words were often so transitory, that she could not retain them until they could be committed to paper; and as she explained herself more clearly, her secret was betrayed, and at last, after much persuasion, what she had written was brought forth, and her friend received permission to read it, but no one else, no not one. Elizabeth crimsoned deeply; it was as if she had committed a sin; she now felt that the whole composition was trivial and child-like. "The Gentleman" read, and was astonished at the clear and vigorous language, and the poetic coloring, but particularly at the descriptions of nature. The work was something more than ordinary; he felt that there was a poetic soul in it, and with a lively and warm praise of it, he pointed out particular passages, and gave a signification to them that she had never thought of, but which they nevertheless conveyed. Priest John's kingdom was the land of poetry and art, wherein the old found the strength of youth, and life's whole beauty again. "The Gentleman" became a commentator, as many have become. His delight gave value, in the eyes of Elizabeth, to what she had written; his encouragement was like the sun's kiss on the flower after rain; his strong interest for her was not concealed, but certainly its cause was, and that must surely be, "He is in love!"

That at least was the old Baroness's idea, and she looked at him with an expression of affection, and shook her head gently.

"My good child," said she, "pray do not go and dream of a wife until you get one. Adam did so, but the wife he got was no good. There are women's hearts that are like a post-bag, which is full of sealed letters, but the letter itself does not know what is in it."

The Baroness, however, came oftener than before to the Councilor's, and spoke in her way, or, as she called it, sensibly, with Elizabeth, who rose more and more in her favor; and suddenly, one day in May, shortly before the Baroness's departure for Funen — she was invited to accompany her.

"For it will do you good," said the old lady; "there you will have peace and quiet, and green woods; there is also a doctor near at hand, and the cuckoo will tell you how long you have to live. We shall go by the steamer; it is one day's voyage, and then you will be half-way home to your island."

She said the same to the Councilor; they talked again and again about it; Moritz was written to, and it was decided. "The Gentleman" found this arrangement excellent; Elizabeth smiled through her tears; it was a separation from her Copenhagen home, but it led to the woods in Funen, to her arrival at home in Oland.

Trina was most pleased about it.

"I wish I could go with you," said she, "and Hansen too. God bless me, I would not travel without him. It is beautiful in Funen; that is my land, though I am a Copenhagener. Remember me to Madame Katrineson; her husband I know is dead. His death was in the papers, with a little verse; and do you know where it was taken from? Why, from my wedding song, which Katrineson himself made! Yes, go to my dear Funen, and God grant that you may inherit the Baroness's property; but, however, it may go with you, do not forget me nor Hansen either; he is a rare man. His cousin the diver spoke about you yesterday, and begged us to give his respects. For Heaven's sake write to me; you know the cellar in Pink Street."

Heimerant was out of spirits. "It was," he said, "as if he were again about to lose one of his children."

" They are all dispersed far and wide : my eldest son is in the East Indies, the second in Archangel ; the two youngest the Lord took from me ; he took them to himself — those two then are the nearest to me."

And the steamer went to Funen.

The weather was fine, the wind fair, so that they hoisted sail ; the sun had not yet gone down when they reached Svendborg, whence they were some miles distant from the Baroness's estate.

That which in Funen so vividly reminds one of England, and in both enchants the eye, is the fresh verdure, the living hedges, and the beautiful groups of trees in the fields, which give the country the appearance of a garden. This sight delighted Elizabeth. The sun, however, had gone down when they drove from Svendborg homewards, but the sky was like gold ; the full moon was quite pale amid all this splendor ; there was a quiet in the whole scene as if all the woods around slept ; and in the villages they passed through, where the bell had lately rung at sunset, were groups of gossiping girls. The farmer's men played at skittles, and the peasant's little daughter came sauntering along with her cow ; it had been grazing all day by the road-side, and was now driven home ; the fields with their spring grain looked like green velvet ; the ditches like the horn of plenty, filled with flowers ; and as they drove on the clouds became paler, the moon assumed a stronger lustre ; it became more and more still on the road and in the villages, and a bluish mist arose from the meadows, like the ghost of that lake which had once extended its waters here. Every remembrance of childhood was awakened in Elizabeth's heart.

She approached the garden solitude, and the old mansion within it ; its jagged gable overgrown with green stood out sharp against the clear air ; a stork's nest was at the very top ; there slept the stork's family, for it was past midnight. Lights moved about within the house ; they saw them through the window-panes. Elizabeth again saw the living espalier within, the old portraits ; the Commander's, with his star on his breast, and the lady with the parrot on her hand. Everything was so familiar, but smaller, much smaller than she had

imagined. The long passage where the floor bulged — it did
so still — was, she thought, but half as long as when she was
a child. A pretty room towards the garden awaited her ; and
when she retired to rest there, the moon shone in at the window, on the hangings, on which bounding stags were represented. She almost thought that her life in Oland and Copenhagen was but a dream ; but in that dream she had become
older, wiser, and had found the invisible thread that went
through hers, as through every human being's life.

CHAPTER XXV.

ELIZABETH was now again in Funen.

She again sat under the fresh green beeches; the whole wood had an aspect of purity and peace, which is refreshing to the eye, and makes the mind young again. The nightingale sang, not funereal dirges, but heart-felt solemn lays, clear as a bell.

A little donkey was saddled for Elizabeth. "The Gentleman" walked by her side, and thus the tour of the garden and the wood was made. Sometimes they drove out, and then it was on frequented roads and through villages, for the Baroness liked to see people. The little peasant boys — they have almost all light yellow hair, and brown faces — gave their comical nod as if they had just received a blow on the back of the head; the girls, great and small, *dipped candles*.[1] This was a pleasure to the Baroness to see.

"They have not been at the dancing-school, like Trina!" said she: "that is natural courtesying; I could do it once, but I have lost it through years and idleness."

They visited the rich peasants, where they sat in the great room between high-made beds, where one disappears in the down; they saw what was "spun and won," what linsey-woolsey and wadmel were made. But they also entered the poor peasant's clay-floor cottage, where the hen had a corner by the family bed, and where there was often under the bare loft so much goodness and honesty, that more than the Almighty might have regarded it. This the old lady spoke of, in her way. At the door of the sick she stopped and asked how they were going on; the best wine from her cellar was not too good here. The simple words in the poor man's thanks, the

[1] Made a quick courtesy.

eyes that spoke, when the words could not find utterance, forced their way to the heart, and did good, like the sunshine and the fresh green woods.

Herman, who, the day after his grandmother's arrival, paid her a visit, was a constant guest every Sunday, although his estate was full twelve miles distant, towards the Great Belt. He and "the Gentleman" had only seen each other many years before, when they both, though differently treated, were the guests of Count Frederick's father. They soon understood each other's abilities. When they spoke of art and poetry, Elizabeth always approached nearer to them, but they could never induce her to join in the conversation. In Herman's presence she quite undervalued herself, and could only say a word now and then. One day she felt this: the Gentleman of the Bed-chamber led the conversation to compositions of the kind to which her writings belonged, and she thought Herman's judgment severe and that he fixed his eyes searchingly on hers ; and yet he did not know her "only fault," as a poet has called it.

"It is not enough," said Herman, "to be able to write down one's thoughts correctly,— that belongs to the refinement of our age,— but the main point is what those thoughts are ; it is not enough that they give a reflection of what we already possess ; a new flower must be added to the tree of poetry ; or a weaker leaf must be strengthened and developed."

"I too think," said the other, "that that poetical work, during the reading of which we are not enriched by a new thought which is either perfectly presented, or which before lay indistinct in ourselves, is a mediocre work. But *you* seem to demand an entirely new art of poetry ; to expect a Messiah in our time in the world of poetry ! — and can we do so ? "

" I think that the time has not yet come," answered Herman ; "there is so much intimated that is not yet executed ; there is so much that must be first brought to light and truth. In novels and romances, I would not have events alone, but characters and poetry ; a novel that contains only events is read but once ; the unexpected, the surprising, which was the life and soul of it, is departed, dead after perusal ; on the contrary, where the human character appears forcibly and nat-

urally drawn; where thoughts exist in living words; where
poetry has its imperishable growth,— to such a work we return
again and again: that book is read and reread; one comes
from it refreshed, as from a ramble in the woods in spring."

"But have we not in part, such an author in Jean Paul?"
inquired "the Gentleman."

"He is very near it," answered Herman; "and would be
one of the most interesting, if he were not the most fatiguing
author I know. He can indicate, but he will not be the Columbus of this age, to lead us to the coast of a new region of
poetry; the voyage is long enough, and has its brilliant natural
wonders, but we are ever in suspense or expectation. He has
no firm ground; the persons we meet with are not flesh of
our flesh: the soul conceals as it were the body from us; we
feel, if I may use the expression, the fragrance of the flower,
but do not see the flower itself — that bodily comprehensive-
ness which we perceive in Walter Scott. This author and Jean
Paul, so different in their productions, and yet so alike in
poetical power, would, I think, could they coalesce and be
brought into a compressed representation, be a type for our
age's new poets. Everything must be true, clear, and concise;
encircled with that fragrance which exists in our national ballads; that lyrical power which beams around Calderon's
dramas, and this may even be breathed into the tale of prose:
it is not the metrical interweavings of the words, but the
metal in them that speaks to the hearts of nations."

Whilst Herman spoke, Elizabeth's thoughts rose to the *ideal*
he pointed at, and she felt what child's play her writings were.

"The Gentleman," on the contrary, found in them an un-
conscious approximation to the standard laid down, which
Herman would acknowledge if he read them, and that he
must do; therefore he begged her to let Herman read them;
but she blushed deeply at the request, and refused it in the
most determined manner.

"And you can think and say so, after having heard his
words to-day?" said she.

But he returned often to the same point; his conviction
was sincere, it gave weight to his words, and with fear and a
mingled feeling of desire and disinclination, she offered them

to him, on condition that Herman, if he found, as she was convinced he would, that they were worthless, would never speak to her about them.

And weeks passed away.

"Herman finds them excellent," said " the Gentleman."

" I do not believe it," replied Elizabeth ; "he did not say a word to me about them the last time he was here. You do not know how uncomfortable I felt myself; it was as if a mountain were interposed between us. I did not venture to be alone with him."

" And by that means you were yourself the cause of his not having the opportunity of speaking with you and thanking you."

"Herman has regarded them as what they are, the occupation of an invalid," thought she ; and yet she treasured up every word of praise that " the Gentleman " delivered as Herman's. These words were regarded as a metal which she did not know whether to consider as genuine or false, and which therefore must not be cast away.

One Sunday afternoon, as Elizabeth sat in the garden under the red thorn, Herman approached. They were alone.

" I thank you for your confidence in me," said he. "What you have written is pretty and natural, and excels particularly in what most writings in our time want — piety. I ought to congratulate you, because I really, as an elder brother, am fond of you. You have an eye for nature and mankind ; you have a heart and purity, as woman should have both; and yet with these great gifts, and whilst they shine forth with a desire to produce something, I am grieved for you. In all sincerity I speak to you : you have courage to come forth before the world, as it were to share with it what God has given you; but remember, that from the moment you do so you no longer belong to yourself — you must be prepared to find that your best feelings may be misunderstood. You know that I have always upheld the good that is in our native land, but now is the moment when I must point to its opposite. Good-nature is not, at least at this time, a characteristic of the Danish nation ; there is in us a tendency to deride, which is far more conspicuous. We have a keen sense of the ludicrous, from which cause we possess a literature of comedies; but amongst the multitude this sense is perverted into a desire to turn things inside out or upside down, — to turn everything into ridicule. Have you strength and courage to bear the derision of the fool? nay, even the best and noblest may vex you. Well then, I will not say a word more. What is a divine mission will make its way; but do not call forth these feelings in you, do not cherish a flower that deteriorates the good soil, and prevents the thriving of that which might be perhaps more useful and better."

" I know you mean well and kindly towards me," said Elizabeth, — "*you* I believe most firmly and sincerely; but believe *me* also, when I say that I have never found anything more in writing than the pleasure I have had when alone in singing a song that came into my mind! but I may have been led astray by hearing another, who placed his own poetic soul in my written words. I assure you, that from this moment I will never commit anything similar to paper."

" That would be an injustice towards me, towards yourself!" said Herman; "yet your good sense will guide you. What I said was from an elder brother's heart; let it be a counterbalance to you, against the perhaps too great enthusiasm another feels for you; and now give me your hand as an assurance that you have received my words in as good part they were offered — that we are friends."

" Still more than ever," exclaimed Elizabeth, with a vivacity and a warmth that almost terrified herself — and she only pressed the hand gently she herself had seized.

It was the 14th of August; that day which the old Baroness liked best in the almanac, as she said, and had chosen as her birthday, when the poor came in the forenoon and got their presents, which was still the custom, and a great party was invited to dinner. Early in the morning she went to the private chamber, but this time she took Madame Krone with her, who was not a little surprised at the invitation.

"No one sees when sleep comes," said the old lady, "and still less when death comes. It is good to have one's house in order before one lies down; so I will do that to-day, and you must help me, Madame Krone. I have thought of it ever since I bade farewell to King Frederick ; he was no warrior, however fond he may have been of soldiers, neither will I be. I will conclude a peace, and that on my birthday. There sits my father-in-law," and she pointed to the old portrait that was set up on the remains of the wooden horse. " He looked just as angry, nay, still worse. He is the first I can remember from my childhood ; he stood in such a red coat as you see there, with his horsewhip in his hand ; it cracked over my head, it made a long blood-red blister over my head and neck, and I was a little innocent child creeping about the pavement under the wooden horse, which my poor father rode on with stones bound to his legs. I can remember how terribly my mother screamed, and he there in the red coat kicked the poor sick woman, so that she fell on the pavement. I never could forget it ; I have had the scream many a time in my ears ; I have felt the blow of the whip burn over my temples ; and that I have not become mad is not my fault. But we must be Christian beings ; I would willingly be so, but we are not rightly fitted for Christianity, Madame Krone ; the will is not sufficient. But now that time is past. King Frederick lies in his tomb, and I certainly keep my last birthday to-day ; so I will not be borne from under the roof with him there, without having first settled accounts and pardoned him."

She took the portrait, which was half loosened, from the worm-eaten frame.

" It shall be put under the poor man's soup-kettle," said she — " it and all the wood there : help me, Madame Krone. I will burn him, and when he becomes ashes, I will hope that he may not burn elsewhere. See how fresh the plank still is ; it was the horse's back ; it shall not be burnt. I can make good use of it ; it is no nonsense, it is a charitable thought."

" You have always been good and charitable," said Madame Krone ; " and it is right and sensible to have all this burnt — it ought to have been done long ago."

" He acted ill to me and mine, towards every poor child ; yes, towards his own flesh and blood ; his own son was good from the hands of the Lord, but was bungled and spoiled, and for that I have wept many a time ; but *that* I have found out of late. The dead man does not sleep so soundly, but that there is some part of him that hears and knows what happens here. He who lifted his horsewhip has been obliged to lie still in his coffin and see poor Dorothy drive into the court-yard with four horses, — see his son and his name die away, and Rasmus's daughter become a Baroness. After me there will come another name, and then there are none who will know the race. Another name, which perhaps is not even the right, the honest one " — She stopped, and a bitter smile passed over her lips.

"Do not say anything more against Baron Herman," exclaimed Madame Krone ; "the very thought is sinful ! "

"And those we have many of," said the old lady ; "I have myself said it to him once. I shall be glad if I may be permitted to beg our Lord pardon for it. But my daughter's child he is, and therefore he will be master of the estate here, when I leave it for the church."

"His mother shed salt tears over him, when he was an infant," said Madame Krone : "his mother was as angelically pure as any on this earth."

"Yes, don't make me think otherwise of her," said the old Baroness, with great vehemence ; "she was pure and honest in her very heart and thoughts ; but my meaning, nevertheless, is not built on air and false words. She was pure as an angel, that I say, and she is with God. I have more guilt ! — one should always fear God and keep to the high-road : if we had been on the high-road to Naples, it would have been better for us all together. I have never told you rightly about it, Madame Krone ; it is not pleasant to talk about. I was in Rome with my daughter, where she was betrothed to Bunke-Rönow, the Holsteiner. They were married early one morning, and we set out in the carriage directly afterwards for Naples ; but I would not go by the high-road — I would go over the mountains. We were there in the middle of the day ; in the afternoon we continued our journey ; we were all mounted on asses, and the guide ran by the side. It looked very wild and romantic ; it was solitary, and evening came on, and we were constantly getting more and more followers ; our party became too great ; they had both knives and guns ; and just as I was thinking what would happen, our guide ran

away. One gun only was fired, and Rönow's servant, who
was tall and strong, was shot dead. There were three to each
of us; they bound Rönow's hands — it was a fine marriage-
day he had! At last we had all to walk between stones and
bushes. It was up and down: one of the robbers, a young
active fellow, helped my daughter; he was handsome of his
kind. There were some caverns in the mountains like stables,
into which we were taken, and there they talked their slang;
and then Rönow was unbound. He was to procure money by
a certain hour, and bring it to a place they appointed? and he
had one of the robbers to accompany him. I and my daughter were obliged to remain there. They did us no harm; they
gave us meat and drink, and I told them how hard it was, and
that it was not Christian-like. I told them, too, that it was
my daughter's marriage-day; that she had been married that
morning. 'Poor child!' said the rascal who had helped her;
and then he laughed with those eyes of his: they were still
blacker than Herman's, and his teeth shone as white as those
in Herman's mouth; and so we remained there in the stable.
I got a hole to lie in; it was a fine night's sleep I had; he,
with the black eyes, took care of my daughter. Next evening
the ransom came, and we were politely and safely conducted
to the road, set on asses, and told that we were to follow the
path we were on, and we should then come to the husband,
and we did so. The first we met with was Rönow, who was
compelled by them to wait for us where we found him. But
before we parted from the rascals, he with the black eyes and
the white teeth came, and kissed my poor child, who was as
pale as death. He said words to her that I have hidden in
my heart; hidden with that smile he had, and the appearance
of his person when he stood up on the stone and waved his
red neckcloth as we rode away. Yes, so it was — but you
must not let this story be printed, Madame Krone, nor will I!
Now take the rest of that wooden rubbish; I have taken what
I can, and then we will go to the kitchen, and get it to blaze
well under the poors' soup-kettle."

Before they left the private chamber, Elizabeth, who could
now take a walk without a stick, had left the mansion and
gone into the wood, whence she followed the path over the

meadow to the church. The door to the church porch was open, the organ sounded sweetly to her; she knew it was "the Gentleman," who often took the key of the church-door and went there to play alone. She stopped by a grave; it was Katrineson's; one of the verses he had written for Trina's wedding, and which was printed in the newspaper with the announcement of his death, was also inscribed here as an epitaph: his verses were thus put to use. From the grave Elizabeth went into the church, and straight up to the altar, where the tones of the organ could be best heard.

It was a pretty village church with whitewashed walls and vaulted roof: in the choir was an old painting representing a man in the dress of an ecclesiastic, with a long beard; he stood between his two wives, and all his children, the sons to the right and the daughters to the left: the youngest stood in the foreground: they were all dressed alike and with folded hands. Opposite this, in the choir, was the family chapel, separated from the church by an iron-railing; within this the coffins were placed in rows, but in the middle of the floor there stood the magnificent marble sarcophagus, brought from Italy, in which were the remains of the wicked Baron, the old lady's father-in-law. Here, when alive, he had rioted with his brother revelers; here he had sat in the open coffin and drunk the most reprobate toasts, and had suddenly been silenced in the midst of them. He sat there dead, with his face of a dark blue color. Now it was still and peaceful here; a sunbeam fell through the window on the old suspended banners, and the white marble coffin at whose foot two carved angels wept; but there came no tears from the eyes, said the peasants, "for there could come none for that fellow."

The last tones of the organ died away; and "the Gentleman" came into the church to Elizabeth.

Herman had arrived at the manor-house at the time they were in the church; his horse was put into the stable, and he himself went from room to room: there was no one to be found.

"The Gentleman of the Bed-chamber is most likely in the church," said the footman, and Herman went there. He did not hear the organ, but the door to the porch was open; there must be some one. As he walked up the aisle he saw

Elizabeth and "the Gentleman" sitting on the kneeling bench before the altar, in conversation.   They did not observe him : a thought struck him and he turned back to the porch, whence one could ascend into the loft up a little open staircase.   The vaulted roofs rose here, like one baker's oven by the side of another.   Herman, however, found the way to the part that was directly over the choir, and where, by taking a board noiselessly away, he made an opening directly over their heads, from which he could see and speak to them.

The organ had ceased playing only a few minutes before Herman came, and "the Gentleman" had gone down to Elizabeth.   They looked at the portraits of the Clergyman's family, and Elizabeth found that the Clergyman in particular was painted so life-like, that it seemed as if he would walk out of the frame and speak to them.   " But now, this morning, in clear sunshine, I do not think that it would terrify me !"

" That depends on what he might ask you, does it not ? " said " the Gentleman," with a smile.

"I have heard that one should answer spirits briefly and firmly ; then they have no power," said she ; "besides, I do not know by what question I should be frightened."

"One could certainly be found."

" And that would be ? " — she asked.

" If he now placed himself before us,"exclaimed "the Gentle-man," "and asked you, — yes, he might do so, — 'will you give your hand to that man who sits by your side, and be his wife ? ' "

" Then I would answer, 'We are not betrothed, and we do not think of being so !' "

" But now if *I* thought of it," said "the Gentleman" seri-ously, and seized her hand. — It was just at that moment that Herman looked down to them from the opening above, but he did not hear a word ; he did not hear what was said. "Yes, Elizabeth ! you are so very dear to me, I could indeed be happy with you, unspeakably happy — I venture to tell you so in this holy place ! — be my wife ! "

No, Herman did not hear it, and yet he started back invol-untarily, surprised at the cordiality with which " the Gentle-man " seized Elizabeth's hand — perplexed at having, per-

haps as an eaves'-dropper, intruded upon a secret   He stood
for a moment, uncertain whether to speak or be silent, to go
or to stay ; he durst not push the board over the opening, as
he might perhaps awaken their attention by the noise ; he
would steal gently away.   What had been said ?   What connection was there between their words and what he had seen ?
They were still talking, but he did not catch the words — he
would not hear them — when at that moment his own name
was audibly pronounced by "the Gentleman."

   "Herman ! you love Herman !" said he, — "answer me !"

   And Herman heard it ; the blood mounted to his brain :
he would have hastened away, but stumbled and fell ; he
crawled awkwardly over the vaulted roofs back again, and
when he reached the bottom of the stairs he stood still for a
moment, in doubt with himself whether he should remain or
retire.   Just then steps were heard ; the door to the church-
porch was flung to ; it was Elizabeth who had hastily broken
off the conversation, and now left the church followed by "the
Gentleman."

   When Herman arrived at the porch he found himself locked
in : perhaps there was another place of exit from the church
itself; at least he could escape through one of the windows ;
they were, however, very high.   His thoughts were in a ferment ; he sat down before the altar where the two had sat just
before.   "You love Herman !" he repeated to himself ; and
what had she answered — what had caused that exclamation?
What connection was there between those two?

   His thoughts descended from his brain to his heart ; he
walked a few paces, and remained standing before the iron-
railing in front of the open chapel : the nearest coffin was the
least ; a withered wreath of flowers lay upon it ; it was renewed every year.   It must be Herman's mother who rested
there ; the coffin by the side of it contained his father.   The
sight deeply affected him, for it was the first time he had ever
been to the burial chapel, and yet so near his deceased parents.   He could not remember either of them, for he was but
little more than a year old when they died.   He remembered
what his grandmother had said years ago, in bitterness, about
his birth ; and the image of the robber clad in silk and velvet,

on the way to the place of execution appeared to his imagination — his own mirrored image, with the dark eyes and shining white teeth. To this figure another succeeded; it was Elizabeth's father, as he stood in the billiard-room and wiped his eyes with the woolen tassel of his cap.

And now the two who lately sat here before the altar, and what had been said, — all passed with the rapidity of thought through Herman's head and heart too quickly to put words to them, but even without words we may understand them. He had stood some minutes, when a key was turned in the little door which led from the chapel into the church-yard; the door was opened, and the old Baroness and Madame Krone entered. They looked at him with astonishment.

"Herman!" said his grandmother; "you here!"

"I could find no one in the house," he replied, "and so I came over here, and have been locked in. I certainly did not expect that you would come here. This is not the place to pay you my greeting on your birthday."

"O, never mind; you can congratulate me," said she. "Do you not yet know that this was never my birthday? It was not registered when I was born, but this date has been remembered — this day, when he there in the marble coffin, did my father, my mother, and me, cruel wrong; therefore I have done poor folks good on this day. But you shall not praise me for that, for I will not be praised. I had malicious feelings in my heart against him, but now old King Frederick has prayed to our Lord for the lords of the soil, as he here prayed for the peasants."

Herman nodded to the old lady kindly and sympathizingly.

"Now, this morning I have rummaged out and put my house in order," continued she, "and I have put all to rights in my own heart, for that one should always do. I came here to say that the past is forgotten, and now I will not come hither again until I am borne hither. I will tell you what, Herman: I should like much to lie outside the church, and not to have my coffin standing for show, like a chest of drawers. Give me your hand. Here sleeps your mother; she was pure and innocent as God's angels! — make her happy and make me happy, by being good towards the poor. We are all of one piece — all made of the same clod of earth ; one came in a newspaper, another in gilt paper, but the clod should not be proud of that. There is nobility in every class ; but it lies in the mind and not in the blood, for we are also all one blood, whatever they may say : what runs in the veins near the heels has before been through the heart, and will come there again ; it is even so within us, and it is even so with those around us. Remember that ! And now we will go, **my son.**"

CHAPTER XXVI.

THE SEPARATION AND THE MEETING.

THE peasants got their presents of woolen and linen, of provisions and playthings, in the great hall at the manor-house. — "And the Baroness spoke freely with us," said they. Herman sat at the breakfast-table quite alone ; "the Gentleman" had excused himself from coming, as he was composing ; Elizabeth, however, made her appearance, and shook hands with Herman ; but she wore a slightly disturbed aspect. She had some arrangements to make, she said, and Herman was again alone. He went into the garden, and "the Gentleman" suddenly stood before him, so free, so lively, and cordial ; it was not as if anything had lately moved him strongly. He spoke of his music, his last composition, and how well it proceeded.

" I lie here as in a quiet harbor," said he, " and roll about by myself, without being disturbed from without ! They have been productive months for me, but my nature is not formed for such continual peace ; during the last few days I have at times felt a disquiet and desire to travel ; to-day I have had such an attack. There is something of the nature of a bird of passage in me ; that instinct by which it is inexplicably driven from its comfortable nest compels it thence on the very finest day. I believe I shall also fly before I know it myself."

" I have known the same at an early period," answered Herman ; "it lies in the mind of youth ; and you, with a strongly gifted poetic nature, have preserved it longer than I : it is an instinct that must be the same as with the bee, to fly forth and gather honey."

Whilst they thus strolled about the garden, in conversation concerning inclinations and situations, which, however, did not touch on the events of the morning in the church, one carriage rolled into the yard after another with guests. They did not seem to notice their arrival, until the footman came to inform them how late it was.

Herman got a place at the dinner-table by the side of an old acquaintance, who was happy in sitting by a man who had seen so much of the world.

" It accomplishes, it instructs one," said he ; " how have I not wished myself in your place, for I know what it is to travel. I have visited most parts of Germany, have been in Hamburg, Hanover, Frankfort, and other places ; but what is that compared to your travels ? "

He was the Councilor from Odense, whom the reader may perhaps recollect seeing at an earlier period of our story. He had become visibly older ; his gray hair was thin over his forehead : his companion through life's voyage had left him — he was a widower.

Elizabeth sat on the opposite side ; she did not once look at Herman ; on the contrary, it appeared to him as if she regarded "the Gentleman" several times with a sad and thoughtful look, nay, that once, even tears forced their way into her eyes, which, however, she restrained.

" And he can believe that *she* loves me ! " thought Herman ; " he can forget what a difference there is between her age and mine ; she sixteen, I thirty-four ; double — yes, more than double ! She, that child whom I have borne in my arms and pressed to my heart ! But is *he* not older even also than myself? Yes, he must be so ; but his years are not to be seen in his face, or in his mind ; that is young, like hers ! The soul is, however, the root and flower of our life's tree ! "

His eyes were cast down thoughtfully, and when he again looked up it was at Elizabeth, who sat opposite to him in all a maiden's loveliness and beauty. Yes, he felt that man was formed after God's image ; *hers* imprinted itself upon his thoughts, to follow him to his home, and there, like the sun's rays when concentrated in the burning-glass, to work with stronger power.

The same evening, after the party had broken up, " the Gentleman " had a long conversation with the old Baroness, and it was in consequence of this that Madame Krone, next day, received a small lecture, which will bring us a step further on with these events. It was a lecture on "matrimony."

"One should not play the Lord," said the Baroness; "one should not pair folks together. It is not right, Madame Krone, and I have never done it."

"Nor I either," answered Madame Krone; "nor do I know at all why you say this to me."

"Because I say it to myself," said the Baroness. "I have read in an old book, or I have myself imagined it—I don't rightly remember—but it is indifferent, for it is not to be printed, that every person is a sort of half ball which is rolled about the world, and will have the right half part that belongs to it, so that it may be whole."

"Yes, but of what use is that?" said Madame Krone.

"Then they roll better," said the Baroness; "there comes one half part, and ther ecomes another half part; they come together directly, but they do not fit rightly! they roll badly, and often separate, and that is not the worst of it. Thus I thought about my good child 'the Gentleman,' and little Eli·abeth, that they were two halves to a right whole: I have not brought them together, and would not play the Lord, but I set them on the road and thought,—now they may run. For it is bad, Madame Krone, when one half rolls about in Greenland, and the other half in France—they don't find each other. I have thought in my way, but I have thought wrong. They will not run together: he has been set in motion all at once, and will roll away to Paris, and now she can trundle to Oland: I shall not meddle with it!"

The day was fixed for the departure of "the Gentleman." He would go—he must go.

"I am not so selfish that I should wish to keep him here," said the old Baroness; "he belongs to the world? he is a wine that must be kept in a golden bowl, and not stand here in the slop-basin. He shall travel; I will have it so." And tears came into the old lady's eyes.

It was as if that restlessness which drove him from the manor, had also seized Elizabeth. She was now perfectly recovered, and almost a whole year had passed since she left her home on Oland, — but how rich had not that time been! She felt that she had become an entirely new being. The time of her childhood appeared to be far, far distant; she was elevated high in thought and seriousness, yet all the while in sunshine and gladness. Kind eyes had looked on her; all had met her cordially and with friendliness; but during the last three days it had been otherwise; it was as if she had humiliated a man who was sincerely good towards her, and for whom she felt as for a dear brother, not less, but yet not more.

It was the last evening "the Gentleman" was at the old manor: there was a life, vivacity, an activity — a restlessness about him, as if he already stood with one foot in the midst of Parisian life. The "Marseillaise" sounded again from the piano, and that infernal theme from "Robert le Diable," and Beranger's songs, the most striking of them, — "Reine du monde, O France, O ma patrie!" The old Baroness was just as lively as ever, but when the clock struck ten, the usual bed-time, or rather the time when they themselves broke up in summer, her smiling face assumed a grave expression, and the tears stood in her eyes.

"Farewell, my good child! be honorable and clever, as you have always been! I shall not get up early in the morning with the sun; so I will now bid you farewell once for all!" She took hold of his cheek: "Let me see your face rightly, see if I have it, and can remember it wherever I may be. God bless thee, my good honest child! Go, go! farewell!"

And "the Gentleman" was obliged to hasten his departure. He had just time to press Elizabeth's hand, but not to speak: the old lady motioned towards the door; his eyes dwelt for a moment, tenderly, sadly, and kindly on Elizabeth; he looked at the Baroness, nodded, and was out of the room.

When Elizabeth went to her chamber, she sat down directly to her writing-desk. She could not do otherwise; she must express herself freely, openly, to her friend, her brother, and bid him an affectionate, hearty farewell! She told him with perfect innocence and sincerity how afflicted, how sorry she was; she begged him to forgive her, to be good and kind to her as a brother! A lover would have read hope and happiness in these lines, but he would assuredly have been mistaken.

She had made a purse of tricolored silk; it had been finished a week already, and destined for "the Gentleman," when they separated; but in the hurry with which his departure had been determined, Elizabeth had forgotten this little *souvenir.* It was taken out, the letter was placed in it, and she went to bed in order that she might get up early the next morning, and bid him farewell a second time. Sleep would not visit her eyes; the hours passed slowly by under heavy floods of sorrowful thoughts. At daybreak she dozed a little, but started from her sleep, for an open carriage drove into the yard: it was the one that was to convey "the Gentleman" to Assens, whence he would reach Kiel by the steamer the same day. Elizabeth sprang out of bed and dressed herself in haste; she took her letter out again; she must read it through once more; when just at that moment the carriage drove out of the yard. "The Gentleman" had everything ready when it came, not to keep it waiting for him. Elizabeth sprang to the window, having stuck the letter quickly into the purse. "The Gentleman" drove out directly under her, so that she could have cast it into his lap. She thought so, but wavered in her thoughts, and then he was some distance from the yard; he turned round and looked up to the window.

"Farewell, farewell!" she cried, with emotion. He answered by waving his hat; but she held the purse and letter fast in her hand; the carriage turned round by the farm-buildings, and out of the first gate. Elizabeth looked at the clouds; they were tinged with red from the rising sun.

The following week Elizabeth was to return to her home in the Halligers. Moritz would then meet her at Flensborg, on the day of the steamer's arrival there, but she must travel alone from Funen by the steamer to Flensborg. She could not see Herman's estate, though this visit had frequently been determined on whilst "the Gentleman" was still at the manor. It had, however, always been put off, from one cause or the other, and now it was quite given up, but not by Madame Krone, who liked the place so well, and would have Elizabeth to see her birthplace.

"Yes, now it looks quite different; instead of the old, ruinous manor-house, the muddy, overgrown moat, there is now a little paradise, the prettiest country-house imaginable, and so

delightfully situated, with a prospect over the Belt and Langeland."

It would be a sin if Elizabeth should not go there, was Madame Krone's meaning, and therefore, three days before the
time for Elizabeth's departure, she had, by her diplomatic
talent, got it settled that Elizabeth and herself should pay a
visit there. The Baroness, however, would, as she said, be
free of them both, and amuse herself at home.

There was a distance of about twelve miles to drive, but the
country was very pretty, particularly after they had left the
main road; they then came into a hilly and woody district
which, at several points, had something of a park-like appearance: the way led past declivities, where one looked through
the tops of old, high beeches down into great mill-dams. The
water-mill lay so far down that the blue smoke, which ascended from the chimney, had a long way to rise past the
dark, elevated woody ground behind. Beautiful grass-plains
stretched along the hills, surrounded by woods, and where an
old willow-tree stood close by the wayside, so gnarled and
split, that one would think it must fall; it bore in its split
trunk and rugged top a whole wilderness of raspberry-bushes
and wild flowers, grown up from seed that the wind or birds
had borne thither.

" It is unspeakably beautiful ! " exclaimed Elizabeth ; "here,
at least, is blessedness and peace."

Her eyes shone as she spoke, but at the same moment sad
thoughts passed through her heart.

" Here my poor mother wandered, sick and alone," thought
she ; "they have buried her somewhere about here in a
church-yard; I know not where — no one knows her grave."

Madame Krone also found the district most beautiful, but
that she had always found. She said, —

" If we were only through the sack ! "

What Madame Krone called the sack was a long lane with
hedges, the finest that were to be found in all Funen : the
sweet-briers, whose green leaves give forth a scent like the
apple, hung so luxuriantly forward, with their thorny branches,
that they struck the sides of the horses ; large burdocks lifted
up their gigantic leaves ; the elder-trees bent down with fruit ;
and the hazels were as if over-sown with five and seven clus-

tered nuts ; whilst the convolvulus, or, as the peasants called
it, "crawl-up," vied with the hop-bine for mastery.

There was a turn in the road, and before them lay a pretty
little country house, the corners of which were bounded by
two towers ; a fine old linden-tree, the same that the young
seamen saw in the old ruined court-yard of the manor-house,
was the chief ornament before the entrance.

Herman came out to meet his guests, his face beaming with
pleasure. This dear visit was no surprise to him.

"At last! at last !" he exclaimed ; "this is kind, and I owe
it to Madame Krone."

"Quite so, entirely to me !" she replied, and they were led
into the Pompeian painted rooms ; here everything was neat,
tasteful, and comfortable. The breakfast-table was laid in the
round corner room, whence they could see out over meadow
and woodland. This was the very spot where Elizabeth was
born ; and here her greeting of welcome was now heard. So
absorbing was their talk, that they did not rise from the breakfast-table ; it was as if they forgot that the house and garden
were also to be seen, and the hours flew on. It was almost
near sunset when Madame Krone remembered the "Tingsted,"[1] the remains of a memorial of antiquity that stood
close behind the dairy, a name which the building near the
house still bore.

"My best prospect," exclaimed Herman, "the amplest of
them all ! but this day seems to have been in a strange hurry:
what has become of the time ?" and he offered his arm to
Madame Krone. She was tired, and they followed a path
under elder and hazel bushes, loaded with nuts. A natural
wall rose on the right ; it seemed impossible that horses could
go before the plough here, the declivity was so abrupt, and
yet they had done so, as the ripe corn showed, which now
waved over the ploughed furrows. They soon stood before
the "Tingsted," which presented a number of large stones
arranged in an oblong circle. The sloe-thorn and bramble
bushes formed a little thicket here ; a flock of crows flew
cawing away over the landscape, which, in smaller hills and
dales, was filled with cornfields and meadows, environed by
woods.

[1] The place of assize or assembly.

" The mill-race down there," said Herman, " was once a large stream that bore the Viking's ships far up into the country ; one can clearly see the whole bed of the stream.

" Here the old giants and heroes sat and held council, each on one of these stones, and the chief sat on the largest. The strong men are all gone, all forgotten, — their names and even their age. Also he who lies up there : he was certainly a king, no one knows the name of " — and Herman pointed to a high mound of stones that lay behind them, where the natural wall suddenly broke off ; three immense stones, with an enormous top-stone lay there, which seemed to hang suspended in the air.

" From there," said he, " we have a still wider prospect, — a perfect panorama ! "

" They ascended it, and the Great Belt with a few sails here and there, the coast of Sealand, and Langeland lay extended before them. Madame Krone would not climb so high, she therefore sat down by the hazel bushes. Elizabeth stood on the top-stone, which was broad enough to admit of Herman's standing by her side ; the sun sent his last rays before setting, and the wind blew fresh and free ; they stood there on the stone, in air and sunshine, as Elimar and Elizabeth had once stood in the rising sea. Where were the thoughts which then had birth ? where were the thoughts that came to life here ? It stands in the Scriptures " that fire and whirlwinds are the Lord's servants ; " the warm sunbeams and the mild winds also announce his message. They bear many a word that is too holy to be heard by the ears of the multitude, words that inclose poetry like that which Petrarch transferred into his sonnets, like that which every young impassioned poet thinks he throws into his first verses.

Herman and Elizabeth had sat down on the top-stone ; there Madame Krone found them, as, not having heard her call, they remained sitting, and she came to them.

" You let me sit and sit," said she ; " you did not hear me at all, nor did you come. Is it then so delightful here ? "

" Immeasurably so," exclaimed Herman, with an expression of rapture : " it is enough to make one dance ; " and he swung Madame Krone round, who laughed and looked astonished at his mirth. He then led her to Elizabeth, who had risen from her seat, her cheeks burnt blushing red, — it was as if tears were in her blue eyes.

What had happened? — yes, two days afterwards it was no longer a secret; they were bride and bridegroom.

"I have said it, and it is my meaning," said the grandmother; "'rather from the milk-pail than from the court calendar,' and Elizabeth belongs rather to the former than to the latter. She is a poor man's child, and so am I too, but I suppose we have a kind of genealogical tree! She will always be a good Christian, and she can teach the young Barons, when they come, that they are akin to the poor man. I shall also give them something to make them remember. They may call it 'Grandmother's Bridal Gift:' it is something out of my life and adventures; it is the flower of my genealogical tree, which shall teach a good lesson."

And what was "Grandmother's Bridal Gift?" It was brought on the marriage-day, — that day towards which we are hastening rapidly; the end of September — that day when the friends sat together in the ruinous old manor-house, which was now a comfortable, spacious, and delightful home, — the anniversary of that day when the friends heard that infant cry and Herman pressed it to his heart — that child who was now his bride, his wife. The portrait-painter chooses the happy moment to take the image of the person he would represent; we choose the happiest, "the marriage-day." Elizabeth stands before us; a plain white satin dress enfolds her, her glossy brown hair is worn in a natural plait: she is somewhat pale, but her eyes sparkle, the soul beams from that countenance, and we see that she is only sixteen. The poor man's child, in corporeal beauty nobly born, in intellect and appearance a daughter of the mind's nobility, stands here before us.

Still so short a life, and yet a history for many pages; as yet only a quiet life, but a consistent whole, as far as it has gone; as yet only an every-day story, but which, in all its fragrance and beauty, was seen and seized by a poetic soul on its best bright day of sunshine.

She remembered Moritz's words about the red thread, that passed through the cordage, great and small, to signify that it was the property of the crown, and that invisible thread which passes through every person's life, great and small, and showed us that we belonged to God. She saw it in the years she had lived ; she saw how necessary, how rich in blessings, every heavy day of change had been to her ; she understood that in her solitary life on Oland, divided between nature and her Bible, a richer seed was sown in her soul than by possibility could have been in the old manor-house with the wealthy, strange Baroness. Even the meeting with the widow-lady was to be. The drive with Adelgunde led her a little over marshy ground ; but the marsh had its lilies, the invisible thread lay in the filament. Elizabeth's heart rose up to God with gratitude and confidence ; ours will, also, when we each seek, like her, the invisible thread in our own life's history.

"Grandmother's Bridal Gift" stood in the centre of the table, hidden in a little casket, which was not to be opened before her death ; no one must see before that time what she called the flower of her genealogical tree, or *the reminder* for the coming generation. The gift could not be of great bulk. "That is my treasure," said she, "and you must promise me to make use of it in the family on the fourteenth of August."

Was it gold and valuables that were to proceed thence? Was it an ornament that Elizabeth was to wear?

"You shall know its destination in due time," said the old lady, and tossed her head.

"The guests assembled around the breakfast-table. They were Moritz, Hedevig, and the Clergyman, who had performed the marriage-ceremony. There were no others ; it was Herman's and Elizabeth's wish ; the grandmother would also have it so, and we may say Madame Krone too. The full-moon was their torch-bearer, when the happy pair, early in the evening, drove to their home — Elizabeth's birthplace. The way might have been a hundred miles long ; they would not have felt it, not have thought of it. The little casket lay in Elizabeth's lap ; what did it contain ? We will hasten to that point of time when it is to be opened, the day of the grandmother's death ; but that is not yet. The full moon that lights the bridal pair home shines into the chamber of the strange old lady, who bends her knee before the bed, and sends up her prayers to the Almighty.

17

CHAPTER XXVII.

A LITTLE ABOUT THEM ALL. — THE GRANDMOTHER'S BRIDAL GIFT.

WE will again fly out of that quiet, happy home, — fly far abroad, in order to come back again wearied, so that we may the better enjoy rest, and comprehend in thought the whole picture that is delineated in these pages. We will look up our old acquaintances, and see how they are going on, now that four years have elapsed since Herman and Elizabeth's marriage.

The widow lady is in the house of correction ; there she is in security, and is accustomed to police air.

Adelgunde — yes, strange things occur in this world — but it is so, and it cannot be otherwise — she is married to Holger, — that *she* understood how to bring about. He is postmaster in a provincial town, and she is now postmistress ; and that the button was the cause of ; that unfortunate button which fell off, or else Holger would perhaps have now been sitting with Clara by his side ; Clara, who now lives in and for art and the great world, who has her box at the Copenhagen Italian Opera, is an enthusiastic admirer of the Italians, casts wreaths of flowers regularly on the stage to them, and is happy. The great world is so, half of Copenhagen is so. She is also as enthusiastic as ever for the exterior of Thorvaldsen's museum, and that, notwithstanding she is not painted on the walls.

Frederick has left the provincial representatives for the vessel of state : he has also become tired of his youthful passion, the steersman's art.

Little Sanne has been confirmed some three years since, and has been twice engaged. Her present sweetheart is now employed at the steam-washing-company's establishment, and it must be a pleasure to us, on little Sanne's account, as there is a chance of her yet becoming clean.

The Organ Man, Elizabeth's father, yes, — she knows nothing of him as yet, nor he about her ; so well had he " grouped " his stories that we were for some time thrown quite off the right track. He is, however, in Copenhagen, and married to little Sanne's sister. Her first husband died, and this one has got his office, not to deliver the newspapers, but the more important one, that of being the responsible publisher ; he even announces a new paper, with family secrets and wood-cuts ; it will have subscribers !

But let us hasten far away from these to the fresh open sea, to the quiet Halligers, for there also we have acquaintances.

Everything on Oland was the same as when Elizabeth set off from there : even Piltitz lay in the same chair and looked up to the picture of Grandmother Osa, whose eyes Elimar had put out, — Elimar who was now married to the wealthy widow. Jap Lidt Petters had courted Keike, but they had not come to terms. Everything was as before, only the gooseberry-bush at the parsonage was withered ; the spring no longer unfolded its fine green leaves ; and the sea had cut off a still greater piece from the old church-yard.

But in Funen, every season of the year brought riches and happiness. At the small estate in Funen lived Herman and Elizabeth, every year still happier, if it were possible to be so. What she had dreamt, the night King Frederick's body was taken to Roeskilde, returned to her thoughts. She now remembered that it was Herman who took Elimar's place, when she in her dream read her book of the future. She believed in it, and thought that her happiness in reality was a continued dream. There was a blessing in and around that little home, as if good elves, which the legends tell of, nourished every root and plant. The fruit-trees bent in their fullness, the corn had the heaviest ears, and in the canal before the house, there Elizabeth's favorite flower abounded, the white water-lily, the lotus plant of the North. It lay like a great swimming bush in the middle of the water, a whole flowery tale.

In that corner of the house where Elizabeth was born stood a magnificent rococo closet, and therein the unopened casket, containing " Grandmother's Bridal Gift," was placed. One day Elizabeth also placed some written leaves there, — it was

Grandmother's history brought down to the young folks' bridal day. It was a true and interesting picture of the old Baroness, — it might be called a novel ; and in that the poet's problem was really solved, by opening the eye to the poetical in the every-day-life around us ; by pointing to the invisible thread which in every person's life signifies that we belong to God , by letting us see the peculiarities in the nature of ourselves, our family, and in mankind ; by finding the impress of God, even where it is hidden under the fool's dress, or the beggar's rags.

Herman raised his finger threateningly, and smiled : "Then you have not yet killed the author in you ? " said he.

"One cannot kill the mind ! " she answered gayly. "Let this, however, be an explanation of 'Grandmother's Bridal Gift,' whatever it may be. It reminds one of her."

"And of my dear foundling ! " said Herman, and he pressed Elizabeth to his heart ; "of her and *thee*, 'The Two Baronesses ! ' "

We will visit the elder of the two, the singular old lady ! There, at the great manor-house, she still resided, the Grandmother and Madame Krone. It was the time for roses ; the great rose-bed in the court-yard, where the wooden horse had formerly stood, was in its richest flower. In the field outside, the red clover stood, so thick and fragrant with its flowers, that it seemed as if they would also be roses. The air was warm ; the clouds so soft and transparent, they might all have been painted, they were so exactly what they should be. The bees flew humming about, and the willow twigs bent under the flocks of sparrows ; there was life and movement ; and during all this there approached, — not that tawny-white skeleton with his scythe and hour-glass, as he is painted on the church wall, — no, but the renewing angel, the winnowing of whose wing brings from the unknown land an air, within whose breath our earthly body is gently prepared for corruption.

The old Baroness had been in delicate health for a couple of days ; she had now recovered her usual liveliness again, and this was still more increased, when she one day, shortly before dinner, got a letter from her good child "the Gentleman." — a letter which told her that he should not die a bachelor; an excellent girl was now his bride, a Scotch girl, sister to Knox, whom we may remember during his visit to the parsonage on Oland. His new opera, founded on Shakespeare's " Tempest," had been brought out in London, and had caused a great sensation.

" Hurra for England and Scotland! " shouted the old Baroness. " We will drink that toast, Madame Krone! "

And she filled the glass and emptied it; her eyes were so large, so clear. " Hurra for England and Scotland! " she repeated: it was the lamp that blazed up; she smiled, and sat still, as if she thought of something that made her inwardly glad; her eyes then closed of themselves — she opened them again.

" It is remarkable how tired I am! " said she. " Sleep comes over me all at once. I am not, however, strong even to bear pleasure. I will now sit a little back in the armchair."

And she sat there, and appeared to sleep, but only for a few minutes; she then opened her eyes suddenly and exclaimed; " Where is Herman? where is 'Lizabeth? I shall not live to see them — I am dying! Do not let me lie in the chapel, but outside; there is a fine prospect there! *I* shall not see it, but *they* can who come there, and so they will, at least, have some pleasure of it. I have given my bridal gift, but I would have said a few words with it; *now* they can open the casket. What do you think there is in it? there is only a wooden spoon; but it is cut out of a plank from the wooden horse that my father rode on. It was on the 14th of August; on that day they shall always take it out for the young lord of the manor. When he comes, they shall lay it before him, and tell him from whence he comes, that it may teach him we are all and every one poor men's children before the Lord! "

She nodded, — there was a smile on her mouth, and the old Baroness was dead. The warm sun shone out-of-doors; the clouds were brilliant, and the roses were in full flower.

A white butterfly flew heavenward from the rose-bed; as if accident would preach immortality, — which shone from the countenance of the old woman, and shines in every believer's heart.